THE DEMON
FROM YESTERDAY

Suddenly the invader was there. It weaved, advancing in an erratic zigzag, seemingly as drunk as the revelers. Spindly appendages were tipped by splayed, metallic feet. Wispy, floppy things might be tentacles. How many legs and tentacles—eight, ten, or more? Dan McKelvey couldn't be sure. The thing was huge. Its hide was a patchwork of rusty plates.

The invader rocked crazily, staggering, but gaining the top of the pit. There it tottered wildly, occasionally slipping off the edge of an excavation and stepping on people who were fleeing in pandemonium. Some were so panicked that they ran right in front of the monster.

Then there was a shrill scream from the leader of the natives, "Demon! The demon!" His voice blasted Dan's eardrums. "It is the demon of the Evil Old Ones!"

By Juanita Coulson
Published by Ballantine Books:

Children of the Stars:

THE PAST OF FOREVER

BOOK FOUR OF THE SERIES

CHILDREN OF THE STARS

JUANITA COULSON

A Del Rey Book

BALLANTINE BOOKS • NEW YORK

Home they came, those ancient hunters
When the day was nearly done;
Huddled round their cave-mouth fires,
Watched the setting of the sun;
Slept and found their dreaming haunted
By the Old Ones' ogre calls;
Saw a host of red eyes gleaming
From the shadows on the walls.

"This was ours, we came before you;
Fought the bear, built place and clan.
This is ours, we claim possession;
Fear us yet, O new-come man!"

> —*Apodosis*, Canto I
> Anonymous

With much, much thanks to Jim Allen, Gary Anderson, and John Miesel, for unending encouragement, for technical advice, and for badly needed inside info.

And most especially to Kay Anderson, for the original inspiration. It finally made it, twin.

Table of Contents

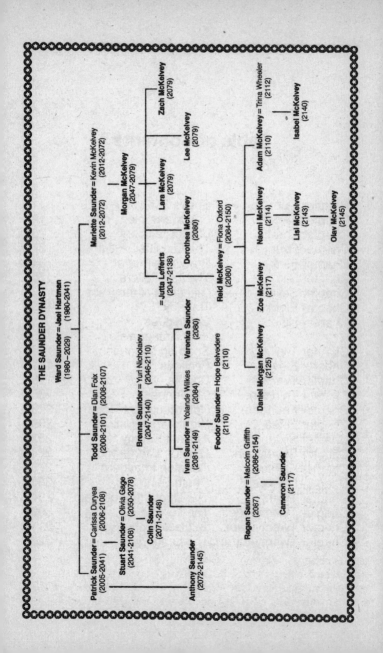

THE SAUNDER DYNASTY

Ward Saunder = Joel Hartman
(1980–2029)   (1980–2041)

Patrick Saunder = Carissa Duryea
(2005–2041)   (2006–2108)

Todd Saunder = Dian Foix
(2008–2101)   (2008–2107)

Marlette Saunder = Kevin McKelvey
(2012–2072)   (2012–2072)

Stuart Saunder = Olivia Gage
(2041–2106)   (2050–2078)

Brenna Saunder = Yuri Nicholaiev
(2047–2140)   (2046–2110)

= Jutta Lefferts
(2047–2138)

Morgan McKelvey
(2047–2079)

Colin Saunder
(2071–2148)

Ivan Saunder = Yolande Wilkes
(2081–2149)   (2084)

Varenka Saunder
(2080)

Dorothea McKelvey
(2080)

Reid McKelvey = Fiona Oxford
(2080)   (2084–2150)

Lara McKelvey
(2079)

Zach McKelvey
(2079)

Lee McKelvey
(2079)

Anthony Saunder
(2072–2145)

Regan Saunder = Malcolm Griffith
(2086–2154)

Feodor Saunder = Hope Belvedere
(2110)   (2110)

Daniel Morgan McKelvey
(2125)

Zoe McKelvey
(2117)

Naomi McKelvey
(2114)

Adam McKelvey = Trina Wheeler
(2110)   (2112)

Cameron Saunder
(2117)

Lisl McKelvey
(2143)

Olav McKelvey
(2145)

Isabel McKelvey
(2140)

CHAPTER ONE

∞∞∞∞∞∞∞

Space 2155

Dan McKelvey completed his check of spacecraft systems. Some independent haulers let servos tend to such chores, but a smart spacer didn't trust his life entirely to machines. Satisfied with the readouts, Dan put circuits on standby and cycled through the airlock. He swam to a nearby gantry platform and turned to look back at his ship.

Major carriers' megakiloton ships dominated the orbiting garage. They made single-stage FTL starhoppers like Dan's *Fiona* seem tiny. Size wasn't everything, however. *Fiona* had come to him secondhand, but she had proved solid, better for his needs than a spacegoing behemoth. He threw her a grateful salute. Thanks to *Fiona*, he'd be able to pay off his debts in a few more years. Then? Maybe he'd go partners with a fellow tech-mech pilot. They could invest in another ship or two, plus some planetside transports. Why not? Dream big! Several of his ancestors had created now-powerful Saunder-McKelvey Enterprises Interstellar from the ground up. And S-ME's competitors, Le Société Famille Universel and Nakamura Kaisya, had built their present-

1

day successes on similarly humble foundations. A "little guy" still had plenty of opportunities to make it on Terra's starlanes.

Yeah. That was what he ought to be doing right now. But instead, he was loafing around Free Port Eighteen, watching other indies grab his slot on the dispatchers' outbound lists.

Dammit, Adam, where are you? You promised that you and Dad would meet me here five days ago. Don't you know—or care—how much you're costing me by these delays? Show up soon, or I'll load cargo and lift!

Dan sighed. He was kidding himself. He couldn't leave, because he didn't want to miss this chance to see his father and brother. No matter how late Adam was for the appointment, Dan had to stay, and continue losing money.

A movement at the edge of his vision made him glance toward the end of the gantry ramp. A Whimed hovered there, readying a skimmer sled for takeoff. Dan switched his suit com over to Terran-Whimed channels and hailed the alien. "*Irast.* You at the sled. Are you traveling to the torus? May I ride with you?"

Felinoid eyes shimmered behind the Whimed's faceplate as he considered the request. Dan explained, "The bus doesn't arrive for another solar mark. I don't want to wait."

He wouldn't have wasted that argument on a contemplative, slow-moving Vahnaj. As for the other species using the Port, Lannon were too unpredictable, and Ulisorians and Rigotians operated on such nonhuman wavelengths that Dan was uneasy dealing with them. The Whimeds, though, shared many traits with *Homo sapiens,* including impatience.

The alien gestured to the sled's jump seat. Dan climbed aboard and locked his safety tether only seconds before the Whimed fired thrusters. The sled shot off the ramp and out into glaring sunlight. Dan winced and keyed his helmet's polarization to a darker setting. He envied the Whimed; felinoids had unbralaca pupils that permitted them to look directly toward a bright star without pain, as the sled's driver was doing now.

Free Port Eighteen was a galactic crossroads, a satellite complex orbiting Terran Settlement World Clay. Torus, garages, warehouses, and human and e.t. trade HQs wheeled majestically against velvety blackness. Small intraport vehicles darted like metallic insects among the planetoid-size structures.

Main Docking was busy. The Whimed's sled took its turn in line with a horde of other craft. Buses and skimmers delivered incoming passengers from the parking garages or on-loaded those heading to departing shuttles and FTL ships. Finally, Traffic assigned a berth, and the sled Dan rode edged forward. He admired the driver's touch on vernier jets and retros and the smooth way he cut power and let them coast into the bay. Inertia and the Hub's adherers did the rest.

Dan expressed his thanks, expecting no acknowledgment. The felinoid headed for his species' mercantile check-in area as soon as the sled was secured. Dan took another access, one connecting to the rental lockers and lifts. He stowed his much-patched pressure suit and caught the first upbound car, squeezing in beside four Terrans and a trio of Vahnajes wearing diplomatic robes.

The Terrans were crewmen off an S-ME liner. They eyed the muscular, sandy-haired, independent pilot scornfully. Dan returned an amiable smile, amused by their snobbery. He wondered how the crewmen would feel if they knew he was related to the owners of S-ME Interstellar. Not closely related, true, but part of that famous clan, just the same.

As the car began to move, riders reacted to the gravity shift from free fall at the station hub to nearly Earth-normal at the outer torus. Dan gulped hard, relieving the pain in his ears. He had to touch his med patch five times during the ride, graphic proof of Free Port Eighteen's size; it was a long haul from Docking to the "upper" levels.

When the car stopped and doors whispered open, he let the others exit ahead of him. They, no doubt, had schedules to meet and places they needed to be. Not Dan McKelvey—nothing to do but spend parking fees and cool his heels.

The concourse was as busy as Docking. Most of the crowd was Terran, though neighboring stellar civilizations were well represented, too. Dan moved through polyglot chaos. Dozens of languages, dialects, and chittering translator devices yammered at him. He bumped elbows with Port staffers, military personnel, traders, recent immigrants, ships' crews, indie haulers, techs, mechs, Terran and alien officials and diplomats, and a smattering of tourists from every sector.

Wending past the worst of the confusion, he eventually reached the Traffic dispatching offices. He wasn't seeking a cargo today, but this section of the torus was a gathering spot for any independent pilots currently in Port. Dan dodged a knot of congestion at the dispatchers' desk and entered the lounge, seeking an empty chair.

"Hey, McKelvey!" a veteran spacer yelled. "Still playin' non-contrib, huh? You one of them trillionaire tourists from Earth?"

The old-timer's buddies took up the game.

"Yeah, what a do-nothin'!"

"Uh-huh! Y'see how he turns down everything a dispatcher offers him? Wish *I* could afford to do that!"

"Aw, them McKelveys and Saunders can always dip into their private fortunes when they run a little short . . ."

Dan forced a tired smile. "Come on, jettison that," he pleaded. "You've got me mixed up with my rich relatives."

"Sure we do!" the others jeered. Their laughter was friendly, though. Dan chuckled with them. Being a good sport was the fastest way to get them off his back. The pilots were well aware that he was no better off financially than they. However, ragging him was a ritual, one Dan had to endure as part of the price he paid for his lineage.

The Saunders and their McKelvey cousins were humanity's prime movers and shakers, influential in nearly every field and backed by enormous wealth. In a century, the family had risen from nothing to become Terra's uncrowned royalty, regarded as *the* representatives of mankind and of Earth by many aliens as well as their own species.

There *were* embarrassing exceptions to that pattern, rare, failed stars in the constellation of conspicuous power. Dan's father, Reid McKelvey, had made some very bad investments and lost his inheritance and a big chunk of that of his kids, as well. Dan's older siblings had been adults when the roof fell in. They'd coped fairly well. He had been twelve. And his father's bankruptcy had meant the collapse of his universe. There had been an abrupt end to his private tutoring and no more servants, luxuries, or first-class tickets. His dreams of completing his education at a prestigious institution and becoming an engineer-inventor disappeared almost overnight. While his rich cousins continued to be treated as princelings, he'd learned a humbler, common settler's life-style. He'd gained apprenticeship as a tech-mech, sometimes hiring out as a brawn laborer to pay the bills. He'd earned his pilot's regs the hard way, without benefit of a sponsoring kinsman or a fat credit account. A few years ago, he'd spent what remained of his trust fund to buy *Fiona*. She'd provided him with a decent if modest income since then. But it was light-years from what he had once imagined things would be. Even now, the loss of his birthright hurt, a lot.

Yet his fellow haulers always put him through this verbal gauntlet, accusing him of slumming.

Didn't he wish he were!

Finally, the game ended. Conversation turned to other topics. Relieved to be out of the spotlight, Dan listened to the gossip. Indie pilots competed for jobs, picking up crumbs left by the major carriers. No independent hauler could possibly handle all the cargo headed for isolated Settlements, so they passed tips on to their cronies—if that didn't dent their own profits. It was an efficient grapevine, often getting the news long before the big com networks did.

". . . fresh load of purgatio coming up from Clay Settlement, they say. . ."

"Yeah? Wish my name was on top of the list. I'd sure like to load some of that stuff on my junker. . ."

"Anybody know where I can get a good replacement unit for a T-45 oscillator?"

"There *is* no such thing as a *good* T-45 . . ."

". . . as bad as trying to deliver a cargo to Earth since those damned Renaissancers put through the last tariffs . . ."

". . . ain't you heard their slogans? They're just 'keeping the Mother World safe for generations yet unborn.'"

That brought a chorus of groans. The veteran spoke for them all. "Heard their slogans? We're sick of 'em. Those New Earth Renaissancers are a bunch of crazies. Let 'em have the fornicating Mother World, if they're so in love with it. Who wants Earth, anyway? Give me a Settlement planet or space, any day!"

The group agreed emphatically. As talk drifted to the upcoming trade fair in the Luyten's system, Dan was surprised to hear himself paged. Across the room, a dispatcher beckoned.

He hurried to the desk. As he reached it, the dispatcher said with a nasty smile, "Still cluttering up the Station? I'm sure sick of you using our library and rec facilities and our commissary. Why don't you get an honest job?"

Dan swallowed a retort. The woman wasn't teasing, as the indies had been; she hoped to sting him into an angry reaction. He couldn't afford to take the bait; dispatchers had the go-or-no-go say on whether an indie got cargo to haul. Shrugging, he said,

"Well, it's just one of those things. I *did* file my layover plans, remember, when I pulled in."

"Oh, sure!" the woman growled. "Commander McKelvey's baby brother knows how to fill out all the forms. Learned it from the Fleet, didn't you? That's how *they* work. By the book, and to hell with justice." Her manner turned very ugly. "I had friends on 61 Cygni Settlement. Your brother rounded them up during that insurrection there in '53. Sentenced them to fifteen years on a mining asteroid. That's death. No way they can serve out that time, and he knew it."

Dan studied her warily. Many Portside staffers hated Space Fleet. They resented the military's high pay, prestige, and clout. This dispatcher, though, was nursing an extra grudge on top of the normal animosity toward the service. He said, "Uh . . . sorry about your friends. But from what I recall of the case, Adam didn't pass sentence; he simply carried out the Council's judgment."

"That's the way the media told it," the woman said bitterly. It was plain she didn't believe the reports or Dan. "Doesn't matter. I only brought it up because every time you come in here and loaf, you remind me of your damned brother. Well, that's over. After today, I don't expect to see your face for a while. That cruiser you've been waiting on? She's docking. So you tend to your business and ship out pronto. No stalling. Clear?"

"Adam's ship? It's here?" Dan exclaimed. "But . . . but his last message said it'd be two more days . . ."

"Never trust a Fleet communiqué," she said, her voice dripping acid. The dispatcher tapped a vid monitor. "There's the ETA. Just posted. You've lost your excuse for wasting our equipment and time." With a smirk, she added, "Better hurry, or you'll miss your big rendezvous."

He was happy to take the advice. Dan made his way around the torus to Fleet's visitors' lounge and checked the update monitor eagerly. TSS *General Ames* had indeed docked. But none of her passengers had arrived at the torus yet, and unauthorized civilians couldn't use the elevators, so he couldn't ride down and meet his family halfway. Curbing his impatience, he sat and waited.

He and others in the lounge appeared to be suspended in a starfield. Tri-di technology created the illusion that people, furnishings, and even the transparent floor floated in deep space. A thousand points of light danced on the inner surface of a black sphere. Some lights were marked by standard chart identifier codes. Those points represented thriving Terran and alien solar systems. Far more suns lacked inhabited worlds. Barren, they shone among bright islands of humanoid civilizations. The display illustrated the vastness of the universe, and its emptiness.

Dan made a leisurely visual survey of the display and admired the ingenuity of Fleet's engineers. He watched a newscast. He planned how he'd get an outbound cargo, after meeting with his family. And he waited. And waited.

At last the elevators began disgorging officers, enlisted crew members, and military liaison e.t.s from the cruiser. Dan searched the mob for an older man in civvies. Where was Reid? He couldn't spot him anywhere.

"McKelvey? Dan McKelvey?"

He turned to face an ensign, a stranger. The junior officer smiled and held out a small object. Dan started to ask what was going on. Then he knew. With great reluctance, he took the package. "I see. A holo-mode letter?"

"Yes, sir. The Commander wanted it hand delivered. He regrets he won't be able to meet you."

Disappointment cut at Dan. He felt compelled to say, "My Dad and brother aren't on that ship out there, are they?"

"Oh, no. Commander McKelvey and his entourage transferred to the *Invincible* last week. Didn't you get the message? New orders from the brass. The Commander is making an inspection tour of Terran-Whimed treaty regions en route to his post. You know how these last-minute assignment changes are," the ensign said cheerfully.

Dan snapped, "No, I don't know. And nobody told me about this change of plans, either. Adam probably didn't think I was worth the price of a com signal." He heaved a sigh and went on, "Just ignore that. It's not your fault. And thanks for bringing the letter. Did you happen to see my father while he was still on board the cruiser?"

Belatedly aware that he'd been the bearer of bad news, the young man was anxious to make amends. "Reid McKelvey. Oh, yes. I saw him and the Commander almost every day . . ."

"How was Reid? In good health?"

"He seemed pretty spry," the ensign assured Dan.

"Li!" The call made the officer jump. A captain gestured sharply to him.

"I have to leave now. Glad to have met you . . ."

Dan nodded absently, opening the package and sliding the holo-mode out onto his palm. So this was the long-anticipated rendezvous! A letter! He was tempted to hurl the wafer against the bulkhead, but mastered the impulse; this holo was going to be his only contact with loved ones for the present. If he smashed it, he wouldn't have even that.

Resigned to the situation, he found an unused monitor and fed the letter into its playback slot. Images formed: Dan's father, Adam, and Adam's family.

"Hi, son! Too bad we can't make connections this trip. We'll get together soon, boy, count on it!"

Commander Adam McKelvey's tone was stiff, as usual. "I assume this will reach you with minimal delay. Li will explain our altered schedule. It's not possible for us to stop at Port Eighteen, as we originally planned. It's off our new course."

"I suppose it also wasn't possible for you to notify me any sooner than this, so I wouldn't waste my time waiting for you," Dan grumbled. It was childish to complain to a tri-di, although that *did* help boil off anger.

Trina, Adam's wife, spoke for a few minutes then. Like Adam, she was a Fleet officer. Unlike Adam, she was a warm person. Dan was genuinely sorry not to see her in the flesh today. He *wasn't* so certain he regretted the missed linkup with Adam.

Isabel McKelvey said "hello" in a bored voice. She was fifteen, and Dan suspected his niece would have preferred to be elsewhere flirting with her father's male cadets.

"This sure has been a long trip, son," Reid said, waving an age-spotted hand. "We traveled clear back to the Mother World a few months ago. Did I tell you that in my last letter? Or . . . was that when we were on our way *to* Earth?" Frowning, the old man scratched his head. "I guess it doesn't matter."

A painful lump filled Dan's throat. His father looked much worse than he had in that last letter. Ensign Li thought Reid was okay. An honest mistake; the officer hadn't known Reid McKelvey in his prime. Dan, however, could see the years taking a toll. Since his wife had died in 2150, Reid had gone downhill fast. That once-strong body was frail, his mind faltering.

"All in all, things aren't too bad on Earth, Danny. Oh, they're

8

stagnating, but they've been doing that quite a while. What they need is a shot of pioneering. That'd keep 'em in shape like us real Terrans. Remember when we homesteaded on Arden? And that time we helped the stasis ship colonists unfreeze and adjust after they reached Kruger 60?"

Reid's memory *was* going. Dan hadn't been born yet when his parents and older siblings had assisted the Hiber-ship settlers. Like many old-timers, his father suffered from increasingly fuzzy recollections. His hands trembled and occasionally his gaze wandered, further evidence of time's cruelty.

Dan consoled himself with the fact that his father was well cared for. Officially, Reid was part of Adam's entourage. And a Space Fleet Commander was entitled to plenty of perks for him and his, enough to keep them in comfort. The younger siblings also chipped in a share toward their dad's support. Dan's contribution to the kitty was necessarily the smallest, which made him feel guilty.

"Your sisters and Lisi and Olav want to say 'hi.'" Reid's image put a recording wafer in an illusionary projector. Four small figures—Zoe and Naomi McKelvey and Naomi's kids—appeared, holo-modes within a larger holo. A doll-like Zoe looked very spiffy in her medic's uniform. Naomi wore a uniform, too; she'd recently been made Chief of Shuttle Operations for Alpha Cee Settlement. Dan hardly recognized her children. They were growing so fast! The kids waved enthusiastically to Uncle Dan.

Though the holo was miniaturized, voices were boosted to near normal. Dan's sisters, niece, and nephew sounded as if they were in the lounge with him, chattering on and on. Dan propped his chin on his hands and stared morosely at the holo. Zoe's gossip, Naomi's news, how they and the kids looked—all of it distant history, recorded weeks or months ago on separate planets light-years apart from each other and from Free Port Eighteen. And at this instant Reid, Adam, and Adam's family were traveling farther on out into the galaxy.

Dammit! Dan wanted to embrace his father, kiss his sisters and sister-in-law, tell Isabel how pretty she was, advise little Lisi and Olav to study hard. Dan even longed to give Adam a bear hug. That would shake up stiff-necked big brother and be a hell of a lot of fun!

But . . . he couldn't touch them. They weren't real, any more than that starfield on the bulkhead was real.

The starfield put things in perspective. Sol was shining, bright and golden. Scattered around her were the suns of Terra's Settlement Worlds, and beyond those, the stars of neighboring alien planets. The room-size map encompassed six civilizations. How could humanity—or any similar species—hope to maintain close ties with its roots and families in so large an arena?

Frontiers continued to expand. Indie haulers like Dan helped that happen. He was one of thousands of spacers keeping open the communication and supply lines to outlying planets in the Terran sector. And yet he himself was becoming more and more isolated from people and places he loved.

Abruptly a paging message with Dan's name and pilot's reg number flashed on the monitor. Sighing, he pocketed the wafer and cued the system. That grudge-carrying dispatcher's face filled the screen. "McKelvey? You done with your big get-together? Want a cargo?"

Hastily he shifted mental gears. "I wasn't expecting . . ."

"You're at the top of the list—again. Unless you turn this one down the way you did the earlier ones."

"No! That's—that's great. Thanks!" Dan said. "I really appreciate this. What's the load and where's it bound?"

"Machinery. Prepaid. Destination, System T-W 593."

He glanced at the bulkhead starmap. Quick calculations made him whistle. "That's a Terran-Whimed Protectorate Listing, right out on the fringe."

"If your ship lacks the range, I'll bump you down."

"Hey, the *Fiona* can do that easy," Dan lied. The job would be a stretch for his starhopper, and fuel costs would reduce profits to a bare minimum. But he was in no position to be choosy. After that long layoff waiting for Adam, he needed a paying cargo quick. If he rejected this one, they might hand him a worse consignment later on.

"Okay, you got it. Lots of luck!" The beginning of a grin showed on her face as it faded from the monitor.

Dan frowned. Why should *she* seem so pleased about it all? Unless she thought he'd be stretched too far and have to call for a rescue. That didn't seem logical. Then he shrugged and tried to dismiss it from his mind.

Numbers flickered on the screen. Dan studied the invoice. The customers were an archaeological expedition. That rang a bell. His cousin Varenka had a nephew who was an archaeologist, and the last Dan had heard Feo was working somewhere in the Terran-Whimed sector. The name on the manifest, though, wasn't that of a Saunder. So what? A delivery was a delivery. This cargo had been in storage at the Port for months. Those scientists on T-W 593 ought to be grateful to see it—maybe grateful enough to give a fat tip.

He looked forward to spacing again. It would wash the bad taste of this botched rendezvous from his mouth, for one thing.

Dan was very busy for the next couple of hours, entering nav data on *Fiona*'s boards, moving her to the warehouse satellite so automated stevedores could transfer cargo to her hold, and paying bills. Parking fees were especially heavy because of Adam's lack of consideration. Another bite went for the fuel package. Normally, before a lengthy starhop, Dan stocked up on entertainment and educational vids in the local shops. This time, feeling poor, he restricted his purchases to a few documentaries on archaeology. He'd never visited an archaeo Settlement before and he didn't want to sound like a total fool when he met his customers.

He was still bothered by that dispatcher's smile. With her grudge against him, it should have been a sign of something nasty to come. But everything seemed to move smoothly. There wasn't even a delay from Traffic in giving him clearance, once the *Fiona* was loaded and primed.

Dan eased out of Port, nudging power, reaching toward FTL hop point. Big interstellar craft had to stand at least thirty kilometers off station before using hyperdrive. An indie ship, with its much smaller energy field, was allowed to engage at ten.

Final checklist showed all boards green. *Fiona* warped space and time, leaping across the light-years.

CHAPTER TWO
⊙⊙⊙⊙⊙⊙⊙⊙⊙

Saunderhome

For a time, Dan was busy fine-tuning vectors. But everything was going smoothly. He settled back, took out the holo-mode wafer, and stuck it into the slot beside his control board. He skimmed quickly over the part he'd already seen.

Reid's image on the screen removed the holo of Dan's sisters from the projector and inserted another wafer. "I wanted you to see this, Danny. Our kinswoman deserves our full cooperation. Now pay attention."

The new scene almost filled the screen, an overlay that almost hid the other figures. A hawk-faced, elderly woman peered at Dan. As she started to speak, it took him a few seconds to pinpoint her accent: Earth, a Slavic inflection mixed with Basic.

"Greetings, dear ones, from Varenka Saunder-Nicholaiev. To those not conversant with our complex intrafamilial relations, I am the daughter of Brenna Saunder and Yuri Nicholaiev. My mother was the beloved granddaughter of our clan's noble forebears, the inventive genius Ward and that immortal visionary, the tragically martyred Jael Hartman Saunder..."

She needn't have bothered with the elaborate and boastful intro. Dan hadn't met his cousin since he was a boy, but everyone knew who she was—one of the richest and most powerful of the Saunder-McKelveys, a force to be reckoned with, particularly on Earth. When she said "Jump," Terra's political and business leaders went into orbit.

Varenka began walking. The lens stayed in tight focus, following her through swaying trees and colorful beds of flowers. Behind her lay a white beach washed by dark waves. Tropical sunlight drenched everything. The landscape was on Earth; no other planetary environment quite matched *Homo sapiens'* Mother World.

The old woman climbed a grassy slope to a ruined castle. Its glassene and stone were badly weathered, encrusted with vines and mosses.

"Look at it, Saunder-McKelveys!" Varenka cried. "Isn't this disgraceful? This is Saunderhome. Yes, Saunderhome! This is where our family began a historic, unparalleled rise to eminence. We must treasure this shrine. Saunderhome is our *soul*!"

Dan snorted derisively at the highfalutin language. Why had his father insisted he watch this? Okay, so that was their stuck-up relative Varenka showing the viewer Saunderhome and weeping because it was falling to pieces. So what? Judging by the news from Earth, whole cities there had been in the same sorry state for a long time.

". . . an absolute desecration, brought about by neglect. I will not go into detail regarding the inexcusable legal problems that have prevented our acting to correct this situation until recently. You all know the story." Dan was tempted to say *he* didn't, nor did he care. Varenka went on. "I am sure you are thrilled to hear that the New Earth Renaissance Foundation has gained clear title to this sacred edifice. We intend to merge this restoration project with our much-heralded campaign to clone a living replica of our magnificent ancestress Jael. Both efforts are well underway. Naturally, funds are needed . . ."

Dan gasped in exasperation. So that was it—a pitch for money! She was hitting up all the Saunders-McKelveys, including impecunious distant cousins like Dan, for donations.

The New Earth Renaissance! That head-in-the-sand bunch! Back to the "good old days!" Renaissancers yearned for a return to Earth's "glorious past" and had done their best to cause trouble

13

for the Chartered Settlement Planets and the expansion of Terra's stellar frontiers. Varenka was president of the N.E.R. and often stated her goal was to "bring humanity's heart home again, where it belongs." She had her nerve asking spacer-oriented relatives who didn't share her feelings about that "shrine" to chip into *her* charity! She wanted to restore Saunderhome? Fine! Let her and her rich friends pay the bills.

She continued to conduct a guided tour of Saunderhome, or what was left of it: fallen ceilings; obscene graffiti everywhere; and animal droppings on the floors. Most of the furniture had been stolen; the rest was a wreck. No settler on a backworld would house livestock in such a ruin!

"Terrible! Terrible!" Varenka moaned, dabbing at her eyes and sniffling. "This cannot be tolerated. We must return our Saunderhome to its former beauty, make it once more the true capital of mankind. I know you will be generous . . ."

Reid McKelvey was an easy touch. That was one of the reasons he'd lost his fortune. Undoubtedly he'd sent his cousin some credits he should have kept in his pocket.

Well, that snooty old woman would wait till Sol froze before Reid's younger son sent her any money!

Years ago, when Dan's father was in desperate financial straits, Varenka and other wealthy relatives had pointedly looked the other way. Like too many successful Saunder-McKelveys, she'd been on top of the power ladder so long she tended to ignore the family's losers—except when she wanted donations for her silly hobby!

To add insult to injury, she wasn't doing anything worthwhile —just rebuilding a ruin and cloning a long-dead ancestor for purely sentimental purposes.

Dan scowled in contempt. Maybe Saunderhome *was* a historic monument, as Varenka was claiming. But nobody could eat history. History wouldn't pay off the debt on his starhopper or buy him a much-needed replacement spacesuit. As far as he was concerned, they ought to forget that cloning project and tear down Saunderhome for salvage. Why waste more money on the thing?

Varenka hadn't chipped in to help Reid, back when that could have made a big difference. So Dan wasn't going to ante up for her "sacred causes."

Her segment of the letter ended, and Dan leaned forward, hoping for more personal news from his immediate family. But his father merely signed off, promising to get in touch when Adam arrived at his new post. Dan withdrew the wafer. It was a poor substitute for real interaction, but it would have to do.

Then the boredom of a long trip settled in. A week later, he'd reread the vids several times and was dipping into his library. Days clicked on. Dan wondered how the old-timers had coped, back when interstellar journeys took months rather than weeks. Starhopping must have been an ordeal in those days.

Seeking diversion, he scanned the subspace channels, eavesdropping on Terran and alien conversations from the star groups he was passing. He didn't join in. That was too expensive.

He replayed his collection of holo-mode letters, usually dimming the lights to enhance the illusions. Thanks to the magic of tri-di, he could even see his mother again. The images reunited Reid, Fiona, their children, and the grandchildren, erasing death and distance.

Once he forgot to cut off the projector soon enough when Varenka's segment appeared on the last letter. The repeat viewing made her sales pitch still more annoying. He found himself wishing Saunderhome would collapse around the woman's ears. As for her hopes of cloning her ancestor, the history vids warned that Jael Hartman Saunder might not have been a martyred heroine, but a murdering tyrant who merited extinction. It would serve Varenka right if her precious clone turned out to be a vicious beast.

Fiona entered unfamiliar stellar regions where most of the com chatter came from Whimed Federation worlds.

When T-W 593's star finally locked on the nav screens, Dan reduced the length of the FTL pulses, then went sublight.

Destination was on the grids! He'd be damned glad to make planetfall. This had been a hell of a long haul.

He knew that few frontier Settlements employed a full-time sparks, so he requested landing coordinates while he was well out from the system's fourth world.

Then he had nothing to do but wait—and begin worrying. The grin on that dispatcher's face still bothered him. Maybe she'd known the archaeology site had been abandoned and there would be no one to sign his manifest. That equipment had been waiting for delivery a long time. Maybe down there they'd ordered and received supplies from other sources. A hundred possibilities began nagging at him, all leaving him stranded with the trip a total loss. And that could spell the beginning of ruin.

It was hours before anyone responded.

"Hello? Independent hauler *Fiona*? This is Praedar Expedition. Uh . . . T-W 593. If you're peddling supplies, we don't need any." The signal was scratchy. The face of the blonde who was answering Dan's hail jittered all over the frame.

He wasn't surprised by the lack of formality and sloughing of com procedure. It was normal for remote colonies. "I'm not selling," he answered, gratefully letting his worries evaporate. "I've got a machinery shipment for you. Where do I set down?"

The silence on the other end of the connection went on so long that Dan checked his receivers to be sure there was no malfunction. At this range, com-time lag was minuscule. The scientists should be able to get back to him almost instantly.

The blonde eventually came back on line. "You've got our machine replacement parts? Where the hell have they been all this time? Come on in! Oh, you need coordinates, don't you? Hang on. Kat, where's that tape we play for the supply shuttle?" A second, darker Terran woman came into view alongside the blonde. The two whispered together a moment, then the data feed started.

That, too, was sloppy. Dan had to ask for several repeats. He supposed these big brains were occupied with heavy subjects and couldn't be bothered to maintain com gear in top condition.

A bare-bones nav satellite orbiting the planet cross-linked with the coordinates, guiding him in. He put *Fiona* into descent mode and started final approach.

Whenever he made planetfall, he thanked Brenna Saunder. Her company had developed the one-man single-stage starhoppers. Of course, she'd intended those to serve as a subsidiary flotilla for S-ME Interstellar's full-size craft. Those big guys needed shuttles to offload cargo or passengers for planetside delivery. Single-stagers combined FTL and shuttle functions, though their kilotonnage was severely limited. As things had turned out, that limitation made them too unprofitable for major carriers. But the little ships were perfect for independent haulers —and a new profession had been born on the starlanes.

Fiona demonstrated her versatility now. Her FTL drive on standby, atmo wings extended, she dropped toward T-W 593. With each successive, lower orbit, waters and landmasses became more distinct. Dan saw deserts, rugged mountain ranges, and shallow seas. There were no cities or roads. The only sign of civilization was the local Settlement, a tiny dot on the equator. Its landing strip was a few kilometers to the east, atop a mesa.

Crosswinds made touchdown steering tricky. There was no tower, ground guidance, or landing grid. The situation demanded seat-of-the-pants skill. Dan relished the challenge. *Fiona* kicked up a lot of sand and dust as she taxied to a stop. He swung her around, aligning for later takeoff, and began shutting down non-essential systems and running routine environmental scans. On the exterior monitor, he noted surface vehicles—a two-seater rover and a fat-wheeled truck with a scoop welded on its front end—bucketing through the flying grit. But he completed his chores before he cracked the hatch and stepped outside.

The blonde and brunette he'd spoken to on the com were dismounting from the rover, a Terran male and two Whimeds from the truck. "Hi!" the blonde said. "Welcome to Praedar's planet." She tossed Dan a supplementary med patch. "Local bugs are fairly benign, and the air's tolerable. But there's a fungus that likes to chew on humans, so you'd better use that." He nodded and slapped the patch on beside his embedded boosters.

Four additional passengers sat in the truck's scoop. The naked little male humanoids alternately panted or grinned inanely. Their eyes were yellowish ovals, their complexions flushed. Wrinkled skin formed folds around their necks and ribs and the wrists of their shovel-shaped paws. They had no ear flaps and mere bumps for noses. Aborigines? Very probable.

The rest of the welcoming committee was thoroughly scruffy. Both humans and Whimeds wore frayed and dusty jumpers, the legs cut short and sleeves detached. Neck scarves and headbands were sweat-stained; their boots were dirty. The Terran women's hair had been braided messily. The felinoids' topknots were so long that strands flopped in their eyes.

Dan held out a hand, said "Hello," and told them his name.

The scientists exchanged startled, cryptic glances. The busty blonde responded, "I'm Sheila Whitcomb. That's Yvica and Drastil, our honeymooners. This is Joe Hughes and Kaatje Olmsted."

Dan wasn't aware he'd reacted particularly to the intros, but as he took the brunette's hand she snapped, "Kaatje is Old Earth Dutch. If it's too tough for you to pronounce, you can call me Olmsted or Kat."

Irked by the patronizing tone, he said, "I'm no tourist. I can handle anything but Ulisorian."

"Give him time to acclimate before you lecture him," Sheila said. Kat glared at her. The blonde winked and went on, "Open the cargo bay and let's see what you've got, McKelvey." She made that a blatant double entendre.

Pleasantly flustered, he unlocked the hold. The settlers trooped inside. One of the little shovel-pawed aliens hopped off the truck and loped up the boarding ramp after them. The other e.t.s tagged along, moving much more slowly than their leader.

Dan, too, moved slowly. Compensation meds could do only so much; it would take time for him to adjust to T-W 593's nine-tenths Earth gravity and somewhat oxygen-thin atmosphere.

"By Kruger's hills, it *is* the stuff we ordered last year!" Sheila chortled over the hold's contents. "Won't this curdle Feo's milk?"

"Feo's *and* Hope's," Kat Olmsted agreed. "It looks as if everything's here. Amazing! Right out of the blue, after being missing all that time. Now maybe we can fix the skimmer and get that vacuum dredge back in operation."

"Maybe." Joe Hughes sounded pessimistic. "*If* we can figure how to install the parts. Well, let's start unloading . . ."

Dan coughed to get their attention. "Before you do, I'll need a receipt. A palmprint will do, if a signature isn't convenient. I have to have proof that the delivery was accepted by the correct party, so I can register it with Terran Traffic Central when I return to a main port."

Hughes and Sheila smiled slyly, and Sheila said, "Praedar will sign. Why don't you take McKelvey to camp and take care of that, Olmsted?" Kaatje shot her another glare. Dan suspected he was being dragged into an in-group joke at Kat's expense. Sheila anticipated his objections. "Don't worry about your ship while you're gone, handsome. We'll leave her so tidy you won't know we've been here." The blonde's blue eyes twinkled with mischief. The Whimed couple uttered those wheezing chuckles that passed for felinoid laughter.

Dan felt ill at ease. He *was* unhappy at the idea of leaving *Fiona* in strangers' hands. After all, she was his livelihood. Could he trust these people?

That emotion must have shown in his expression. Kat said, "Oh, nobody's going to damage your spacecraft! How clumsy do you think we are? We use far more complex equipment than this every day!"

Despite her boast, he doubted the scientists knew as much about a starhopper as they did about test tubes and fuss-fancy scanners. But if he said so, he'd have a word brawl on his hands —and there would go his hopes of a tip. Without enthusiasm, he said, "Well, I guess it's okay."

Sheila smirked. "Our guest is all yours, Kat. *Do* be a gracious hostess, hmm?"

Kaatje spat a word Dan recognized as a pithy Whimed obscenity; then she trotted down the exitway. Sheila's grin did nothing to reassure him. He was now certain that the blonde had shoved him headlong into a private squabble, and there was no escape hatch in sight.

CHAPTER THREE

✦✦✦✦✦✦✦✦

Blacklisted

Sheila yelled, "Kat! Take the N'lacs with you. They'll get in the way here." She told the most energetic e.t., "Chuss. You digger fellas go along by Kat and McKelvey, huh huh."

Chuss galloped to the two-seater. His companions trailed him, strolling. As the humans climbed aboard the vehicle, red-faced e.t.s swarmed up onto the rover's hood.

Joe Hughes backed the now-empty truck into loading position at *Fiona*'s ramp. Dan winced when the rig groaned in protest. That machine needed repairs. But he couldn't offer to fix it at the moment; Olmsted was firing up the rover. It roared away, leaving a small sandstorm in its wake.

The road was unpaved and rutted. Dan grabbed at the safety bar, steadying himself. Kat dodged the worst of the bumps, however, and after a few minutes he began to relax and enjoy the scenery.

Purple foliage dotted the mesa—brush, grasses, and grotesquely gnarled "trees" with snaky tendrils. The sandy soil was rust-colored. Beyond the plateau, a dark line of jagged mountains boxed the area.

As Kat drove northwest, Dan cupped his hands over his brow and squinted at the dashboard chronometer. According to that, it was late afternoon on this meridian. The temperature, though, was still murderous. Kat didn't seem to mind the heat. Neither did the N'lacs. They ignored flying dust, grinning, and clung to the rover's hood as if their pawlike hands were equipped with adherers.

Dan studied Kaatje Olmsted sidelong. Her profile was sharp, accented by a pert nose and pointed chin. A form-fitting jumper outlined her slim figure. Girlish pigtails and a smudged face made her look younger than she probably was—about Dan's age, thirty. She was attractive, under that grime.

"Well?" she said waspishly, not taking her eyes off the road. "Do I pass inspection?"

"Top score. But it wasn't an inspection, only a friendly survey. That's not permitted?"

After a pause, Kat shook her head and managed a weak smile. "Sorry. I had a blowup with a colleague shortly before we drove out here, but I shouldn't take it out on you, McKelvey." She glanced at him curiously. "McKelvey? What's someone like you doing piloting an indie starhopper?"

"Someone rich, you mean?" Kat heard the anger in that and nodded, on guard. Dan said, "I'm not rich. And there are times when I wish I wasn't a Saunder-McKelvey. It gives me too damned much trouble. As for my piloting *Fiona*, that's what I do for a living. I work, instead of wallowing in the lap of luxury like my wealthy relatives." He described his background briefly and finished on a lighter note. "If you were planning to hit me up for a loan, you might as well save your breath."

"Damn," she said in mock anguish. "And I was counting on you for a hefty grant, too. All right. I promise I won't make any more cracks about your name. I'll warn you, though, some members of the team may be very hostile at first, when they learn you're a Saunder-McKelvey."

"*Very* hostile?" he asked, puzzled by the emphasis.

Kat pretended she hadn't heard him. "There's the complex," she announced, steering the rover down a slope into a broad, sun-baked valley. They parked near a collection of plasticene insta-cells. The lightweight polygonal structures were popular on

21

the frontier. They were cheap, easy to transport, and could be used as individual housing or linked into community buildings.

The camp showed a lot of wear and tear. Insta-cells, solar panels, and deep-well windmill pumpers were sand-scoured. Vehicles and metalline hangars were streaked with temperature stress cracks.

T-W 593's population was a multispecies mix. Terrans, Whimeds, Vahnajes, a Lannon, and dozens of N'lacs. Dan was surprised that there was so little visible friction, far less than he would have expected from such a disparate bunch.

In those ed-vids he'd bought, archaeological sites were neat diagrams and pictorials recorded when digging was done. This place was in full operation and it was a mess: piles of dirt and rubble; partially uncovered ruins; a haphazard clutter of tools, vehicles, and unidentifiable stuff; middens of broken storage crates; and labyrinths of stakes and strings.

One especially large domed edifice caught Dan's eye. It was half buried, sitting uphill from the insta-cells and dominating the landscape. The thing reminded him of a supersized Asita Hosi Settlement, creepy-crab emerging from its burrow.

Kat led the way into camp. Chuss loped out in front. His buddies ambled along in the rear, as did Dan. Heavy with fatigue and short of breath, he rubbed his med patches. Even after he got a boost from grav compensation drugs, he made no attempt to match Kat's stride, not this soon after planetfall. Only a greenie would do that.

The brunette leaned in the door of an insta-cell and asked where Praedar was. Dan peered over her shoulder, hoping to watch exotic experiments in progress. Instead, he saw a lab full of catnapping Whimeds and a few bored-looking Terrans. One pot-bellied scientist sat at a monitor, his nose nearly touching its screen. He glanced at Kat and chuckled. "Praedar? Up at the dome dig. Say, if you see the hunting party while you're there, hurry 'em along. Frank wants to fry something good for supper. I'm hungry for boomer lizard, myself." Others in the room made disparaging remarks. The paunchy Oriental scratched his groin, gobbled a blue fruit, and produced a spectacular belch.

Bemused, Kat moved on, telling Dan, "Don't be impressed by Chen's little act. He likes to stage that for visitors."

"Uh . . . no . . . I wasn't . . ."

She was setting a rapid pace. He had to push not to fall be-

22

hind, stumbling occasionally. The valley floor was uneven, and Kat was leading him through an obstacle course. Dan dodged tools and crates, coming abreast of a trench. He slowed, then halted, gawking. A Terran male and a Vahnaj female were inside the excavation, heaving shovelsful of dirt up and out.

Dan was astonished. Vahnajes were elegant beings in floaty robes. They never performed grubby manual labor or wore dirty jumpers.

This one did.

Her Terran co-worker was shoveling just as hard and getting just as dirty as she was; but, in his case, that was far less shocking.

Two Terran males caught the soil as it sailed out of the pit. They shook it back and forth on a screened box, now and then picking small objects from the debris. That done, they dumped the contents and readied themselves for the next shovelsful.

None of the quartet looked at the others. They knew this choreographed routine by heart.

Dig. Throw. Catch. Sift.

Dig. Throw. Catch. Sift.

"I thought you needed proof of delivery." Dan woke out of a trance. Kat stood arms akimbo a few meters beyond the trench. She tapped her foot impatiently.

He dragged himself away from the scene. "Uh . . . what are they doing?"

"Helping Getz's students sift for effigy fragments and any potsherds that might have been missed earlier."

Dan thought hard, mentally reviewing those ed-vids. "Oh. Potsherds. Pieces of pottery. Right?" Kat nodded and raised her dark eyebrows. "Effigy. That's related to fetishes, isn't it? Small representations of humanoids, often with religious or sexual connotations."

"Where did you . . . ? Yes, that's correct. The potsherds are nothing out of the ordinary. The effigies, though, are unique. Dr. Getz, an expert in that field, has come here solely to analyze them."

Dan peered again at the dig-and-sift team. "So you're working on a primitive culture?"

"No! A highly developed civilization," Kat said with heat. He wondered why she was so fiercely defensive. Abruptly she dropped the topic and hurried through another maze of shallow excavations. "These are dud pits. Dead ends," she explained. "But these ahead *did* prove out, so watch your step." Dan dutifully obeyed.

Each rectangular depression was framed by numbered stakes. Pegs and strings separated them from each other and from the path. Kat threaded her way among them, climbing toward the partially buried dome. A circle of Terrans and aliens stood at the top of the trail. They were engaged in a loud multilingual argument. Chuss and a gaggle of young N'lacs hunkered on the sidelines, enjoying the show.

"Praedar!" Kat's bellow momentarily silenced the crowd. As a tall Whimed left the group, noise resumed, full blast. Frowning, the woman said, "We'll have to find a quieter place to talk. Come on."

Dan followed her and the Whimed along the hill's crest and hastily rearranged his thinking. Why had he subconsciously assumed the expedition's leader would be a Terran? That was a chauvenistic attitude worthy of Varenka's New Earth Renaissancers, and those hidebound bigots weren't people he wanted to emulate. He resolved to be more open-minded in the future.

Reaching a spot out of earshot of the debate, Kat wheeled and said, "Praedar, this is Dan McKelvey, the pilot who brought in our missing machinery. Dan, Dr. Praedar Effan Juxury."

The Whimed regarded him intently. "You are a Saunder-McKelvey?"

Dan blurted, "Yeah! I'm a son of Reid McKelvey and Fiona Oxford. My grandfather was Morgan McKelvey. And my great-great-grandparents were Ward and Jael Saunder. Anything else about my antecedents you need to know? Or am I automatically a pariah on this planet no matter what I do?"

Kat spoke up fast. "I'm sure he's all right, Praedar. He doesn't strike me as one of Feo's or Hope's flunkeys."

"You talking about my cousin Feo Saunder?" Dan demanded.

"None other." Kat added scornfully, "Your illustrious kinsman."

"Damned near *all* my kinsmen are illustrious," Dan retorted. "That's no ID. Feo. Hmm. Haven't seen him in years. He and I don't exactly move in the same circles. My sister tells me Feo's digging somewhere in this sector. He's in archaeology, too, I hear. Just like you people."

"*Xeno*archaeology," Kat corrected, sniffing. "And it's questionable if the Saunder-Nicholaievs' project equates with ours. Their selectivity is, to say the least, highly tainted. If they'd open their eyes and actually *read* what we've published concerning our findings here, they'd . . . oh, what's the use!"

"They have faith in their theories," Praedar said, "as we do in ours."

"But *ours* are *correct*," Kat insisted.

Dan was confused. Weren't all scientists in the same game—trying to solve the mysteries of the universe? Yet these people and his relatives obviously were involved in a competition, stepping hard on each other's toes. Because of that, Praedar's expedition distrusted any kinsman of Feo Saunder. The whole thing seemed self-defeating; wouldn't both groups accomplish more if they cooperated?

Kat said, "From what he told me, I can practically guarantee Dan's not one of their spies."

Whoa! All stop!

Was this a joke? She made it sound like a war, with espionage agents stealing enemy secrets!

". . . and anyway, he wouldn't be the first person in this camp with a link to the Saunder-McKelveys."

Before he could ask about *that* cryptic comment, Praedar smiled and thrust a calloused hand at him. "Apologies for my rudeness. You are most welcome here, Dan McKelvey." The alien's Terran English was impeccable, with only a hint of a Whimed accent.

"It's okay. Glad to have been of service, Doctor. That's what I get paid for."

Kat laughed. "Cute! Dan needs a signature on a receipt."

Whiskery hairs at the edges of Praedar's brows and eyelashes pinched together as he grinned. "*Stransir cheleet!* We must attend to that obligation at once." He took the receipt pad from Dan and signed twice—in Whimed characters and in Terran. It was an impressive feat by an impressive being.

Dr. Praedar Effan Juxury was unusually tall and lean for a Whimed. Dan stood a meter and three-quarters, and he had to look up to meet the scientist's starburst-pupiled eyes. Praedar's face was strong and bony, framed by striped red and silver hair. A felinoid's most distinctive feature was the crest, that barometer of its owner's emotional state. Praedar's crest was jet black, and at present it flopped limply, showing he was in a mellow mood.

If he'd been upset, the mane would have been a crown of spikes.

Signature taken care of, Praedar wanted to chat. What type starcraft did Dan fly? How far had he journeyed to T-W 593? What other planets had he visited recently? Occasionally Kat put in a query, too. Both scientists listened to Dan's replies with flattering attention. It made him a trifle uncomfortable, as if he were a specimen under examination.

When there was a break in the small talk, he said, "How about a swap? May I play tourist? Look around? This sort of Settlement is new to me."

Praedar's eyes gleamed. "*Aaaaa!* You also are an explorer. It is a reasonable request. Kaatje will be your guide, since she has been so kind as to vouch for you."

"I didn't go *that* far," Kat protested.

"An impartial observer would interpret your responses so, Dr. Olmsted." Praedar laughed silently, then sobered and said, "I must mediate the discussion regarding the temple dig." He turned on his heel and trotted back to the still-noisy debating circle.

Obviously envious, Kat watched him go. Dan said, "You needn't play nursemaid. I can sightsee on my own."

"What? Oh, no bother." Seeing his skepticism, she added, "Honestly, I can't contribute there. They're arguing over architectural concepts. Not my discipline at all. I'll wait till they arrive at a consensus, then read the report. That way, I miss the excitement of yelling myself hoarse at Armilly."

One debater was Lannon. The hairy procyonid was louder than anyone else on the hill. Dan pointed at him discreetly. "Armilly?" Kat's expression confirmed his guess. They listened to the uproar awhile and Dan noted, "Praedar's not doing much talking."

"He's absorbing. When they're through, he'll assemble key decisions into a coherent whole." Hero worship glowed in her brown eyes. Dan had seen Fleet cadets stare at his brother that way, when Adam had saved 61 Cygni Settlement from civil war. Kat straightened her shoulders, focusing her energy. "All right. To business. The camp rules. First: Time limit. You can stay forty-eight local hours, then you have to leave. That applies to all our guests. It's a clause in our dig permit. Besides, our funding is tight. We can't afford to feed and house outsiders longer than that." Dan said he'd eat and sleep aboard his ship. She brushed that aside. "It won't change anything. You might as well take potluck with us instead of wasting your time running back and forth to the landing strip."

He was disgruntled. These people were awfully damned inhospitable.

Kat continued, "Second: Until you leave, you have the freedom of camp, barring sensitive areas, which I'll point out to you. Third: Don't stand on the backfills, or any other piles of dirt. They may contain valuable artifacts we haven't extracted yet. Fourth: Don't walk on marker strings. Fifth: Don't move anything unless a team member tells you to. Is that understood?"

Saluting, Dan said, "Very clear. Further orders, ma'am?"

She wasn't amused. "These rules are important. If you break them, you may accidentally destroy years of work. That covers the basics. Let's go."

He was stung by her condescending manner. Big brain! That didn't give her the right to talk down to him.

It took him several minutes to get over his sulks. The path topped the dome hill, meandered down a gully, then leveled and widened on the far side. By the time they'd reached that spot, he was willing to try restarting the conversation on a friendlier note. "I know what you mean about visitors messing up things. I have to warn passengers to keep their hands off the boards, or they'll scramble my nav settings and life support feeds."

Kat asked interestedly, "You carry passengers? I thought indie haulers were strictly cargo transporters."

"Mostly, but sometimes I have a rider. A merchant in a hurry to get somewhere the major lines don't serve. I'm his taxi."

She looked as if she were putting the info into a file crammed with similar trivia. "I didn't know that. It may be useful someday; though I can't imagine how. To change the subject—our dig currently covers the area from the complex to that vacuum dredge there and from the mesa to that riverbed to the west."

"River?" Dan said, eyeing the arid, rough terrain to the right of the camp.

"It *is* a river, during the short rainy season," Kat said curtly.

She sure was touchy! He said, "Yeah, I'll bet it is. I've lived on a few desert worlds." He swung around, surveying the area she'd indicated. "So your Settlement's a couple-three kilometers square?"

"At present. We've shifted location, over the years. Praedar's initial investigations were twenty kilometers upstream, where the

N'lacs' village was originally. As our dig moved down slope, the N'lacs have followed us." Kat smiled, as if that fact pleased her. "A lot of sections were like those dud pits. Empty. But *this* site is absolutely full of potential. We've concentrated here these past three seasons."

She headed along the trail again, lecturing as she went. "The ruins were once part of an ancient city. When Praedar arrived, everything was buried in centuries of windblown drift. For example, until very recently that dome was completely hidden. Armilly's deep scanners showed us there was something there, but we couldn't be sure precisely what without excavation. And because that dredge broke down last season, we haven't been able to probe it as soon as we'd hoped.

"During its heyday, two millennia ago, the city was probably its world's capital. A wonderful find. Lower strata date to twelve thousand years before present. Indications are that this is one of the oldest inhabited sites on the planet. If only we had the funds to do justice to this dig! We'll have to be content to open a bare tenth of it. But we're on our way at last. Praedar's earned a payoff, after eleven years' work."

"Eleven?" Dan whistled, awed.

"Barely scratching the surface. When you strike xenoarch gold, as Praedar has done on T-W 593, it's the project of a lifetime. Of course, not all of us are in for the duration. Most of the students will finish their postgrads here and move on to their own careers elsewhere. And we have some short-term researchers like Dr. Getz, who's here solely to catalog the effigies we're finding. Even full-timers like me have to go offworld now and then—to touch base with families and our training institutes and beat the bushes for sponsorship grants. We're holding our breaths right now, praying the licensing Council renews Praedar's permit and our funding. If they don't . . ." Kat's face pinched with worry.

Dan sympathized. He'd done his share of scrambling for credits. It couldn't be easy for these scientists to do their work while sweating out money problems. Conditions on T-W 593 didn't demand huge injections of terraforming capital. But undoubtedly they demanded money as well as energy. Most alien environments did.

Overhead, the sky was a pale, blue-green bowl. A large moon hung like a ghostly face over the eastern cliff. The tendrilled "trees" and purple bushes growing everywhere digging hadn't

28

uprooted them were wilting beneath the local star's blazing glare. People and objects shimmered in heat waves.

Dan fought thirst and fatigue. This was an educational opportunity, expanding his horizons. He soaked up Kat's words and drew aerial maps in his mind's eye, getting an overall view of the project. Plainly, direct routes weren't important here. Buried ruins were. Those dirt paths meandered between dozens of trenches and pits and bracketed the boulders left by the desert river's rare floodings. Without any straight lines connecting excavations and complexes, a tour of the Settlement meant a long, hot walk.

"...most likely this continent's governmental center," Kat was saying. "We've found huge collections of data records. Our xenocrypto specialist, Ruieb-An, is deciphering them. And Dr. Chen is studying what was once the subbasement of a museum. Simply marvelous material! The N'lacs can be proud of their ancestors."

"Slow throttle!" Dan cut in. "Are you claiming those red-faced little e.t.s built all this?"

"Yes. At least their species did," Kat amended. "I'll admit not everyone agrees. Your kinsman Feo is stubbornly convinced the N'lacs are a lower order, distantly related, if that, to the race that created this splendor."

"He might have a point." Dan, gasping a bit, boosted his meds and said, "The locals haven't impressed me as super-thinkers. Chuss is the only one who—"

"Behaves with what we're arrogant enough to call true intelligence?" Kat snapped. "Don't underestimate the N'lacs. They're not stupid. They're simply operating under tremendous handicaps. And there's an excellent reason why Chuss seems so bright." She took a deep breath that did attractive things to her breasts. Dan stifled his hormones with effort.

"Intelligent life is so rare in our galaxy. Too many technologically gifted species eliminate would-be competitors, as mankind nearly wiped out the apes and cetaceans before we came to our senses. That's why preserving the N'lacs and their ancestors' history is so imperative. At least the Terran-Whimed Xenoethnic Council has classified them as relatives of the once-dominant local species. That'll protect them, for now."

"Level Two, huh?" Dan said. "Like the Flahni, those amphibians on the Vahnajes' home world, or the Rigotian bird folks?"

"Exactly!" Kat quoted standard Level 2 criteria. "Simple cognitive abilities, opposable thumbs or manipulative appendages, rudimentary speech. As if that's all the N'lacs had!" She grimaced angrily. "Chuss will prove otherwise. He's a forerunner, a successful test case. Once we get sufficient funds, we'll make the Saunder's and Praedar's other critics see they were wrong. In the meantime, we watchdog the N'lacs' development and discourage squatters. Too much contact with untrained outsiders at this point would be a catastrophe for Chuss' people. We can't let that happen."

Dan muttered noncommittally. Primitive species often *did* suffer cruelly from too much exposure too soon to outside influences. But was that the sole reason this expedition was keeping other offworlders away? Another aspect of the setup had occurred to him. He'd seen N'lacs toting baskets of dirt and doing general scut work for the scientists everywhere. "Yeah. It's a fair exchange, I suppose. You protect the N'lacs and they provide slave labor."

"Slaves? That ridiculous!" Kat exploded. "This is a symbiotic relationship. We supply the N'lacs with medicine, food supplements from our stores and greenhouses, a reliable water supply, and we nourish their history, their pride. That's critical to their survival. Can't you see that? And they *want* to help us. They volunteer to do those simple chores. Do they look exploited? I assure you, their health and their general welfare are *enormously* improved over what they were when Praedar first came here. Is that slavery?"

She talked a good defense. But Dan couldn't help thinking she overdid it. Was she feeling guilty, deep down?

Kat marched away, her head high, outrage stiffening her spine.

He decided it was smarter not to pursue the matter. As far as he could tell, the N'lacs weren't being abused. And he was a guest. He shouldn't kick his hostess's shins on such weak evidence.

Anyway, there was plenty else to command his attention on this tour—wildlife, for one thing. He'd seen lizardy animals with ruffled fringes at their throats; countless insects, some spectacularly large and colorful; and fuzzy critters, many of them camouflaged. That didn't protect them from flying predators. A diamond-shaped, leather-winged meat eater pounced on a victim and carried it to its lair on the cliff face, zooming past almost under Dan's nose. The flyer's wings made an eerie ripping sound that lingered in the hot air, echoing faintly.

"The N'lacs call that a duto," Kat said. Her anger had apparently simmered by now. "They're more or less harmless to humanoids, though they will bite and drink blood, if they find you asleep outdoors at night."

"Charming. Any other nasties?"

"Major predators? None except us. There are numerous marsupials, a few avians and reptiles, but no snakes. And billions of these pests the N'lacs call oony." She slapped at a cloud of midges, but her glare was aimed at Dan.

He maintained a prudent silence for a time after that, plodding in her wake, nodding as she pointed out items along the trail.

Gradually Dan grew uneasy. Something about the landscape seemed skewed. It was a familiar, nagging sensation. Other humans had felt the same thing, ever since humanity first left Earth and landed on alien planets. Evolution installed key recognition factors in the brain—factors tied to the world where a species originated. When that species dealt with a different environment, even a nominally terrene one, instincts revelled. Normally Dan overruled the reaction with his forebrain. On T-W 593, an unidentifiable undercurrent squirmed beneath his skin disconcertingly, refusing to let go.

Aside from that, it wasn't a bad place. He'd known far worse —the plains of Asita Hosi, the salt flats on E Indi Settlement, and a wind-torn wasteland on a Whimed world named Chayn. Pioneers could put up with incredible hardships if there was prospect of reward, such as precious metals, exportable flora and fauna, new trade routes, or new products. Others sought the freedom to follow an unusual life-style, to set up experimental political systems, or to create havens for offbeat religions.

None of those motives applied to Praedar's expedition. The scientists weren't mining or tilling the soil. They weren't manufacturing anything. They didn't behave like religious mavericks or political rebels. Their only reason for being here was to dig up this buried city.

The search for a long-lost civilization seemed as impractical and noncontributory as Varenka's projects to clone her ancestor and restore Saunderhome. Praedar's team would probably approve of her plans; she and these xenoarchaeologists were equally obsessed with ancient relics. It all seemed a waste of time—hobbies for rich folks.

And yet . . .

Kat said Praedar's funding was tight. And these people certainly weren't New Earth Renaissance dilettantes. They mingled freely with other races, coped with an alien world, and weren't afraid of hard work. Dan had seen the offworlders hauling rocks, digging with hand tools, and crawling in filthy rubble, unearthing their treasures. He tried to imagine Varenka grubbing in the dirt like that. Hah! Not even to save Saunderhome!

Kat delivered a running commentary. "We think this was an administrative structure . . . group residence . . . housing unit . . . educational center . . . a temple . . . government building . . . market . . ."

Dan saw none of those things. Kat pointed to rocks, sand, and crumbling lumps that *might* have been walls worn down to their foundations. Even fairly intact structures were little more than shells. It seemed impossible anyone could figure out what they used to be. But Praedar's team claimed to have done so. Marker strings stretched between pegs, outlining the ruins. There were signs everywhere, in Terran and alien languages, warning passersby to keep off the "constructs." Dan tried to envision a thriving e.t. population center on this site. Kat made it almost real. Almost, but not quite.

Occasionally she stopped to chat with colleagues. Their shoptalk went well over Dan's head. "Strata . . . the gnathic materials . . . hyperbarics . . . paleomagnetism . . . crystal dating . . ."

The path took a long loop past that disabled dredge and curved back to the main camp. By the time Dan was climbing the slope near the dome, he was getting winded. Kat said, "I hope I didn't go too fast for you."

"Nah, I'm fine," he lied. Kat smiled archly.

There was a mob scene in camp. The truck had returned from the landing strip. Team members were unloading cargo, hampered by the N'lacs, who got underfoot. Praedar and the debaters had joined the crowd. Kat, too, elbowed her way into the thick of things. Dan was content to be a spectator. He'd already done his job, delivering this stuff.

Praedar fingered a crate's shipping tag. *"Durin kwilya!* How long we have waited!"

"Indeed!" chimed in a scientist with a heavy Martian colony

accent. "A most costly delay. Our preparations for the Xenoarch Assembly have been thrown completely off schedule . . ."

Kat turned to a sad-faced Vahnaj. "Now you can repair the dredge, and we can finally make some progress excavating the dome."

"Urr . . . I do not mer-it rep-ri-mand, Ka-at-yuh," the Vahnaj argued. "Dredge is op-er-a-tion-al . . ."

Sheila guffawed. "Ruieb, when a machine doesn't run, most species say it's *not* operational." She broke off and shouted at the N'lacs. "Chuss! You fellow get them diggers 'way from truck!"

"Hoosh! Motherless thieves!" Armilly, the loudmouthed Lannon, waved his hairy arms and growled, "Stolen expedition's property. Thieves! Evil Deo and Hoop."

"Feo and Hope," Praedar corrected him. "An unprovable charge. The machinery was not stolen. Observe. It is here."

"Then how about 'deliberately mislaid'?" Kat asked. "Or 'kicked into the back corner of a warehouse for a year'?"

"That must be what happened," Joe Hughes said. The black man lifted a box and started toward the insta-cell storage shed. "Somebody paid shipping clerks plenty to look the other way. I just wonder why this stuff surfaced *now*."

Dan was wondering that himself. Worry crawled through his gut.

Sheila suggested, "Maybe Feo was too cheap to bribe-bury it permanently."

"Miser!" Kat said with withering scorn. "He's a billionaire. He and Hope don't apply for grants. They could buy the whole planet they're digging on by peeling a few hundred thousand out of their petty cash . . ."

"Urr . . . brib-ery is illegal," Ruieb-An chirred.

The Terrans and Whimeds grinned. Sheila said, "Yes, but authorities get corrupt or greedy. That never happens in the Vahnaj sector, huh?" Ruieb-An looked uncomfortable.

"You can bet Feodor Ivanovich Saunder-Nicholaiev didn't get his own hands dirty bribe-burying this," Kat said. "He probably sent his fair-haired boy, Greg Tavares, to make the payment under the table . . ."

Dan sidled away from the group. What if the accusations were true? He'd better find out.

He'd gone a few meters when Sheila Whitcomb caught up with him. She swatted his rump and said, "This is a fine comment on our hospitality, McKelvey. Are we boring you already?"

Kat, Praedar, and a number of others were staring at him. Embarrassed, Dan stammered, "N-no, it's not that at all. I have to get back to my ship."

"Chow's on soon. Better hang around," Sheila invited. "If you don't eat with us and bitch about Frank's cooking, you'll hurt his feelings."

"Uh . . . I'll pass tonight. Have to make a subspace call."

"Use our com," Sheila said.

Smiling, Dan replied, "No offense, but I want a clear signal, and your unit isn't up to that."

The blonde was taken aback for a second. "Kroo-ger, you're fussy! Okay. If you say so. But the sun's too high for you to walk it. Take the rover."

It was his turn to be taken aback. "You'd let me borrow it?"

"Sure! Kat might not, but I will, and I'm the one talking to you, handsome. Besides, I'm a paramed, and I'm not eager to nurse a heat-stroke victim. You wouldn't be any fun, flat on your back and unable to rise."

Laughing at her lewd crack, he broke into a run and yelled, "Thanks! I'll bring it back in the morning!"

He drove out of camp at top speed, bouncing up onto the mesa, putting readouts in the red, punishing power systems. When he reached *Fiona*, he skidded to a stop beneath her wing and raced into the cabin.

Once seated at the com, though, he took his time composing the outbound message. This priority call would cost him plenty. He needed to be precise and concise, in spacer's lingo, to get his money's worth. Finally Dan drew a deep breath and fed the signal starward.

Then he waited. Terran Traffic Central's nearest base was a light-hour away via an indie's skimpy subspace equipment. He'd have to keep busy in the interim, or tension would eat him alive.

He did a walk-around inspection of his ship and found that the scientists had shut the cargo bay doors, as promised, but had left an adjacent hatch open. That thing never *had* closed properly. He spent a quarter hour, local time, getting it buttoned up again to his satisfaction.

Another couple of walk-arounds passed. He watched the sun set and a second moon rise to keep its bigger sister company. Minutes ticked by.

He was back in the cabin long before the com glowed to life. A disinterested voice said:

"Terran Traffic Central Base 444, responding to query from IHS *Fiona*. Status of McKelvey, Daniel Morgan Saunder. Reading. Terran Reg #IH-447820. Starship operator's license #899312-47. Free Port Eighteen has filed a question concerning possible unauthorized transportation of cargo. Pilot will be notified when a decision is arrived at in this matter. Base 444, out."

For a long while, Dan was too stunned to move.

The scientists were right. That cargo *was* supposed to be bribe-buried. But somebody had unburied it. And they'd used it to nail him to the bulkhead.

Free Port Eighteen. The complaint had been filed there. That dispatcher! The one with the grudge against Adam—and against Adam's baby brother.

The Saunder-McKelvey clan bragged that blood was thicker than water. Now that kinship was squashing Dan.

The dispatcher set me up. Why didn't I see it! The timing on this cargo was just too damned convenient, coming after that long layover. If only I hadn't been so preoccupied with Dad's letter. If only I'd used spacer's intuition to smell the garbage she was dumping on me. If I'd checked with Traffic earlier, maybe I could have figured a way out. No, who am I kidding? There's no way out. There never is from these things.

The dispatcher had her revenge. Dan was blacklisted.

He pulled the ident receipt from his pocket and gazed at Praedar's signature. Nice and neat—and worthless, for now.

Dan had seen this happen to other indies who inadvertently broke the unwritten dispatchers' code regarding bribe-buried cargos. He knew when he made his next stopover, a clerk would duly record the receipt. Then the record would disappear for an indefinite period. No funds would move from the expedition's accounts to Dan's. Dispatchers would overlook him when they assigned cargo loads. That situation would continue until the dispatchers decided he'd learned his lesson. That could take months.

Without money, he couldn't make payments on his ship. She'd be repossessed. He'd be out of the hauling business. Then? If he was lucky, he might find a job at the bottom of the tech-mech labor heap, starting all over again.

Dan went out and sat on *Fiona*'s debark ramp. He stared dejectedly through wispy clouds at the stars.

The stars . . .

For five generations, the Saunders and McKelveys had led mankind outward and onward to those stars. Since the days of Ward Saunder, Dan's great-great-grandfather, his family had served in the forefront of Earth's leap into the galaxy. He'd kept up those traditions, in his modest way. True, he didn't operate a fleet of spacecraft or own a multiplanet conglomerate like Feo's sister Ulrica or his cousin Phil McKelvey, to name just a few. But he'd treated his customers fairly and always paid his debts—until now. His ancestors had broken the chains binding humanity to Earth and the solar system, and Dan gave his customers and their cargoes interstellar wings. He was his own boss, a spacer.

Not anymore.

What was he going to do? Ride his sisters' coattails, or Adam's? He cringed, hearing Adam say, "I knew it would happen. You're a loser, just like Dad."

Other alternatives? Sell *Fiona* for whatever he could get? Losing the starhopper would hurt, but he'd have little choice. He didn't have enough financial cushion to ride out this blacklist.

When he launched from T-W 593, he'd vector into limbo.

And he would have to leave soon. His visitor's pass was limited to forty-eight local hours, and he'd already used up more than six of those.

He didn't want to go, and he couldn't stay.

Dan was trapped. Whichever way he turned, he'd face a dead end.

CHAPTER FOUR

✪✪✪✪✪✪✪✪

The Outsider

He drove back to the valley at dawn. Sunlight filled the mesa, but below the cliff the only illumination came from solar storage lamps and the N'lacs' cook fires. Dan parked the rover and picked his way along a barely visible path, trying to avoid the pits and string markers he'd seen yesterday.

Suddenly he collided with a living form. Atavistic alarms jangled in his brain.

Someone laughed, and a human voice said, "You gotta watch your step when you don't know the trail, McKelvey."

"Hughes?" Dan said sheepishly. "Yeah, I guess I should. Say, have you seen Praedar, Kat, or Sheila this morning?"

"You're headed in the right direction. Look in at the cook shack."

"Thanks, I . . ."

The man had vanished. Hughes had moved on, becoming just another shadow in a valley heavy with shadows.

Dan shivered, then swore softly. Why was he so jittery? Sure, he had to stay on his toes in this new environment, but he didn't need to imagine each noise and object was a monster. He squared his shoulders, determined not to let things rattle him.

All the same, he breathed easier when he reached the lighted area surrounding the buildings. The cook shack was the biggest of the linked polygons and served as a communal meeting room as well as a diner. At the moment, it was cluttered with eating stations, most of them empty. Vahnaj privacy cubicles and a Lannon "platform where one ingests" stood bare. Dan looked around and didn't see Praedar or any other Whimeds. A few Terrans, Kat and Sheila among them, sat at the tables at the far end of the room. As he approached the women, Sheila said, "You're an early riser, handsome. Kroo-ger! You look like leftovers from a lizard's breakfast!"

That was a painful reminder of what had happened last night. He muttered, "I didn't sleep well. I . . . I wanted to catch you before you started work. Have to ask something . . ."

"Shh!" Sheila gestured toward Kat and an older man and whispered, "Let me hear how this comes out first."

Kat was saying, "Oral tradition based on genuine tribal history is a given in our profession, Dr. Getz."

"Not with the N'lacs. Not yet. I'm unpersuaded." Getz was a pudgy, balding type, very sure of himself. "You xenosocios who study with Harte never *do* take these primitive legends with sufficient salt and cynicism."

"Chuss is a very reliable interpreter," Kat retorted. "And I'm fluent in N'lac. I guarantee he's giving us an accurate rendition of Sleeg's narratives."

"No doubt you do. I've observed your quaint selection process for a full dig season now, Olmsted, all those so-called tale-telling sessions." Getz sipped from a disposable mug before he recited in a bored tone: "'We traveled long-long time through Big Dark to escape Evil Old Ones. We come home here. If we do not please gods, Evil Old Ones will send demons to catch us and take us back to the horrible place.' Bah! Sleeg's spinning yarns for the N'lac kiddies. Don't forget Chuss himself is a N'lac kiddie, barely more than a pup. He's bright, yes, thanks to Hughes' experiments, but far too impressionable for Praedar to base an entire hypothesis on."

"You agree Sleeg's legends correspond closely with aboriginal myths from Earth's Western Hemisphere," Kat said, refusing to retreat.

Getz made a rude noise. "Where's the evidence? You need material to measure and analyze . . ."

"Of course. Measure and analyze—and ignore any anomalies that don't fit one's preconceived ideas. A few people on this project think you use that system in your effigy classifications, to the detriment of science . . ."

Sheila bit her lip, afraid that Kat had pushed her arguments over the edge. She was right. Dr. Getz, his face alarmingly flushed, got to his feet and stomped out of the room.

Kat smashed his abandoned mug into a messy puddle. A be-whiskered cook, gathering trays, complained loudly about people who played with their food and made extra work for him. That drew a taunting chorus from the breakfasters. "You call this stuff food, Frank?" The cook gave as good as he got. Ribald insults flew.

Their banter eased Kat's mood. She managed a lopsided grin and said, "Well, at least sparring with Bill gets my adrenaline flowing in the morning. Far better than caffa."

Sheila regarded her friend with amusement. "Suit yourself. But that was a low blow, accusing him of unprofessionalism about his effigies. He *is* the expert."

"Maybe he's too cocky because of that. It won't hurt him to consider others' opinions and doubts for a change. I'm sick of his brushing off everyone else's theories—including those concerning the N'lac legends."

"He can be a pain, true," Sheila conceded.

"More than that. He has to modify his claims," Kat said. "If he doesn't, Feo and Hope will tear his data to shreds at the Assembly. That is, if we even get to the Assembly—if something else doesn't crop up and spoil our plans." She noticed Dan and said, "Good morning. You look terrible. Did you bring back the rover? Is it in one piece?"

"Yeah, and in better shape than it was. That power switch was a mess. Why don't you people take better care of your equipment?"

Kat shrugged. "We have more important matters to attend to."

He wanted to shake her out of that indifferent pose. But smart beggars didn't antagonize potential benefactors, and he was here to beg a favor. Dan cleared his throat and asked with careful courtesy, "Could I have an extension on that visitor's pass, please?"

The women exchanged weary glances, then headed for the outer door. Kat said, "Sorry, no. This isn't a tourist world. You heard the rules."

Dan pursued her and Sheila, talking earnestly. "I don't want to play tourist. All I'm asking for is a longer layover permit, and maybe a chance to work."

No response.

He went on, explaining his problems with the blacklist, emphasizing that he wasn't requesting charity.

Still no response.

The trio ducked through the insta-cell's low exit. Dan was momentarily blinded by sunlight. The air was heating up fast, a scorching promise of what it would be like at midday. However, the atmosphere by the cook shack was as cold as Kat Olmsted's face. She repeated, "Sorry. All our personnel must be fully accredited members of the project."

"So I'm not a scientist. I can still be useful here."

They smiled at him patronizingly and Dan bristled. Sheila said, "We're sure you're good at what you do, but we don't need a pilot."

"Hey! You think I was born at a starhopper's controls?" he exclaimed. "I'm a qualified tech-mech, all branches, fifteen years' experience. I can repair any rig and most circuitry. Terran, Whimed, Vahnaj, you name it, I'll fix it."

"Not necessary," Sheila said with the same superior smile. "We take turns keeping our machinery in good order."

He opened his mouth, eager to remind her that the rover, the com, and that broken vacuum dredge showed they weren't doing a terrific job at that.

Kat cut him off. "It's not that we're unsympathetic. We simply have no place for you."

Frustrated and angry, Dan quit worrying about stepping on their toes. If they were going to turn him down anyway, he might as well speak his mind. "I see. No place for an ordinary spacer, since you've already got plenty of slaves."

The women's bland expressions altered. Kat yelled, "I *told* you the N'lacs aren't slaves!"

"Then how did you know I was referring to them?" Dan said, and went on with heavy sarcasm. "Excuse my pitiful lack of education. I know I can't join your exclusive club of the big-brained elite. I'm just a stupid tech-mech. You make your own

40

definitions, dressed up in fancy words. You want to call it a symbiotic relationship? Fine! How could I? Why, I can't even flaunt a degree from some important institution . . ."

The brunette spluttered, speechless with indignation. Sheila tugged her friend's arm. "Come on, Kat. Let's not waste the morning in this pointless jabbering . . ."

Dan blocked their path. "You owe me, dammit! The least you can do is give me that pass extension as partial payment."

They gawked at him, amazed. After a lengthy silence, Sheila said, "How do you figure we owe you anything?"

He jerked a thumb at the camp's supply sheds. "That cargo. That's what got me in bad with the dispatchers. I'm mixed up in your feud with Feo and Hope Saunder, whether I want to be or not. Maybe I ought to take the machinery back to Port Eighteen. That might pull me off the hook and reinstate my regs."

It was an empty threat. A lone man couldn't cart away kilotons of cargo under the noses of an entire Settlement. But the rest of what he'd said seemed to make the women reconsider. They frowned and conferred in whispers, eyeing Dan thoughtfully.

On edge, his senses drawn taut, he awaited their decision. He became keenly aware of sight, sound, and smell: sunlight reflecting off polygonal housing and labs; the odors of freshly dug earth, sweat, smoke, and food; and the multiple sounds of men and N'lacs starting the day's work. In the distance, a machine coughed; Ruieb-An, trying to get that dredge operational, using the parts Dan had delivered? He hoped the noise would underline the debt these settlers owed him.

Kat finally threw up her hands and grunted sourly. Dan braced himself for a rejection. But to his surprise, she said, "Your point is well taken. You *do* appear to be an innocent bystander who was dragged into our dispute with Feo and Hope." He started to thank her. Kat held up a warning hand. "That doesn't mean you get the extension. It means we'll talk it over with Praedar. No promises. Agreed?"

"Agreed!"

"Hmph! I should think so!" Kat peered at her wristvid and said brusquely, "Until you hear from us, you're on probation." Then she hurried on up to the trail to the dome. Dan got the impression she was fleeing before he could come up with any more demands or disturbing cracks about slavery.

Sheila said, "Pretty slick blackmailing there, handsome.

41

You'd better not try it often. Olmsted has a short fuse." She winked and ran to catch up with Kat. The blonde's long legs easily matched the smaller woman's pace.

Dan swung a roundhouse punch at nothing, releasing pent-up tension. They hadn't said no. They'd said maybe! A reprieve! His hopes soared. He even allowed his hormones to romp, watching Kat and Sheila walking away, enjoying the movement of their bodies, bare legs, and bouncing braids. Snooty, sure, but they were sexy women. If Praedar let him stay, he might become better acquainted with them. Not a bad deal.

If Praedar said okay.

No matter what sort of work the expedition assigned him, it was bound to be an improvement over mooching dregs at Settlement Labor Offices or living on Adam's crumbs. Also, he'd be able to hang on to *Fiona* for a while longer. No creditor would come clear out to this back-of-nowhere world to repossess a secondhand starhopper.

A lot depended on Praedar's generosity. Whimeds were funny beings, similar to Terrans in certain ways, totally alien in others. How could he encourage the expedition's boss to decide in his favor? Obey camp rules, naturally, and avoid annoying the scientists or getting in their way. It seemed wise to scout the territory and learn as much as he could now. Then he'd be primed to step in and prove he could contribute when Praedar gave the go-ahead.

There was considerable activity at the dome this morning. That was as good a place to start as any. Dan climbed the hill and stood on the sidelines, observing. The xenoarchaeologists had set up a dirt-removal assembly team. Offworlders shoveled and N'lacs scooped with their webbed paws. Rubble went into hand carts or baskets and was taken from the deepening excavation to a nearby dump pile. The process was steady but very slow.

The scene appalled Dan. He empathized with the scientists' aching muscles. And although he still wondered if the N'lacs weren't glorified slaves, he had to admit that the e.t.s weren't being bullied or doing any heavy stuff. The offworlders handled that, and it was damned rough work. Obviously this was why the team had been so glad to see those replacement machine parts. Once the dredge was repaired, it would suck away this mound of earth in a hundredth of the time it would take via hand labor.

Not everyone was shoveling and hauling. Armilly, the Lannon, hunkered amid a forest of monitors, checking on what lay under the remaining soil. Dr. Getz and his students were poking through the accumulating rubble heap, searching for effigy fragments.

Dan sidled nearer the site, craning his neck to see. The team was gradually clearing a ramp that sloped toward the hidden base of that huge dome. Eavesdropping, he learned that Armilly's gear was mapping underground structures for them, showing precisely where to dig. Those remote scans weren't good enough for the group. They wanted eyeball contact, and were willing to strain their backs to achieve that. With the dredge out of commission, they'd had to resort to hand tools.

Work progressed in fits and starts. At times it came to a dead stop while the scientists used miniature blowers to expose finds. They crowed over these "life-style artifacts," "socio-indicative litter," and "ethnic constructs."

A wall bordered the ramp. As dirt was removed, team members cleaned its surface and sprayed it with protective mists. Writing and pictures began to emerge.

Despite Dan's feelings about the foolishness of salvaging Saunderhome and this buried city, he was intrigued. This was fascinating! How many years had these things been locked in the soil? Now they could be studied and might tell Praedar's gang more about the civilization that made the dome, the ramp, and the wall—the civilization of Chuss's ancestors, if what Kat had said was true.

Dan longed to join the party. It would be a thrill to make such a discovery, like finding a wrecked starhopper and tinkering her back to spaceworthiness after everyone else had given up on her.

His shoulder blades itched, an odd, unnerving pressure. No, it wasn't an itch. He was being stared at. Someone was boring a hole through his spine.

He turned and came face to face with Praedar.

The tall Whimed's jumpsuit was rumpled, his crest unkempt. He looked as if he'd just awakened. Whimeds, a polyphasic species, grabbed short catnaps around the clock instead of sleeping for long stretches, as monophasic Terrans did. The boss no doubt had been taking a snooze. Now Praedar was out and about, and pinning Dan with that unblinking, piercing stare.

A Whimed's starburst-shaped pupils were weapons. No human, Vahnaj, or Lannon could match the felinoids in this game of locked gazes. Dan didn't even try. He lowered his eyes and pretended that he really wanted to examine a chunk of rock by his boot. He allowed a number of seconds to elapse in order to regain his composure, glanced up, and said, "Can I help dig?"

"No." Praedar softened that with, "I would prefer you do not at present. You do not know what we are seeking or how to seek it. That requires much advance preparation and training."

Plain enough. Ego deflating, but plain.

It was unusual for a Whimed to take that much trouble to explain his reasons to a non-Whimed. Praedar's patience was necessary, if he was to lead a diverse, multispecies team. He waited, silently demanding a response. Thoughts of that visitor's pass danced in Dan's head. He clung to the implications in the phrase "at present," hoping that meant Praedar would accept him eventually. For now, he'd occupy himself elsewhere, and stay out of the alien's crest.

As Dan retreated, Praedar joined the diggers. He relieved a fellow Whimed, who flopped down to catnap in the shade of the portable canteen. Changing of the guard.

None of the scientists looked at Dan or told him "See you later." They'd barely been aware of his presence while he was on the site and didn't seem to notice him now that he was leaving. A N'lac elder sat on the refuse pile, and he scowled at the pilot. The wrinkled little e.t. reminded Dan of the old codgers lounging on benches fronting many Settlement municipal squares. Did this N'lac gossip with his cronies and gripe that the younger generation was going to hell, too? Maybe. At any rate, he was the only being here who paid any attention to a departing Terran.

Dan kicked at pebbles, feeling grumpy. He was an outsider with no training, just in the way. Okay! He'd teach himself, starting with an educational walk through the entire valley.

It would be a lonely walk. Kat was busy on the dome dig today. So were most of those scientists Dan had met on the trails yesterday.

He set off on the same path Kat had shown him, then branched off, exploring, drawing additional maps in his mind's eye. It was the same method he'd used to pass his pilot's regs, so it ought to work in this situation, as well. He built on the scraps he'd acquired from the ed-vids, soaking up info and getting a feel for Praedar's world.

Bright orange insects clicked and hovered about his head.

Boomer lizards sprang between the rocks. A furry quadruped moved stealthily through a copse of purple "trees" beyond one of the larger soil dumps. Dutos, those leather-winged predators, drifted in lazy circles overhead, riding thermals and seeking prey. Several times Dan was startled when bushes made a loud snapping sound. The effect was that of immense jaws closing. After a while, he got used to the peculiar natural phenomenon.

The air was a thirsty sponge. He stopped often in the shadow of a ruined building, a "tree," or a flood-dumped boulder. The path hadn't been this tough yesterday. But then the sun had been well past the zenith. Now it was climbing, and so was the temperature.

As he reached the far turn of the trails, near the disabled dredge, he found he wasn't alone out here, after all. Ruieb-An and another Vahnaj were fussing with the big rig. Dan watched them with a critical eye. The lutrinoids were as inept at this job as he would have been attempting an advanced xenoarchaeological technique. Squirming, he said, "Uh . . . honored persons, Ruieb-An, may I offer my assistance?"

The Vahnajes regarded him owlishly. Ruieb-An said, "Most honored Dan-iel McKel-vey. Good morn-ing. Wel-come. Most kind of you. Urr."

Dan bowed and bobbed.

The Vahnajes bowed and bobbed.

The courtesies went on and on, until Dan realized the aliens were deliberately stalling. Burying him in an avalanche of politeness. Their expressions were serene. Pointy-toothed smiles shone in their flat, gray faces. But their nostrils were pinched shut and their sideburns were flattened. Those were emotional barometers, like a Whimed's crest. Ruieb-An and his companion were annoyed by Dan's offer, and refused to accept it.

"The hell with it," he muttered. "Do it your way. But I'll warn you—that thing will chew you to pieces if you align it wrong, the way you're doing it."

The Vahnajes bowed and bobbed a bit more, then turned back to their tinkering. Dan jammed his hands in his pockets and stomped off on the eastern leg of the trail.

There were fewer marker stakes near the cliff and less for him to look it. The path did give him respite from the sun, and Dan walked in the shade of a rocky overhang wherever he could. A few times he sat on a stone shelf and rested and boosted his meds.

Getting his second wind, he headed northward, still compiling his mental map. The trails formed a rough triangle. One leg went past the dome to the dredge, then took a sharp angle eastward there. A return leg followed the sheer cliff wall as far as the N'lacs' village. Then another major trail cross-connected at that point with the insta-cell complex.

At the spot where the path swung west, he came out from under an overhang and stopped, staring up apprehensively. The cliff was particularly steep here, and an enormous boulder perched on its summit. The thing was an ominous giant.

To Dan's left, a deep, narrow excavation gaped. He couldn't see the bottom. Rickety brushwood ladders leaned against one of the sides. A canvas sun shelter sat close to the rim. Dr. Chen, the pot-bellied joker, was sorting through a tote box of small objects he'd brought up from the pit. Joe Hughes and one of the N'lacs looked on interestedly as Chen assembled his finds.

Hughes glanced around at Dan and smiled. "Admiring our landmark? Don't worry about Hanging Rock. It's the camp pet. According to Baines, our geologist, it's stood there for ages. Hasn't moved a millimeter in all that time. Perfectly safe."

Dan still didn't feel easy about the landmark. He tried not to stare up at it as he made his way to the sun shelter. The N'lac squinted at him and suddenly brightened, crying "Kelfee! He Kelfee!"

"That's right, Meej," and Hughes patted the youngster's bald head. "Him fellow McKelvey. Your brother fellow Chuss meet him last sun time."

Meej thrust out a paw. Dan took the childike hand. The webbing between Meej's tiny fingers was less obvious than that on other N'lacs'. Meej was on tiptoe, studying the pilot with a wide-eyed, nearsighted gaze.

"Now that you've been introduced, you'll have to shake hands with him every time you meet," Hughes warned. "With the other N'lacs, too, once they get to know you. They love to shake hands. It's a Terran custom they've adopted with a vengeance. Why don't you come into the village and I'll show you the drill? I've got work to do there, and I'd appreciate the company."

"Sure. Thanks. You're the first person who hasn't told me to scram today."

"They're wrapped up in the dome dig right now," the black man said. "On top of that Sleeg, the shaman, objected to the excavation on religious grounds, and they had to placate him."

"Hah! Praedar smoothed his feathers," Chen exclaimed. "Good boy. Taught him everything he knows. Smart kid, for a Whimed."

Dan certainly hadn't thought of charismatic Praedar Effan Juxury as a kid!

Chen sealed his specimens into the tote, reserving one chunk of pottery, and stumbled toward the trail junction. Hughes, Meej, and Dan followed him. The Oriental held the potsherd scant centimeters from his eyes, poring over it, heedless of where he put his feet.

"Can I help you, Doctor?" Dan asked.

The scientist turned his head in Dan's direction. His stare was even more myopic than Meej's. "Dunno. How good's your eyesight, boy?"

"I'm a pilot," Dan replied, believing that was sufficient answer.

It was. "Then you can see too damned good for *my* purposes. You'd be as bad at examining these little bitty museum treasures as Praedar is. All those Whimeds are farsighted. Can't see worth a damn without a ton of expensive gadgets. Me, I carry all my equipment right here." Chen tapped a forefinger on his orbital ridge. His grin widened. "Nice of you to make the offer, though. I knew you were the right sort, boy. Don't let anybody here bluff you. Hear?"

They had reached the trail junction. Chen veered left toward the insta-cell complex. He continued to examine the potsherd, weaving all over the path as he did. Hughes shook his head in amusement. "He'll break his neck one of these days, doing that. Crazy eccentric!"

As he followed Hughes into the N'lac village, Dan said, "He's a real character, okay. I like him."

"Everyone does. That's why we play his old curmudgeon game with him. Chen particularly enjoys treating Praedar like an apprentice, and Praedar doesn't seem to mind. I suppose Chen's entitled to take that stance. He and Praedar have worked together for years. Praedar actually started as one of Chen's students. That's unusual, for a Whimed. Of course, Praedar's long since surpassed his mentor..."

47

"Is Chen really nearsighted?" Dan wondered. The concept was strange, in these modern times. Prenatal engineering and postnatal adjustments, including corrective surgery, eliminated most of the physical glitches that had plagued humanity in the past centuries.

"Oh, yes, and proud of it. His personal design, having his eyes converted to acute myopia." Dan's jaw dropped. Hughes nodded and went on. "Had it done when he was an undergrad. One of his heroes was Sir Arthur Evans, a Terran archaeo who excavated in the Mediterranean in the early 1900s. Evans was profoundly nearsighted, and famous for using his eyes as a microscope. In Chen's case, it's a stunt, but a useful one. He truly doesn't need any sophisticated gear to analyze the stuff he's bringing up from that ancient N'lac museum basement."

Dan, Hughes, and Meej made their way through draperies of tendrilled trees into the N'lac community. Round-roofed, mud-brick huts nestled under the cliff's overhang. Women tended crops in tiny garden patches. Naked children played in the dirt. Clay pots clustered around a communal firepit. Stretched hides were drying in the sun. Village elders squatted in the shade, swapping yarns. It was a textbook version of those aboriginal habitats depicted in the ed-vids.

When the villagers saw the Terrans, all of them retreated briefly toward the huts, then turned and waved exaggeratedly, as if just that moment discovering their guests. Their actions had the look of an elaborate social ritual.

Hughes waved back at them while telling Dan "About the crew snubbing you this morning—don't take it personally. As soon as Ruieb-An gets that dredge repaired . . ."

"Don't hold your breath for that," Dan warned. "He doesn't know straight up about the rig."

"Hmm. Sorry to hear that. Ruieb was indulging in Vahnaj braggadocio, I guess . . ." Then Joe Hughes broke off as villagers huddled around them, grabbing his hands. He introduced Dan. True to his prediction, each N'lac then had to shake the pilot's hand. He noticed most of their fingers were extremely club-tipped, unlike Chuss's and Meej's.

It was Dan's first close-up view of the e.t.s They were red-faced, wrinkle-skinned, and panting, mouths open wide, revealing bright red tongues and mucous membranes. The N'lacs sweated so profusely the desert air couldn't evaporate their perspiration fast enough. Except for Meej, they were all very paunchy. And all of them except Meej moved in apparent slow motion, as if action lagged behind thought. They plucked at Dan's clothes and gawked at his hair, several muttering in pidgin that he was like "Sheila fellow on head top."

Meej flapped his skinny arms and yelled, "He fellow Kelfee! Come fly-fly. Zwoop! Down quick! Skirsh! Chuss see him. Kelfee come out. Come Praedar's camp. Come from high-high." The N'lacs giggled, delighted with the account.

"That makes you all right," Joe said. "N'lac legends claim that only bad strangers come out of places in the ground. They think we offworlders are great, since we came from the sky."

"But their houses," Dan argued, pointing to the half-circle of miniature domes. "The floors are below the doorsills. They live underground themselves."

"Nobody ever said myths are logical."

The edge taken off their curiosity, the N'lacs drifted back to whatever they'd been doing before the Terrans arrived. Women returned to gardening. Bigger kids picked berries. Babies played in the puddles around a well spout. The codgers resumed swapping lies. Dan saw no able-bodied males. He assumed they were all out hunting or helping at the dome dig.

It was a textbook village, a living museum. No wonder the Terran-Whimed Xenoethnic Council had licensed Praedar's expedition to protect these people. Few primitive species enjoyed that privilege. Most of the aborigines shown in the pop science edvids were now extinct, victims of conquest, disease, or both.

Kat said the team supplied medicine, food, and a reliable water source. The last was very apparent. In fact, it was the center of village activity. A shiny, automated, windmill-driven pump filled pots and its overflow provided those puddles for the babies' play. But the well was a jarring anomaly in the simple scene.

"Thinking that's an intrusion, a tampering with local ecology?" Joe asked, shrewdly assessing Dan's reaction. The pilot nodded and followed as Hughes went to check the pump's readouts. "This well is a major reason these people are still alive. When Praedar landed, they were in the grip of a severe drought. Praedar imported this pumper. The N'lacs' ancestors used to make windmills, so they accepted a new one without any culture shock. Sometimes they even try to make their own windmills, but without much success. They've long since lost the technology. See?"

Dan looked where Hughes pointed and saw several wooden towers half hidden in the purple foliage. The structures were pathetic toys, imitations of the real thing. They couldn't turn, could never pump water for this thirsty tribe. Dan conceded, "They sure need a well. I lived on Asita Hosi for a while, and I know how it is. Without water, a desert settlement is dead."

"Meej? Dooch? Where's Soong?" Joe counted noses, rounding up three N'lac children. "Ah! There you are, sweetie. Come along, kids. Time for your boosters."

The youngsters eagerly trailed Hughes to one of the huts. The villagers watched the parade with blank-faced disinterest. Dan puzzled over the differences between them and these bright-eyed kids and Chuss. It didn't make any sense. Damned near an entire community of retardates?

Joe steered the three kids through the hut's door. They jumped down across its threshold, calling out to someone inside. Then the man cued controls and the door shut behind them with a heavy thunk.

Dan started. This looked like the other mud-brick homes, but the walls were plasticrete. "What the hell?" he exclaimed, and touched a porthole-shaped window, checking its thick glassene. "A . . . a pressure chamber?"

"Hyperbaric," Joe Hughes said. "Standard issue medical. I did my best to blend it in with village housing. Not bad, huh?" he added proudly. Hughes peered through the window and waved at the hut's occupants. Dan stared over the scientist's shoulder. An exceedingly pregnant N'lac woman was stirring a cook pot hanging over a firepit—a pseudofire, an artificial hearth. The kids clustered around her as the women filled their bowls. Baskets and simple furnishings were scattered around the room. The interior was exactly what Dan would have expected to see—except that the N'lac family was locked in and their "fire" was a sophisticated copy of the real thing.

He confronted Hughes angrily. "That's a test lab. You're using them as guinea pigs!"

Hughes didn't deny it. "In a manner of speaking, yes. But before you slug me, you ought to remember that I warned you not to go too fast when you don't know the trail." He waited for Dan to digest that, then went on. "I assure you, everything you see is both legal and benign. Do Loor and her kids look tortured? In pain? Did I force them into that hut? And do you notice anything different about them, compared to the rest of the N'lacs?"

The last question, in particular, made Dan backpedal. "They're a lot brighter."

"In all ways. More intelligent. More alert. Healthier. More adaptable. And they'll reproduce more easily and more safely than their playmates. On Loor, the mother, the effect is modest. She was an adult when this experiment began. Hyperbarics has a dramatic effect on her kids, though." Joe warmed to his topic, his dark eyes sparkling. "They're so damned smart we really have to hustle to teach them. Chuss is the eldest, not quite an adult, in N'lac terms. Yet he's already the village leader in many respects. The N'lacs recognize his abilities and are willing to follow him. They know Chuss and his siblings are . . ."

"Freaks?" Dan had visions of the Frankenstein monster and all-too-real Earth history—mutant warfare labs and the genetic purity leagues of the first decades of the twenty-first century.

"No. They're normal. The way the N'lacs *should* be." Joe waited for that to soak in and penetrate Dan's revulsion and outrage. "Loor volunteered to participate when we told her what the chamber might accomplish. She hatched each of those kids and Chuss in there and is about to hatch another. We've got other N'lac women clamoring for their own hyperbaric houses now. They want to have smart, healthy kids, too. I won't go into the biomechanisms. Suffice to say that pressurized gestation enhancement won't work with *Homo sapiens*, Vahnaj *lutrinis*, or Lannon. It does work with certain primitive relatives of the Whimeds. Praedar spotted the similarities between felinoid and N'lac morphology, and we decided it was worth a try."

"Slow throttle," Dan said. "All I see is that you're tampering with these people, playing deity."

"Nothing new in that. Humanity saved the cetaceans and great apes and made partners out of them. We manipulated their genes to boost intelligence and break through communications barriers. Was that so bad? The results are their own vindication, wouldn't you say?"

"I . . . I don't know," Dan said slowly.

Hughes grunted. "But Praedar and I do, and so does the Xenoethnic Council. They support this experiment, and they wouldn't, if it hurt the N'lacs."

Still troubled, Dan asked, "How long do they . . . ?"

"Stay in the hut? Six hour boosters a day, for the kids. Twelve for Loor, though she often opts to stay in much longer."

"Hyperbaric pressurization accelerates her fetus's development?"

"Right! I'd be glad to take you on as a xenobiology trainee." Hughes checked the hut's controls and waved again at his test subjects.

Dan was torn. Was Joe conducting cruel experiments or rescuing the N'lacs from a life of dull-wittedness? And did a Council light-years from T-W 593 have the right to choose what happened to these e.t.s?

"Coming along nicely," Joe said. "So I think I'll have lunch. Care to join me?"

"Here? In this heat?"

"This is winter," Hughes said scornfully. "You want to experience *heat*, come back a few months from now, after the rainy season. Right now it's not too bad. Besides, I have to hang around and monitor the chamber."

"Glad *I* don't have to. I don't tolerate this much sun well. Must be the lack of pigment," Dan said with a grin. That was an old joke among light- and dark-skinned Terrans. Hughes laughed, relishing his superiority on that score.

"Then you'd better head for camp," he suggested. "Humans will be folding very soon, and so will Armilly. In a while even the Vahnajes and Whimeds will head for the complex. No stamina!"

"Me neither," Dan said, moving away.

There was no shade whatsoever on the cross-valley trail to the dome dig. Dan paced himself, putting one foot in front of the other methodically, his tongue thick with thirst. The outlines of the insta-cells wavered in the heat. So did the figures of the N'lac diggers and the scientists.

He stopped at the hill's portable canteen and drew a large mug. The distilled water was one of the most refreshing things he'd ever known. Recuperating a bit, Dan knelt in what little shadow there was near the canteen and watched the excavating.

Chen, oblivious to the temperature, was leaning over the cleared face of the ramp trench. Praedar stood beside his former teacher, pointing out a detail on the wall. They chattered in an odd mix of Terran and Whimed.

Work was winding down fast. Xenoarchs took increasingly frequent rests. The N'lacs sat on their haunches, panting, their webbed fingers in their mouths. Dr. Getz picked tiredly over the rubble pile. Sheila swore at a colleague who stepped on her foot. Kat pushed hair off her sun-reddened forehead. Armilly scratched at his fur and stared bleary-eyed at his monitors.

Then Sheila shouted, "Hey, Kroo-ger! He did it!"

All work halted. Everyone turned toward an approaching behemoth. The vacuum dredge. Ruieb and his assistant sat at the controls. Slash-mouthed smiles creased their gray faces.

Dan frowned. Had the Vahnajes taken his advice after all? That was the only explanation. There was no way they could make that temperamental machine operate right unless they'd aligned it the way he'd told them. Amid the team's congratulatory cheers, he heard a subtle shift in the rig's power, a growl replacing the purr.

"Watch out!" he roared, gesturing frantically.

Too late.

The dredge bucked, lurching forward, rapidly gaining speed. Fumes boiled from under its cowling. Ruieb fought the controls; then he and the other Vahnaj were bounced out of the cab. They fell safely behind the charging monster.

Others weren't as lucky. They were directly in the machine's path. They screamed, tripping, running, trying to escape.

Full throttle, no one at its helm, the dredge thundered toward the dome—and toward the hapless dig crew.

CHAPTER FIVE
∞∞∞∞∞∞∞

Praedar's Planet

Memories of past disasters flogged Dan—of a buddy crushed under a lumber hauler and of frontier shanties buried by a runaway transport, with broken bodies, blood, injury, death.

He gauged his stride, gulping for breath, and lunged. The fender was slick with dust. He fought for a handhold, pulling himself upward painfully. Lungs and muscles protested as he crawled across the cowling and into the empty cab.

Time ticked in milliseconds. The dredge's howls drowned out the shrieks of its potential victims.

Dan operated on reflex, years of training taking over as his hands flew across the controls. Shunt transmission, in sequence. One. Two. Three. Four.

Die, damn you. Quit!

Lights stuttered on the panels. The giant rig hiccuped and then squealed like a mortally wounded beast. The sound quavered and began to fade.

Inertia carried the dredge on. But with its power off, friction

54

created more and more drag. That gave the offworlders and N'lacs a chance to dodge.

Dan clung to a stanchion, riding out the last few meters helplessly. He was only a passenger now, bracing for impact. Spewing smoke, the dredge plowed its nose deep into the refuse pile. Its treaders gave a final whine as it stopped.

There was a gritty pattering noise around Dan—sand, thrown up by the rig, settling back onto metal surfaces. Plating snapped, cooling.

Dan rested his head on his crossed arms and commanded his pulse to return to normal. Eventually his heart quit trying to pound its way through his rib cage. He slid out of the cab and off the fender and sat on the ground. He made no attempt to stand; not yet. He wasn't sure his legs would support him.

Some scientists were cursing. Others retched nervously. Many simply sat, repairing their shattered energies, as Dan was doing. Whimeds flexed their fingers instinctively, felinoid genes making them "claw air" to release tension. Armilly curled into a furry ball. Vahnajes fussed with their sideburns and chittered. The N'lacs wailed, a shivery ululation that raised gooseflesh. Praedar, Sheila, and Kat led others in checking for injuries. Fortunately, the worst damage appeared to be bruises, scrapes, and rattled nerves.

Sheila rushed past the dredge, fire in her blue eyes. She homed in on Ruieb-An and his assistant. The two Vahnajes were brushing off their jumpers, taking great pains in a typical lutrinoid pose—focusing on trivialities to avoid confronting an upsetting uproar.

The uproar had come to them in the person of a furious blond Terran. Sheila shook her fists under Ruieb's small nose. "You gray-faced fornicating fool! You cretin! You told us that thing would be okay! That you'd have it working perfectly! Kroo-ger! What an egregious, mother-hating liar! You and your whole damned species! You damned near wrecked the dome . . ."

"He damned near wrecked *us*," Kat put in. Her voice was hoarse from shouting warnings earlier.

"Most regrettable." Praedar spoke calmly, putting on a good fearless-leader performance. His self-control was awesome. Only his spiky crest revealed his turmoil.

Sheila continued to berate Ruieb, hammering him with a lexicon of startling expletives. Abruptly Ruieb turned his back on her and walked toward the complex. Every Vahnaj on the team followed him. While the rest went on assessing damages, the Vahnajes emerged from the insta-cells carrying travel gear. They loaded the baggage in a truck and headed toward the mesa. Sheila pursued the vehicle halfway up the road until she realized her chase was futile.

Kat stared at the departing Vahnajes. "Oh, marvelous! They'll sit out there and sulk for days. Meanwhile, nothing gets done on Ruieb's translation data."

"This was to be anticipated," Praedar said. His crest was softer now. "Association with other species is difficult even for progressive Vahnaj scientists. Ruieb-An has endured much criticism from his colleagues because he chose to join this expedition." The unspoken implications sobered Praedar's listeners. Like Dan, the other Terrans were very aware of an age-old enmity dividing Whimeds and Vahnajes. It was precedent-breaking for Ruieb-An to be here, working with a team led by a felinoid. Praedar sighed, sounding resigned. "Within his institutional community, his faction are rebels. Such are always quick to react to loss of face. Sheila pointed out his error. McKelvey corrected his mistake. Ruieb cannot tolerate such disgrace in our presence. We must wait while he retreats and purifies his shame. Or until we apologize."

"Apologize, hell!" someone said. "Why should we cater to his tender feelings? He blew it!"

"Bunch of prima donnas," Getz growled. "You never should have allowed those fish-faces into this project, Juxury." The pudgy Terran fussed over the rubble heap. "That machine scattered my specimens. A whole morning's work wasted!"

"What about *our* work?" another crew member griped. "Look at that! Pushed half the dirt back into the ramp. We'll have to shovel the whole thing clear again!"

Then a new crisis struck. The N'lacs stopped wailing and began trotting toward their village. Dan assumed they were taking their midday break, but the scientists' reactions showed him that wasn't the case.

Kat hurried after the N'lacs, pleading "Hooni, hooni. You fellow not afraid, huh-huh? Machine not hurt. Machine not belong to Evil Old Ones. 'Member? Machine come from sky, like Kelfee's flyer. Hooni! No go!"

Chuss and other young N'lac males grinned and nodded, agreeing. The older males, though, were all for getting while they could. Their shaman, Sleeg, headed the exodus.

Kat finally gave up, standing arms akimbo and yelling at the disappearing marchers "You are a pup, Sleeg! A fool! Machine is not demon. No demons here. Come back!"

"Save your breath," Getz advised. "Sleeg's showing us he can still make the N'lacs obey whenever he says 'boo!'"

Sheila was trudging up the path to the dome. She eyed the N'lacs and said, "So they're bailing out, too, huh? Kroo-ger! What a stupid mess!"

Kat wiped her smudged face with her forearm. "Don't worry. Rosie and I will powwow with them later and get them back on the job. Just give us some time . . ."

"Yes," Praedar said. "That is best. Let them recover, as we must." Then he swung around and stared intently at Dan. "I have not thanked you, McKelvey. You saved our work and our lives."

Dan levered himself to his feet and leaned against the fender. "Glad I was here to help."

The felinoid's starry eyes glittered. "*Irast*, you are *aytan*."

Aytan. Ethical. The highest possible praise, coming from a Whimed. The compliment made Dan blush. "Thanks. It's too bad this happened. It shouldn't have. I met Ruieb out in the valley and told him he was installing that linkage wrong. I guess he didn't believe me."

While the crew picked up broken tools and tended minor wounds, they added a storm of complaints about the Vahnaj. Apparently this wasn't the first time the lutrinoid xenoarchaeologists had refused to take instruction from a non-Vahnaj and caused problems.

Praedar interrupted the gripe session, asking Dan "Can you repair the dredge?"

The boss. Cutting to the heart of the situation.

Dan weighed options. How much did he dare guarantee? And how far could he push his bargaining power? "Maybe. That depends on what Ruieb did wrong and on what the emergency shutdown did to the rig."

Sheila groaned. "You mean he may have wrecked the replacement parts? Damn! We'll have to wait *another* year to get more. And we're already way behind schedule excavating the dome because that damned dredge was out of action . . ."

Kat broke through her friend's lament. "All right. Let's assume the damage isn't fatal. How about it, McKelvey?"

Terrans and aliens regarded the pilot anxiously. He shrugged and said, "If I fix it, am I on the roster?"

Guffawing, Sheila cried, "Blackmailer!"

Praedar, too, seemed amused. "*Aaaa!* Kat explained your difficulties to me. The matter of the cargo. Unfortunate that our disagreements with the Saunders hurt you, as well."

"More than a coincidence, if you want my opinion," Dr. Getz said.

Chen muttered, "Do we have a choice? You'll tell us your opinion anyway . . ."

Getz ignored that. His manner dripped suspicion. "Funny. McKelvey gets here yesterday. And *this* business happens today."

"Don't be ridiculous," Kat snapped. "Ruieb's the one who fouled the repairs. Why pick on Dan?"

"Because he's a Saunder-McKelvey." The effigy expert's pointed reminder triggered an uneasy murmur. Scientists who'd expressed gratitude to Dan earlier now looked wary. Getz said, "He's Feo's kinsman . . ."

"Yeah, sure. Fine," Dan countered. "Have it your way. Listen. I don't have a damned thing to do with Feo Saunder beyond having the same ancestors. But if you think I'm in a conspiracy with him, repair your own dredge."

He turned to go, but Praedar blocked the way. The Whimed forced him to meet that alien, hypnotic gaze. "Dr. Getz's statements are not a consensus, Dan McKelvey. *I* do not question your honesty in this matter. Kaatje does not accuse you, nor does Sheila, nor many others." Praedar smiled and said, "I will offer a . . . a deal. Repair the dredge, and I will amend your visitor's pass. There is space on our license list for . . . a . . . *aaaa!* . . . for a maintenance specialist." Dr. Chen slapped his knee and cackled.

Dan imagined Praedar juggling reports. A committee on a distant world wouldn't know a maintenance specialist from a skyhook inspector. And what the stay-at-homes didn't know couldn't hurt Praedar's right to dig on T-W 593. Smart! He was tempted to demand some extra perks, but it was better not to push his luck. Dan said, "I'll do my best. I can't make any promises until I check the rig."

"Accepted." The Whimed held out a hand. That was a Terran form of contract, not a felinoid one. Most Whimeds disliked touching other species. Praedar's grip, though, was solid. Dan was willing to bet the big alien could bow and bob his way through a convoluted Vahnaj conversation, too, and hoot and hop with Armilly if necessary. He was definitely something special.

"How soon can you start repairs?" Kat asked. "Not that we want to push you, but we have a *very* keen interest in getting that dredge operational."

Dan investigated the machine and found that Ruieb had left its tool kit out where the dredge had been parked. Yvica offered to fetch it, since she was less bothered by the heat than a Terran would be. Dan helped the scientists finish tidying the dome excavation—covering the delicate paintings, stacking hand tools and carts. One by one, humans wilted and fled for the complex. One student complained, "It's not fair. When I was an undergrad, they told me this was a cerebral profession. Nobody said anything about frying or collecting bleeding blisters . . ."

"Welcome to the real universe," Sheila taunted.

When Yvica returned, Dan took the kit and propped open the dredge's cowling and used it as a sunshield. He wrestled the misaligned linkage from its niche and toted it and the kit to the insta-cell cluster. By then nearly the entire crew was bottled up in its clime-controlled interior. Sheila showed Dan the access to the vehicle workshops. He scrounged for test gear and began tinkering.

For a while, he had an audience. Scientists rubbernecked and nagged him with questions. He dumped a blizzard of tech-mech jargon on them. It was an amusing reversal of roles. This time *they* were the ones who didn't understand the in-group terms. Annoyed, they got the message and finally left him alone.

He needed that solitude. Linkage repairs were a bitch. A mistake could wreck an element. He worked until his eyes complained, took a break for a snack and a short nap, and continued the job. Another short break, and back to repairs.

Time blurred. He was vaguely aware the afternoon had slipped by. It was twilight before he was done.

As he carried the linkage to the dome dig a darkening bluegold sky glowed overhead. A few stars were escorting T-W 593's tiny moons, climbing lazily above the valley. Solar reserve lamps winked on, illuminating key areas. Across the way, fires flickered in the N'lacs' village.

The crew had resumed work at the ramp, shoveling dirt and hauling it to a new refuse heap. When Dan climbed onto the dredge's fender, they stopped and eyed him apprehensively. He assured them, "Nothing to get excited about yet. I'm only reinstalling the unit. I'll let you know before I fire up."

"It will function?"

The question came almost in Dan's ear. Praedar stood beside the dredge, looking hopeful.

"Maybe. I gave it my damnedest." Dan squirmed under the cowling and fitted the linkage in place, setting adherer locks. Shoving the tool kit ahead of him, he wriggled out of the cramped spot, shut the cowling, and hunkered on the fender. "The unit's kinda bent. I've operated rigs in worse shape, but it's always a gamble. Ready to give her a try?"

"Her? *Aaa!* The machine. Yes!" Praedar's colleagues moved out of the way, just in case. He got up on the fender and leaned in the cab door as Dan settled himself at the controls.

"Systems green," the pilot announced. He felt a subliminal tingle. Lights glowed across the board. Anomaly frames stayed dark. He touched the engage circuit and it tied in without a hitch. "All go. You're in business."

"Aaaa!" That happy Whimed stammer hinted at Praedar's hunter ancestors pouncing on prey. "Excavate!" Dan cued the intake hoses. Flexible snakes extruded from the forward vents. The scientists seized the guide rings and aimed at the pile of dirt the dredge had shoved back into the dig at noon. "Begin small," Praedar said.

"And with extreme gentle pressure? So as to pamper Dr. Getz's specimens?" Dan adjusted the feed levels.

Silent laughter shook Praedar. "Yes. Gentle. You understand well. Excellent." He jumped off the rig and hurried toward his team, taking his place on the work line. They shouted in triumph as suction removed earth and pebbles to the dredge's tanks. Dr. Getz pointed to a place beyond the original rubble pile, and Dan tapped the control to pay out the exit hoses. Getz's students steered them to the new dump site. As debris poured from the outlets, night breeze coated Getz's people with dust, making them sneeze. They were too busy—finding effigies—to care.

Dan stayed in the cab for a time, monitoring circuits. Jerry-rigs had a bad habit of falling apart unexpectedly. But this one held. Eventually he felt it was safe to put systems on auto. He sat on the fender and watched the scientists. Praedar let the dredge run for nearly an hour before he signaled a stop. Unlike the previous situation, this was a controlled cut. No stress on the newly repaired linkage was indicated. In sequence, panels went on standby. "That it for tonight?" Dan asked.

"And how!" Sheila said. "Plenty! It'll take us days to record all of this!"

The Whimeds stowed hoses in the ports. Getz and his students gathered their treasures and trooped to the complex. Other scientists moved portable lamps into position, shining them directly on the now-exposed ramp. Several took the time to thank Dan for his help. He nodded and waited by the dredge, uncertain whether he was supposed to scram now that his job was done, or if he'd be in the way if he hung around.

Praedar cocked his crested head. His eyes were iridescent jewels. "Do you wish to see what it is you have helped us uncover?"

Dan didn't need a second invitation. He followed the Whimed down the slope. It looked as if most of the xenoarchaeologists planned to be there all night. Their enthusiasm was an aroma. A few N'lacs sat nearby. Chuss gawked curiously at the scene, plainly puzzled by all the excitement.

A three-meter-wide incline had been opened an equal length toward the hidden base of the dome. The structure itself was an ominous shadow, looming over the excavation.

The team panned cameras along the painted wall, sprayed fresh preservatives, and picked away lingering crumbs of soil. A row of figures seemed to emerge from interment; half of the last shape in line was still buried. Squiggles and dots framed the pictures. One of the students said, "Too bad Ruieb's bunch isn't here. We could sure use him to translate this . . ."

"Okay, okay, I shouldn't have jumped him. So kick me," Sheila grumbled.

The byplay was vocal white noise to Dan. He was staring at those figures. Slender, round-faced, golden-eyed humanoids. Humanoids! A rare lifeform, as Kat had said. And he remembered her statement regarding the N'lacs' kinship with these ruins' builders. This was a civilization that had been unknown before Praedar's expedition began digging here. A race lost to history! What a breakthrough!

The figures marched across scenes of a high-tech culture, showing great cities, continent-spanning transport networks, advanced satellite navigation aids, aircraft, and spacecraft. Silvery ships, leaping away from the planet, reached toward a glowing dot, a distant star.

"These people . . ." Dan murmured, his thoughts jumbled.

Praedar anticipated him. "They ruled this world and a colony, T-S 311, where your kinsman is excavating."

Dan found himself wondering how the nonhuman members of the team saw these paintings. They viewed it with eyes and brains different from *Homo sapiens'*. He imagined wearing another being's skin, exploring the universe in an alien body, with the outlook of another race. This must be what xenoarchaeology was really all about. The scientists' enthusiasm had infected him, too. "Another star system," he said. "If they did that, they had FTL. What happened. Where did they go?"

"They're here," Kat said, without turning from her work.

"The N'lacs? But why did they degenerate so much? Those villagers couldn't have built a ramp like this, couldn't have painted those pictures or written those inscriptions. Not the way they are now."

"Their society collapsed," Praedar said tonelessly. "Their colony on T-S 311 collapsed, as well. We believe the colonists abandoned T-S 311 and returned to T-W 593, their home. Your kinsmen dispute that interpretation of events."

Dan was more and more caught up in the drama. "How long ago did this happen?"

"It is not possible to be precise. We can date matters to within fifty *niay*. The approximate time of collapse, in Terran terms, is two thousand of your years before present. Feo Saunder and his wife agree with our findings at least in *that* respect." The Whimed waited. For what? For Dan to arrive at some brilliant conclusion about those facts, which the xenoarchaeologists had already reached much earlier?

If only Reid hadn't lost his fortune, his younger son would have had a decent education, and Dan wouldn't be so afraid of exposing his ignorance now. He peered intently at the wall, envying Dr. Chen his microscopic vision.

The painted figures' faces weren't flushed like their modern-day descendants'. Their fingers were graceful, unwebbed, and unclubbed. Minds as dull as the average N'lac's could never have created those cities and spaceships. However, Chuss and his siblings, properly educated and reared in a technologically oriented culture, just might have.

"Was . . . ?" Dan hesitated. "Was there a catastrophe? Some kind of environmental upheaval or a drastic change in atmospheric conditions?"

"No." One of the scientists, Rosenthal, added, "Our biota analyses of the time period prove that conclusively."

"It doesn't make any sense," Dan protested. "If Joe can raise a N'lac's intelligence by pressurizing a gestating fetus . . ."

Kat studied him narrowly. Praedar said, "Yes. You are indeed an explorer, Dan McKelvey."

"Much more open-minded than his relatives, as well," Kat put in.

Dan sighed in mild exasperation. "I just want to know how things work and why. This history you've described implies a severe alteration in this planet's environment. I've seen what that means on some Terran Settlements, when pioneers homesteaded at the wrong altitude or skimped on breather apparatus. They didn't usually end up as bad off as the N'lacs, but . . ."

"Few current stellar colonies have endured an apparently inhospitable environment for as many generations as we theorize the N'lacs have," Praedar reminded him. "Interesting, is it not? The solution demands what xenoarchaeology refers to as selectivity. A most careful examination and interpretation of data to develop a correct hypothesis of a newly discovered civilization."

"The *right* selectivity," Kat stressed, making it sound like an oath. "Not the selectivity Feo and Hope are using."

"Can't you tell me . . . ?" Dan began.

A predatory grin split Praedar's features. "You must learn from your own effort." Dan blinked. Was that a brush-off or a quaint Whimed homily quoted to chasten an inquisitive amateur? The alien gestured sharply and headed back up the ramp. With reluctance, Dan followed, glancing over his shoulder longingly at those mysterious pictures. He wanted to stay. Yet if he did, he'd be useless, as the scientists had been while he was repairing the dredge linkage.

At the top of the slope, Praedar halted and said, "You fixed the machine. You will remain as our maintenance specialist."

Rattled by the sudden, welcome decision, Dan stammered his thanks.

"I can pay little. Food. Quarters. Fifty per hundred-day. It is enough?"

That was bare bones, right at the Chartered Settlement

Planets' recommended bottom base wage. Before this starhop, Dan would have turned it down with a sneer. Now, blacklisted and in a corner, he couldn't afford to. He suspected Praedar would get the money out of his personal funds, which probably were already heavily involved in this dig. And from the way these scientists scrimped along, *nobody* was getting rich from the expedition. The offer was fair, given those factors.

Also, this job would be a hell of a lot more interesting than what he'd find for a similar wage anywhere else in the sector.

"That's fine," Dan said.

"You will repair other vehicles."

"Sure, if they're repairable."

"There is a skimmer." The Whimed was wistful. "It has not functioned for a local year."

And Kat and Sheila said they didn't need a tech-mech here! "I'll see what I can do . . ."

He started the next morning, taking inventory of the equipment. Some of it required only maintenance. Some qualified for major fix-it schedules. A small number were hopeless cases. They got shunted to the mechanical graveyard west of the complex.

It was impossible to set up a routine work timetable. Dan had to play things by ear—and according to what parts he could scrounge, make himself, or locate substitutes for.

He took daily drives to the landing strip and ran his system checks on *Fiona*. That was just common sense, whether he got back into indie hauling or was forced to sell her, further along the line; no one would pay him a counterfeit credit for unspaceable junk.

Most of his waking hours, though, were spent in camp. It was no ordinary Settlement. Little by little, he became acquainted with its people and its habitats. There were a dozen or so families with children among the offworlders. The majority, however, were singles. Accomplished scientists, up-and-coming young xenoarchs, and students tended to their special disciplines and assisted in others'. The multispecies team—nocturnal and diurnal races, monophasics and polyphasics, mammalian Terrans, Whimeds, the currently absent Vahnajes, and the marsupial Lannon—worked together. Thanks to uniformly casual dress, they actually looked remarkably similar, as well. Rumpled jumpers were round-the-clock wear—in the labs and cook shack and on the dig, whether day or night; the only changes involved attaching the garments' sleeves and legs during the colder hours.

Whatever their species, the scientists were characters, each with individual quirks. Those patterns came out in their speech, dress, and their working and sleeping quarters. Many team members wore "primitive jewelry"—a potsherd pendant, arm- and legbands of bright furs and feathers, clay ornaments braided into Whimed crests or human hair, the Lannon's neck ropes of dyed natural fibers. Kat's area of the xenosocio's office was full of native masks and models of grisly rituals. Sheila's lab featured a graffiti-accented sonic potsherd scrubber. Praedar's contained a striking assortment of artifacts from Whimed history, including his grandfather's *oryuz*, a garish anti-esper helmet, a leftover from the time of the Whimed-Vahnaj interstellar cold war.

Camp operations never ceased. Scientists kept shifts going night and day. As a result, there was always an empty bunk where Dan could log a few zees or bench space for him in the cook shack.

He did his best to fit in, memorizing names and relationships. Reactions to his presence ran the gamut from amiable acceptance to Dr. Getz's open dislike. It wasn't easy to get close to these people. They had little leisure to nursemaid an untrained newcomer in camp. There was extra pressure on the expedition at present, especially. They were preparing for a big upcoming scientific conference, the Twelfth Xenoarchaeological Assembly, to be held on Feo Saunder's dig world. The prospect of facing their rivals on the rivals' home territory made for touchy tempers. Conditions weren't improved when a three-day sandstorm confined the entire crew to the complex. During that period, Dan lived in the repair sheds and kept a very low profile.

In his rare free time, and when a monitor was free, he poked into the Settlement's library. He hoped for a self-taught crash course in xenoarch. But many entries were code-locked. The generally available material only showed him how much he had to learn and made him hungry for more.

He read through professional journal back-issue vids by the dozens, getting an overview of the field, of important past and present digs, and of prominent scientists. Feo and Hope Saunder came in for a lot of coverage—too much, in Dan's sour opinion. Many of the articles dealing with them and their expedition sounded like standard Saunder-McKelvey PR releases. Frequently Dan's kindred gave interviews calculated to play down their status as members of "Terra's uncrowned royalty." In fact, they went overboard to present an image as common, hardworking xenoarchs. The tactic was effective. Editors and reporters praised the Saunders' dedication and their self-sacrifice in plowing thousands of their own credits into their work. As if Feo was bankrupting himself by doing so!

Greg Tavares, a handsome redhead about Dan's age, was the Saunders' protégé. He appeared again and again in those interviews, always alongside his mentors. Each time Dan saw Tavares' picture, he recalled Kat's description of the man as Feo's dirty tricks expert, the one responsible for bribe-burying that cargo.

Halfway through Dan's second week on the job, the N'lacs returned to the dome dig. Kat's powwows had obviously been successful.

Dan was having his own share of success in the repair sheds with scout bikes, trucks, rovers, scanners, monitors, balky clime-control units, circuits, and other tools and gadgets.

The skimmer was his most difficult assignment. She was a derelict. At some point, she'd been belly-landed, damaging vital components. There weren't enough replacement parts to mend her, so he resorted to more jerry-rigging, calling on his training and a lot of ingenuity. He was well into his third week on Praedar's roster before he felt he had the problem licked.

The next day, he rolled out at dawn and gobbled breakfast, then hurried to the hangars, passing the morning shift of scientists headed for the dome dig.

Dan opened the shed doors wide and took care to remove any test equipment and all connecting lines blocking the skimmer's exit path. After an obligatory walk-around, he climbed into the cockpit and did a thorough systems check—three times, to be on the safe side. Green showed across the panel.

Canopy locked, power cued, the flyer lifted smoothly, riding a column of air, awaiting commands. Taking her slow and steady, Dan steered through the doors. The skimmer soared to meet the rising sun. Lamps were winking out and shadows retreating fast. Moment by moment, the valley brightened. He put the little craft through her paces, banking, risking stalls, pushing her responsiveness. There were a few glitches, but nothing major. A duto dived and zoomed around the metal invader, casting a puzzled compound eye in Dan's direction. Laughing, he applied more thrust and sailed away.

He hovered above Dr. Chen's museum excavation, Hanging Rock, and the village. E.t.s gathered at the pump, pointing excitedly at the skimmer. Joe Hughes was a dark face amid a sea of wizened red ones. Dan returned the N'lacs' happy waves and flew on.

The shakedown cruise tracked thirty kilometers upstream from camp and back again. It was Dan's first look at where the team had dug in previous years. He was delighted to find that he could pick out shapes of ancient buildings and the N'lacs' earlier village locations from the air. Maybe he *had* learned something from studying those vid journals, after all!

At the end of the test run, he drifted in to a perfect landing near the dud pits below the dome. Excavation halted. Scientists and native diggers rushed to greet him. Chuss' crew swarmed over the flyer, chattering and patting the craft investigatively. Dan hastily shut the canopy to prevent small webbed hands from touching something they shouldn't.

As he stood on the wing, Sheila reached up and swatted his rump playfully. "Not bad, handsome! I never thought you'd get this thing up."

"Interesting congratulations you give. I'd *heard* you Kruger 60 women are insatiable."

"Oh, it's true, it's true!"

Praedar studied the skimmer narrowly. Dan could almost see wheels turning in that crested skull. Saluting, the pilot said, "One skimmer, fully functional and ready for action, boss."

"That's Dr. Juxury to you," Getz growled.

Dan was taken aback. Had he been too chummy? He'd adopted the team's patterns of address without asking permission. That might have been a mistake.

"Not important," Praedar said, intent on the aircraft.

Getz argued, "It *is* important. You must demand respect appropriate to . . ."

"Oh, go classify effigies," Kat said tiredly. "Get your respect from them. If you're in the lab, you won't be nitpicking everything we do at the dome."

Getz left in a rage. Looking rueful, his students tagged along behind him. A few scientists smiled in relief and gave Kat a thumbs-up. Getz rubbed a lot of people the wrong way.

"It's really okay now?" Sheila asked, nodding at the skimmer.

"I'm flying her. If she isn't A-One, I'll be the first to know."

Kat winced at that old spacer's joke. Then she turned to Praedar. "This means we can pull fresh core samples and take readings at the other sites."

"Yes." Praedar's chin dug into his bony chest in a sharp nod. "Update of correlations. Preparation for Assembly. We will need tools, maps, charge-coupled cams. You and I."

There was a brief, noisy protest. Praedar vetoed others' attempts to join the party. He had decided, and that was that.

"We were going to enlarge the ramp," Baines, the geologist, said. "Use the dredge . . ."

"Hell, I can do that," Sheila said, sniffing scornfully. "We don't need McKelvey. Now that handsome's taught me how to manage the rig, no sweat."

"Do not proceed further with the image wall," Praedar ordered. "Clear the eastern face. We will reveal the structure there which Armilly has scanned." Sheila made an "O" with her thumb and forefinger, grinning.

Most of the N'lacs had already lost interest in the skimmer. They squatted listlessly, waiting for someone to tell them what to do. Only Chuss was still bright-eyed and alert by the time Dan, Kat, and Praedar finished loading survey gear aboard the aircraft. Kat took the elevated observer's seat, Praedar the second pilot's chair. Dan locked the canopy, and outside noises muted. As the skimmer rose, Chuss and the scientists standing near the dud pits sent them off with cheers.

"Which route?" Dan inquired.

"Site TWP-30 to TWP-40, then return," Kat instructed.

Course lines rippled on the nav screens. The skimmer's guidance system tied in to the planet's nav-sat and logged the data. The sky boat swung around, aiming due north. As they passed a badlands area at the bend of the dry river, Dan boosted speed. The flyer's needle-nosed shadow raced ahead of them over scrubby uplands.

"Very good. Excellent repairs," Praedar said. Kat's reflection smiled at Dan from the control panels. He smiled, too. A step up the ladder! Still a long way from being a student xenoarch. But at least now he was the team's resident tech-mech.

Cameras and scanners soaked up info: precisely measured weather figures; land contours; elevations; moisture variations;

vegetation quantities and types; and shadow configurations. Dan tapped that last entry and said, "That's an ancient town line there, right? And that looks like a buried road."

"You *have* been studying, haven't you?" Kat exclaimed. She leaned forward, pointing out details on the flowing map. "This was a population core, not as big as our city, but fair-sized. That depression was probably a market square. The structures are long gone, of course, but with the optimum lighting, they're apparent. I wish we'd been able to make these aerial surveys more frequently, at all times of day, to get the overall picture. But because the skimmer . . ."

"Suffered a belly landing," Dan supplied, "you couldn't. Too bad. You missed a lot of data. Better let me fly her from now on. I can't fix *everything* you people inflict on her."

Kat blushed prettily. Had she been the one at the controls when the skimmer crashed? She rushed on, covering her chagrin. "Every trip adds material we lacked before. We really appreciate what you're doing to repair the machinery, Dan."

"I aim to please. I *told* you I was more than a rocket jockey."

"Far more." Kat grinned.

When they approached the first selected site, Dan took manual control and landed flashily. Once on the ground, though, he became a spectator. Kat and Praedar drew cores and calibrated and set up their monitoring gear. Dan wandered around the grassy knolls for a while, then sat in the shade of the skimmer, daydreaming.

He saw time rushing backward two millennia. A bustling city rose where meadows now lay. Chuss' ancestors hurried about their daily business. Transports and aircraft hurtled toward distant N'lac population centers. Suborbital vessels arced through the dark sky. An interplanetary ship stabbed up and out to the N'lacs' colony world, T-S 311.

It had been a thriving, progressive people, on their way, with all that implied. There must have been the usual humanoid intraspecies competition, some angling for power. That was an inevitable side effect of aggressive growth, and any culture that achieved FTL had to have that kind of drive.

As humanoids expanded into the universe, they also, inevitably, encountered other humanoid races. That demanded a delicate balancing act and mutual compromise—or disaster could result. It took a lot of adjustment for species that had evolved light-years apart to learn to tolerate the very different behaviors and customs of their stellar neighbors. Sometimes that contact was so difficult that diplomacy and trade could be carried on only in a cultural "neutral zone." One aspect of Praedar's expedition that awed Dan was the way five species had managed to work together with so few clashes.

The same self-interest and energy that drove humanoids to the stars made them pugnacious, and that could lead to belligerence. Whimeds and Vahnajes had teetered on the brink of war far too many times in recent centuries. Terra had also had its tense collisions with non-Terrans. Fortunately, intelligent beings generally understood the terrible risk involved and backed off before the point of no return. The Whimeds and Vahnajes had contrived complex game rules, administered by both species' saner factions—playing at espionage and limited, surgical strikes without dealing mortal wounds to their enemies. Terra, Lannon, Rigotia, and Ulisor had cooperated, mediating, helping the felinoids and lutrinoids maintain that dangerous equilibrium, for the benefit of galactic survival.

The N'lacs, though, had never had to cope with those problems. Their starbound civilization had collapsed before they'd even made a good start on interstellar development.

When Kat had told Dan how important the expedition's work was, he thought she exaggerated. Now he realized she hadn't. Knowledge was a weapon in a hostile universe. It *was* important that Praedar's team learn what had happened to the N'lacs and make sure it didn't happen to other humanoid races.

At the second site, things went pretty much as they had at the first. Dan waited and the scientists measured and collected.

Surveys complete, they stowed the equipment aboard and flew homeward toward N'lac Valley.

For a time, they rode in silence. Then Praedar said with aching regret, "So much yet to study."

Kat stroked his crest. The intimate action disturbed Dan more than he wanted to admit. A Terran woman shouldn't caress a Whimed male that way. It wasn't quite . . . human. Kat said, "Wait till we make our presentations at the Assembly. You'll see. We'll get new grants and new volunteers. With any kind of luck, we'll be able to field a crew at every likely dig in this hemisphere."

Praedar murmured, "Perhaps." Responding to Kat's touch, he

made a deep rumbling noise in his throat, a basso purr. However, his voice was sad. "I will not live to see the conclusion. This is the work of several lifetimes."

"No, none of us will," Kat agreed. She gazed at the desert horizon. "But we'll have the satisfaction of being the initiators. We're making history here, Praedar."

The Whimed shook his big head. "No fame endures. In ages, our civilizations will end. During future millennia, other races will explore our ruins as we explore the N'lacs'. The cycles will continue." He spoke calmly, very relaxed now.

Dan shivered. Xenoarchaeologists were used to dealing in terms of thousands and thousands of years, historical infinity, with species being born, living, dying, then rediscovered long after they were dust. To Dan, it was an uncomfortable reminder of his mortality and mankind's. Were all the seemingly permanent peoples and objects in his universe mere blinks of a cosmic eye?

Kat was saying "It's possible to be remembered. Look at Schliemann's work at Troy on Earth. And your grandsire's on Dobend in the Whimed Federation. No one will forget them, and they won't forget your achievements, either. We'll prove your theories to everyone. They'll have to admit you're right." She pressed Dan's shoulder and added, "*You* recognized the link between the wall paintings and the N'lacs instantly. If an untrained layman can do that, your relatives ought to be able to, too."

"Umm. Maybe Feo has a card up his sleeve," Dan said, playing devil's advocate. "Something that contradicts your findings, new stuff he's found on T-S 311 . . ."

"Feo is foolishly stubborn," Praedar cut in. Dan was surprised by the Whimed's angry tone. "Saunder will not concede he has located a colony of this world. He continues to insist that the ruins on T-S 311 predate the cities here. He selects only evidence to support his own ideas and completely ignores the results of Joe's gestation experiments; the Saunders will not accept that the N'lacs are the true descendants of the race that built this culture."

Dan said, "Sounds like Feo and Hope are as bullheaded as a few other members of my clan. Huh! Chuss is no monkey, no stupid offshoot of the main local humanoid tree . . ."

"Exactly!" Kat exclaimed. "Feo's claims are an insult to the N'lacs. Worse, he and Hope have tremendous clout in the xeno-arch community. It's not fair! They don't need the extra backers or the credits. Being a Saunder doesn't automatically make them right. But because they are Saunders, they command respect *and* money. Meanwhile, we scrimp and limp and beg for a hearing; and we're selecting better data!"

"I guess people always want more money," Dan said. "Even when they're as rich as my kin. Like Varenka, trying to tap my Dad for a donation to clone Jael Saunder and restore Saunderhome..."

The scientists pounced on his statement. "Saunderhome? Varenka Saunder-Nicholaiev?" Praedar's eyes shone brightly. He and Kat prodded Dan for more info. Sorry he'd said anything, he told them about the holo letter.

"Views of Saunderhome? *Current* views?" Kat was delighted. "Wonderful! May we see them? The last report in *The Journal of Archaeo-Architectural Restoration* was several years ago. Rumor has it that Varenka's sending a rep with an update to the Assembly. But it would be great to get an advance peek."

"I'll make you a copy of the letter," Dan said, shrugging. "Nothing much to look at, though. Saunderhome's a rotting wreck. That old woman's throwing good credits after bad."

"How can you talk that way? You're a McKelvey."

"A *poor* McKelvey," he reminded her. "Varenka never scratched my back or Dad's. I won't scratch hers."

"But this is *history*!" Kat seemed horrified by his disdain. "The Saunders. The McKelveys. It's *important*. It's as if you were throwing away priceless relics of the Egyptian dynasties, or of Alexander's empire, or the Romans'. Don't you have any pride in your family's significance in the human time stream? The Saunder-McKelveys are Earth, a distillation of mankind's brightest and best..."

"Like Feo Saunder? Nope. I don't see how the family's reputation in and out of the Terran sector affects me. I'm not included in the show, or the wealth."

Dan was torn between bemusement and annoyance. Kat was cute when she was fuming. On the other hand, she was getting steamed up over nothing. Saunderhome! A pile of junk!

She abandoned the argument, sitting back and pouting. Her angry reflection shimmered on the control panel throughout the rest of the flight. As Kat sulked, Praedar eyed the pilot sidelong. The scrutiny was unnerving. Was Praedar probing him, as he'd probed the ground at those remote sites? And what did the

Whimed think he was looking for in Dan? A hidden, sincere interest in Varenka's plans, despite Dan's apparent contempt? If so, Praedar had things pegged wrong!

They entered the valley from the west, banking steeply above the complex and landing lightly near the dud pits once more.

Scientists ran to meet them. Dan gawked in dismay. It was almost midday. The heat was awful. But Terrans, Whimeds, and Armilly all courted sunstroke—running! They banged on the skimmer's hull and gestured urgently, nagging the riders to get out of the cockpit.

The instant Dan cracked the canopy, Sheila leaned inside and shouted, "We found a second dome! A much more recent construct! Come on!"

Praedar and Kat jostled Dan in their haste to scramble out. They and the other offworlders raced up the slope to the dome. Dan's curiosity warred with good sense. The smart thing to do was stash the skimmer in the hangar and then hole up in the complex's air conditioning. But . . . what was going on at the dig?

He yielded to temptation. As he approached the hill, he saw that the entire N'lac village had come to view the discovery— Chuss, his mother, his siblings, scoop-pawed workers, elders, women, kids—everybody. The N'lacs knelt reverently, patting something that was concealed by the mass of wrinkled bodies. Scientists crowded close behind the e.t.s, using scanners and talking loudly.

Dan scaled the packed earth on the opposite side of the ramp and stood atop the painted wall. It gave him a broad overview of the crazy scene below.

He wasn't the only one who'd taken that high road. Sleeg knelt beside him, keening.

On the ramp, Sheila was screaming to make herself heard above the din. "We'll use the dredge to finish clearing it. I got this far and figured we'd better shut down till you had a chance to assess the setup. Look how intact it is! Fabulous preservation!"

Dan shielded his eyes with his locked hands, peering down into milling confusion. N'lacs were petting a dirt-encrusted wooden door. The portal peeped from a surrounding mound of soil. Dan mentally erased tons of earth, imagining how things would look when the vacuum dredge completed its job. As Sheila had said, it was a dome, smaller than the one farther south. This dirty door didn't appear to belong with the high-tech material of

73

that larger ancient building. Yet it was far more sophisticated than the villagers' mud-brick huts.

"Date?" Praedar demanded. Someone yelled that the door tested at five hundred Terran years before present.

"Definitely made by villagers . . ."

Dan was bewildered. Chuss' people had built this? How? Ordinary, dull-witted N'lacs were incapable of that. Chuss might have the necessary intelligence and drive, but he lacked the knowledge, and was only a single N'lac pup.

And the date was wrong. Praedar said the civilization collapsed thousands of years ago, not five hundred. Which date was right? They both couldn't be. This was crazy!

Sleeg chanted. A few words of pidgin Terran crept into his crooning litany. "Evil Old Ones! Big Dark! The place of the many fathers-ago. Bad bad! We be punished!"

Cottonmouthed, blasted by a merciless sun, Dan listened to the old N'lac and felt icy cold.

CHAPTER SIX

⊗⊗⊗⊗⊗⊗⊗⊗

The Tale-tellers

The celebration/lamentation came to an abrupt end when Armilly keeled over. Subdued, murmuring nervously, the N'lacs retreated to their village. Dan and four other muscular male offworlders carried Armilly to the cook shack and laid the procyonid near a cooling vent. Once he had rested a bit and swilled a couple of liters of foul-smelling, fruit-laced water, he perked up.

By then the entire expedition was jammed into the room. The medical emergency over, bull sessions began. Dan had hoped to take a siesta after lunch, but the debates were so noisy they carried even into the bunk area. So he sat on the sidelines as the marathon arguments and theories raged around him.

"... fits perfectly into previously collected legendary material ..."

"... not necessarily. Data. We must have more data ..."

"... why did this have to happen *now*? Why not last season? It's such a short time till we have to leave for the Assembly. How can we get this new stuff in presentable order by then?"

"... run a prelim, whet their interest ..."

". . . no, it'd never work. The Saunders won't be sitting on their hands. They'll crucify us, claim it's only speculation . . ."

". . . have to include enough N'lac holos and artifacts to prove our case . . ."

". . . can't overlook Sleeg's religious fears or offend the people's taboos. Interference with cultural integrity . . ."

". . . such a thing as overdoing this noninterference routine . . ."

". . . give Sleeg time to adjust. His myths are coming true before his eyes . . ."

". . . and ours!"

". . . dating is so exact. Did you see the figures? Superb!"

After a while, the conversations became repetitious. Dan dozed off and on. Each time he awoke, the team seemed to be rehashing something they'd discussed earlier. Praedar looked patiently pained by all the verbal circling.

It was late afternoon, and temperatures outside surely had begun to moderate. Dan made his getaway, moving quietly. He was a few meters from the cook shack when Praedar overtook him and asked, "Where are you going?"

"Flying the skimmer out to my starhopper. Okay?"

"That is where you have the recording concerning Saunderhome?" Praedar was a big, hungry cat, lusting to get his claws on Varenka's views of that rotting mansion.

Smiling, Dan said, "I'll make you a dupe."

"Very good." The Whimed nodded, staring fixedly at the domes. He muttered, "So much to do. Truth. We are the preservers."

It was an oath. Dan edged away carefully. Praedar was still gazing at the domes when he reached the skimmer. To Dan, the alien appeared to be in a trance.

Dust devils and thermals were everywhere on the valley floor. Dan rode the latter up to the mesa. Long shadows, thrown by the tendrilled trees, snaked across the sand. He took a roundabout route to the landing strip, enjoying the scenery. Every day he felt less like a stranger here.

At *Fiona*, he ran his maintenance checks and played back the auto com monitor. There wasn't much news to tell the camp, this trip: a plague scare on Mars; a Vahnaj ambassador threatening to boycott Terran products if Loezzi Settlement traders didn't stop alleged favoritism toward Whimed merchants—more of that ongoing age-old cold war between Vahnajes and felinoids; and an arrest of a smuggling ring in Terran sector seven. Adam McKelvey, the fleet officer commanding that operation, would probably get a medal. Dan grinned proudly. He didn't begrudge Adam the reward. Big brother earned it, putting his life on the line for Earth and the spacers. Their sisters were doing pretty good in their careers, too. The sole foulup among Reid McKelvey's brood was the baby of the family.

Like father, like son? Both were unlucky. Reid's lousy judgment had bankrupted him. Dan had struggled up from an apprenticeship toward a decent future and had wrecked it by being stupid and hauling one bribe-buried cargo.

Now he'd just have to start climbing all over again.

He shoved aside depressing thoughts and got busy duping Varenka's segment of that letter. On a whim, he let it run in real time, watching.

Saunderhome! What must it have been like to live there when it was in its prime? He didn't think any of his direct ancestors had resided in the tropical palace, but Dan wasn't sure. After five generations, the Saunder-McKelvey family tree was crowded and complicated. His wealthy relatives hired genealogists to keep track of the various connections. That took an expert; the clan was scattered from Earth clear out to the sector's fringes.

According to Varenka's tearful account, the last occupant of Saunderhome had been Colin Saunder, Jael's great-grandson. He'd left the rotting hulk in favor of more modern quarters back in 2120, thirty-five years ago! By now the place wasn't just a wreck. It was ancient history. No doubt that was why Praedar wanted to see it.

Another reason was its association with Dan's family. If an alien knew of any Terrans, he knew of the Saunder-McKelveys. Kat called the clan a distillation of mankind's brightest and best, and to a degree that was true. Amid those dilettantes Dan scorned were giants. Ward Saunder's inventions had paved humanity's path to the present era. Ward's wife Jael had consolidated his patents and created an enormous fortune, built Saunderhome, and made sure that Ward—*and* Saunderhome—became immortal. Their son Todd had established the first contact with extraterrestrials. His daughter Brenna and her cousin Morgan perfected the FTL drive. Anthony Saunder, clone of Todd's brother, led the Settlement planets in their breakaway from crippling economic and political ties to Earth. Ethan pioneered in new world development. Geoff, martyred in the *Ad Astra* spacecraft sabotage tragedy, became a posthumous trigger for peace negotiations that averted interstellar war. Brenna's daughter Regan, managing far-flung S-ME Corporation . . . Regan's son Cameron, executive of Pan Terran Media Network . . . Wileen McKelvey, tamer of ocean worlds . . . Lara McKelvey, governor of Vaughn Settlement . . . Nathan Saunder, the sector's favorite entertainer . . .

The list went on and on. Little wonder Praedar, like Varenka, regarded Saunderhome as a historic shrine and the Saunder-McKelveys as Earth's uncrowned royalty.

Dan chuckled bitterly. *He* didn't feel at all like royalty!

He completed the dupe, then cued a final scan of the monitors. On this go-around, he spotted an item he'd missed earlier. With a frown, he told the comps, "Repeat traffic blip." The screen blinked. A dot froze on the grids. Analyzers ran checks and double-checks to confirm.

Dan leaned back in his web couch, studying the display. The local nav-sat had noted a vehicle's entry into planetary orbit. But what sort of vehicle? Configuration didn't match anything in the United Species recognition keys. The object was too small to be manned and didn't follow normal ident formats. It had dropped over the horizon and off the sat's scanners. A meteor? No, the vector spiraled in, a controlled descent.

He scratched his blond mop and decided the blip had to be space junk. There was plenty of that out there. Most of it was marked on the charts, but occasionally something slipped through the grids. This was probably a maverick. No one could identify her now. She'd have been a spectacular little flash in T-W 593's atmosphere, then splattered herself on the surface or one of the seas.

Why had it taken him so long to spot this? The thing had registered on the monitors days ago. Was his brain asleep when he'd run previous checks? Well, no matter. He had it logged at last. Dan closed the file and headed back to the skimmer.

The terminator was well west of N'lac Valley. He flew home in deepening twilight. The complex's lamps and a huge bonfire near the dud pits welcomed him. He touched down by the hangars and walked to the cook shack. To his relief, the debating club had adjourned. Most of the offworlders and a number of N'lacs were gathering by that bonfire. Praedar, Kat, and several others were finishing work at the painted wall. Dan went up there and gave Praedar the dupe of Varenka's sales pitch, then peered around.

Scaffolding, calibrators, charge-injected imagers, and tools cluttered the ramp and the apron in front of the newly revealed small dome. The pictures on the wall seemed to draw Dan's hand like a magnet. He asked, "Is it okay to touch it?"

"This part, but don't rub it," Kat said.

Tentatively he made contact. The wall resembled stone, yet felt like metal or, rather, metalline. Strange stuff! An alloy? Tingly warmth spread up Dan's arm. He fumbled for words. "Is there a . . . a power source here? A current of some kind?"

"No, no power," Kat said. "Our instruments would note it if there were. The effect is psychological."

Praedar, too, was caressing the wall. His expression was feral; his spidery hands probed carefully.

Beautiful, sad pictures showed a star-roving race, reduced to this. Fate had locked the N'lacs in limbo. Could the same thing happen to humanity? Did *Homo sapiens* face the same mysterious dead end Chuss' people had landed in? Lost, forgotten, waiting for xenoarchaeologists of the forty-first or forty-second century to dig up the fragments of their civilization . . .

Dan recoiled. He told himself the N'lacs had simply been the unlucky victims of a cosmic catastrophe—disease, radiation, fatal gene mutations or some other one-in-a-trillion blow. Not anything likely to strike again at Terra.

But what if . . . ?

The spooky images were giving him disconcerting ideas. Maybe it was the result of rubbing elbows with all these scientists. That could twist an ordinary spacer's view of the universe.

Kat pressed his arm. "Yes, we feel it, too." Startled, he stared down at her. "We wish we could go back in time and prevent their collapse," she said. "But we can't alter the past. We can only learn from it—or try to." She gestured toward the bonfire. "I have to set up my equipment before Sleeg begins his tale-telling. Are you going to join us there, Dan?"

"What is it? A party?"

"Not exactly." Kat's manner was solemn. "It's an aftermath of finding the small dome. The N'lacs need a safety valve."

Praedar said, "They will remember what they were. We will know what we may become." With that, the Whimed headed

79

down the hill. So did Kat and the other scientists. After a moment, so did Dan.

Brushwood fed green and purple-tinged flames. The strange colors didn't detract from tempting food aromas rising from spits suspended over the fire. Dan eyed the food hungrily, but he hadn't been part of today's hunting teams, so he had to wait his turn. Once the nimrods took their shares, the rest dug in. Dan filled his bowl with roast lizard and crumbly bread and looked around for a place to sit. Sheila beckoned invitingly. He settled beside her and the blonde handed him a mug of "diggers' brew." That was a mild concoction fermented from native berries and grains, with enough spunk to make him happily mellow.

It was a pleasant multispecies picnic, lacking only the Vahnajes' presence to complete the scene. Each race had its own food favorites, mostly used as dessert or taste-topper for the simple fare. The mood was atavistic and oddly comforting. Terrans, felinoids, and procyonid—stepping back through the millennia to the dawn of their civilizations and joining the primitive N'lacs in this open-air meal. It didn't matter if one were a famous scientist, a stony-broke indie pilot, or a descendant of those golden-eyed former masters of T-W 593. Here they were all people, well fed, content, and among friends.

The circle wasn't rigid. Now and then children crept off into the bushes to relieve themselves. A few couples strolled away arm in arm, responding to another natural urge. Other offworlders ran errands to the domes or the complex, then returned to the fire. Several times the Whimeds indulged in their custom of compulsive "huddling"—embracing one another violently and growling in apparent fury, or ecstasy, then breaking apart. For the most part the crowd ate and digested, talked, and watched sparks sail into the night sky.

After an hour or so, Sleeg started swaying rhythmically and chanting. His tribe chanted with him, a susurrating undercurrent. Kat, Rosenthal, and the expedition's xenoethno students switched on recorders. They acted as if they'd been through this ritual many times but hoped to collect something brand new. Terrans, Whimeds, and Armilly hummed along with the N'lacs. The sense of community was very strong.

"Kat," Sheila whispered, "give handsome a transbutton so he can understand." The brunette fished a miniature listen-plug from her equipment case and offered it to Dan. He inserted the button in his ear, picking up an English rendition of Sleeg's story in midword.

"... pened in the days of the many-fathers-ago. There! At the temple place—the big dome place where Sheila's people dig when sun is high. Our many-fathers-ago build little dome there, when they came Home from slavery in the Evil Old Ones' place..."

Sheila nudged Dan, speaking softly. "Notice how Chuss anticipates what Sleeg's going to say? He even helps the old boy whenever Sleeg forgets a phrase. The torch is being passed. Kat calls it oral history in action. The Vahnajes evolved a different form of prehistoric bonding. But for us and the Whimeds and Armilly, this is a graphic demonstration of how things were in our species' early stages."

Dan murmured, "And Chuss will probably memorize the stories even faster than Sleeg did, won't he, thanks to Joe's work?" Hughes was sitting close by, and he grinned.

"Right!" Sheila agreed. "Not bad, handsome."

"... Evil Old Ones came to us in the many long-agos," Sleeg crooned. "They took us to their place. Their world. Bad bad place! We live there many long-longs." He contorted his wizened face, waving his skinny arms for emphasis. The horror of N'lac captivity gripped the villagers. Young and old alike echoed the shaman, crying "Bad bad!"

One scientist grumbled, "Have to clarify that in our presentations to the Assembly. Feo's faction will insist that we heard the N'lac myths first and worked backward. They won't believe we arrived at our theories independently..."

"Then we'll shove it down their throats," Sheila said grimly.

Sleeg's tale crossed species lines, dragging Dan into the narrative. "Evil Old Ones lost their hands," the elder—or the translation of the elder's words—said. "Long-long-long-long time ago they lost hands. They take N'lacs and those like N'lacs to be their hands. We are their slave-hands..."

Revulsion roiled Dan's gut. Handless? That hinted that the Evil Old Ones were nonanthropomorphic—and slavers to boot. Of course, humanoids weren't too clean on that last score. Yet the effect was different. Even egg-laying Ulisorians, with their float bladders and extra arms, and the trisexed, blue-skinned Rigotians were human*like*. When humanoid enslaved humanoid, it

81

was despicable, but familiar. What Sleeg was describing was a sickening perversion of natural order.

"Evil Old Ones. No bones. Bones outside. Round. Tall. Tall tall!" Sleeg sketched in the air, drawing an upright, bulbous form encased in an exoskeleton.

Dan's nausea grew. A bunch of insects! Big worms with lattice-shaped outer shells. Ugh!

His reaction astonished him. He'd dealt with alien critters of all kinds since he was a toddler. Sleeg's story shouldn't disturb him this badly. It was hitting reflexes so deep Dan hadn't been aware he possessed them. Maybe it was due to the diggers' brew. He put the stuff aside. N'lac fairy tales and alcohol didn't mix.

"Evil Old Ones have demons with many arms. Demons find, hurt N'lacs." Again, Sleeg drew pictures in the air. Chuss copied him, the apprentice tale-teller learning his trade. Their drawings involved another upright oblate, though a more angular shape than that of the Evil Old Ones. "Demons move like sand crawler. So!" Sleeg parodied a reptile's serpentine waddle, and N'lac kids squealed.

"Demons shiny," Chuss added. "They machines. Like Kelfee's fly fly."

The shaman considered his apprentice's comment, then waggled his jaw, the N'lac form of nodding. The tribe gazed worriedly at Dan. He hoped they weren't lumping him in the same category as Sleeg's many-limbed demons and Evil Old Ones.

Chuss said, "Round. Not pointy like Kelfee fly fly." The N'lacs sighed collectively, smiling.

"That lets you off the hook," Sheila whispered.

He shook his head. "Were these things they're talking about real?"

Kat put in, "In all probability, yes. Most legends are based on past events, often on a violent clash of cultures. This situation certainly qualifies."

"What situation? There wasn't anything about a triggering cause in your library vids," Dan said, aggrieved. The scientists looked amused. He went on irritably. "Okay. It's a professional secret why there's a gap in N'lac history. Two thousand Terran years ago to the five hundred years ago you pegged that small dome at. But right now I'm interested in how that ties in with Sleeg's tale. Were these demons servo robots? Chuss said they were shiny. That implies metal, to me."

"To us, too," Sheila admitted.

"And it's no secret," Kat said, on the defensive. "It's just that we prefer to keep those particular hypotheses in secure files, for the time being, until they're positively confirmed."

Dr. Chen and Praedar were sitting together across the big circle. They listened to the exchange with a conspiratorial manner, aged Oriental and enigmatic Whimed. Their all-knowing attitude bothered Dan, underlining his novice, outsider status.

Sheila said, "Sometimes the N'lacs make models or sand pictures of the Evil Old Ones and demons. The latter sure look like robots. Mechanical eggs on stilts. God knows how they were manufactured."

"Or if they were," Dan said skeptically. "Maybe Dr. Getz is right, and these are just scare stories."

"Arguable," Kat retorted. "Bill's not an expert in xenoeth."

"But he is in *his* field," Sheila said, scowling at her friend. Then she wriggled seductively and squeezed Dan's thigh. Her lips tickled his earlobe as she murmured, "I'll bet I know one of your fields of expertise. How about a moonlight stroll later?"

His hormones roused. "Daddy warned me about you Kruger 60 women. Spacers say because you settlers are polygamous, you're supersexy."

"We are." Sheila winked. "Hey, if your fathers and mothers were frozen in a stasis ship for years and thawed out and told to populate a planet, they'd pass on interesting reproductive ideas to you, too. Care to find out the straight dope about us Kruger fems?"

Dan grinned. "Sounds exciting."

"Then when Sleeg finishes, we'll . . ."

"Here!" Dr. Getz shoved his way between Dan and Sheila and plunked down a box full of his effigy specimens. "You and Rosie hand these out to the N'lacs for their ritual, Whitcomb. And be sure to collect 'em all, when they're through. I have something to do at the refuse pile. Olmsted, make certain I get copies of the N'lacs' attempts to mold their own effigies," he said imperiously, and hurried up the trail to the domes.

Sheila got to her feet, running after him. "Bill, wait! I want to ask you about that . . ."

Dan was irked. Did he have a date or not? Kruger 60 women might be hot, but this one was threatening to be a tease. Didn't

Sheila care if she nudged a man's hormones and left him up and nowhere? Hell of a note.

Sour and disappointed, he watched Rosenthal pass around the box. Each N'lac adult and adolescent took one of the effigies. After a few minutes, Dan began to forget his annoyance with Sheila, fascinated by the N'lacs' actions. As Sleeg continued to chant, his people dabbled small amounts of water onto loose dirt and molded the soil, copying Getz's specimens crudely.

". . . Evil Old Ones had many people to be their hands. Many N'lacs and not-N'lacs. No one get away. Only our many-fathers-ago escaped." The elder thrust his webbed hands into the air, ticking off a few dozen beings on his clubbed fingers. "They ran to the Below. Came through the Big Dark, where the People cannot see or hear or feel. The Big Dark is many-many-many far aways and it is many-many stranges. Dark! DARK! The People came from Below to here. Back to Home . . ."

The N'lacs responded, "Up from Below. Home! *Shree!*"

"And when we came here, we made the holy things, the magic things . . ."

Dan frowned. Magic? Like those mud models they were making now? How many generations of N'lacs had sat by similar bonfires, inspired by their tale-tellers, molding little shapes? The scene was poignant—dull-witted humanoids, earnestly attempting to duplicate the objects of their ancestors.

"The effigies," he asked Kat. "How old are they?"

"Difficult to say. Glass resists precise dating."

". . . magic things made world go," Sleeg told his people. "Made sun come into our houses. Made wind come in. Made the warm. Made the cool. Made the water . . ."

Hair raised on Dan's nape. The old e.t. was talking technology. Light. Air circulation. Heating and cooling systems. Automated water-supply systems. The words sounded eerie, considering the source.

Rosie had left Getz's box sitting an arm's length away. Dan peeked inside and took out several specimens that were lying in the bottom. Getz was so proprietary about his collection that this was Dan's first opportunity to get a close look at the things. He studied the glass, hollow-cored, brachiate forms. Then he chuckled and began fitting pieces together. Some were difficult to match up. Others worked fine. By trial and error, he quickly assembled a fair-size unit.

Sleeg's tale-telling stuttered to a stop. The N'lacs quit chanting. Startled, Dan realized all the villagers were staring at him. Chuss scuttled around the firepit and hunkered directly in front of the pilot. The boy's big eyes locked on the glass objects Dan was holding.

By now the scientists were staring, too. Conversation faltered. Kat turned her scanner in Chuss's direction.

It was an unfortunate moment for Dr. Getz and Sheila to return from the domes. Getz froze, then stabbed an accusing finger. "Rosie! How dare you let him tamper with my specimens?"

Sheila hurried around the circle and knelt beside Dan. "I thought you had better sense. You know how touchy Bill is. What did you think you were . . ."

Sleeg howled. The cry shocked the offworlders to silence. The N'lacs erupted, babbling. An incoherent storm blasted Dan's ear. He'd almost forgotten he was wearing the transbutton.

The shaman bellowed, "Magic! *Shree!* Like the many-fathers-ago magic! They did so. My grandfather's grandfather's grandfather told it so. Kelfee knows the magic!"

Praedar was moving along the edge of the fire, a stalking hunter—and Dan was his prey.

Getz leaned over the pilot and shook his fists. "You bastard! I knew you'd be trouble!"

Dan scrambled to his feet. "Just hold it. *You're* the one who's been pulling funny stuff. Now I know why you hide these things." He thrust the glass units under Getz's nose. "So no one can see that they're nothing but fluidics elements."

All the scientists talked at once, some siding with Getz, others intrigued by what Dan had said, asking colleagues if *they* knew anything about it.

"Give me that!" Getz lunged, grabbing and shouting curses.

Dan fended him off easily. Angered, he defiantly demonstrated his discovery, twisting the glass pieces apart and putting them back together again. "See? Flange to flange to insert. A Schmitt trigger here. A fluid amplifier on this end. NOR gates. AND gates. Even a flip-flop or two. No big mystery. Some of the elements are pretty badly made. The makers must have used lousy molds. The rest, though, are fine connectors . . ."

"They're *effigies*!" Getz roared. "Of *course* they interface, you cretin! The poorly made ones are a degenerate form, more recent artifacts. The better ones were constructed during the initial stages of the ritualization, centuries ago. The objects you are holding—and *without* my authorization—are rare, early finds. I lend them to the N'lacs solely for their quaint little ceremony, as a favor to naïve xenoeths like Olmsted. Don't be deceived by the natives' reactions. This isn't the first time they've been excited by the effigies. They did the same thing when *I* showed them how these could be either mutability fetishes representing a single being or joined to comprise a symbolic communal . . ."

"Jettison that out that waste tubes," Dan cut in rudely. "You can't see the truth when it's right in front of you. Look. Channel here. Shunt here. This unit is obviously a power linkage, probably to a pump of some sort. So forget that stuff about 'mutability fetishes' or 'symbolic communal' garbage . . ."

Getz swung. Dan ducked. The blow missed him by a good half meter.

He cocked a fist, then thought better of it. He couldn't hit this thick-headed old scientist, even if Getz was picking a fight. Sure, Dan had the advantage of youth and weight, and he could wallop the shorter man with no problem. Then what? He'd be pegged as a bully. What a no-win mess this was!

Praedar flung out an arm, blocking Getz's attempt to close with Dan again. Casually the Whimed shoved the Terran xenoarchaeologist aside. Getz's jaw dropped. Praedar paid no attention to him. He bored in on Dan instead. "Where have you learned this thing you speak of?"

"Tech manuals. History of systems. Alternative power feeds. That's *my* field of expertise," Dan added, shooting a belligerent scowl at Getz.

"Explain the process." Praedar's words were flat, lacking his normal, elegant diction.

"They're switches and relays, mostly. Slow, compared to modern equipment, or even to old-fashioned chips and electronics."

Rosenthal brightened. "Like optic fibers? I've read about . . ."

"Nah! Those are quaint, too, nowadays. Museum fodder. Fluidics carry air, not liquid, not electrical signals. Most humanoids have used them, at some time in their developed stages. Fluidics are ideal in applications where heat is a problem." He admired the glass pieces. "It's an efficient concept, and doable on a frontier. You know, the Romans might have hung onto their empire longer, if they'd stumbled onto these. They had the necessary knowhow . . ."

A gabble of discussion arose. Dan yanked the transbutton from his ear. He didn't need that distraction. Doggedly he continued his explanation.

"With these you have the interruptible jets and back pressure systems, great for controlling machinery, pipelines, maybe even com links. They're explosion-proof, vibration-free, and immune to outside electrical noise and radiation. If the N'lacs' ancestors used them, they probably weren't bothered by the slow response factors. Milliseconds would have been fine, in these conditions. They didn't need the usual nanosecond speed rating. Yeah! And they had sand, a solar power source, all the ingredients for . . ."

"The construction of the effigies has never been in question!" Getz was alarmingly flushed. He stared daggers at Dan but wasn't willing to go through Praedar to get at the pilot. Getz said, "Do you take me for an illiterate fool like yourself?"

"I'm neither illiterate nor a fool." Something in Dan's tone made Getz, other offworlders, and the N'lacs back away from him.

Still riding his specialty, Getz ranted, "The N'lacs have long since lost the capability their ancestors commanded—if indeed they ever had it. I am not convinced Olmsted's theories on these primitives is correct. For all we know, the villagers stumbled across these effigies and have concocted their own elaborate myths to claim them. They've reduced everything to these pitiful tales concerning 'magic.' That's why they make those mud copies, or whittle effigy models in brushwood . . ."

"Where are the glass ovens that produced the fluidics elements?" Dan demanded. "There's nothing in your library about ovens. Where did the locals *make* these?" He held up the glass pieces challengingly. Several scientists exchanged uneasy glances.

"Unimportant," Getz sniffed. "I'll locate them, in time . . ."

"Praedar's been here eleven years, Kat and Sheila and others almost as long. *They* apparently haven't found the manufacturing unit. And *you*'ve been here a full season," Dan said. "By your own brags, you've cataloged thousands of these elements. And you're too blind to see what they are, or to dig hard enough to find out where and how they were made? Huh! Before I came up with a whole bunch of wrong-headed ideas about 'symbolic communal fetishes,' I'd want something solid to base them on. I'd want to eyeball the glass molds. I'd want to see the complete system and see if it was a shaman's assembly line for magic objects or a frontier factory for turning out energy-channelers."

Kat and Praedar nodded, obviously impressed.

Dan rushed on. "Hollow construction. Flanging. Snug interfaces. Damned sophisticated for use as 'religious figures.' Not to mention unnecessary. If they're effigies, why are they hollow? Why do they have valves? Where are the humanoid features all the journal articles say effigies have? And aren't effigies clay or ceramic? These are glass. You want to chop me down, you'd better get some bigger ammo."

"Those *are* pertinent questions, Bill," Kat put in. "They've bothered many of us." Sheila shook her head warningly.

Rosie and a number of others Getz had rubbed the wrong way dived into the argument. "That's right! They don't fit the criteria. And they're strata intensive. Right at the five hundred B.P. level and nowhere else . . ."

"There are none in the ancient N'lac museum," Chen noted, his eyes sparkling. He seemed to enjoy Getz's discomfort.

"Can't you see?" Getz yelled. "This is one of Feo's tricks!"

Praedar asked Dan, "These fluidics could drive complex devices?"

Joe caught the Whimed's drift. "Could you power a pressurizing system with them? Say . . . to increase atmospheres within a hut, as I've done in the village, for Loor?"

"Sure! Pumps. Resistors. Detectors. Monitors . . ."

"Why are you doing this to me?" Getz whined. "Feo sent him to discredit me, disrupt my work. Why are you ganging up on me? I go through hell, researching on this end-of-nowhere dump, and for what? So you can conspire against me and steal my data!"

"No one steals." Praedar's voice was a basso thunderclap. "What McKelvey suggests is new. He speaks from a technological discipline, one none of us shares. It offers us much for our consideration."

"Wiping away my sacrifices on Chrow and Noviy Settlement and those damned Vahnaj outposts," Getz said, snuffling. He rounded on Kat. "And you! You've always doubted me, now you're stabbing me in the back!"

"Calm down, Bill," she soothed. "We're here to find the truth. Dan may have shown us an aspect of that which we didn't know existed. We have to examine it. Haven't we wondered what aided the N'lacs' adaptation to this environment, when the slaves first escaped from the Evil Old Ones' domain . . . ?"

"You have. *I* haven't. And how can you forget the most vital fact of all? He's a *McKelvey!*" Getz shot an indicting finger toward Dan.

"And my mother was Colin Saunder's lover," Kat said. "I may be his daughter. You know that. It hasn't affected your opinion of me, has it? Do you think I'm Feo's spy? Neither is Dan. Quit allowing your temper to impede your reason."

"You . . . you're a *scientist*," Getz protested. "But him? He's not one of us. We hardly know him." Several offworlders nodded, eyeing Dan warily. He felt walls going up against him again, separating him from the club members. "That story about a blacklist. Ridiculous! Who ever heard of a poor Saunder-McKelvey? He just wants to hang around here and cause trouble, and that was a handy excuse. Well, he didn't fool me!" In a frenzy, Getz ran around the campfire, sweeping up effigies, knocking N'lacs out of his way. Shrieking, the e.t.s fled.

Dan hastily pocketed the fluidics unit he'd assembled, hoping Dr. Getz would overlook it. He did. Clutching his trophies, the effigy expert stumbled toward the insta-cell complex, crowing "You won't get *my* data! Hah!"

Kat and Praedar moved to follow him, but Sheila waved them back. "Not you. You've done enough damage, supporting McKelvey instead of him. Bill's got a right to be upset. You know how Jarrett, Ishyu, and Lizenka have been attacking his classification record recently. Now this! Talk about kicking a man in the balls! You keep clear. I'll make peace, if I can. He knows I'm not his enemy."

The blonde, Getz's students, and a dozen other Terrans hurried after him. They closed ranks, glowering at those who'd taken the other side of this argument. Ugly words flew as the two groups edged apart.

Praedar sighed tiredly. Dan didn't envy the Whimed's job. The boss would be justified in blaming his maintenance specialist for causing the latest uproar in this expedition crammed with squabbling, multispecies, professional egos. But Praedar gave no such indication. He said, "Sit by the fire. If we pretend to be civilized, the N'lacs may return."

Chastened by his sarcasm, the others obeyed. Out in the dark, in the scrub brush, in dud pits, and behind parked machines, the N'lacs' golden eyes gleamed. Dan put himself in their place. He'd been caught between a bunch of procyonids while their matriarch had hysterics once. That was a terrifying experience for a non-Lannon—trapped among huge, hairy aliens. Getz's rampage must have been just as scary for the N'lacs. They were probably afraid other offworlders would go berserk, too, gauging by those loud arguments they'd witnessed.

Whimeds, Terrans, and Armilly sat and put on a performance for their spectators. Amateur musicians on the team brought instruments from the complex and led singalongs. The emphasis was on lighthearted, cheery tunes.

Gradually laughter and music had a soothing effect on the participants, even if it hadn't yet persuaded the N'lacs to join the party. Praedar's topknot was soft now. He chatted quietly with those nearest him. "Most distressing that Bill behaved so."

"But not surprising," Chen said. "Whitcomb's word for him is touchy. And then some." The Oriental nodded owlishly. The antique corrective spectacles he wore when he wasn't examining museum finds slid down his nose, giving him a comical appearance.

"Sheila will settle him," Kat assured them. "She's got a damned sweet tongue, when she chooses to use it. Remember the Vahnajes' brawl at the Eleventh Assembly, four years ago? She cooled Ruieb until the main lutrinoid faction got their reps in check."

Dan gaped at her. Vahnajes? Brawling? He'd heard spacers' gossip to that effect, but never believed it. Maybe the gray faces were no different from other humanoids, despite their elegant way of moving and their rigid social etiquette. Pushed far enough, they might turn nasty. Apparently even Vahnaj scientists weren't above that. Dan had spent years out here, dealing with aliens as well as humans, and he was still learning. Well, he'd always said when he quit doing that, he'd be dead.

Kat went on. "I'm afraid of another snag, though. Bill may pull his data out of our presentation package for the upcoming conference."

A buzz of protest arose around the fire. Rosie said, "He should, if his datum are incorrect. That would give the Saunders something to beat us with and to cast doubts on the rest of our material."

"Okay, a lot of us suspect he's made mistakes," Baines, the geologist, noted. "That doesn't mean things are hopeless. His effigy classifications are in the data banks. The comps could pull those files and test them against McKelvey's fluidics theory, if that proves out."

"A big assumption," someone said.

Praedar told Dan, "Do not be offended. We are obligated to question your thesis."

"Thesis?" Dan said weakly. "I didn't . . ."

Kat walked on his words. "Let's be honest. We've all thought Bill's adjusting his findings to suit his prior expectations. Bad selectivity. Bad science. The Daust Effect. A researcher trying to repeat his past successes and altering his interpretations accordingly."

"But on the other hand," Rose said, "McKelvey's a rank amateur."

"In many ways, so was Schliemann," Joe Hughes cut in. He started to explain the reference for Dan's benefit.

"I know," Dan said curtly. "A romantic nineteenth-century Earthman. He believed ancient legends were based on fact, and went looking for Troy. To the then-establishment's chagrin, he dug up ruins exactly where he'd said he would. He wasn't a professional and his excavation methods were a disaster. But he taught the scoffers that they couldn't ignore either mythology or maverick theorists."

He was gratified by the stunned expressions on every side. A flicker of new respect moved across the scientists' faces. Kat smiled and said, "You *have* been busy studying. Don't tell us; you read that somewhere."

"It's one of my small talents, naturally, as one of the notorious Saunder-McKelvey family," Dan retorted. "I do read."

The team squirmed uncomfortably. He hoped he'd made a dent in a few hard-core snobbish attitudes. Lacking an institute degree didn't mean a Terran was fried-brain stupid! And it was time they conceded that fact.

Praedar said, "Maruxa of my home world died proving that the Dread Regions are indeed the birthplace of all Whimed. She, too, was scorned and disbelieved, at first."

Kat nodded. "It's an old problem in this field, Dan. People like Schliemann often wreck as much as they find. But sometimes the scientific establishment wears blinders. They refuse to

91

look at fresh aspects. They become tenured, timid, unwilling to take chances, waiting for some recognized brave soul to break the barriers and publish *the* definitive paper, so they'll know it's all right to add a new concept to the accepted view of the universe.

"Yet there are dangers in being too daring, as well. For instance, because the N'lacs are still living on this dig world, we could—without meaning to—alter their history and mythology and insert ourselves into the data. That's a constant risk in such situations. And we can't do certain normal xenoarch work, like examining graves, even though there are thousands of burials available in this region. We worry that we're moving too fast, endangering the facts and the N'lacs' integrity, simply by being here . . ."

Baines said, "It's impossible to study a culture without contributing to its future." Was he quoting a famous law of his scientific branch?

Praedar added a Whimed adage: "To listen well and walk cautiously is a gift of those who will learn."

At the edge of the fire-lit shadows, N'lacs crept forward. Singers played their instruments softly. The conversationalists smiled encouragingly. One by one the N'lacs took their former places in the circle. They were still edgy, however, and the offworlders continued their talk at a soothing, low-volume level.

Kat explained, "Dan, the best time to get involved in a discipline is when it's in flux. That's when things are happening. And that's xenoarchaeology, right now, making new, exciting finds, like these civilizations out here on the known stellar boundaries. You landed in the middle of one of the hottest debates—and poked your finger in Bill Getz's pride. Oh, we know you didn't do it deliberately. But it's too bad, all the same. He's a hard worker and has a number of significant publications to his credit. But he's afraid he's slipping. His normal abrasiveness is being made worse by challenges from young, ambitious colleagues. He's scrambling to stay on top, and that may have made him careless about identifying those glasses as effigies. *May.* Your ideas concerning fluidics are a long way from being proved."

Dan pulled the linked brachiate form from his thigh pocket and turned it over in his hands. "I'm not wrong. And I'm damned sick and tired of being treated like a lying greenie because I don't have a fancy degree and because I'm related to Feo Saunder." His harsh tone shook his listeners. Again they eyed one another uneasily, and with some embarrassment.

Praedar said, "Truth is all. If you spoke truth, it will be confirmed, in time. We will investigate fluidics and see if this fits previous findings regarding N'lac civilization. We will know." He tilted back his leonine head, gazing at the stars. "Larger patterns—all elements must support the larger pattern."

Dan nodded. "I see. The big picture. Assemble the components of a gigantic unit."

The Whimed swung his arm in an arc. "All the universe— life: Whimed; Terran; Lannon; Vahnaj; Ulisor; Rigotian; and those whose lives ended before our knowledge touched them, the lost ones. We reach. We will learn what occurred here. The N'lacs' story may echo what has happened before on each of our home worlds and what may happen in time to come."

In his way, Praedar was as much of a mesmerizer as Sleeg. He went on in a musing voice. "We must be alert in our selection of data to support our theories. Much may be misinterpreted, if one is not wary. The Evil Old Ones—" Praedar glanced at the N'lacs. "—may not have been at all evil, as the term is understood by Terran or Whimed. Alienness is its own reason, and the reasons of a nonanthropomorphic alien perhaps are unfathomable to humanoids."

"But slavery..." Dan said, troubled.

"Was it slavery to the Old Ones? Had they initiated and planted humanoid races eons ago for eventual harvest, as we seed crops and domesticate animals for our use?" Firelight shimmered on the tapetum layer of the felinoid's eyes, making iridescent mirrors. "Did the Old Ones consider their world and others teeming with humanoid life their property, to be taken as they willed? Had they indeed given humanoid races their first tastes of existence and merely collected a debt owed them?"

Dan saw that he wasn't alone in being rattled by the Whimed's cold speculation. Several scientists shivered. Drastil looked at Praedar with obvious dismay, wanting to reject his suggestions. So it wasn't just the Terrans who found these ideas unsettling.

"How did the Old Ones think and feel? We shall probably never know," Praedar conceded. "Yet we shall strive to learn."

There was a heavy silence for a long while. Then Sleeg resumed his taletelling. Dan picked the transbutton up, dusted it off, and reinserted it in his ear. Sleeg was saying "We who have hands. We made things for them. They made us build their demons, demons that punish us when we disobey the masters. Old Ones changed the N'lacs and the not-N'lacs. They made us into better hands for them. Long ago, in the forever time . . ."

Night breeze ruffled Dan's hair, an eerie touch by an unseen presence. Enslaved humanoids, forced to build their masters' police robots! And the masters had changed their captives to make them better slaves. Genetic alterations? Compared to that, Joe's hyperbarics experiments were truly benign. Despite Praedar's warning against being judgmental about the masters' motives, Dan thought they were thoroughly evil.

"We got away!" Sleeg exulted. "Demons not find us! Got away in the Big Dark!"

Dan muted the volume on the transbutton and turned to Kat. "Where's their spaceship? Their ancestors must have used one to make their escape. An FTL craft, most likely. Have you dug it up yet?"

"No, we haven't. We *did* find the ships and shuttles the ancient N'lacs destroyed, just before they were carried off to captivity."

Nonplussed, Dan said, "Huh? They destroyed their own ships?"

"Analyses and dating confirm it." Kat's expression was stiff with tension. "Not alien destruction. N'lac explosive residues. They wrecked every vehicle on the planet, as far as we can determine."

"Got away from Evil Old Ones!" Chuss shrilled.

Dan gazed at the brunette in utter confusion. *"Why?"*

She shrugged in annoyance. "We don't know. Cultural madness? Maybe the Evil Old Ones forced them to do it, as they'd forced them to construct robot policemen. Two thousand years before the present, the N'lacs wiped out their entire fleet. Then they vanished, presumably into the holds of the Evil Old Ones' ships." Kat gave Dan a rueful smile. "Trust you to ask *another* question I don't have any answer for."

Sensing he'd pushed her into a corner, Dan said lightly, "Well, that's one of my lines of expertise, as Sheila calls it. Speaking of which, do you think she'll be back? We sort of had an appointment."

Kat made a wry face. "I'll bet. You and she will make a great

94

pair. You think alike—with your gonads. No, I doubt she'll return to the circle tonight. She's a champion romper, but she's also thick-skulled loyal. And Bill Getz needs stroking more than you do."

Accepting his disappointment with as good a grace as he could manage, Dan asked, "How about you? Would you care for a moonlight stroll on the cold desert sands?"

Chuckling, she said, "The idea is tempting, but I'm too busy. Another time?"

He brightened at that half-promise. Then he recalled something Kat had said earlier and sobered. "Uh . . . was your father really Colin Saunder, my cousin who lived at Saunderhome?"

Her manner was reserved. "Possibly. My mother's secret. Are you worrying about consanguinity problems? We'd be remote kin if Colin was my father. It needn't concern us unless you plan on reproducing. Then we ought to do a genetic check, just in case."

Was she teasing him? Her cool, scientific stance toward such intimate matters jarred. Dan narrowed his eyes, studying her. "No, I wasn't . . ."

"We'll talk about it later," Kat said briskly, concentrating on the taletelling once more.

"Safe! Safe at Home!" Sleeg patted a mud copy of a fluidics element and said, "We make the magic as the many-fathers-ago did. Demons will not follow us and punish. Never never again. No more Evil Old Ones!"

A guarantee? Or a hopeful prayer? Nothing Dan had heard in the legends claimed that the Evil Old Ones had been wiped out. To the contrary, Chuss' ancestors had escaped—and the enemy might still lurk out there in the stars, waiting, still greedy for humanoid slaves.

The desert air was a knife, slithering against Dan's bones.

As Praedar had, he looked up at the stars. How fragile humanoid civilizations were! Seen on a stellar time scale, Terra and Whimed and Vahnaj were mere heartbeats. That didn't mean they wouldn't survive and thrive indefinitely. But it laid down no laws about a continued existence, either.

There could be an unavoidable astronomical disaster or war, disease . . . So many things could go wrong. Mankind and its peers must be ever vigilant and willing to defend themselves if they hoped to prevail.

Somewhere out there, unknown species, so alien that their motivations appeared to be abominably evil, could be on the move. Extinction, or as near as made no difference, could lie in the wings. If they struck, *Homo sapiens*, like the N'lacs, were looking at oblivion. Mankind—dust, less than a memory, and irretrievably lost in its own "forever time"!

CHAPTER SEVEN

Glimpses of the Past

For the next few days, Dan steered cleared of Dr. Getz and those who supported the effigy expert. Even those scientists who were curious about fluidics were discreet; they waited until Getz was elsewhere before they quizzed Dan on the subject. Praedar learned that Dan had some fluidics tech vids in his library on board *Fiona* and requested copies, which the pilot supplied. But after the Whimed and other team members read the texts, they remained uncommitted. Dan couldn't tell if that was because the concept was so new for them or because his reliability was still iffy. He didn't worry about it. There was too much else to keep him occupied.

Excavation around the domes went on at a painstaking pace. The diggers worked with extreme care, constantly consulting Armilly's subsurface scans of buried structures and materials. And certain areas weren't touched at all. Future scientists would have better equipment, better methods, and be able to extract more from those sections than the present expedition could. In leaving the sections alone, Praedar's team served knowledge, though they frustrated their curiosity.

One itch they *did* intend to scratch was the newly discovered dome. On the scheduled morning, everyone assigned to the job arrived very early. Dan fine-tuned the dredge to optimum and sucked away a final pile of earth blocking wide access to the door. He shut down the rig as Armilly made a complete survey of the building's interior and announced it was cleared for entry.

But first the N'lacs' ancestors—and their ghosts—must be appeased.

All the villagers came to see the show, joining Chuss' work gang at the site. Joe Hughes hovered anxiously near Chuss' pregnant mother, monitoring her with hand-held med gear. There were greetings and handshakings for half a local hour. Dan lost track of how many webbed paws he'd held and how many times he responded to "Hello, you fellow."

Social amenities attended to, the N'lacs used the dirt dump for a grandstand. They gabbled and jostled for the best seats. Sleeg, Chuss, and the top hunters stayed near the small dome's door. The taleteller laid an object on the ground, fussing over its exact placement. Then Sleeg and the others began marching around the bundle. The N'lac onlookers yelled enthusiastically, getting into the spirit of the occasion. Occasionally Sleeg picked up a pinch of sand and flung it to the breeze, reading omens.

Dan hid his amusement. The N'lacs were so serious about this nonsense!

But none of the scientists were laughing. They were intent on the ceremony. Like the N'lacs, they seemed caught up in the purpose of the ritual. Whimeds and Terrans hummed the marchers' song. Armilly patted his big feet.

Sleeg's song was hypnotic and it also set Dan's teeth on edge. He was relieved when the parade finally stopped. The group waited while an elderly female hobbled into the marchers' circle. The crone slashed away the vines binding the mysterious package, using a stone knife. She gathered the wrappings and tottered back to her seat on the dirt pile.

Dan stared at the revealed object—a crudely carved wooden ovoid a meter and a half in length. Spindly sticks protruded from one end of the model, forming a radiating pattern. Those sticks were attached to other sticks in a parody of ten jointed legs. A network of painted lines laced across the sticks and the "body."

Suddenly the shaman screamed. His mouth gaped, a wine-red maw. The entire tribe screamed with him:

"MARAA!"

Dan flinched, stunned by the predatory rage of the cry.

Without further preamble, Chuss, Sleeg, and the hunters attacked the model. Clubs shattered the stick "legs," obliterated intricate carvings and painted tracery. So much work had gone into the thing. Yet they smashed it with murderous glee. Villagers cheered them on with the N'lac words for "demon" and "kill." When the marchers lowered their clubs, the model was reduced to a pile of splinters.

Chuss grinned and said, "O-kee! Is *durin*, Pwaedar. Demon fellow all gone. All safe. O-kee!"

Praedar spread his hands, palms upward, in a Whimed gesture of friendship. "Most thanks. We are grateful." He repeated the phrases numerous times in N'lac, shaking hands with the demon killers. No Vahnaj could have behaved with more excessive courtesy.

Student scientists passed out gifts, payment for the killers' services. Sleeg got the largest present. He peeled off its plastic wrapping and licked the lump of fat from the complex's storehouse. Other N'lacs chattered happily over their shares of the same lardy stuff. Dan understood the logic behind the strange handouts. A desert world made its inhabitants voracious for fat to supplement their diet and lubricate sun-parched skin. N'lacs rubbed their red faces in the presents, slathered them in their mouths, heading back to the village in noisy, lip-smacking celebration.

Joe Hughes stood near Dan, and the black man tipped an imaginary hat to the expedition's boss. "Nice job, Praedar. Keep 'em happy." He winked at Dan and said, "Not bad, huh?"

"The fat, sure. But that business about killing a demon?"

"Doesn't hurt to take out insurance. I only hope smashing one ritual object was enough."

Dan blinked. "You're kidding, aren't you?"

"Am I?" Joe's face was a dark mask. "You'd better spend a bit more time in primitive cultures before you sneer at their customs. They know things we don't."

"Yeah . . ."

"I mean it. Don't laugh. This is another trail you aren't familiar with," Hughes warned. "When in doubt, get your go-ahead from the local shaman *before* you dig." Joe again tipped that nonexistent cap, then followed the departing villagers.

Praedar's team crowded close to the dedemonized dome. Rosenthal crawled on hands and knees, collecting pieces of the smashed model for analysis. Others pushed on the door, with little result. Armilly's instruments said there was no obstruction, but the barricade refused to budge.

The Whimeds waved aside the Terrans, then tackled the door with Armilly. Felinoids and Lannon had evolved on planets with a higher gravity than Earth, and genetic factors gave them the muscle to force the door partway open.

That done, the Whimeds and Terrans squeezed through. Armilly shoved his recording gear inside and tried to follow it. He got stuck. Dan helped scientists shove until Armilly popped through, leaving tufts of hair and flecks of blood on the wooden frame.

The remaining Terrans then trooped indoors. Dan waited for an invitation to join the gang. None came. So he returned to the dredge and flopped down in its shadow, mildly irritated. Odds were, if he went to the equipment sheds and started his day's repair chores, Praedar would need him back here at the site again, and he'd have a hot walk up the hill. Sighing, Dan closed his eyes, intending to take a short nap.

Loud sounds jolted him. Terrans staggered from the dome. Many were coughing desperately, half choking. Others wheezed for breath. Some bent double, retching.

Sheila reeled to the dredge and sat down hard, shaken by paroxyms. Dan knelt beside her anxiously. "Hey! Do you want me to fetch the med kit?"

The blonde gestured voicelessly, ordering him to stay put. When she could finally speak, Sheila said hoarsely, "I'll . . . be okay . . . in a minute." That was followed by another bad choking spell. She wiped her eyes and complained, "Whole dome is packed solid with dust and fungi. Should have known it. Ran into the same stuff in other enclosed digs here. This one's *awful*. Not lethal, but Terrans can't take those conditions for any length of time . . ." She paused, sucking in air, and wheezed, "Damn! This means Praedar's cat folks and that fur ball will discover all the goodies while we stay out here and cough ourselves silly."

Dan marveled at her lack of imagination. "Why don't you run the dredge on negative pressure and clear the stuff out? Even if the dome isn't airtight, you can cut down a lot on the junk."

Sheila glared at him. "It . . . it can't be that simple. Hell! I know the manual says you can do other things with that rig, but . . ."

Chuckling, Dan said, "To borrow from you—Kroo-ger! You big brains aren't so smart. If you can't figure out what a glass piece is, you call it an effigy. You can't read tech-ese, you say the dredge won't work. Do you want the air cleaned up in there or not?"

Still glaring, Sheila nodded grudgingly. Dan cued the machine and guided an intake hose to the dirt-encrusted door. None of the Terrans sitting nearby offered to help. Most of them continued to cough. They all regarded Dan with misery-loves-company expressions, hoping he was on a fool's errand and would be forced to beat a hasty retreat, as they had.

Getting through the door took some careful maneuvering. Dan lifted the hose over snags and squeezed through the splintery opening. Inside, he faced an abrupt change in lighting. Armilly and the Whimeds had set up lamps, but the interior remained dim. Sheila hadn't exaggerated; the murky room was thick with drifting crud. Dan's throat tightened and his nose began to itch.

"Do not step on importants," Armilly boomed. The Lannon's warning made dust motes dance, adding to Dan's growing distress.

He fastened the hose to a ledge above the door and, fighting an urge to cough, cured intake circuits. Imperceptibly at first, an outward flow of air started. Dust and fungus particles diminished, sucked to the dredge's tanks.

Now Dan could see Armilly's "importants." Broken furniture and pottery lay everywhere. The Lannon was rigging strings and pegs, marking pathways through the debris.

Poking his head out the door, Dan said, "Clear breathing." The Terrans approached warily. But once they were inside, they relaxed a bit, then got busy. All of them except Sheila thanked Dan. He was puzzled by her reaction. Plainly she was mad at him. Why?

Moving with great care, the scientists used hand-held vacuums and tiny brushes, removing ages of soil and grime. Sheila and Chen examined postsherds. Armilly scanned the inward-curving walls with his monitors. Wherever the beams paused, writings and pictures seemed to leap off the ancient surface.

"Probably a reception area," someone speculated.

"No, it was lived in," Rosie argued. "Notice the eating utensils, the sleeping furniture."

Kat pointed to the walls. "A bulletin board? Inscriptions are layered. The lowest strata are very crisp. See how the writing deteriorates with each later stratum? The last entries are mere scribbles. What a wonderful support of Praedar's theories . . ."

"I wish Ruieb were here," Rosie said. "The comps can separate this, but it'll take a top linguist to decrypt it."

"Well, Ruieb *isn't* here," Sheila snapped. "Okay. Don't look at me like that. I know it's my fault and McKelvey's that Ruieb's up on the mesa sulking in his tent, like our other Achilles."

"It's not the same," Kat said. "Bill Getz's work is his own project, an adjunct to ours. Ruieb-An's an integral member of the team." She and the blonde debated loudly as they went on with their jobs.

Dan gazed at the wall inscriptions curiously. Suddenly a shudder racked him. Startled, he analyzed the reaction. He'd felt no draft. In fact, the temperature in the dome was comfortable. There was no reason at all for him to shiver. He could almost hear his mother quoting a family superstition: "Somebody walked over your grave."

That thought added to his disquiet. When Kat paused in her arguing and brush wielding, Dan asked, "Did you feel a . . . a breeze in here?" She frowned and shook her head. "Like an air current. Or maybe . . . an odd power source. It was the same feeling I get when those big Vahnaj molecular-shifter FTL drives go into gear. Weird."

Sheila snorted. "You believe in ghosts, too?"

"Just because we didn't feel it," Kat said, "doesn't mean it doesn't exist."

"There's nothing on the scanners," Sheila said flatly.

Dan scowled. Dammit, he wasn't making this up. Why was the blonde being so doubting?

From deeper in the dome, a Whimed called, "Is McKelvey here?"

"Yo!" Dan brightened. At least someone appreciated his presence!

"Come. Inspect. Tell us what this is."

He detached a hand lamp from the banks of illuminators and made his way into an alcove at the rear of the big room. Praedar, Yvica, and Drastil stood by an inner door. It was a lot more solid-looking than the entry. Praedar stabbed a bony finger at a patch of crumbling wall beside the frame. Dan wedged himself in among the felinoids, grateful that they, unlike Vahnajes, had no strong, alien body odor.

The light picked out a peculiarly shaped gadget and dangling glassene fibers. Dan canted the lamp at an angle, peering behind broken elements. The Whimeds hovered, their impatience tangible. Straightening, Dan said, "I'm not sure. It could be a switch. Really a crazy design, if so. Never saw anything to match it."

Praedar nodded. "In all likelihood it is the work of the N'lacs' ancestors. They had no contact with known civilized sectors."

"Yeah, that would explain why it's an unfamiliar technology." Without touching the mud-plaster wall, Dan traced a line. "I'm guessing at function, but it probably provides a linkage about here. Maybe I can tell with the adjustable power identifier in the repair shed. That can be reset to detect glassene and similar substances . . ."

The Whimeds' eyes were starry pools. Gooseflesh prickled on Dan's arms. Felinoids were low-level espers, and their ancestors had been rapacious carnivores. Occasionally Whimeds radiated emotions on wavelengths humans could sense. Praedar and his students were tremendously excited. Was there that much difference, on esp channels, between enthusiasm over a scientific discovery and delight at being close to edible prey? Fight-or-flight alarms raced along Dan's nerve endings.

"Can you repair it?" Praedar asked, his calm tone mocking the pilot's fears.

"I don't know," Dan said honestly. "I'd be working blind. You got any ideas what it controls? The door?" Yvica and Drastil agreed eagerly. Did they know, or was that wishful thinking? Dan went on. "It could activate other circuits instead, ones we couldn't begin to guess at."

Praedar spoke solemnly. "Sleeg tells of a golden era when the N'lacs lived entirely below this world's surface. Armilly's scans show another room and a tunnel beyond this door. We must explore them. The N'lacs do not object. The demon has been slain. What lies within may provide the key to this entire story—why their civilization fell, where they were taken, whether the Old Ones truly existed, how the slaves escaped and why their descendents have degenerated so seriously . . ."

The poor lighting prevented Dan from seeing the Whimed's

face clearly. He longed to read the boss's expression. Did Praedar, like Joe, take every N'lac myth seriously? Apparently so. All these big brains, whatever their species, did that. Only Getz remained skeptical. And Dan wasn't sure he wanted to be on the same side of anything with Getz. Maybe he, too, should accept the legends and believe.

"I'll give it a shot," Dan said, shrugging.

"Not today, McKelvey," Sheila cut in. She stomped into the alcove and grabbed Dan's arm, tugging hard. "Let's go. Something we have to take care of . . ."

He dug in his heels, refusing to move. "The boss wants me to fix this."

"Hell! He didn't mean this moment! We have kilotons of prelims to do before we can even think about digging into the dome's guts. Translating that wall takes priority. The results might tell you how to open this friggin' door, so come *on!*"

Dan hoped Praedar would overrule the blonde. To his dismay, the Whimed said, "Yes. Ruieb-An. Translations are needed. Go. I understand."

"I'm glad somebody does," Dan muttered.

Sheila tapped his shoulder, digging into the flesh. "That means us, fly boy. The two of us rubbed Ruieb's nose in his mistake. We're the ones who have to fluff his sideburns. Quit stalling."

Grumpily he followed her out. As they walked through the string-marked entry room, Kat eyed them with concern. "Take it slow, Sheil," she said, then shifted her glance to Dan. "You, too."

That didn't bode well. The blonde needled him constantly while they prepared for the trip. Dan tried to let her nitpicking and nagging roll off his back, but it wasn't possible. She scraped his already-taut nerves raw.

They were in the skimmer, ready for lifting, when Sheila found yet another way to irk him. She said, "Maybe we just ought to drive up and find the Vahnajes instead of taking this thing." He gawked at her, astonished, and she went on slyly, "The winds are tricky in that gorge where they camp out. You might splash us."

"I'm no amateur. I can handle any landing site. And have you looked at the time?" Dan demanded. "It's midday. I'm not driving *anywhere* in this heat, Whitcomb. If you want to, fine. Go alone!"

"No taste for adventure, huh?" She grinned mischievously and fed nav coordinates into the skimmer's boards. "What are you waiting for?"

He got them airborne without further conversation. Dan didn't trust himself to speak for the entire ride.

The Vahnajes were roughing it ten kilometers northeast of N'lac Valley. From the prerecorded coordinates Sheila had provided, Dan knew this had been a favorite sulking spot for Ruieb-An throughout the years of the expedition. As the skimmer neared the canyon, they encountered the winds Sheila had mentioned. Dan let the little craft sideslip, then touched down without a hitch. Only readouts told them they were on the ground, he'd brought her in so smoothly. "This where you wanted to park?" he asked with mock innocence.

"It'll do." And Sheila climbed out. His annoyance building again, Dan followed her to the lutrinoids' camp. They were almost there when the blonde said, "I hope you talk Vahnaj. I won't waste my time interpreting."

"I can manage," he retorted, seething.

Some Vahnajes were eating when they arrived. Pale with anger at being caught doing such a filthy thing in front of humans, the Vahnajes hastily hid their food and rose to greet their guests. Ruieb-An's crew stood rigidly erect, hands clasped tightly to their slender waists, their expressions coldly reserved—the very picture of proper lutrinoids. However, unlike the compulsively neat Vahnaj diplomats and traders Dan had met on his past travels, Ruieb's bunch was rumpled and dusty. Even such a fastidious species had trouble staying clean on a frontier world.

Bowing opened negotiations. They exchanged "Honored Persons" and "Esteemed Colleagues" for more than half a local hour. These social forms were as obligatory as N'lac handshakes.

The canyon was shaded, but still oppressively hot. Ruieb made the Terrans suffer another hour before he offered them water and food. Naturally, the aliens averted their eyes while the humans indulged. The water was tepid, the food bland, though ample. It was obvious the Vahnajes were living fairly well during their self-imposed exile. Dan wondered if they kept a gourmet camping kit packed at all times, ready for when they stormed out of the complex in a snit.

Refreshments finished, the Vahnajes' hospitality must be praised at great length for another hour of polite murmuring, bowing, and scraping.

How had the Vahnajes ever got anything done on their own planet, let alone had the get-up-and-go to conquer space and conduct an active interstellar trade?

Different modes for different species, Dan conceded. This leisurely, excessively ritualized style had served the Vahnaj Alliance well enough to enable them to pioneer at contacting younger races such as *Homo sapiens* and Ulisorians. They were in the forefront of sector-wide trade and efficient enough at conducting their age-old cold war with the far more aggressive, quick-acting Whimeds. However irritating their behavior to non-Vahnajes, plainly, the system worked.

It was late afternoon before Sheila could steer talk around to the reason for her visit. The Vahnajes knew why they were here. They had enjoyed making the Terrans grovel.

"Much shame, Honored Ruieb-An. *Pla chur nyo re sterla.*"

Ruieb was fairly fluent in Terran English. But he forced Sheila to deliver the apologies in *his* language. The game went on until she decided she'd smoothed the aliens' feathers enough. Then the blonde switched to Terran. "We regret our unseemly actions. We request that you return to the expedition, Honored Ones."

Dan had done his share to that point, putting in apologies now and then in his skimpy but adequate command of Vahnaj. As weary of the time-wasting as Sheila, he jumped in, trading blatantly on his family connections. "Indeed. I would be at fault if I did not beg you to agree, Esteemed Ruieb-An. Vahnaj scientific mastery has been admired on all Terra since the days of my kinsman Todd Saunder." The lutrinoids chirred, visibly affected by the magic name. Dan hammered at the point. "Todd Saunder, you know, discovered the first Vahnaj interstellar probe to my Mother World. Relations between our people were begun. I would follow my kindred's many examples of friendly cooperation with the great scientists and explorers of the mighty Vahnaj Alliance. Please. Will you not maintain the link that binds my family to your species?"

The Vahnajes were teary-eyed. Dan made a passing-off gesture to Sheila and whispered, "Your turn."

Recovering her poise, she hurried to describe the discovery and opening of the small dome. When she mentioned the wall

106

inscriptions, Ruieb couldn't hide his interest. He wriggled in anticipation, his sideburns fluffing with eagerness. "Honored Whitcomb, it is . . . urr . . . per-haps use-ful if we re-turn."

"Very useful," Sheila agreed, and elbowed Dan.

"Oh, yes, very useful!"

Nevertheless, the powwow dragged on till sundown. Having dithered so long, Ruieb decided his people might as well wait and go back to camp tomorrow. After all, they shouldn't be hasty.

With exquisite courtesy, the Vahnajes invited the Terrans to stay for another meal. Both sides were relieved when Dan and Sheila begged off. They made their escape to the skimmer before Ruieb could think of any further reasons for bowing and scraping.

While Dan flew them homeward, Sheila contacted the complex, relaying the outcome of their parley. Rosie took the message and promised to pass on the word. "Nothing much happening here at the moment. You peacemakers needn't break any speed records getting back."

As the circuit winked off, Dan said, "In that case, I'll detour by *Fiona* and run my regular checks. Okay?"

Sheila said contemptuously, "Why should I object? I figure small amusements for small minds."

He boosted power feed, channeling his anger. They zoomed past wind-sculpted rocks, banking steeply along cliff faces. Instead of being fearful, Sheila laughed, thrilled by the tooth-popping ride. She taunted him, and his anger grew. The woman sneered at everything he did. She'd offered no thanks for his help at the powwow, and now she was in a thoroughly nasty groove, jabbing him with putdowns about his flying skills and intelligence.

When they landed at *Fiona*, Dan hurried into the cabin, hoping he'd find anomalies that would hold his attention long enough for him to cool off. He was determined not to blow up at Sheila. That was probably just what she wanted! Damned if he'd give it to her!

Unfortunately, the self-repair servos were working fine, with monitors in nominal ranges and comps purring.

Sheila sauntered up the ramp. Dan pretended to concentrate on the screens, wanting an excuse to avoid facing her. Tension was a vise, tightening around him. Sheila prowled the cabin and hold access tunnel noisily. Then she came forward and dropped into the second chair. "So this is your precious ship. The way you rave about this hulk, anyone would think it's a yacht, not a—"

Dan spun around. "Hunk of junk? Spacegoing coffin? For your info, she's a damned fine starhopper!"

"Hah! So you're one of those pilots who just *loves* his vessel. How kinky." Sheila stretched voluptuously, her breasts jutting. "You're too close to your darling to see her straight. For instance, facilities. I'm used to *modern* appointments. The supply ship that takes us out to conferences has brand-new flight couches. I'll bet this tub's equipment is years old . . ."

He got to his feet, glaring down at the blonde. "What's this all about? Having fun, insulting me and my ship?"

She stood up and moved very close. There was something new in her manner—sexual challenge. Sheila swiveled her hips seductively. She toyed with Dan's belt, saying "Call it a test, handsome. You're too damned easygoing. I had to find out if there was any fire in there. And there is! You've been so busy tinkering with the machinery. How about tinkering with *my* equipment for a change? We never *did* take that stroll. Kroo-ger! Are you still waiting for *that*? Believe me, romping bare-ass in the desert is no fun. I speak from experience."

"No doubt." Dan fought a rising hormone level. "Tests, huh? Crazy mean ones."

The pressure of her breasts and hips was overwhelming his resistance. By now his erection was painfully obvious to both of them. Sheila grinned. "Crazy, because I like to spice up plain old-fashioned fornication?"

"The insults, the bitchiness . . ."

"Got you mad, didn't they? Physiological data prove that anger-aggression responses are quite similar to—"

"Screw your data," he growled, and gave in to the inevitable.

Normally, Dan preferred lighthearted romps. But Sheila's tactics had made that impossible. Reflexes took over. They were rutting animals, ripping at clothes, tumbling into the pilot's web chair.

Sheila was eager, yet continued to scratch and sham kick, as if she couldn't shut off the bitch act even though she'd gained her objective. Her face contorted with ecstasy.

Locked in the rhythm of pelvic thrusting, Dan realized with a small part of his brain that she had manipulated them back to these gonadal basics. Sheila reveled in the results, loving the violence and lack of finesse. Physical urgency swept her, removing traces of civilization. Then he, too, was caught in her frenzy.

Release was a shuddering collapse. They sprawled in the chair, savoring detumescence.

Gradually Dan became conscious of the outside world, the silent, glowing banks of monitors, the servos, and exterior scans of the desert and the stars winking into view above the darkening mountains. Sated, but badly rattled, he sat up. Sheila stretched once more, sighing in contentment.

"Very good. You're a real beast, McKelvey, when you're sufficiently prodded. That must be how your family got its rep. The Saunder-McKelveys—Earth's champion achievers. Drive. Ambition. Animal instincts."

"I'm hardly a champion," Dan muttered. "Do you mind if we don't do this quite this way again? It isn't my. . . ."

"Sure it is." Sheila drew her short-cut fingernails lightly down his chest, making him shiver. "All it takes is pushing the right buttons. Admit it. You had fun."

"Yeah, but . . ." He forced a weak smile, regarding her curiously. "Tell me, if we had taken that stroll the night of the tale-telling, would it have ended up like this?"

"Probably not. We'd have had an ordinary romp, which is tame, from my point of view. I'm adaptable, though. We'll do it your way, next go-around," Sheila finished, her blue eyes twinkling. She fetched two cups of caffa from the food storage unit and returned to the chair, snuggling cozily beside Dan.

Bemused, he said, "You're nuts."

"Sure! What else could I be, with my upbringing? The whole Kruger 60 Settlement was a mess from the word go. Our elders spent decades in frozen stasis to reach the planet. They expected to make history as Terra's first interstellar pioneers. But FTL was discovered while they were en route. They were obsolete before they landed. That warped their attitudes, and that of their kids.

"Picture it. When they left Earth, humanity's only contact with aliens was a single Vahnaj Ambassador. By the time they arrived on Kruger 60, Terrans were all over the starmap, wheeling and dealing with races the Hiber-ship crew hadn't even known existed when they launched.

"Oh, they were taken care of, nursed along, until they could cope. The Saunder-McKelveys had a guilty conscience. Your grandfather and Brenna Saunder invented FTL and wrecked my parents' dream. So Brenna turned Kruger 60 into a reservation. She guarded us poor anachronisms from the world-grabbers while we tried to catch up with the settlers who had a head start on us. In other words, we were a charity case." Sheila's joking tone didn't hide her bitter resentment.

Dan eyed her thoughtfully. "Yeah, my dad was part of the family team assisting the Krugers after planetfall. He reminisces about those days. Says the Hiber-ship bunch were real fighters, sure to prosper."

Sheila drew her legs up, clasping tanned arms around her knees. "Huh! The main thing they prospered at was breeding. That was first on their agenda—hatching kids in a hurry to build a viable colony. The Hiber-ship project was a polygamous design —studs and harems, all genetically cross-calculated. It worked. Healthiest kids in space! But hell, the way other Settlements treat us because of that system, you'd think we bred with slime worms!" She gazed into nothing and said, "I admit, when I was growing up, there were times when I had trouble remembering which woman was my mother. But I always knew who my father was. He reminded us of it constantly. Captain Derek Whitcomb, the hero," she intoned with heavy sarcasm.

"I hadn't realized . . . wow! A decorated Fleet officer and member of the original FTL breakthrough group, *and* commander of the Hiber-ship. He *was* a hero," Dan said.

"Still is, to hear him tell it." Sheila's expression was sour. "Don't forget. He's still in good shape, even if he was born in the 2040s. Being frozen let him skip a few decades. Nowadays he spends most of his time whining about how he was cheated out of his place in the history vids. But it was his own option. He bailed out of the FTL project too soon. Your kin got the glory, and all Derek got was Kruger 60 and his harem. Not a bad deal, despite his griping. He still gets a chance to do some tupping, when Kruger Council wants an older bloodline cross to mix the gene pool." Again her manner was a blend of admiration and scorn.

"He was luckier than one member of the FTL team," Dan said softly. "My grandfather."

"Morgan McKelvey. But people idolize him. They pity us Krugers."

"They pitied Morgan, too," Dan said, "when he got mangled in that early FTL test flight. Every pilot's nightmare. He came out alive, but in a plastic body. Some glory! Is that what your

110

father wishes he'd shared? At least he's alive and romping. Morgan only survived the accident by a few years, and he never..." He touched Sheila's hand and added, "He couldn't have done what we just did."

"But he had kids. You're his grandchild."

"Oh, yeah. The Saunder-McKelvey dynasty must go on. They selected four women to bear Morgan's kids. Artificial insemination from cryo-preserved sperm. My dad got Morgan's genes, but none of that Saunder-McKelvey financial knowhow. He's been broke since I was twelve. I might as well have been a Kruger kid, despite my name," Dan finished.

There was a long silence. At last Sheila said, "Interesting. Gives the Saunder-McKelveys a personal touch, not like the news releases. Just the same, there's a difference—for one thing, Kruger's mixed-up generational factors. By normal reckoning, I ought to be your father's contemporary, not yours. I'm out of synch with the rest of humanity."

"It's happened to others," Dan reminded her. "Look how much prejudice Anthony Saunder had to overcome because he was a clone of Todd's brother. That was tough. Yet he changed people's way of thinking in his favor."

Sheila shrugged impatiently. "He always had the family to fall back on. So do you. That's being part of the time stream. The stasis trip took that away from the Krugers. For us, Day One was planetfall. Before then? Nothing. I'm a settler from nowhere."

An odd smile twisted her mouth. "A psych scanner once told me that was why I took up xenoarch. According to him, my entire career is a subconscious quest to become part of mankind's time stream, to belong. Maybe he was right, but he sure was a lousy lay," she said, laughing.

Her unpredictable mood shifts confused Dan. He empathized with her problems, but felt wary. "I hope I'm not," he muttered in response to her last statement.

Sheila gave him a lingering kiss. "I said you were good. Don't fish for compliments." Her expression softened and she said, "I'm sorry for being such a bitch. I hate myself for doing that, but I can't seem to help it. I'll make it up to you. Maybe I'll tell Olmsted what she's missed and send her your way. Kat needs to cut loose and she's not going to get that from Praedar—not the way she wants it," the blonde said.

Dan supposed a casual, share-the-wealth sexuality was typical for someone born and bred in a polygamous settlement. The idea shook him a trifle, though. "You needn't advertise on my account."

"No trouble. Glad to. By the way, that's not all you're good at. Not by a damn sight. You were terrific with Ruieb. That stuff about your relatives floored him. It surprised me, too. I never heard you do anything but badmouth your family before. A McKelvey princeling pose suits you."

"I can trot it out, if I need to," Dan said. "Frankly, considering your feud with Feo and Hope, it's seemed smarter to clam up about being a Saunder-McKelvey while I'm here."

"Nobody blames you for that," Sheila said, briskly donning her clothes. "Well, hardly anybody. This has been fun, but I have stuff to do in camp. You coming?"

Jarred into activity, Dan dressed and put ship systems on standby. Sheila noted his library catalog and exclaimed admiringly. "Dumb tech-mech! What a liar! With this in your brain, you've got damned near a postgrad degree—or two! Why don't you drop that uneducated pose and act your ability?"

"It's not on paper," Dan countered, torn between pleased embarrassment and a contrary pride in his self-made indie hauler status.

"That could be mended," Sheila said, then swept on out to the skimmer. She showed no inclination to elaborate on that final comment, and her genial mood continued. So Dan let it drop, relieved that there were no more taunts or verbal jabs.

Landing was routine. As they walked toward the complex, he braced himself for a ribbing. Everyone would know why they were late, and no doubt they'd put him and Sheila through a ribald gauntlet run.

Halfway to the insta-cells, he forgot that. A horrible sound raised hair on his nape. Dan stopped in his tracks.

"That's Armilly!" Sheila cried. "What the hell? That's his 'I'm mad and lost, Mommy!' screech." She pointed at Hanging Rock. Armilly perched atop the landmark, howling.

How in the universe had the Lannon scaled the boulder? And why was he yelling his lungs out?

Sheila gestured urgently, breaking into a lope, Dan at her side. They had to detour around a snarling mass of Whimeds. The felinoids, clutching one another, whirled about, ugly, primitive noises issuing from their throats. Praedar, normally so cool, was screaming in fury. Dan had never seen Whimeds so enraged. He gave them a wide berth.

Beyond them, at the dud pits, the Terran scientists were expressing anger in their way—cursing, hurling rocks at the pits, stamping, shaking their fists—general uproar. Dan slowed his steps, uncertain about wading into this melee.

Armilly moon baying? Whimeds huddling furiously? Terrans cursing "them"? "They" had done it. "It," apparently, was one more rotten trick. Another collective gripe session aimed at Feo and Hope Saunder? Whatever had happened, it had obviously been a beaut.

"What is it?" Sheila demanded.

Kat stood arms akimbo. "Welcome back. You just missed the news. Our pickup has been 'unavoidably delayed.'"

"What?" Sheila yelped. "They can't do that!"

"They did." Dan muttered a question and Kat explained. "Our transportation to the Xenoarch Assembly. We paid for our tickets months ago. Fifteen of us are scheduled to go. We've been working our tails off, getting our presentations ready, preparing to woo our sponsors. Now, with barely more than two weeks to go, our ship says sorry, they can't make it."

"Damn them!" Sheila was an explosive device about to detonate. "I'll bet Feo's fair-haired boy is behind this again. Tavares bribed someone else—at the transport office this time. He's burying us, the way he buried that cargo!"

"Hey, call in the Fleet," Dan suggested. "There are laws. You have to have a transport lifeline. That's regulations. Tell 'em you've got a medical emergency..."

"Oh, they'd come, all right," Kat said. "To transport the patient and *only* the patient. And if it's a fake emergency, they'll slap us with a whopping fine and maybe yank our license. No, we can't go that route, and Tavares and the Saunders knew we couldn't." She rubbed her brow, pushing back dark strands of hair. Kat mimicked their professional rivals shedding crocodile tears. "'So unfortunate that you won't be at the Assembly. What a shame!'"

"Message in your data then," Dan said.

Sheila growled and Kat replied, "We'll have to. That's all we have left. But...you're a tech-mech. You know what a holo relayed across a parsec looks like. Convincing?"

"Uh...not very," Dan conceded. "Distance plays hell with

realistic images. I see your point. If tri-dis alone aren't enough, maybe . . ."

"Forget it." Kat sighed tiredly. "There's more involved than the data. Xenoarch thrives on a cult of personality, and Praedar has one of the best. We count on him to sell this project and keep our funds flowing. Sure, we'll message in our material. And some secretary will play the vids for the attendees, and they and our sponsors will yawn and put their credits back in their pockets."

"Damn them!" Sheila repeated with vehemence.

Kat agreed. "Yes, damn them. Feo and Hope have their own share of charisma and enormous prestige with both alien and Terran attendees, not to mention the media. With Praedar absent, they'll have the Assembly eating out of their hands. All that Saunder money and power—and dirty dealing—is killing us. No one will care whether we publish our findings or not. This project will fold, and we'll have to pull out."

CHAPTER EIGHT
○○○○○○○○○

Tragedy

Night winds blew off the mesa. Somewhere in the distance the Whimeds continued their huddling, ignoring the temperature drop. Armilly, protected by his fur, was ignoring it, too. Thin-skinned Terrans, however, were gradually driven to seek shelter. Soon only Dan and four of the scientists remained by the dud pits. All the others had retreated to the complex.

Suddenly Praedar walked up to the diehards. The humans jumped in surprise. No one had heard the Whimed approaching. He seemed to have materialized from nothing. It had obviously taken extreme effort for him to break free of the huddle. Praedar's breathing was harsh, his eyes glistening. When he spoke, his accent was noticeably thicker than usual. "A solution to our problem occurs to me. A starhopper is already on planet. Would not need to summon here. Pilot would not tell us he is delayed."

The Terrans digested that and turned to Dan. Kat said, "Of course! We've been so upset we didn't consider the obvious."

"Slow throttle," he protested. "*Fiona*'s a cargo hauler, not . . ."

"You told me you've carried passengers."

"Rarely. She's a one-man ship," Dan said. "If I take on super-cargo I have to adjust the life support systems, load extra supplies, extra pressure suits..."

"Hell, we've got suits," Sheila put in. Kat, Joe, and Rosie nodded as the blonde went on. "A suit's one of the first things a xenoarch field digger buys. We never know where we'll ride or what sort of planetary environment we might encounter. As for extra flight couches, you've got those, McKelvey. I saw 'em."

"Did you try them all out, Whitcomb?" Rosie asked, winking at the others. Sheila laughed, unoffended.

Praedar concentrated on the main point. "It is possible for your spacecraft to carry people from there to T-S 311?"

"Yeah," Dan said, then shook his head. "But I can't." As the scientists argued, he held up his hands, demanding a hearing. "I'd like to help. I really would. But you've forgotten something: I'm blacklisted. I know how my rich relatives operate. I'll bet Feo's built himself a full-scale spaceport on his world." His listeners' faces told him he'd guessed correctly. "Uh-huh! That place will be crawling with people during the Assembly. Media types. Staffers. Spacers who ferried the attendees to T-S 311. If there's just one freelance repossess artist in that crowd, my ship's gone."

"You're dreaming up excuses," Sheila said.

"No excuse. You don't know how things are on the space-lanes. The dispatchers have my credit locked. My bills are over-due. A repossessor can legally seize *Fiona* to satisfy paper holders. I'd be an indie hauler with no starhopper—and *you'd* be stuck on T-S 311, maybe for a long time. Or do you think the Saunders would strain themselves to buy you a ride home?"

That question stopped the scientists for a moment. Then they brushed qualms aside and again clamored that Dan had to transport them, no matter what.

He drowned them out, shouting "I can't take the risk. I'm sorry. Dammit, see it from my angle. If my ship's repossessed, I'm bankrupt."

"If you don't, this project is," Sheila retorted.

"So it's a standoff. A nowhere vector for everybody..."

Praedar said in an achingly deep voice, "We are indeed requesting a great sacrifice of you. However, it is in a crucial cause. Our failure to make presentations at the Assembly will

116

have grave consequences for the N'lacs as well as for the expedition."

"Yes, they'll suffer the most, Dan," Kat chimed in. "We *must* get to T-S 311, to meet our backers."

"Without funds and support, work ceases," Praedar said. "Our permit will lapse. We will depart. The N'lacs will be alone."

Dan felt cornered. "Well, they survived okay for centuries before you got here . . ."

In that same hypnotic tone, Praedar said, "Their numbers had steadily declined recently. They had reached near-extinction threshold. If we leave, they will cross that threshold."

Wincing, Dan stammered, "I-I have to think about this," and sidled away. Praedar wasn't playing fair, hitting below the belt, appealing to his emotions like that.

The team members stared morosely at him. Kat said, "While you're thinking, think about the N'lacs and their future." She wasn't playing fair, either!

He trotted up a trail from the complex, not caring where he was going, wanting only to escape from those accusing stares. Behind him, he heard the group trying to restart the conversation. Rosie asked, "By the way, Whitcomb, when are the Vahnajes coming back to work?"

"Tomorrow," Sheila said listlessly. The contrast with her normal sassy tone added to Dan's guilt.

"Good. Then Ruieb can get busy on those inscriptions."

"Why not? Even if our funding's gone, we can cram in as much research as possible before we have to pack and go."

"It's not the end. There will be other projects. Life goes on, people."

"Sometimes . . ." That last was from Kat, underlining bleak reality, a potential death sentence for the N'lacs.

Dan walked faster and the voices faded, swallowed in a moaning wind. The sound conjured images of Chuss' ancestors. Their graves hadn't been disturbed, thanks to the high principles of the team. But their spirits seemed to line the path, watching Dan, haunting him. He broke into a run, not stopping until he reached Dome Hill. There, catching his breath, he gazed around.

From that height, he had a panoramic view of the central valley. Two cores of light dominated—the complex and the village, where brush-fed fires danced behind the tendrilled trees, high-tech community and primitive culture, side by side. Five disparate species were living and working together. This was the ideal of humanoid coexistence on the galactic frontier—the ideal the politicians of all the civilizations so often espoused, but that was too rarely fulfilled.

Had he once suspected the xenoarchaeologists of enslaving the N'lacs? He'd since learned his error. This really *was* a good, symbiotic relationship. Damned good. And it deserved to continue.

Dan walked down the ramp to the lamplit painted wall and gazed at those figures, showing the N'lacs' days of glory. If they hadn't been conquered, Chuss' people would occupy seats on the Pan Sector Council right now, up there with Terra, the Whimed Federation, the Vahnaj Alliance, and others.

But the Evil Old Ones had come, nonanthropomorphic invaders. Only a handful of the N'lacs' many-fathers-ago had ever escaped from their bondage. And their descendants had been on the brink of extinction when Praedar had rescued them.

The N'lacs were about to be conquered again, victims of a scientific rivalry this time.

Without Joe Hughes' hyperbaric treatments, Chuss and his siblings would sink into thick-witted lethargy. Their ability to think and to lead their people would trickle away through their paws like dust. Without the offworlders to teach them how, the N'lacs couldn't maintain the wells, cope with disease, or survive bad hunting seasons. They might scavenge off the expedition's debris for a while, but that was a finite resource.

If Praedar's dig license lapsed, the Terran-Whimed Xenoethnic Council, with assistance from Space Fleet, would take control of T-W 593. Even when they meant well, such groups were generally bad news for native subhumanoids. At best, military officers and bureaucrats would treat the N'lacs as pets. At worst, they would hasten the N'lacs' extinction, because local e.t.s were an obstacle to settling this world with Terran and Whimed colonists.

And the N'lacs *would* be classified as subhumanoids, thanks to the Saunders. Dan's kindred were at the bottom of this crisis. Naturally, the Council and Fleet would accept Feo's and Hope's interpretations and act accordingly. The Saunders were eminent scientists, weren't they? They wouldn't bend the truth for petty purposes.

Dan knew different. And he knew the N'lacs were true humanoids. He'd worked with them, laughed with them, shaken their hands, heard their myths, learned a bit of their language. He'd testify to their right to full Level 3 status.

Who'd listen to him? Nobody. He was only a self-educated tech-mech pilot without a single scientific credential to his famous name. Feo and Hope Saunder-Nicholaiev had all the odds on their side.

When he was a kid, Dan had seen what happened to monkey-like creatures on a planet his brother had administered. Adam's soldiers hadn't slaughtered the clever little beings. Nothing so crude. But Fleet's presence had finished off the locals. Most of the e.t.s withered away and died. Others became pathetic copy-cats of the Terrans.

Was that what lay in store for the N'lacs?

Cold raked at him. Dan sealed the cuffs and neck of his one-piecer more snugly. Then he decided he might as well head back to the complex. There was no percentage in hanging around here. Freezing his ass off wouldn't solve the N'lacs' problems or his.

He had taken only a few steps when he heard furtive noises beyond the top of the ramp. Dan peered around its corner curiously. It took him several seconds to locate the source of the mutterings. N'lacs hunkered in the shadows near the small dome —Sleeg, Chuss, Meej, and seven adolescent males. They were whispering, obviously wanting to keep their activities secret.

If Dan left the site now, the N'lacs would see him and think he'd been spying. To avoid offending them, he moved back out of their view and stayed put, watching.

Sleeg's voice was a muted warning. The tale-teller was holding a little "demon," a half-size version of the one he'd smashed that morning. Dan didn't need a transbutton to figure out what was going on. The scene was straight out of a docu-vid—the shaman instructing the tribe's youth, showing them how to protect their people with sympathetic magic. When the models were destroyed, any demon robots nearby would be, too.

In Dan's opinion, magic was a poor substitute for a few of Adam's battle cruisers in orbit around T-W 593. Those would keep the N'lacs safe.

Or . . . would they?

The N'lacs' ancestors had spaceships, presumably armed ones. But they'd wrecked all of them. Why? Kat's speculations rang in his thoughts: "Maybe the Evil Old Ones forced them to do it."

Psi powers? The Vahnajes had employed tech-enhanced psi devices in their espionage cold war games against the Whimeds. That was why Praedar's race had developed countermeasures, like the *oryuz* helmet decorating the wall of Praedar's office; his grandsire, he said, had used it to ward off such esper attacks, years ago.

Had the Evil Old Ones invented far more potent versions of the Vahnajes' psi assaulters? Had the Old Ones compelled the N'lacs to wipe out their planetary defense, leaving themselves helpless before the invaders?

In retrospect, Dan was ashamed he'd laughed at the N'lacs' demon-smashing ritual. Why shouldn't they believe in such stuff? Their ancestors' high-tech civilization had been wiped away, almost overnight. Who could blame the villagers for now relying on magic and mysticism?

They weren't the first humanoids to take that course. *Homo sapiens* had often trusted in mumbo jumbo and miracles. Even today, in 2155, a few Terran Settlements had rejected science, putting their faith in a back-to-the-good-old-days, fringe-cult religion. The N'lacs had as much right, and far better reasons, for doing the same thing.

The youngsters listened intently as Sleeg, with Chuss' help, taught them the arcane rules. The tale-tellers' susurrating voices lulled Dan. His mind drifted into nightmares.

What if the Evil Old Ones and their robot demons and unknown weapons were still out there someplace? Did they need new slaves? If so, would they strike on the same vectors they used millennia ago?

The alien monsters would find slim pickings on T-W 593 and its former colony world nowadays. But there were other planets, with larger humanoid populations, in the core stellar regions. Trillions of Terrans, Whimeds, Vahnajes, Lannon, Rigotians, and Ulisorians. Prime stock, with hands, for the Old Ones' slave markets.

Would modern civilizations' star fleets stand up to that non-anthropomorphic invasion any better than the N'lacs had?

Questionable.

Acknowledging that, Dan shuddered. He felt . . . what? More than cold. Pressured by something he couldn't put a finger on.

It was unseen, but there, a living presence, incredibly ancient —older than the N'lacs, older than mankind or perhaps than any other humanoid species. It was soft-bodied, bulbous, a sickening excrescence encased in an exoskeleton . . .

He swallowed a curse. What the hell was the matter with him? He was beginning to believe Sleeg's fairy tales—just like a gullible N'lac pup! Evil Old Ones! Demon robots! Invaders from the stars! Vid fiction scare drama, local style.

Wasn't it? That uncertainty increased the load of ice chilling Dan's veins. He chafed his arms to stir circulation and waited impatiently for the lessons to end. That took awhile. Sleeg made each boy repeat the magic phrases over and over before he was satisfied. Finally, when Dan ached with cold, the elder allowed the kids to smash the toy demon. In single file, the teenagers followed Sleeg back to the village.

Dan didn't try to unkink his muscles until the N'lacs were well out of sight and earshot. Then he stood up with a groan, stretching. What an evening!

And it wasn't over yet.

Suddenly wary, he searched the darkness. He wasn't alone on Dome Hill. Two glowing starbursts hovered to his left.

Whimed eyes!

The silhouette was of a large crested head and a tall, lean body. Beside it was a smaller figure, pot-bellied. A chuckle gave Chen away. The taller being, naturally, had to be Praedar.

Dan's fear faded, replaced by annoyance that he'd been so jumpy.

"It is a memory." Praedar's words startled him anew.

"Wh-what do you mean?"

"The old teach the young." Praedar moved as silently as dust drift, coming forward, halting an arm's length from the pilot. Dan took a step backward. He knew, intellectually, that the Whimed wasn't going to attack him. Eons of evolution, though, shoved his instincts hard. With a much heavier tread, Chen topped the slope, standing beside his alien friend and the Terran.

"It gives the people to the children," Praedar said. Lamplight from the ramp glowed palely on his arm as he gestured toward the small dome, where Sleeg and the kids had sat. "They will thus remember what has been."

"Oral tradition," Chen murmured. "Mm!"

Dan nodded. "Pride of heritage. Maybe pride of species, too.

I know. When I was little, my dad used to tell me about the Saunders and McKelveys, about how our family helped Terra reach the stars. It made a big impression. It's probably what inspired me to become a tech-mech and a pilot."

Chen nudged the Whimed. "Uh? Uh? Predicted, didn't I?"

"Yes," Praedar agreed. "My grandsire instructed me and my twin as your father did you, Dan. I was taught of Maruxa and of how she proved the Dread Regions were Whimed's soul. From her example and my grandsire's, I learned to seek truth, to make the unknown known." Chen grunted emphatically, emphasizing the point.

"I guess we're alike in that," Dan said. "All humanoids."

"Terran, Whimed, N'lacs," Praedar murmured, then added with a touch of disdain, "Not Vahnaj. They do not teach their young in this manner. Ruieb-An does not fully understand N'lac ritual."

Dan smiled. Lurking prejudice was a chink in Praedar's armor. He was a genius at handling this multispecies team, but he wasn't immune to that age-old enmity between Whimed and Vahnaj. That comment on Vahnaj child-rearing methods made the boss seem, if not more human, more humanlike.

"Heritage," Praedar said, pointing again at the dome. "Kaatje tells of Earth peoples who crossed a glaciated northern continent to settle in warmer, more southerly areas."

Dan recalled the references in the library vids. "That must have been the Native Americans."

"Their descendants preserved the story of the journey, and generations later spoke of a land of endless cold where the sun did not shine."

"Not in winter, in a polar region," Dan confirmed.

"Their legends said that in that place many of the tribe's children died of cold and were eaten by large canine beasts."

That involuntary shiver shook Dan again. "Wolves, probably," he said. "When they told those legends, they lived in temperate zones. They couldn't have had any personal knowledge of what a polar climate was like or memories of events thousands of years earlier. Yet they kept the story going."

"They saved the truth," Praedar noted.

Chen put in, "As the N'lacs attempt to do."

Dan didn't offer his kinsman's counterargument—that the N'lacs weren't remembering true history because they weren't actually related to the species that built these ruins. He weighed various possibilities, letting his mind chase leads. "It still seems odd to me that Sleeg doesn't describe the ship the slaves escaped in. And that you haven't found traces of one. Where is the getaway vehicle?"

The silence lengthened. At last Praedar said, "Time. The place the ancestors returned. Here."

With surprising ease, Dan followed his logic. "Yeah! That must be it. They cannibalized the ship to make temporary shelters. Maybe they took fluidics molds off its equipment." More and more enthusiastic, he repeated, "Yeah! It fits. You didn't find fluidics elements—pardon me: effigies—below the five hundred–year stratum. And no ship. But right then's when the small dome appears, *and* the fluidics elements. It *has* to indicate a master job of N'lac cannibalization and conversion of materials!"

Praedar rocked with noiseless laughter. Chen was less reserved. He cackled gleefully. For a second Dan was irked, thinking they were amused by his naïveté. Then Chen said, "Oh, indeed! Indeed! Astute! Very astute! You *do* learn remarkably quickly, my boy. And you try to claim you have absolutely no education. Tsk! What a sham! He's as good as you are, Praedar, at seeing the big picture. No, Dan, there are no glass artifacts in the 2000 B.P. museum stratum I'm investigating. None in the following periods. It's just as you said. Everything begins when the legends say the N'lac slaves returned Home from slavery. Coincidence? We hardly think so!"

The felinoid's eyes were bright, starburst ribbons. "You see and speak with a fresh viewpoint, starship pilot. You would behave as you have suggested, had you shared existence with the escaped slaves?"

"I wouldn't have had a choice, if I wanted to survive," Dan said. "From what Joe's work shows, those genetic alterations the Evil Old Ones did to the N'lacs would have made readapting to this planet's environment a life-or-death struggle for them. They probably managed okay for a while, but . . ."

Praedar's head jerked down in a characteristic Whimed nod. "True. Their numbers apparently multiplied for several decades, in and around this immediate area. Gradually they began to suffer from soroche. Remote probes of graves spell out the progress of altitude sickness. Symptomology: a severely lessened mental and

123

physical capacity; great increase in blood volume, particularly in oxygen-carrying components; nausea; vertigo; and retinal hemorrhaging, which is observed in present-day villagers. There are also visual distortions, impotence, infertility, frequent spontaneous abortions when gestation *does* occur, and slow development of infants who do survive birth. They also show sensitivity to heat and cold and inadequate compensations for humidity fluctuations. All evidence indicates the body is desperately attempting to adapt for an oxygen content well below that of the atmosphere in which the species evolved—or which it was genetically changed to accept."

Dan winced at the grim recitation. The escapees' descendants had been trapped in a hopeless downward spiral. The pressurized dome had been a temporary refuge. But as their supplies dwindled, they had been forced to make longer and longer foraging trips away from that shelter. The environment had taken its toll, sapping them, and dulling their wits. With maintenance knowledge lost, they couldn't remain in the refuge and hence abandoned it to time and dust drift.

"They still try to build domes, don't they?" Dan said, touched. "Those round-roofed brick huts, to them are the right shape for a house. That must be why they took to Joe's hyperbaric model with so little fuss. They vaguely remembered when pressurization was the way of life for their ancestors. The rest of it is reduced to legends about the magic that made things work; and the domes are sacred places." He paused, then added, "They're in awe of them and afraid of them, as if this is where their civilization came to an end, as well as where their ancestors escaped to Home."

Praedar and Chen nodded, an almost comical contrast of forms and species.

Dan was deeply affected by the N'lacs' history. He imagined Terrans—his own family—sinking under the weight of circumstances as the N'lacs had. This was something xenoarchaeology could teach modern stellar cultures—how to step into another race's boots and appreciate what they'd experienced. Those New Earth Renaissancers and the lucky settlers on safe, prosperous worlds needed an occasional humbling reminder, to keep them from getting cocky.

Praedar abruptly shifted focus. "When we find portions of the escapees' ship, you will analyze them?"

Taken aback, Dan said, "Well, sure, if I can. At least I could tell you what was different about the pieces from known technology. But . . . don't you want an expert to do that?"

"You will be our expert," the Whimed said flatly.

Dan's ego took a quantum jump. Damned right he'd do the job! If the expedition didn't have to close up shop long before it ever got within digging length of those long-lost escapee ship fragments.

The team was about to be squashed by Feo and Hope Saunder. The N'lacs were facing extinction or pethood. Compared to those options, was the risk of losing *Fiona* so awful? Dan considered the worst scenario: *Fiona* repossessed; no ship; no credit.

Rough! He'd been there.

And he'd climbed out of that hole. He could do it again. Hell, he was only thirty. He still had the guts and knowhow to accomplish that.

But could the N'lacs and the expedition survive what his relatives were dumping on them? Dan doubted it.

Chen was whispering to his former student. Praedar nodded and turned to Dan. "Would these repossess artists, as you call them, seize your vessel if it were registered to another owner?"

"Huh? Sell her? Nah! She's got too much debt paper out on her, plus my being blacklisted. No buyer wants to hassle a private deal like that."

"Illusion," Chen said. "An illusion that your vehicle has acquired a new owner."

"Fake a sale? I . . . I don't know. It wouldn't fool the debt funders on Procyon Four for long." Even as he protested, Dan was recalling spacer gossip about just such scams. Sometimes they succeeded.

"The illusion need not be sustained indefinitely," Praedar said. Dan weakened. What an outrageous proposal! Borderline illegal, to boot—and crazy enough to work. "I am not able to purchase a ship, in reality," the Whimed admitted. "However, I would pay you pilot's wages for your risks, an appropriate portion of the sum reserved for our transport."

"Hmm. Pilot. The way I'm your maintenance specialist, huh?" Dan said slyly, then sobered. "You can't afford it. You're already strapped for funds. I know how it is . . ."

Praedar's words were harsh. "It will be. Fair Terran-Whimed exchange rates. Less is *sarige-aytan*." Unethical and totally repugnant to a felinoid. The alien was willing to spend credits from his lean purse, engage in the sham of ship-ownership, and make any sacrifice to get to that Assembly, because he wanted the scientific community to know the truth about the N'lacs and ensure that they and the dig went on.

Could Dan do less? His grandfather had put his life on the line to develop the stardrive. Praedar wasn't asking for anything nearly that dangerous. And whether or not Dan helped him, *Fiona*'s fate was iffy. He could say "No," let the expedition fail, and still lose the ship, on down the line. So why not prove he was Morgan McKelvey's grandson in spirit as well as in blood? Yeah! He was a spacer. And sometimes a spacer had to take chances.

Praedar deserved a break. So did the N'lacs.

Thrusting out his hand, Dan said, "You've got a deal."

Chen crowed in delight. Praedar gripped the pilot's hand. "Told you!" the Oriental said. "I told you to go on and ask him! He's good stock. Most of the Saunder-McKelveys are. The best!"

"And we'll split the pay difference," Dan insisted. "It's worth it to me, if I get to see Feo's face when you show up at the Assembly after all."

That sent Chen into fresh gales of laughter. Praedar wheezed in amusement. Dan laughed, too, feeling free, now that he'd taken the plunge. Eager to share their news, the three hurried down to the complex.

The felinoid huddle had broken up. Whimeds were sprawled in the cook shack, nursing headaches and strained muscles. The only Terrans in the room were Kat and Joe. They all looked up as Dan and the scientists entered. Kat studied the trio a moment, then leaped to her feet. "Something's changed! I can smell it!"

"Good little nose, there," Dan teased. "Praedar and Chen twisted my arm. We'll work up a bogus bill of sale to cloak *Fiona*'s identity, and I'll take you guys to the Assembly."

Whimeds forgot their headaches and howled in triumph. Kat flung her arms around Dan's neck, kissing him. Joe pounded him on the back. The uproar brought other team members running from every area of the insta-cells. When they heard the news, pandemonium took over for a time. Kat finally let Dan come up for air. He grinned and said, "We'll have to do this more often."

Sheila was smiling, not at all jealous. She commented to Joe and Rosie, "I told you all Olmsted needed was some priming."

126

"A new man on the dig didn't hurt, either," Rosie noted with a smirk.

As things began to calm down, Joe asked, "What about those repossess guys?"

Dan said confidently, "If T-S 311's Port Authorities quiz me, I'll tell 'em the official title transfer on the ship is in the pipeline. That might even be true, given red tape. In fact, it's fairly common on the frontier. By the time anyone digs deep enough to suspect it's a fake, we'll be on our way home."

Kat frowned. "That sounds as if you're still operating under a sword of Damocles."

"Nah! The grapevine isn't that speedy. And while we're there, Feo's going to be too busy hosting the Assembly to bother checking the fine print on my registry papers." Dan put a bright face on matters for the sake of the scientists. He himself was fatalistic. With luck, he'd come out of this without attracting a repossess artist's unwanted attention. And he'd do his damnedest to hang onto *Fiona* for the foreseeable future. But if someone saw through the scam and tracked him back here and took her later, well, that was part of the risk. He'd known that when he'd made his commitment to Praedar. That promise came first. He was no weaseler.

"We'll make sure the Saunders are kept *very* busy," Kat said. Other scientists chimed in, fervently agreeing.

Praedar sliced away unimportant aspects. "How many beings can your ship transport?"

The mood shifted. Everyone stared anxiously at Dan. He took a deep breath. "That depends. Armilly going to be a passenger?"

Kat answered for the team. "No, he's an outcast from his fur-kinship. And his matriarch's aunt will be at this Assembly. Armilly will send holo-mode material with us, but he doesn't want to attend and take a chance of meeting her."

"I see." Dan did some quick calculating. "Then I could take five Terrans, Whimeds, or Vahnajes."

"*Five!* That's *all?*"

Dan struggled to make himself heard, spelling out the laws of single-stager FTL physics. ". . . limits capacity and life support systems, and I'll be stretching fuel thin. That transport that was supposed to haul you could make the jump overnight. It'll take *Fiona* a good three days, even if she *wasn't* overloaded with specimens and exhibits, as you're planning. Hey! If a single-stager could haul as much as the big guys, I'd *be* a big guy and a quadrillionaire!"

Again the tone of the discussion altered. People now jockeyed for position. They cited credentials, seniority, and preparedness as reasons why they deserved one of the precious berths rather than someone else. Friends eyed one another as rivals.

Getz broke in, announcing loudly "Whoever else goes, one of the tickets is mine. No options." The effigy specialist and his students took a storm of verbal flak. Getz drowned out protests. "That was a prior, contracted condition of my coming here. Juxury will confirm." The pudgy scientist swung around and exited the cook shack before anyone could argue further. His students made a hasty getaway as well.

"He has no right," Baines, the xenogeologist, said hotly.

"Unfortunately, he does," Joe countered. "Remember? He had it put in writing, when he joined us to study those effigies. It didn't seem important, when we had several dozen transport tickets . . ."

Amid the angry confusion, it struck Dan that Getz had done the team a favor; he'd concentrated animosity on himself and made would-be rivals for starhopper seats allies.

Praedar chopped off the gripe sessions. "We will decide the exact composition of the representative team when we have weighed all factors. In the interim, it is unquestioned that certain exhibits will be taken, no matter which beings attend. Full cooperation in preparation is necessary to assure success."

The group closed ranks. That undercurrent of rivalry lingered, but for right now the scientists were willing to work together for the common good.

Their normal schedule was heavy. It got much heavier.

The morning after the big change in travel plans, Ruieb-An's crew returned. When they learned the news, they got busy translating the latest finds. The Vahnajes behaved as if there had never been a blow-up.

Armilly rejoined the gang that morning, too. He looked like an enormous, hungover raccoon. But he pitched in immediately to ensure that those making the trip would have plenty of ammunition to throw at the Saunders. Dan fine-tuned the Lannon's scanners and occasionally assisted Armilly in processing the results.

Labs were jammed. Scientists analyzed, cataloged, holo-moded, packed, and consolidated exhibits. Terrans gobbled stims to keep going. The polyphasic Whimeds skipped their usual cat-naps, and their huddles became terrifyingly violent releases of tension. Vahnajes stuck to their translation comps until several of them were badly dehydrated and had to be ordered to recuperate before they went into shock.

Dan flew constant aerial surveys with Praedar. He sat in on powwows with the N'lacs. Kat used the pilot's growing popular-ity with Chuss and the young e.t.s while she recorded telling audio-vids showing just how fully humanoid the N'lacs were.

Along with all the other rush-rush chores, digging at the domes continued at a controlled pace. Though constrained by the "go-slow" rules of their profession, the team was determined to collect as much new raw data as possible for the Assembly. Dan helped when and where he could. He also coached Sheila and several other scientists in the care and maintenance of the vacuum dredge; they'd be totally responsible for its function while he was taking the expedition's reps to T-S 311.

The "importants" in the small dome's entryway were recorded and removed, some for shipment to the Xenoarch conference. Kat was mildly surprised when Dan didn't question the team's haste in doing that. He shrugged and said, "You're what's called a full-range dig, right? Broad-overview researchers. How did that ed-vid description go? 'Generally selective rather than specifi-cally selective,' like the Saunders. To you, this stuff is more valuable as part of a wide collection instead of individual treas-ures. So you want to take as much as you can, across the boards, to show off. That it?"

The brunette studied him with a crooked smile. "Sometimes I wish you weren't such a fast learner. One of the reasons I enjoy xenosocio work with the N'lacs so much is that I'm a teacher at heart. I thought I'd be your tutor. But you're boning up so thor-oughly I can't tell you anything."

"I wouldn't say that," Dan said, winking.

Praedar broke up that encounter before it could develop into a more interesting conversation. "The inner door," the Whimed or-dered. "Open. Scan is complete. No obstacles within. Air is not unique. We will see what is inside before we depart."

Dan sighed, watching Kat hurry off on another task, and got busy on the assignment.

It was a brain-busting challenge, the type he liked. No other tech-mech, in any sector, had taken a crack at this particular problem. Trying to figure out the alien fibers and circuits—and *were* they circuits?—got his juices pumping. Dan had been intrigued by work-blind tinkering ever since he was a boy. This was as close as he was likely to come to his one-time dream of being a breakthrough engineering genius.

He called on all his skills. The door unit was a much tougher chore than dismantling and reassembling Adam's pocket vidder from scratch—which he'd done when he was nine.

Ruieb-An's translations of N'lac texts weren't any help. Dan needed manuals, not inventories of food stocks or paeans to the ancient leaders of this world. And Ruieb's data was mostly in that vein.

The N'lacs were no help, either. The majority of them were afraid to enter the small dome or even look at the door. Chuss and Meej did, but their knowledge of their ancestors didn't extend to their technology. The two brothers did hang around, though, getting under Dan's feet, poking into crannies, babbling, and making nuisances of themselves.

The original materials in the wall linkage were useless. Dan requested replacement fluidics elements from Getz's "effigies." Getz, predictably, turned him down. And Sheila refused to aid what she called a rape of Bill's artifacts. Praedar and Kat, however, weren't so fussy. Unlocking the door took precedence over Getz's outraged feelings.

Kat brought Dan the elements and leaned over his shoulder awhile, watching him work. Her presence was distracting, but she didn't play hormone games, as Sheila might have done in the same close quarters. It was just as well, though, that she didn't stay long. Dan needed to focus his attention solely on the job.

He cleaned elements, installed them, learned that position didn't work, pulled elements, realigned, and reinstalled them. He tried again.

And again.

And again.

Time was a weight, prodding the back of his skull. He fought its influence, fearing it would make him clumsy. One bad mistake could ruin chances of getting into the dome's interior with minimal disruption. Without the door access, the expedition might have to bash down a wall to get inside and damage irreplaceable evidence of N'lac history.

After days of disappointment, Dan found the right combination. Everything finally fitted. Valves tripped. Air flowed into fluidics units. Circuits dead for centuries glowed to life, and dormant mechanisms readied for action.

Praedar had insisted that he be informed before Dan opened the door. He wasn't the only one interested in the event. Kat, Sheila, Baines, Rosie, and a dozen other scientists crowded into the tiny alcove. With a flourish, Dan triggered alien systems. The door opened slowly, like an aged being waking after a long sleep.

"No significant air shift," Dan said. "Indications are it was pressure tight once, but it's lost that."

"The N'lacs no longer knew how to maintain the seals," Praedar said absently, then swept forward.

Dan accompanied the xenoarchaeologists inside. They fanned out, moving in centimeters, scanning the floor. The dredge's hoses cleared interior air for the humans' comfort. Porta lamps were set up. Recording gear hummed.

In contrast to the outer room, this was surprisingly bare. It looked as if the N'lacs' ancestors had removed the furniture before they'd left the room permanently. Light beams raked across a fine layer of grit—sand drift from mesa and desert. No, this long-abandoned sanctuary hadn't been airtight.

Sheila exclaimed with soft excitement and knelt by a bell-shaped structure. The odd-looking thing dominated the far side of the room opposite the entry. It appeared to be built into the wall and filled nearly an eighth of the floor space. A funnel or stack angled toward the dome's roof. But the exhaust duct had collapsed. A small, very heavy door sagged forlornly from the structure's front. Sheila shone a headlamp into the guts. "Kiln? I can't think of what else it would be. Weird design."

"Possibly modeled upon the Evil Old Ones' manufactories," Praedar suggested. "The escaped slaves brought that learned technology with them. Hence the nonexistence of glass artifacts —effigies or fluidics elements—until this stratum." The scientists nodded, conceding the logic of his assessment.

Kat was gesturing to another wall, urging Rosie, "Set to record at peak resolution! This is wonderful!"

A mural ran from the door almost to the glass kiln. Unlike the parade on the ramp wall, this wasn't a catalog of ancient N'lac triumphs. This was more recent history, of what happened when

131

N'lac civilization fell, of enslavement and escape. And of what the N'lacs had escaped from.

Repressing a sickened shudder, Dan stared at the vivid, life-size images of N'lacs, demon robots, and their masters.

Despite Praedar's warnings about jumping to conclusions regarding alien motives, Dan couldn't resist the temptation. The masters in these pictures *were* evil. And they were even more repulsive than what he'd imagined while listening to Sleeg's tales. The N'lac artists who'd painted the mural were talented, and their abilities hadn't yet been dulled by a hostile, oxygen-thin atmosphere.

Monsters! The Evil Old Ones! And their demons—hideous robot copies of their awful masters. Enslaved N'lacs cowered beneath wispy insectile tendrils—nonanthropomorphic appendages. No wonder the Evil Old Ones needed humanoids to be their hands!

At one side of the continuous picture, elegant N'lacs were shown amid grandeur, at the height of their culture. Then they were depicted being sucked into a central frame dominated by Evil Old Ones. They became smaller. Their hands enlarged. Their eyes became myopic, protruding. At the side nearest the outer door, escaping slaves swam through the Big Dark. Their bodies seemed to melt and fragment. Nearer the door still, the many-fathers-ago emerged into a realistically-drawn T-W 593 desert scene.

Two figures in that segment caught and held Dan. An adult N'lac male, genetically altered but not yet suffering the extreme effects of altitude disease, rested his webbed hand atop a youngster's head and pointed to the central box. Dan didn't need a translation. *"Remember, my son, these terrible things. The Evil Old Ones bred us like beasts for their cruel purposes and punished us with their robots. Be ever on guard, lest they return."*

An unpleasant tingling sensation was working its way from Dan's soles to his scalp. It was a lot stronger than the psychological effect, as Kat pegged it, that happened when he touched the ramp paintings. He wasn't touching the mural.

Chuss and Meej had crept into the room. They squatted before the pictures. Fear was a scent, radiating from the young N'lacs. But they seemed unable to break away from its spell.

The scientists argued about the mural, the so-called kiln, and why Chuss' people had utterly abandoned the domes. Not only that, they apparently had fled from this part of the river valley and had located their village far upstream, where Praedar had found them when he first arrived on this planet.

Chuss and Meej echoed all the N'lacs' attitude toward the recently uncovered domes—part reverent awe, part angry fear.

Dan didn't blame them. He felt the same. The mural scenes left him full of shivering dread. *All* of that central panel, with its awful portraits of the Evil Old Ones, was too damned alien! He'd prided himself on being a child of the stars, a true spacer, capable of handling anything the sectors could throw at him. But he wasn't sure he could handle those nonanthropomorphic *things*, even as static, lifeless depictions on an ancient wall.

That annoying tingle he'd sensed earlier was increasing. He dug his fingernails along his forearms, raking irritably. Invisible insects were squirming under his skin. By now, other Terrans were affected by the same scratching urge; the Whimeds, Vahnajes, and Armilly reacted, too. Chuss and Meej scratched listlessly, as if not aware of their actions. Was the sensation caused by a dormant fungus they'd all stirred up when they'd trooped into this long-unused area?

Abruptly Praedar exclaimed, "I must tell Chen!" He wheeled and hurried out of the mural room.

A safety tether seemed to bind him to the other offworlders. As one, they followed him. Chuss and Meej remained by the wall, entranced.

Driven by an impulse he couldn't name, Dan rushed out into blazing midmorning sunlight. Momentarily stunned by the glare, he blinked, getting his bearings. Praedar was already halfway along the cross-valley path leading to Chen's museum dig.

"Come on!" Sheila cried. "Let's hear Chen's reaction!"

Scratching, tagging in a line like mindless geese, they all dogged Praedar's steps.

A rational fraction of Dan's brain told him to stop. This was stupid. What the hell was the matter with him? With all of them?

Ahead, cool beneath his canvas work awning, Chen sat at the edge of the deep-strata excavation and examined the latest treasures he'd fetched from below. As the mob approached him, the Oriental squinted at them curiously. Praedar took long strides, shouting, eager to share his discovery with his old friend.

The insects-under-the-skin sensation rose to an unbearable level.

And as it did, the planet scratched itself. It heaved, undulating.

Dan and the scientists were hurled off their feet. Praedar attempted to crawl, still trying to reach Chen's dig. The quake knocked him back down—hard.

Chen, being seated, was riding out the ground waves with less trouble than his colleagues. His expression was one of bemused astonishment.

The earth shuddered again and again.

Dan, not knowing why, raised his eyes to the top of the cliff, to Hanging Rock. The boulder that had perched there since time immemorial was teetering, a building, breathtaking rhythm to its motion.

Then it was leaning farther and farther inward, toward the valley.

"Shree! Shree! Shree!" Panic-stricken cries echoed from the N'lacs' village. Their high-pitched shrieks warred with the deep thunder of the quake and the groans of that rocking monolith above.

Dan felt the same helpless horror as the primitives. Unable to move, he clung to the bucking ground and watched the inevitable happening.

Time crept, defying his certain knowledge of how Hanging Rock *must* be falling.

With enormous, deadly beauty, it dropped, accompanied by an entourage of smaller stones and a hail of crumbling dirt.

The landmark smashed onto the museum pit, completely covering the excavation. Amid a gentle rain of sand and pebbles, it settled into its new site. The boulder now sat at the junction of the eastern valley's paths—a sentinel guarding the entrance to the N'lacs' village.

The canvas awning, the specimen tables, the collection case, and Dr. Chen were gone, buried beneath kilotons of stone and earth.

CHAPTER NINE
✕✕✕✕✕✕✕✕

Colleagues or Antagonists?

Reality and unreality were frighteningly mixed. The past, present, and future blurred and shifted. Dan was simultaneously an observer and a participant. He saw Praedar burrowing furiously at the edge of the museum excavation. The Whimed roared in futile rage at the thing that had killed his friend. He struggled to free Chen's corpse. Dan, along with many others, was beside Praedar, digging with his bare hands, banging his knuckles painfully against Hanging Rock. And he was fighting tears, an agonizing lump filling his throat.

Instantly, it seemed, it was later. He was operating the dredge, sucking away dirt, knowing it wouldn't matter.

Hanging Rock settled deeper with each load of soil the dredge removed. All they were doing was embedding the landmark farther.

Sheila and Joe shut off their remote med monitors. "No signs of life. No purpose in digging him out. Let him be . . ."

Years reversed, and Dan was on Alpha Cee Settlement, with his siblings and Reid. Fiona McKelvey's wasted body was at rest

135

at last. The lingering xenovirus that had attacked her before Dan was born had claimed another victim. A physician consoled her family, saying "It was very sudden. She didn't suffer. . ."

As Chen hadn't suffered?

Then Dan was atop the cliff, picking over the spot where Hanging Rock had been, seeking answers and finding none. Baines was blaming himself. "There's just no reason! That thing was stable. On bedrock. And there was no identifiable epicenter on that quake. It came from everywhere at once! None of this should have happened!"

Kat was weeping, clinging to Sheila and Rosie, wailing "It's not fair! He can't have died like this!"

Praedar sat by Hanging Rock. He had been there for hours, motionless, inconsolable, untouchable, as Reid had been, when his wife had died.

Dan was watching them both, the big Whimed and his father, two beings he wanted to help and couldn't. Aching for them, and for himself.

And then he was elsewhere in the space of a heartbeat.

There was darkness—the Big Dark—numbing cold, and the mind-boggling expanse of stellar distances. He was melting, fragmenting, as the N'lacs had, transferring from one dot in infinity to another in a nanosecond. He wanted to know method, locations, vectors, and coordinates. But the form he inhabited understood none of those things. He was with a band of fleeing slaves, seeing through alien eyes, reliving their experience.

Then towering, ropy excrescences surrounded him, looming over him. He tried to scream. No sound came from his mouth. He couldn't move. He was trapped by the Evil Old Ones, who preyed upon humanoids, taking them to unknown regions to serve as hands.

Their demons confronted him, too, shiny caricatures of their loathsome masters with lifeless, glittering compound eyes, scanning, on the lookout for disobedient slaves to punish.

Wispy insectile limbs reached for him, threatening to enfold him. His gorge rose as instinctual revulsion racked him.

Then the Evil Old Ones and their robots changed, becoming a giant boulder, falling toward him. Dr. Chen sat beside him, oblivious to the danger. The old man was poring over his finds from the N'lacs' museum.

Dan struggled to warn him, to escape.

Hanging Rock was falling, falling, closer, *closer*!

"Dan! McKelvey! It's okay!"

Panting, his pulse roaring, Dan sat bolt upright. One of the student xenoarchitects was leaning over him, gripping his shoulders reassuringly and repeating "It's okay. It's okay."

With a groan, Dan buried his face in his hands, then swung his legs over the side of the bunk. He sat there sucking in air, quieting the triphammer pace of his heart. Finally he managed to say, "B-bad one. Thanks."

"You must have been wrestling Procyon Five octopi," the student said lightly, plainly relieved the pilot was getting back to normal.

"Worse! Much worse." Dan stared dully at the shimmering spray bandage covering his raw knuckles. That much hadn't been a dream; he *had* hurt his hands while digging at Hanging Rock.

Deciding he was fully awake, the student retreated to his lab and resumed work. Dan watched his rescuer through the nearby door, uncaring what he saw, marshalling energy. It was several minutes before he stumbled to an adjacent soni-shower and cleaned up. Grit and grime—leftovers from the efforts to extricate Chen's body—were ground into his pores and beneath his nails. He let the vibrations work him and his clothing over thoroughly.

Feeling slightly fresher, Dan wandered through the complex, still not too certain where he should be going. His head wasn't functioning in full gear yet. Around him, scientists continued their feverish preparations for the Assembly. The tragedy hadn't altered the schedule. On the contrary, it gave new impetus to the expedition. They agreed Chen deserved that, as a memorial.

Dan noticed Kat and Sheila in one of the insta-cell's offices and stepped in. He looked on as the women sorted through Chen's personal belongings, separating personal articles from professional mementoes. Kat showed a set of solid opics to the blonde and said, "Praedar will probably want to keep this, don't you think? It's souvenirs of their first dig together."

Sheila nodded. "Put it with that stuff from their Institute days. I think I'd better pitch these clothes, or feed them to the recycler. They're too threadbare to save."

"Sad," Dan said, shaking his head. "All that's left of his life."

They eyed him sharply. Both were visibly weary, but they reacted with remarkable patience. "No, he left much more," Kat said gently. "An enormous body of work and the friendship of everyone he ever worked with, ever helped. That's thousands of beings."

"Including me," Dan admitted. He fingered the boxes of opics and trinkets—curios, an unusual potsherd strung on a thong so it could be worn as jewelry, a yellowing program from the first Xenoarch Assembly Chen had attended, a comical clay model of him and Praedar side by side, their individual features exaggerated. "I feel cheated. You had a real chance to get to know him. I only got here weeks ago, was just finding the groove, and now he's gone . . ."

Sheila's expression was kind. "Everyone felt that way about Chen Zihua. Especially Praedar. That's why we're doing this, instead of waiting until he feels he has to. He's had enough pain."

"And it's realistic," Kat said. "An acceptance therapy to ease the dread of our own fates. Other team members will someday dispose of our belongings. Decades from now, if we're fortunate enough to live that long. Joe, Sheila, Rosie, me . . . all us long-termers will probably end up buried on T-W 593. It's common; career xenoarch field workers tend to make their dig worlds home."

There was an awkward pause, one Dan finally broke by asking "Where is Praedar?"

"In the main lab, I think," Kat said. "Working overtime. He refuses to let the grief ride him any more."

"He can't," Dan agreed. "Not with what's at stake." He went looking for the expedition's leader. Praedar was where Kat had said he'd be—preparing exhibits for shipment to T-S 311. The felinoid's crest was a tangled mat. His bony features were drawn from lack of catnaps. As Dan neared him, Praedar glanced up, regarding the pilot thoughtfully.

They said nothing for several minutes. Then Praedar announced flatly, "We continue. The decided-upon schedule will be followed." Dan nodded, and Praedar's starburst gaze dropped to the pilot's bandaged hands. "You are able to work?"

"What? Oh, this? It's nothing serious."

The alien muttered in Whimed, then in Terran: "Humans are so fragile."

A reference to this injury, or to Chen's death? Dan said, "Well, admittedly, we're not as tough as your species. Comes of evolving in a softer environment."

"Yet you strive, with courage, and sincere effort. It is most admirable." Praedar was remote, staring through Dan rather than at him. With obvious difficulty, he brought himself back from wherever he'd been mentally. "You will be a full team member at the Assembly. I will supply your accreditation when we arrive. Here is the conference agenda. Familiarize yourself. You will see certain manners of dress are expected. Joe Hughes will be attending. He has extra garb that I believe will fit you . . ."

Dan had been listening with growing dismay. "Wait a moment. I don't think it's a good idea for me to rub elbows with those top-grade xenoarchs. I'll pilot you there, sure. But I was planning to hang close to the Port, keep an eye on the ship . . ."

"You are a Saunder-McKelvey. Your presence is valuable."

Sighing, Dan explained. "I'm not in the same league with Feo and Hope. They've got years of degrees and prestige backing them. I . . ."

"You are a Saunder-McKelvey," Praedar repeated stubbornly. "This is useful. It serves the expedition." He studied the pilot narrowly, gauging Dan's objections. Then a wan smile curved the felinoid's mouth. "We have never had a member of your family on our team until now. This has possibly cost us important weight with sponsors and licensers. You are a weapon, as truth is a weapon."

Dan said, "My being a Saunder-McKelvey can't cancel out my lack of formal education. I couldn't lecture on fluidics or—"

"Of course not." There were times when Praedar's blunt honesty could be disconcerting. He needn't have snapped up Dan's modest disclaimer so fast! "There is as yet insufficient material to confirm your fluidics theory. And no paper has been prepared. Your purpose will be to wield an emotional effect upon our colleagues and the media."

"Reporters," Dan muttered, unhappy with the prospect. "I haven't had to deal with *that* breed in years. As for your scientific cronies . . ."

"You will assist us." Those hyponotic eyes locked on the Terran. Then, softening his attack, Praedar explained. "Chen planned this, and he was rarely wrong. He assured me that you have depths of ability and assurance you yourself have forgotten you possess. Chen referred to it as protective coloration. Do not disprove his trust in you."

Using the dead man's memory to batter down Dan's resistance

was unfair tactics. "I suppose he meant my adapting so I'd fit into the indie haulers' world, but..." The Whimed's personality chopped more ground from under lingering doubts. Dan sighed and said, "Okay. The name game it is, if that's the way you want it. Against my better judgment. I think you're expecting too much of me."

"I do not. Nor did Chen." Praedar's smile widened. "Consider this: Whatever luster you add to our expedition, it is a gain over what we had at previous Assemblies."

And that was that. The boss had decided. Arguments were futile. Dan was getting more and more used to that pattern.

The next few days, during final preparations for launch, Dan practically lived aboard *Fiona*. By then, the passenger list was completed: Praedar, Ruieb-An, Joe, Kat, and Getz. There was a lot of grumbling over that, though no serious conflict. Scientists helped Dan alter the starhopper's interior to accommodate her extra load, jerry-rigging web couches, modifying a section of cargo bay for additional life support supplies, and cushioning racks in the hold for the delicate exhibits the team was taking. Extra everything was needed.

Dan constantly updated his estimated fuel expenditure and sweated. This was going to be tight. If necessary, he could make the run to T-S 311 and back without a replacement package. But then he—and the expedition—would be stranded until a regular supply ship deigned to stop. Running one's fuel to the bottom was a rotten safety practice. Dan hoped those phony ownership papers would convince Port authorities to grant them a fuel top-off.

An already frantic pace went critical. Nerves frayed. Squabbles broke out. Ruieb-An took umbrage when Drastil sneered at the Vahnaj's bulky array of translation demonstration luggage. Praedar had his hands full averting another mass Vahnaj walkout. Kat was short-tempered. Sheila needled everyone mercilessly. Even easygoing Joe Hughes was snappish. The memory of Chen's death was an additional, if rarely mentioned, trigger. Some scientists, irked by personality clashes, detached their polygonal sleeping quarters from the combined insta-cells and moved them apart from the main complex. That left their former roommates, understandably annoyed, seeking new bunk space.

The N'lacs were unusually subdued. Sleeg held secret ceremonies in the village, barring all offworlders from the rituals.

Many N'lacs sat for hours near Hanging Rock, gazing stupidly at the boulder, as if unable to comprehend why it was no longer atop the cliff.

D Day 0900! *Fiona*'s cargo bay was loaded and locked. Her passengers had completed suit and survival drill to Dan's satisfaction. The launch window was calculated and on the boards.

Nearly everyone came to see the team's reps off. N'lacs chattered, climbed over vehicles, and clutched at offworlders' hands. Dan shooed them away from *Fiona* several times.

"You fella go hunt, huh huh?" Chuss asked him. "Like after rain, when boom crawlers come out of holes? Dutos catch 'em. We catch 'em. Kelfee fly all you fella catch meat, huh huh?"

The likable little e.t. created a vivid picture for Dan—pot-hunting jaunts, communal lizard roasts. He felt a twinge at the idea of leaving T-W 593, even for a few days.

"Catch much meat," Sheila assured Chuss. "Them fellow go catch Feo and Hope and nail them fellow hide to wall."

Scientists chuckled at her grisly comment. The N'lacs didn't understand the reference, but laughed, too, squeaky hiccups of amusement. It was good to see them enjoying themselves, after their melancholy vigils near Chen's grave.

Chuss flung his skinny arms around Dan's waist and hugged him, exclaiming, "You come home soon, Kelfee."

Very affected, Dan patted the e.t.s pate. "I will, Chuss. You take care N'lacs till we fellow return. Huh huh?"

"Yes yes! Take care!" Chuss turned to Praedar, putting his paws into the felinoid's big hands. "Praedar come home," the native said simply, a heartfelt plea.

Surprisingly, impulsively, Praedar embraced Chuss, as moved as Dan had been, in his own way. He murmured inaudibly, words meant only for Chuss. Then the boss straightened and said briskly, "It is time to depart."

There was a last-moment flurry of farewells. Kat and Sheila, who'd often been at each other's throats this past week, hugged. Others exchanged handshakes and noisy backslaps and mock-stern exortations to behave. Then pilot and passengers tore themselves away and entered the cabin. Dan made sure his riders were securely tethered and ran through his systems checks while the well-wishers retreated from the takeoff lane.

Power circuits came to life. Redundancy safety scans noted hatches were tight. *Fiona* swept down the mesa. She reached lift point sooner than the passengers had anticipated. They reacted with a mutual intake of breath.

On the monitors, geographical details shrank rapidly. The complex now resembled a cluster of white bumps on the valley floor. Chuss' village wasn't visible at all. In another few seconds, plateau and mountains were dwarfed by widening horizons. The sky darkened from pale blue-green to turquoise to near black. Though *Fiona* was rising from the dayside, stars began to shine on her forward screens. The curve of the planet's sphere became apparent. Deserts, ancient riverbeds, oceans, and ranges dwindled, blurred by cloud masses.

Dan gazed at T-W 593, remembering that unidentified blip the monitors had spotted weeks ago. Could he backtrack the thing from this high vantage and find where it had impacted? He had actually reached for the comp before he jerked his hand away.

Sheepish, he wondered why he'd started to do such a dumb thing.

Because he yearned to know. Praedar's lust for the truth was contagious.

He ordered himself to concentrate on the job at hand and forget his lingering curiosity about that mysterious blip. There were far more important matters to attend to now.

As *Fiona* climbed, the terminator swung past below again and again. The orbit of the nav-sat and those of the planet's moons fell behind. The passengers adjusted so well to ascent that Dan had to notify them when he approached FTL hop point. None of the riders had noticed the telltale light on the monitors. Under his supervision, they rechecked safety webbing and braced themselves.

He engaged the S-ME patented hyperdrive, and the universe blinked.

Fiona leaped starward. T-W 593 system's sun became a glowing dot as the ship hopped in and out of real space.

The passengers settled in for the journey. From Dan's point of view, this was a short jump. For the scientists, it probably would seem long and uncomfortable, particularly compared to a fast trip aboard a major carrier, which was what they'd originally paid for. The project members were planet-bound people who spent their lives Down There. They were unused to the nature of single-stage starhopping.

Come to think of it, I'm turning planet-bound myself lately,

*staying put on one world and working with the same people all
the time. I kind of like it. Maybe it's Praedar's influence—and
Kat's and Sheila's. Hell, blame the whole damned crew plus the
N'lacs. The place has a grip on me.*

Old-timers said passengers came in two varieties—queasy
and easy. The scientists didn't show any tendency toward nausea,
and Dan didn't have to hold hands. Nevertheless, his riders
weren't easy. They were the most restless beings he'd ever
spaced with. His servo pets and games palled quickly. The vid
library held their interest longer. Kat, looking over the selection,
remarked wryly that now she knew how a mere tech-mech came
by such a well-read background.

When the riders weren't fussing or banging elbows, they
talked about their strategies for the Assembly. Dan eavesdropped.
There wasn't any way to avoid doing that! He was resigned to
playing the name game Praedar had demanded. The protocol of a
big-brain scientific conference, though, daunted the pilot. He was
acutely conscious of his lack of formal training. He listened in
anxiously, picking up every hint on what lay ahead, preparing
himself as best he could.

The passengers' restlessness hadn't quite peaked when their
destination star centered on the nav grids. Then they became
impatient, eager to arrive, nagging Dan with constant questions
on their status.

Fiona entered approach mode. Dan made minute course corrections and aligned the vector precisely. The little starhopper
moved from a high ecliptic starlane onto T-S 311's planetary line,
then went sublight. Grids locked on the solar system's fifth
world. A ship-time hour later, Dan cued the com.

He got a fast response. The voice was crisp and robotic. "T-S
3ll Landing Central. We copy your request touchdown coordinates. Please identify."

Dan hesitated. For the most part, robot navs were simpler to
fool than human operators. But servos came in a wide range of
models. The supersophisticated type could put a pilot through the
gears. His kinsman could afford such a unit, though he might not
have bothered. The expense was certainly unnecessary, out here
in the stellar boonies, with little traffic in and out of the area.

And yet . . .

He crossed his fingers, fed *Fiona*'s new, phony reg listing to
Central, and said, "This is the *Praedar's Project* arriving from

T-W 593. Our party is here to attend the Xenoarchaeological Assembly. Ready for tracking assignment. Over."

There was an ominous pause. Dan uncrossed and recrossed his fingers.

How deep was that robot going to dig before it cleared them?

"Come on, come on," he muttered.

As if it had heard him, the servo answered, "Terran Reg IH 447820, you are cleared for landing. Tracking coordinate grid is Quad Five, down eight. Local time at Port is 1109. For your convenience, if you wish to employ manual setdown, winds are westerly at surface at ten KPH, broken cloud at six kilometers on approach Saunder City F-H S-N. Do you require further assistance? Over."

"Negative. Data on boards. Thank you. Over."

"Very good. Safe planetfall. Over and out."

Dan closed the key and shook clenched fists above his head. "It worked! By damn, it worked!"

"You sound surprised," Kat said. "I thought you assured us that fake title transfer would grease right through, in your words. And what's this *Praedar*'s *Project* stuff?"

"It's a good name for an expedition *or* a ship. And much safer than underlining *Fiona*'s debt status and my blacklisting." Dan craned his neck, looking toward the bobbing web couch where Praedar floated. "Do you object, boss?"

Getz started to retort. Praedar cut the effigy expert off in midword. "It is a device that succeeds. Approved."

Joe Hughes said, "I'd love to be a bug on the wall when Feo gets this news from Port Landing Central. What a shock for him and Hope and their protégé, Tavares. We didn't cancel out after all!" Ruieb-An grinned, baring tiny, pointed teeth. Praedar's smile was predatory. The humans, too—even Getz—relished the situation.

Dan hated to break up the party. "Time to double-check all safety tethers and tie down. Or you'll land in the Saunders' infirmary instead of their Assembly." Hurriedly the scientists obeyed.

Fiona lacked a full-sized shuttle's superfluous baffling. Descent aboard a single-stager kept passengers awake. Her screens crackled with ionization. Atmosphere screamed past the little ship's hulls as she reached lower orbits.

Gradually forward momentum decreased as retros stabilized her fall. Screens cleared, revealing a world of heavily forested landmasses girdled by deep seas. Nav beams targeted *Fiona* toward a city on a bay indenting the coast of the largest continent.

Scans detected vast rain belts. Through breaks in the moisture-laden clouds, Dan stared at the planet. Had T-S 311 been this lush millennia ago, when the N'lac colonists first scouted it? T-W 593 had once been a wetter, cooler place, according to team findings. It might have resembled T-S 311 a great deal, making this look like a perfect place for the N'lacs' interstellar settlement.

Fiona spiraled lower. Dan searched for traces of ancient N'lac population centers. He couldn't be sure, but he thought he could spot a few buried towns and connecting roads, where forests didn't hide all traces of previous occupation. His growing knowledge pleased him. Those aerial skimmer surveys had taught him plenty.

Dan had no trouble locating the biggest set of ruins, the ones the Saunders were excavating. The site was directly south of the port city. An enormous transparent dome shielded the dig from the weather. No frontier style insta-cells here, no roughing it—not for the dig and not for the port! Saunder City F-H S-N's shuttle strips were long and well paved. Her street layout was tidy. Several hundred hectares of agriculture plots had been cleared and fenced east of town. It was very impressive for a Settlement of two thousand and remarkably developed for a colony far off normal trade routes and deep in Terran-Whimed border sectors. Treaty negotiations usually made settlement in such sectors more bother than most developers cared to deal with. However, Feo Saunder needn't concern himself over petty details. He had the money and power to set up a colony anywhere he chose.

The scene below reminded Dan of his approach to another world, years ago. Reid's family had visited his half sister, Lara McKelvey, governor of Vaughn Settlement. Her capital was a bigger settlement than Feo's, and the signs of wealth had been even more obvious. In her mansion, there'd been imported clothes, imported foods. She had spacecraft fleets at her disposal. Big-shot Terrans and aliens fought for invitations to her social affairs. Throughout Reid's stay, Lara had been unfailingly gracious to her impecunious kindred. Yet the contrast between her success and Ried's recent bankruptcy had hit young Dan hard. It was the first time he'd been fully aware that he wasn't rich any more.

Nearly twenty years later, and nothing much has changed. But I'm not going to let that stop me!

He took his own sweet time on final line-up and landing, demonstrating his expertise with a feather-light touchdown. That done, Dan taxied slowly to his assigned berth—at the far end of a row of major carriers' shuttles. Once there, he went methodically through his secure-the-ship checklist. Let Feo's staffers wait on the Saunders' poor relation!

The scientists, too, were stalling. They fussed at length over storing their pressure suits and gear and wondered aloud who, if anyone, would come to meet them.

A small crowd was gathering at the Port control tower. Dan assessed the setup on the exterior scan monitor. He saw pilots. Well, that figured. Uniformed local personnel. That figured also. And civilians, some wearing twinkling holo-lens pendants. Dan pointed them out, asking Kat, "Reporters?"

"From the scientific vid-pubs," she said, nodding. "I won't be surprised if there are a few stringers from the media networks, as well. Normally they wouldn't cover a conference so remote. But the Saunders are hot copy. I mean, after all, Cameron Saunder manages the Pan Sector channels . . ."

Dan grunted sourly. "In or out of xenoarch, *wealthy* Saunder-McKelveys always wield clout."

"Speak of the devils," Joe exclaimed. The others looked back at the screens. Feo and Hope Saunder-Nicholaiev were emerging from the shuttleport's lounge. They led a parade of fellow scientists, reporters, and flunkeys, heading straight for *Fiona*. It was obvious their staff had tipped them off about the Praedar expedition's arrival, and the Saunders were here to stage a grand entrance. Reporters, Dan noted, kept their lenses tightly focused on Feo and Hope. Any prayer of impartial media coverage was a lost cause.

"What a farce," Joe said. "Feo probably ordered that nav robot to assign us a roundabout entry path. That way he and Hope had time to get here and put on this performance."

Getz growled, "Are they xenoarchs or actors?"

"Both," Kat said. "They're also excellent PR manipulators." Her jaw set in a firm line. "Our job is to steal their spotlight."

"We meet them," Praedar said, and waved to Dan. He opened the debark ramp. Team members squared their shoulders and held their heads high as they started down to the tarmac. Dan brought up the rear, wanting to observe, for now, and not attract attention.

Feo and Hope moved with long, athletic strides, easily outdistancing most of the reporters, though not their colleagues. All of the xenoarchs, even portly Terrans and aliens, looked fit, like people who walked their own sites and did much of their own digging. Dan could testify that put a humanoid in good condition. Since the landing, he'd touched his grav compensation med patch only once, and his pulse and breathing rate had rarely been this steady after planetfall.

When the two groups met, there was momentary chaos. Lens pendants winked. Praedar huddled with fellow Whimeds on the welcoming committee. Ruieb-An bowed and bobbed with Vahnajes. A Lannon female boomed "Wal-cooms!" to everyone.

Gradually subtle divisions in the seemingly amicable meeting became apparent. There was definite chilliness between Whimeds and Vahnajes. An undercurrent of animosity separated Terrans, too. They fell into two factions—those supporting the Saunders and those who didn't. Dan made careful mental memos of who was in which category. He was pleasantly surprised that he recognized so many of the scientists, both humans and aliens. Those tri-di illustrations in the expedition's vid files gave him prior acquaintance with some of the biggest names in the field.

A muscular Terran, Jarrett, told Joe, "Glad you're here. We heard rumors that you might not make it."

"We almost didn't," Hughes admitted.

A sharp-faced Whimed asked in heavily accented Terran English, "There are difficulties in your travels?"

"Many obstacles," Praedar said. His starburst gaze impaled the Saunders and the redhead, Tavares, accompanying them.

Feo and Hope reacted with surprise. Dan sought for guilt in their expressions. He couldn't find it. They appeared to be genuinely upset on Praedar's behalf. Tavares, though, *did* have something on his conscience; he was too sympathetic, overdoing it blatantly. Dan resolved to keep a close watch on the Saunders' fair-haired boy. Tavares was probably the one who did his bosses' dirty work, and the T-W 593 team had to stay alert to prevent any more of his tricks.

The welcomers listened in consternation to Praedar's account of delayed machinery shipments and snafued transport connections. The latter, in particular, produced a storm of outrage.

147

"Why, that's the ship we arrived on," Jarrett said. "I'm going to register a complaint with the Council."

"If it happened once, it could happen again. None of us is safe!"

"They can't be allowed to get away with that!"

"Somebody arranged it. The only possible explanation . . ."

Dan's team nodded at that theory, and he noticed that Tavares reddened, confirming Dan's suspicions that the Saunders' aide was behind these problems. The Saunders themselves, however, shared Praedar's anger. That was confusing. Dan had come here prepared to see the Saunders as enemies. Now their seeming innocence muddied the matter.

"Rest assured, Juxury," Feo promised, "we'll get to the bottom of this. The perpetrator will be punished."

Praedar considered the statement, took it at face value, and blinked, releasing his hosts from that unnerving stare. "It would be appreciated," the Whimed said. "It is difficult to conduct research under such handicaps."

"Of course! Say no more!"

The crowd was impressed by Feo's vehement assurances. Dan took them with a kiloton of salt. Typical razzle-dazzle. Squash the "perpetrator?" Sure—a hapless clerk in the central transport office, most likely. The missing machinery? Another clerk's fault. And whatever steps the Saunders took to swat their chosen patsies, it wouldn't make a dent in the dispatchers' code of silence and blacklistings.

Reminded of that, Dan surveyed the mob warily. Any repossess artists among them? It was tough to judge. Those grabbers didn't wear badges. He'd have to stay alert on that front, too, to protect the team's means of getting back home.

Commiseration shifted to an exchange of courtesies all around. Praedar spoke in a warmer tone than he'd used earlier. "We thank you for meeting us, but it was not required. Some of us visited your world several years ago and are familiar with the city and dig. Escort is unnec—"

"Nonsense!' Hope Saunder interjected. "You *must* accept our hospitality."

"Quite right," Feo agreed. He extolled Saunder City's amenities, recently refurbished quarters for Assembly guests, and other specially arranged perks. Was that a sales pitch for the attendees or for the onlooking media?

While Feo talked, Dan compared his relatives with his childhood recollections. There wasn't a lot of change. Both Saunders were darkly tanned. Both wore the just-ordinary-settlers fashion now in vogue with Terra's elite. Both were of medium height. Feo's sand-colored hair framed a broad, Slavic face. His eyes were an undistinguished gray, his nose a sunburned lump. The man worked overtime to create an image as an average hardworking xenoarch. Hope, on the other hand, wasn't playing down her well-bred Belvedere genes. Her iron-gray hair was cropped stylishly close. Skillfully applied cosmetics enhanced good facial bones and her large brown eyes. She was a horsey woman, heavier than her wiry husband, but carried her weight well. Despite their differences, they resembled one another, proving human folk legends about lifetime partners.

"Kaatje!" Hope gushed. "You're prettier than ever!" The younger scientist's smile was weak. Obviously Kat would have preferred a compliment on her xenosocio record.

Joe, Praedar, Getz, Ruieb-An—all came in for a share of the Saunders' flattery. Then Feo frowned, peering about. "Where's Chen Zihua? I thought . . ."

"He is dead. An accident." Praedar's firm announcement put a period to any further questions along that line. He was a living warning sign, telling outsiders not to touch. The Whimed turned and beckoned. "You have not met the newest member of our team."

Taking the cue, Dan stepped forward, holding out his hand. "Hello, cousins. You probably don't remember me. It's been a long time since we last met. I'm Dan McKelvey."

He'd made up his mind in advance how to handle this moment, and the effect was gratifying. Reporters buzzed, shifting their focus to Dan's team. The welcoming committee whispered among themselves excitedly. Feo gawked, speechless.

Hope, somewhat desperately, tried to salvage things. "Of course we remember you, Danny! How you've grown! You were just a boy when . . ." And she gestured waist-high, beaming maternally. She elbowed her husband. "Feo! You know him. Reid's youngest. Morgan's grandson. We and Reid and Fiona and their kids were all at Brenna's picnic, that bash on Mars in '37. Right, Danny?" Feo's continuing stunned silence plainly annoyed her.

Dan nodded absently. Hope's words had triggered a painful flashback.

The picnic was the last big family reunion he had attended. Shortly after that event, the financial roof had fallen in on Reid. Dan remembered his mother standing beside him, guiding him through the social maze of the gathering. He felt her hand on his shoulder as he was introduced to adult relatives, Feo and Hope among them. The pair hadn't made a strong impression on him then. There had been far more glamorous people at the party: Grande dame Brenna herself; the family's entertainment legend, Nathan Saunder; Ivan Saunder, terraforming wizard; and Wright McKelvey, hero of Space Fleet, soon to die tragically in action . . .

Hope was laughing, saying to no one in particular, "Poor Feo! He's so wrapped up in Assembly affairs he can't deal with mere family matters." She smiled conspiratorially at the reporters, inviting their indulgence of her brilliant husband.

At last waking to his duty, Feo seized Dan's proffered hand and pumped it, stammering apologies. "Long time indeed, my boy! Far too long! We hadn't known you were with Juxury's group." Feo shot a worried, calculating glance at the big Whimed.

Again, Hope covered that heavy undercurrent of rivalry with cheery conversation. "You're the very image of Fiona, Spirit of Humanity rest her soul." That was a flat lie, and they all knew it. Dan regarded her with a faintly scornful smile. Hope rushed on, "We'll have a nice chat later and bring each other up to date, won't we?"

Feo jerked a thumb. Tavares bellowed orders. Flunkeys hurried to summon trucks and courtesy vehicles from the Port parking area. Porters bustled forward, ready to offload cargo.

"No," Praedar said loudly. He blocked the porters' way. "We will handle our specimens and exhibits. We only."

"No need for that," Feo said. "They'll take care of donkey chores . . ."

"No," Praedar repeated, more firmly. His crest bristled. Whimeds reacted to that flag, and their own topknots stiffened. Non-Whimeds edged apart from the felinoids, on guard.

Dan understood the boss's suspicions and desire to protect his property. But he also saw problems a planet-bound person wouldn't be aware of. "We had help stowing the stuff, Praedar," he said. "It'll take the six of us days to unload it all."

"Out of the question!" Feo snapped. "Registration and opening ceremonies are tonight. Sessions begin in the morning . . ."

Kat said with sarcasm, "Sorry we arrived so late. Couldn't be helped. The transportation difficulties, you know. I'm sure you can see why all that made us excessively touchy about our displays."

The Saunders brushed that aside. Feo said, "I fail to see any reason that should . . ."

Dan stepped into the gap. He shot a searching look at Praedar's friends among the welcoming committee. "Maybe if we had some extra hands . . ." He left the rest of it—"that we can trust"—unspoken.

Former co-workers and students eagerly volunteered to help. Praedar made his decision with Whimed abruptness. Within minutes, scientists were trotting in and out of *Fiona*'s cargo bay, moving luggage and exhibits to the waiting vehicles. The Saunders, their supporters, and flunkeys stood by, obviously miffed. A few of Praedar's friends traded broad winks, enjoying this opportunity to tweak the Saunders' noses.

Amid the confusion, Dan cornered a Port staffer and got Praedar's signature on the forms they'd need later to requisition a refueling package. That wouldn't guarantee them the top-off, but with luck it would eliminate delaying tactics or excuses by Feo's staffers when the team was ready to depart.

After the cargo was safely transferred, Dan made a production out of locking the starhopper. An angry red light glowed beside the now-secured hatchways. A reporter asked the obvious question.

"That? Oh, just a bit of burglar protection," Dan said offhandedly. "After all the trouble we've had, it seemed like a good idea. Built it myself. Nasty little gimmick. Special tamper-proof guts. If anybody tries to give us any more problems, they'll be very sorry."

Tavares scowled. "This is a *Saunder* settlement. You don't need to worry about theft here."

"Oh, I'm not worried—now," Dan retorted. He turned to Feo and said with a grin, "It pays to be careful, eh, cousin? We Saunder-McKelveys didn't get where we are by leaving things to chance, did we?"

The Saunders, their noses in the air and out of joint, stomped past him to the lead car of the courtesy caravan. Dan got into the vehicle carrying his team. As the parade started out of Port, he settled himself amid heaps of baggage, feeling smug. The look Kat and Joe gave him was very sly.

It had been years since he'd stepped into those haughty mannerisms his family could wield to such daunting advantage. Feo and Hope had been thoroughly taken aback. Dan was delighted at how quickly half-forgotten patterns crept into his speech once more. Cool! Buttery! And that verbal knife, slipped artfully between the ribs. Not bad!

He didn't kid himself that this was a victory. Only a small skirmish, it wouldn't end the rivalry between the teams. But his oneupmanship had temporarily tipped the scales in favor of Praedar's expedition, the N'lacs', and truth's.

CHAPTER TEN

оооооооо

Sparring Matches

His euphoria didn't last. The drive through Saunder City's, single main street rubbed Dan's nose in the sort of privilege that was only a dim memory for his branch of the family. The Port's qualifying call letters—F-H S-N—stood for "Feo and Hope Saunder-Nicholaiev," to distinguish this Settlement from other Saunder Cities scattered throughout the Terran sector. They also branded this frontier village of two thousand as a company town.

Every citizen wore Feo's insignia. The same mark hung over rooftrees and the Port's gate. Vendors' stalls and shops looked tightly controlled, as if a Saunder computer dictated what and when the proprietors would sell and how they'd dress. There were no import-export houses, no major shipping docks, no section where the usual brawler element ran its rougher bars and brothels. The lone, staid amusement area was patrolled by Saunder guards to make sure no one got out of order. The only offworlders on the scene were visiting scientists and off-duty human and alien crews from the shuttles.

The settlement was frozen. It lacked the bustle of a thriving, growing community because the Saunders wanted it that way. Saunder City had one reason for existence—the dig. The Port was there to bring in supplies. Period. No outbound commerce. None of a developing world's entrepreneurial activity. The citizens were to support the dig and provide light diversion for the local team when their work became tiresome. And that was *it*.

It was Feo's private kingdom. FTL and subspace com enabled him to work in this splendid isolation while enjoying contact with the larger interstellar scene and any luxuries he and Hope cared to ship in. The power and wealth on display were ostentatious.

Saunder City had no true outskirts. Offices and residences stopped and agriculture strips began. Farmers tended crops and cut back encroaching weeds from the surrounding forests. Dan envisioned Chuss's colonist ancestors waging the same war against native foliage.

Beyond the farms, woodland crowded close to the paved road. On the left, tangled masses of yellow thorn-shrubs and vines alternated with small patches of prairie. To the right, waves lapped at black stone beaches. Trailing creepers raked at the vehicles' windows, forcing those seated on the landward side to recoil to avoid being scratched. "How much of that stuff is feral?" Dan wondered.

"Much," Praedar said. "Analyses by the Saunders indicate the biota are similar to species found on T-W 593. Our conclusion is the stocks were imported. The Saunders believe otherwise."

Scientists sharing the ride with Praedar's team laughed, and one of them said, "What do you expect? Selectivity, Juxury. Always selectivity. The Saunders select for their theories, you for yours."

Ignoring the byplay, Kat touched Dan's sleeve. "You wouldn't have asked about biota when you first arrived on T-W 593."

"I wouldn't have known enough to, then. I told you I was a fast learner."

A man seated nearby overheard him. "False modesty, McKelvey. Denigrating the head start you had on the rest of us. That's what Feo does—assumes everyone was privately tutored and force-fed knowledge from infancy, because *he* was."

Dan didn't set the man straight. Maybe the misconception that he was on equal terms with Feo would help the team and the N'lacs.

He gazed into the alien forest, imagining N'lac colonists

154

clearing land and planting, establishing a settlement they'd later have to abandon to the elements. They had believed this was their first step into space, the first of many. Other humanoid races had made similar confident beginnings in their starward expansion. But for the N'lacs, everything had ended here. The Evil Old Ones had been waiting in the wings, and the N'lacs were virtually wiped out.

As mankind, the Whimeds, and the Vahnajes might be someday?

Shivering, Dan turned away from the window. Ever since Chen's death and the nightmares that followed, he couldn't get rid of these disturbing speculations. They were an itch impossible to scratch.

The road ended at Assembly Complex, a cluster of one-story multiple housing units circling a main hall. The car carrying the Saunders slowed, taking the caravan on a leisurely tour. Dan was reminded of a Terran core world's institutional think tanks. There were well-engineered lanes, fancy stonework facing on the buildings, and neat beds of flowering shrubs. A park was full of scooters and minibuses, in case guests wanted a run back to town. Elaborate arcades and skyways connected sleeping units with the central structure, and a bigger passage linked the entire Complex with a man-made hill to the south—the Saunders' fantastic, enclosed dig site.

"They've added a lot since we were here in '50," Joe said.

"Yes." Praedar's stare bored holes through that covered dig.

"Must be nice," Kat muttered. "Peel off some petty cash and use cheap local labor to beef up the facilities and impress one's colleagues." Snickers on every side seconded her assessment of how the Saunders had created this amazing sub-Settlement.

"Convenient, eh?" a scientist named Jarrett said. His comment dripped contempt.

Getz snapped. "You're jealous. You'd jump at a chance to have such conveniences on *your* dig."

Jarrett smirked. "As a matter of fact, I wouldn't. You seem to have forgotten the prime tenet of field xenoarch: Nothing worth finding is easily dug."

Reddening, Getz said, "No rule says we have to grub like peasants . . ."

Others diverted the conversation before it got out of hand.

Getz was still glowering at Jarrett when they reached the parking area.

Apparently, during the trip, the Saunders had decided to humor Praedar as they would a short-tempered eccentric. They were ready when his team alighted from their bus. Hope said sweetly, "No doubt you'll want to set up your exhibits before you go to your rooms. Very sensible. Get the tiresome necessities out of the way before you relax at tonight's opening ceremony . . ."

"Quite right," Feo chimed in, snapping his fingers. "Rehan! Your people are to assist Dr. Juxury's expedition. His materials are *very* valuable. Priceless! Nothing must be damaged, or you will answer to me personally. Understood?" Rehan made a low obeisance, eager to fulfill his boss's command. Praedar started to protest. Feo refused to hear. "We won't take no for an answer, Juxury, and that's final."

Hope grabbed hands, saying "We have *so* much to do. We'll see you this evening . . ."

Feo patted Dan's shoulder. "Wonderful that you're here, my boy. Adds a real touch of family to the occasion . . ."

Without giving anyone a chance to reply, the Saunders rushed away, a gaggle of staffers at their heels.

Rehan bowed again, this time to Praedar, awaiting orders.

It took a lot of persuasion to convince Praedar to accept the flunkeys' help. But it was a good thing the team had those extra hands before they were finished unloading and carrying exhibit materials into the main hall. All of the new arrivals had boosted their compensation meds several times during the exhausting process. One by one, Praedar's scientist friends on the welcoming committee made their excuses and left to attend to their own business. Manufacturers' booths and other expeditions' exhibits were shuttered in the darkened display section by the time the T-W 593 team had everything set up. Their late arrival made for an overrushed schedule; and they had little time in which to recuperate, because the Assembly was due to begin very soon.

Rehan showed them to their reserved quarters. Guest units were generally assigned on species lines. One wing of one building, however, housed multispecies groups. There were only two of those, that headed by Karl Imhoff, and Praedar's.

The staffers made pests of themselves, demonstrating the luxurious accommodations, bowing, scraping, and offering to help the team unpack. They were got rid of with great difficulty.

156

Feo had spared no expense. His rivals had a huge suite, with roomlets to house all fifteen team members who were supposed to attend. There were fully stocked food and drink dispensers and privacy eating cubicles for Vahnajes and huddle circles for Whimeds. Praedar peered around the sprawling array and summed it up succinctly: "Wasteful."

"We could operate our dig for months on what the Saunders spent furnishing just this one suite," Joe agreed.

"My cousin's proving how generous he can afford to be," Dan said.

"Intimidating us, you mean," Kat exclaimed.

"Well, it won't work," Getz said. "And you can tell your kinsman that for me, McKelvey." He tossed his luggage into one of the roomlets and went on. "*None* of it will work. Not the Saunders' posturing or Jarrett and his cracks. Oh, I know what he's up to, him and his bunch of young turks. I'll rip them to shreds!"

"Maybe," Kat said, sotto voce. In a normal tone, she added, "We won't even put in an appearance if we don't hurry." She tapped a chronometer. "About one-half local hour to get cleaned, dressed, and back over to the main hall."

They ran through unpacking, sonic showering, and selecting what they'd wear to the evening session. Dan was grateful for the current fad of dressing down; it made his best clothes fit right in with the prevailing styles here. He boosted his meds again, and, only slightly late, he and the rest joined the stream of beings heading across the skywalks.

Feo's architects had designed the passageways to protect while providing an evocative view of their employer's world. Late-afternoon rainfall freshened the nearby alien woodlands, scenting the breeze. Cries of native fauna echoed. T-S 311's blue-white star rested on the ocean horizon, reflecting on whitecaps. The sticky-sweet odor of the flower beds wafted through the skywalk like a heavy perfume. Dan hoped his kinsman was overdoing it. So much emphasis on Saunder wealth might well backfire, making less affluent scientists jealous. That hostility could benefit Praedar.

The main building contained meeting rooms, auditorium, exhibit area, and registration. A small army of Saunder student diggers manned the registry comps, playing junior hosts and hostesses. They were efficient, greeting attendees, passing out ident

157

packets, and recording names and images. Everything flowed smoothly.

Until Dan reached the desk . . .

Procedures suddenly slowed to a crawl. Scientists and news hounds, watching, murmured uneasily. Snatches of their conversation hung in the oxygen-heavy air. "McKelvey . . ." "Saunder's kinsman . . ." "Trying to insult Juxury's expedition . . . ?" "Unheard of . . ." "Rude . . ."

Kat demanded action from the students on duty. "What's the problem? Surely not a shortage of membership packets. We're preregistered for fifteen beings, and Praedar gave you Dan's data when we arrived . . ."

Praedar's mesmerizing stare was in high gear. The registrars squirmed as the alien said, "Our expedition's xenomechanician is an essential participant."

Dan bit back a laugh. Xenomechanician? That was a good one! One of Feo's students stammered that she had no category listing for that specialty. Dan put on his best Saunder-McKelvey princeling tone. "It's a brand-new designation. And perhaps you're looking for my name under the wrong alphabetical division. Try McKelvey instead of Saunder-McKelvey. That's Daniel Morgan McKelvey."

Seething, Kat said, "Hurry up! I'll vouch for him. Didn't the Saunders say you were to render us every assistance?"

"Found it!" a registrar exclaimed in relief. "Sorry for the delay. Comp troubles."

Praedar's smile was frightening. He murmured a barely civil thanks. Feo's students turned to process the next beings in line with indecent haste, plainly glad to be done with Daniel Morgan McKelvey.

Dan looked through the hard-won packet. It contained a thick program book, professional journal excerpts, manufacturers' promos, and bio-files of the attendees. The materials were printed in five humanoid languages—no Ulisorians were members of the United Species Scientific Conference Society—and several important dialects. No one could complain that his or her race was being slighted. The nature of the contents testified to the attendees' literacy.

Kat was still grumbling about the registrars' ineptitude. "Totally uncalled for. What did Feo and Hope think they were doing with that little stunt?" She fussed with Dan's badge, affixing it to his breast pocket.

"No harm done," he said. "I can remember, though, when you tried not to vouch for me."

She sniffed and made a wry face. "Familiarity can breed more than contempt, given enough time." Kat led him to a holo-mode portrait gallery and called up entries. The display offered a full roster of Assembly guests. Transbuttons converted voice-over intros to any language the viewer selected. Lifelike tri-dis formed and disappeared smoothly. The first image was that of a white-haired older Terran male.

"Imhoff, Karl. Doctor of Xenoetymology, Todd Saunder Science Foundation. Life Master, Regan Saunder-Griffith Remote Research Institute. Past President of the Fellowship of . . ."

Kat spoke under the servo voice. "Karl's an old friend of Praedar's and Chen's."

"He heads up the one other multispecies dig here, doesn't he?"

"Correct. Mixed expeditions are rare, too rare," Kat said. "Single species digs have a limited capability of interpreting xeno cultures, as the Saunders' dig amply proves."

A second holo took shape. "Tawnay of Hoyoo, Matriarch of the Combined Exalted Xenoexploration Division Investigating Ruins on Paab . . ."

Armilly's fur-kinship aunt. Dan had met her briefly at the shuttleport. She was a grim-visaged procyonid twice Armilly's size and five times as loud. He didn't blame his expedition's furry young scientist for giving her a wide berth.

The next image was that of a regally imposing Whimed male. "Anelen. Director, Terran-Whimed Xenoethnic Council, Chairman of the Academy of Whimed Xenoarchaeological Endeavor, Founder of . . ."

"One of Praedar's sponsors," Dan murmured, recalling what he'd learned in T-W 593's vid library.

Kat nodded, looking solemn. "He's one we have to sell to renew our dig license. And Anelen also has control of grant dispersals for Praedar's project. His support is crucial. As if we don't have enough problems, Feo and Hope have been cozying up to Anelen shamelessly the past few years. They flatter him in their articles, do favors for his people, you name it. They don't need his grants or licenses. They're simply trying to undercut us.

The one consolation is that Anelen doesn't like most Terrans."
She glanced at Dan and added, "But he may be impressed by
you. That's what we've lacked—a Saunder-McKelvey on *our*
team." Dan scowled, no more convinced that was a scoring point
than he had been earlier.

Another holo showed a burly Terran wearing the badges of
C.S.P. Administration Central.

"Jon Eckard," Dan said, before the voice-over did. "He's your
other major licenser."

Kat muted the gallery's intro. "Yes, a fairly generous guy. But
he's been under pressure lately from would-be colony developers.
That worries us."

"It should," Dan said. He studied Eckard's portrait. "I think
I've met him, but I'm not sure where."

"Maybe that'll be useful. I hope it was an amicable encounter." Kat sighed. "I wish we didn't have to go through these
dances with licensing boards and grant dispensers . . ."

"That's the way the sector functions," Dan said, sympathiz-
ing. "We all have to dance for somebody. For me, it's been dispatchers." He noted the miniaturized attendee lineup and IDs.
"Looks like more than half these people are sponsors, manufacturers' reps, or reporters."

"Typical," Kat acknowledged. "It's a bigger turnout than most
remote-world Assemblies attract. All four of the science vid-pubs
sent reporters. And there are more sales reps than I anticipated,
too. I suppose it's because Feo and Hope are hosting the show.
They *are* a draw."

"So few scientists, in comparison," Dan commented, still
eyeing the board.

"And not all of those are diggers, not by a long-handled
shovel. Many are labbers. They stay safe on their institutes'
home worlds and analyze and publish data shipped in by field
teams." Kat didn't hide her disdain. "Catch any of them taking
the risks we do."

Risks! Some of them unexpected and unavoidable. He knew
she was thinking of Chen's tragic death. Dan tried to get her mind
off that. "I guess I assumed there'd be a bigger crowd."

Kat shook her head. "We're a tiny discipline. The smart students opt for straight archaeology and dig on their origin planets.
We have to hunt all over the sectors for sites of probable unknown cultures. Then we wade through light-years of red tape to

get the permits and funding. The competition is fierce for too few promising sites . . . "

"Like T-W 593 and T-S 311."

"By unwritten tradition, T-S 311 ought to be an extension of Praedar's dig," Kat said, her expression angry. "Money can do amazing things. Feo just 'happened' to acquire a special license permitting his operation here—*after* Praedar had already established the existence of a xenocivilization in this region, years earlier. It's not fair! And look at the way some attendees bootlick Feo and Hope. The Saunders manage a science foundation, handing out grants to deserving candidates. That sort of thing makes beggars out of people I once thought were honest independents."

Taking a deep breath, she cued the holos again, creating and destroying facsimiles: Quas-Jin, a Vahnaj scientist attached to the New Earth Renaissance Projects; Svejar, a Whimed of some fame; Jarrett, an up-and-coming effigy specialist, one of Getz's rivals; York, an expedition leader who criticized Praedar's theories. Retur of Whimed; and a dozen or so more.

Dan watched in silence awhile, then said, "They're giants. I'll sound like a cretin alongside them."

"You have something they don't."

"Being a Saunder-McKelvey? That and a credit might get me a cup of caffa on a backward Settlement. I'd trade the name for some solid scientific credentials," Dan admitted.

"You already have them, so stop whining," Kat scolded. "You're our xenomechanician. That's not a joke. You *do* have a specialized background in a field none of those giants is familiar with. And despite your complaints that you lack an education, you do pretty damned well. That shipboard library of yours proves you're no fool, so it's logical Praedar—and I—expect you to be more than a mere handsome face and famous name." She chopped her hand through the holo beams, ending the show, and stomped out of the gallery.

Dan easily overtook her. "Why didn't you tell me this sooner, charmer?" The brunette peered up at him quizzically as he said, "So you think I'm handsome, huh? And here I thought Sheila was the only woman on the dig who appreciated my sterling qualities." Kat broke into giggles, then clapped her hands over her mouth until she regained her poise. Her eyes twinkled mischievously as they entered the main hall side by side.

The building's central section was designed for quick alteration that could create a number of individual lecture rooms. Tonight the walls had been raised and stored in the high ceiling. A crowd milled around in the resulting staging area. Scientists, media reps, and salespeople collected on dozens of refreshment islands, exchanging greetings with old acquaintances and introducing themselves to new ones. Species tended to congregate with their own kind, though there was some cross-socializing. Transbuttons and the medias' lens pendants were everywhere. Two currents worked against each other. One, a chauvinistic, separatist influence, gathered like minds and races. The second pushed them together, to debate and learn. To Dan, the philosophy of xenoarch ought to make all these beings willing to encounter fresh ideas and contact other species. But that countering current was powerful, raising the tension level considerably.

Many news hounds gravitated toward the Assembly's two multispecies groups, Imhoff's and Praedar's. Their eclectic nature made them sure-fire visual hits. Praedar, in particular, came in for a lot of attention. He fielded questions smoothly, switching languages and tone to suit the interviewer. Dan drew his share of questions, too. Joe and Kat also balanced shop talk with mini-interviews, as did Ruieb-An with Vahnaj "information seekers." Getz played the game with his team for a time, then wandered off and got into a lengthy, heated discussion with Jarrett and his fellow effigy specialists.

The scene was a blend of sight, scent, and sound, wild varieties of clothing and exotic cosmetics, clashes of food, drink, and alien body odors, and muted music of all types. A babble of voices argued with a constant hum of trans devices.

". . . haven't adequately considered K versus R reproductive strategies, and they'd better not publish till they do . . ."

". . . she selected her materials in eroded tuffs. Did you ever hear such idiocy?"

". . . interesting to see if a Lannon can handle that subject calmly . . ."

". . . sourcing wasn't adequate for conclusions, and if he goes public now he'll wind up . . ."

". . . really think there *is* a universality in humanoid facial responses? Wouldn't have imagined it's quantifiable . . ."

Dan wanted to listen to a dozen conversations at once. He couldn't. News hounds continued to corner him, asking the same things, generally innocuous stuff. It seemed odd that they all landed on the same points.

"That's right. I'm Morgan McKelvey's grandson on the Jutta Lefferts bloodline. Feo? He's my third cousin . . ."

And around him, the fascinating give and take went on.

". . . Kaatje, overlook the need for simplicity. Harte's laws of xenosocio extrapolation explicitly state . . ."

". . . understand Quas-Jin is going to report on the latest work at Saunderhome and Varenka Saunder's efforts to clone Jael Saunder. Ought to be . . ."

". . . iconoclast, or so Ruieb-An's viewed by mainstream Vahnaj science. True, Dr. Juxury?"

That thrust came from a particularly persistent pop-sci news hound. Praedar checked to be sure Ruieb was preoccupied with fellow Vahnajes before he replied. "The most successful Vahnaj innovators have always been those you term iconoclasts. They expanded the horizons of antiquarian research to the benefit of every species' knowledge." Diplomatically he glanced at Dan.

The Terran caught the cue expertly. "Quite so. One of Ruieb-An's predecessors in his exploration society sent out the original Vahnaj star probes, centuries ago. If he hadn't, my ancestor, Todd Saunder, might never have made contact with an extraterrestrial civilization. And we humans would still be puttering around our own little stellar backyard. It puts a humbling light on our alleged importance in the cosmic picture, doesn't it?" The reporter looked uncomfortable, and Dan went on. "Dr. Juxury often reminds us that we must keep our focus on the larger scene. That's what xenoarch is all about—relating to the past and selecting the right data so that it all makes sense."

Flustered, the news hound who'd posed that question backed away, mumbling. Other reporters snickered. As they did one of their group, a bright-eyed woman, darted forward speaking to Dan. "Rei Ito, Pan Terran S-ME News. I'm sure you've seen my big sister on our net's scandal channel. She's practically part of your family . . ."

He was acutely aware of the scrutiny of her lens pendant. "Uh . . . yes. My sister mentioned that Miwa is engaged to Cam Saunder."

Ito's competitors glared, resenting her trading on her tenuous link with the famous dynasty. She ignored them, boring in on Dan. "I hope that makes us a bit closer. Perhaps you could clarify

163

a few bio items for me? I'm informed that you are Dr. Juxury's xenomechanician. What is that? Could you elaborate? Where does one train for it?"

For a second, panic knotted Dan's gut. He'd been afraid of this. Then, calling on resources he didn't know he had, he resumed his Saunder-McKelvey princeling stance. "Oh, like most of us—our family, I mean—I was tutored. As for being a xenomech, I've always been interested in inventions, power systems, ways to harness energy. You know the sort of thing. I guess I inherited Ward Saunder's knack, and maybe just a little from Morgan McKelvey."

The magic names. Alien and Terran listeners were awed. There was a cynical glint in Ito's eyes, but to Dan's relief, she didn't press him. Was she restraining her reporter's killer instinct for the sake of about-to-be family ties? Did she know his background and that his tutoring had ended when he was twelve? Ito didn't say. It was as if her queries had been a stunt to call attention to herself, not Dan's failings.

Breathing easier, he said, "When Dr. Juxury offered me the chance to analyze certain alien devices he'd found on T-W 593, well, I couldn't turn him down."

"But how did you happen to be on that planet?" someone demanded.

Ito drowned him out and elbowed him aside. "That's very informative, Dan. Thank you! I'm sure we'll be hearing great things later in the Assembly from you and Dr. Juxury and your colleagues . . ."

He seized the opening gratefully. "Oh, yes. Dr. Juxury's made some amazing breakthroughs . . ."

Media focus swung back to Praedar. Behind the Whimed's back Joe winked at Dan and Kat gave him a thumb-and-forefinger 'okay.' Praedar handled the demands for details with aplomb and a relaxed crest, very much in control. He offered plenty of quotable copy to mollify the news hounds. His linguistic skills and quick adaptability to other species' customs, together with his height and presence, added up to a striking charisma. Praedar would have made a felinoid version of a top Saunder-McKelvey politician or actor.

He wasn't the only expert at the cult of personality. A Rigotian scientist held a crowd, and so did Armilly's aunt. Several other xenoarch "stars" commanded large audiences, as well. The less glib, less confident, and less accomplished circled them in outer orbit, like skimmer sleds around major space stations.

Dan got only brief glimpses of Anelen and Jon Eckard, the team's all-important sponsors. Anelen tended to stick with other Whimeds. He was hawk-faced and a lot more daunting in person than in his holo-mode. Eckard was touching base with a number of people, glad handling, chatting, never staying long in one spot. Dan's sole exchange with him was of the 'Hello, glad to see you, good-bye' variety.

Nearly all of the Assembly's registered attendees were present by now. Lighting dimmed, then brightened directly above a portable dais in the center of the auditorium. Feo and Hope Saunder stood on the platform, surrounded by flunkeys and aides, Greg Tavares among them. The dais revolved slowly, allowing the Saunders to face in turn every part of the large room. Translation devices were busy. Life-size monitors projected the Assembly hosts' images on the walls, so that no one could possibly miss their opening speeches.

Hope punctuated her welcome with smiling pauses. "As humanity has reached out into space, extending the hand of friendship to our galactic neighbors, so we greet you, our fellow searchers of the past. We are here to serve, to make this, the Twelfth Xenoarchaeological Assembly, the best ever. It is in the proud tradition of our family and of our species. Let us all be, for these few days, a larger family, one united not by blood and race, but by unity of purpose . . .

Her delivery was excellent, Dan conceded, not as persuasive as Praedar's, but not bad. It was what he would have expected from Hope Belvedere Saunder. Her breeding and background were almost as royal as Feo's, though her personal fortune was much smaller.

When she finished, Feo took over, giving their guests more of the same, and at too great a length. He wasn't an orator. Some highly paid voice coach had taught him to project and develop all the right phrasing. However, Feo lacked the essential fire that held his listeners and he definitely didn't know when to quit. Several times Hope muttered wifely advice, plainly telling him to wrap it up. Either he didn't hear her or was too pleased with the sound of his voice to yield the floor.

The audience fidgeted. Some aliens switched channels on their transbuttons, effectively tuning Feo out. Terrans whispered, carrying on conversations even though their host wasn't through speaking.

At last, Feo noticed what was happening and hastily concluded, ". . . And so, my dear friends and colleagues, we shall conduct our business here in the true amity of science. Amity! And a sincere reverence for knowledge. I thank you!"

Greg Tavares led the applause. Saunder staffers tried to make up for a lack of enthusiasm in some parts of the room.

Dan was gratified by what he'd witnessed. Feo's money gave him clout, but it couldn't buy him absolute, fawning adoration, at least not in this arena!

The Saunders stepped off the dais and it swirled away into storage. With Tavares at their tails, followed by flunkeys and reporters, Feo and Hope began to tour the refreshment islands and press the flesh with their guests. They stopped frequently, posing for the news hounds. The whole thing smacked of a media session.

But as the pair approached Praedar's team, their tactics changed. The flunkeys fanned out, surrounding their bosses and the Whimed's party, forming a living barricade. Other scientists and the media were shut outside that circle. The reporters grumbled loudly. Rei Ito seemed less upset than the rest. She leaned forward and peered within the island. Dan saw that Ito's lens pendant was top quality. She had it set on peak resolution and supersnoop. The Saunders thought they had shut out unwanted observers, but Ito could capture every nuance of their expressions and every faint comment for later playback.

"Juxury!" Feo said with enthusiasm. "I wanted to tell you in private how pleased I am that you're here. I trust your rooms are satisfactory? And your specimens and exhibits? All installed properly? No damages?"

Praedar nodded curtly, his unblinking stare raking the Saunders and Tavares. "Sufficient. The rooms are excessive."

"Nothing but the best," Feo said. "Enjoy it! We want you to enjoy a few luxuries while you're our guests."

Hope added, "Indeed! As Bill Getz is fond of saying, it's not necessary for scientists to suffer in order to achieve their goals."

"Not everyone agrees with that," Kat said, her eyes narrowed.

Feo shooed away imaginary gnats. "This world, this Assembly complex will be a haven for thought. Teams like yours are forced to operate in such appalling conditions. Have you never

166

considered that working under that sort of pressure may affect your selectivity? It's bound to. Enervating climate, outdated equipment, and even death, as . . ." His wife jammed an elbow hard into his side and Feo coughed, startled. But he did take the hint and dropped what he'd obviously been about to say about Chen. "It's understandable how primitive settings would distort data and create unfounded doubts. One wants to blame someone for the misfortunes. Quite natural. But to imply, as you have, my friend, that other expeditions might stoop to sabotage . . . really!"

"Explanations?" Praedar said flatly. "Alternate answers?"

Hope stiffened. "You . . . you actually believe . . . ?"

Kat cut in, "Who would have anything to gain by delaying our work or preventing our attending this conference? And so *much* to gain! It does look questionable, and not only to us." She glanced at the media, and for the first time the Saunders became aware of Ito's merciless scrutiny, in particular.

"That's ridiculous," Feo protested. "We hadn't heard a thing about this . . . what was it? . . . missing machinery? Or this business of transport difficulties . . ."

"Did you not?" Praedar stared at Tavares, and the redhead took an involuntary step backward. Dan suppressed a grin. The Whimed went on in a deceptively soft manner. "Do you speak for all your staff, Feo?"

The Saunders regarded their protégé. The assessment took mere seconds. Hope said, "We assure you that if there is any basis whatsoever to your suspicions, the matter will be tended to."

Tavares, recovering, parroted his superiors. "That's right! We'll prove we had nothing to do with this so-called sabotage!"

Again, more surreptitiously, the Saunders traded looks.

Dan almost pitied Tavares. But the blacklist—and near certain knowledge of what had put him there—tempered his sympathy. He saw the redhead with clear-eyed detachment.

You fool! They're going to jettison you at the first sign that what you did might rub off on them. Some Saunder-McKelveys are dog-loyal to their people. I think you've linked up with the other kind. It won't matter to Feo and Hope how much you've helped them or how much prestige your published works have brought to their dig. If they need a scapegoat, they'll dump you so fast you'll feel you're in FTL without a spaceship.

Too bad for Tavares. Dan suspected the man didn't deserve all

167

the blame. He might simply have been guilty of being overeager to please. Perhaps he'd overheard the Saunders expressing the equivalent of "Will no one rid us of this troublesome Dr. Juxury?" They'd planted the seed, let their protégé take the risks, and kept their own hands clean. Tavares thought he was carrying out their wishes and that they'd back him if he got caught with his hands in the cookie jar.

Fat chance!

Tavares didn't grasp the subtle shift in the situation. He continued to fawn on his mentors, supporting their every word.

While Hope chatted with Praedar's team and Tavares, Feo suddenly threw an arm over Dan's shoulder and steered the younger man a few paces away from the others. Lowering his voice, Feo said, "I need to speak to you alone. No, please. Hear me out. You owe me that much, for family's sake." After a hesitation, Dan nodded grudgingly. "Good! Hope and I wish you'd let us know earlier that you were interested in xenoarchaeology. We could help you tremendously, Danny. It's not too late. You're more than welcome here. Why don't you join our team? Hmm?"

"Anticipating an opening on your staff in the near future?"

Feo frowned at that oblique reference to Tavares. "You're *family*. You belong with us. We Saunder-McKelveys must stick together, as we always have. Hmm? Hmm? We're winners. And I hate to see you harnessed with a failure like Juxury." He shut off Dan's annoyed protests with a silencing upheld hand. "Not to take anything away from him. Juxury's a fine scientist. But his selectivity? Woefully flawed, I fear. His sentimental attachment to those subhumanoids further complicates the problem. One can't fault him for his idealism, even if it *does* affect his judgment. Sooner or later—maybe at this conference—his theories will come crashing down in ruins. And the collapse is likely to bury his hard-working junior colleagues, as well. A pity. Don't let yourself be trapped in that debacle, Danny."

"History may record a different outcome on whose theories are flawed," Dan said with heat.

His cousin's fingers dug painfully into his arm. "Softly!" Feo smiled at curious onlookers, then spoke in Dan's ear. "This is just between you and me, my boy. No need to share our family discussions with that mob." He was patiently solicitous. "Of course you feel obligated to defend Juxury. He *is* a mesmerizer. But be practical. Think! Hope and I hate to see you on the enemy team,

168

so to phrase it. After all, we could do so much for you that he can't . . ." Feo continued to grip Dan's arm, veiled menace in his eyes.

Alarms jangled along Dan's nerve endings. Feo had massive resources. He could dig up kilotons of ammo against a rival—or against a stubborn young relative. How much did Saunder know? And how much was he willing to reveal to the media if Dan refused to cooperate? Dan's lack of a degree? The faked ownership arrangement of the starhopper? The nastier members of the Saunder-McKelvey clan were quite capable of figuratively cutting a kinsman's throat, if they wanted to.

A buttery grin creased Feo's homely face. "You needn't make up your mind this very moment, Danny. I merely wanted to spell things out for you. Sleep on my offer. Consider it. Won't you?"

Decades of resentment overcame prudence. Dan blurted, "I see. Charity, huh? For the poor cousin. Funny. You could have done the same for my father, when he needed help bad. Instead, you and Aunt Varenka and the other family snobs turned your backs and let him drown."

Feo's expression was ruefully tolerant. "Is that what he told you? Is that what Reid honestly believes? How sad! Myth making on a personal scale. I've dealt with cultural versions of the same phenomenon—actual events blurring and being reversed to fit the desperate emotional needs of a people. Or of a person." The scientist's sorrow seemed genuine. He released Dan's arm and pressed the younger man's shoulder gently. "Reid never asked me for money, Danny. Never. Not any of us. We urged him to take a loan. Again and again. We wanted to help. Spirit of Humanity, he's a McKelvey. How could we *not* want to help a kinsman? But he was adamant. Turned all of us down. No favors, he said. He'd make it on his own, somehow. And you saw where that got him, you and him and your lovely mother. It sounds as if he's convinced himself—and you—that the sole cause of his bankruptcy was our rejection of him. He probably *has* to think that way, to save his sanity and pride."

Dan was stunned. He clenched his jaw, afraid of saying anything and giving Feo yet another weapon to hit him with.

"So sad! In a way, Reid's a practitioner of faulty selectivity. He's blinded himself to the facts, just as Juxury has. You were only a child when your father formed those warped ideas of reality, my boy. You had no control over your destiny. Now you do.

169

Don't make the same mistake Reid did. Remember what I've said. Hope and I would welcome you with open arms."

With that, he stepped back into the main conversational circle, picking up the thread there smoothly. It took Dan much longer to pull himself together enough to imitate his cousin's action. He drifted to the fringe of the group, listening, contributing nothing, his brain still reeling from Feo's assault.

Finally the Saunders said their good-byes and moved on to another expedition's island. Their flunkeys parted the reporters and Feo and Hope swept away. After they and their entourage had left, Dan's teammates regarded him wonderingly. But none of them pried.

Someone else was studying him, too. Rei Ito, the news hound from Pan Terran S-ME Net. She lingered behind the army of media following the Saunders. Her pert, Oriental features were unreadable. Ito touched her capture-all pendant, a tacit reminder that she'd been witness to everything he and Feo had said. A hint of a smile pulled at her mouth. Then Ito wheeled and vanished into the milling crowd.

CHAPTER ELEVEN
ᴑᴑᴑᴑᴑᴑᴑᴑᴑ

Factions

Dan parked the scooter, jumped from its protective bubble, and ran toward his assigned housing unit. Predawn rain drenched him before he reached the lobby. He stood inside the door, stripping off his sodden poncho. Through the window wall he saw a steady stream of Whimeds and Lannon crossing the skywalks. Those races had been in session since last night's opening ceremony. Now lights were coming on in other species' quarters as *they* woke and prepared for the first full day of Assembly.

After tossing the poncho in a recycler, Dan caught a people lifter to the second level. Earlier risers were congregating in the corridors. Slugabeds' rooms' info panels bore "Do Not Disturb" notices. The atmosphere was an odd mixture of think-tank dorm and a prosperous Settlement's best public inn.

Dan tiptoed into his expedition's dimly lit suite. Praedar, no doubt, was still caucusing with his fellow Whimeds. Ruieb-An's roomlet and those of Joe and Getz were shut; apparently they were sacking in. Kat, however, was awake. She was sitting in the window alcove. Dan perched beside her and said, "Good morning. Sort of. Want a weather report?"

She snuggled deeper into her robe. "Not necessary. Praedar, Joe, and I visited here a few years ago. I know what the climate is like." Kat rested her forehead on the glass and traced a raindrop's track with her fingers. "These downpours seem as extravagantly wasteful to me as this posh suite. But that's because I was raised on Mars. Sheila says that's why I don't get fed up working in T-W 593's desert environment."

"Does she?" Dan asked.

"Not really. Sheila simply enjoys griping." Kat regarded him curiously. "Where have you been?"

"At the Port. Checking the ship. She's okay, so far."

"You're still worried about repossession?"

"Damned right." Dan heaved a sigh. "All I can do is lock her, check her frequently, and keep my fingers crossed." He yawned and stretched, then added, "We might get help from an unexpected source." Kat raised an inquiring eyebrow, waiting impatiently. "The Port manager beat around the circle awhile and finally got to the point. He wanted to know if I'm related to the Fleet's 'Iron Fist.' What a joke! Adam hates that title the media hung on him."

"Well?" Kat wiggled. "What did you tell him?"

"The truth. No reason not to. The manager definitely was impressed. If push comes to bash, he may back me against a repossess artist—or against Feo's dirty-tricks boy. That's ironic. I doubt Adam would lean on Port authorities if they gave me trouble. But the manager thinks he would," Dan said with a grin. "That shuttle strip boss sure doesn't want any Fleet Inspectors coming here and nitpicking his logs and procedures and fining him."

He yawned again, more widely. "I also had a gab with a couple of pilots while I was there. It started out as shop talk. Then they kicked a few rocks at the Assembly. The usual stuff. Our science is a waste of time. Xenoarch doesn't put food on settlers' tables and so forth. It's not real work. And I ended up defending us. The pilots backed off. They looked at me as if I'd been talking to them under false pretenses. I . . . I forgot to act like an indie hauler," Dan said, mildly surprised.

Kat smiled. "You dropped your mask." He glanced at her warily as she went on. "When I first met you, you deliberately

172

downplayed your intellectual capacity. I think you even fooled yourself, to a degree. Now you're beginning to let your deeper strata show." She added with exasperation, "What are you afraid of? You're one of the quickest, most adaptive people I know. There's nothing wrong with being a damned fine xenomechanician and an innovative novice scientist."

"Protective coloration, Chen called it, according to Praedar." Dan shrugged, feeling embarrassed. "I've spent almost twenty years on the lower ranks of the Terran status ladder. I took plenty of flak down there, too, because of my name, even though I tried hard to fit in and be just an ordinary spacer. But stuff I learned when I was younger—the Saunder-McKelvey song and dance, for one—sticks with me. I guess it comes out, under the right circumstances."

"Genetics," Kat suggested. "You got a huge dose of your ancestors' genes, as well as a polishing by your parents."

He chuckled sourly. "Great. Why couldn't part of it have been a fortune?"

For a minute, the brunette was silent. Then she said, "Something's been eating you since last night's ceremony, hasn't it? If it isn't too personal, what did Feo say to you?" Dan, a bit reluctantly, described the conversation. Kat gasped in anger. "He was lying! It's another of his tricks!"

"Maybe. Maybe not. My dad *is* too proud for his own good. He and Feo could both be telling the truth, the way they remember it," Dan admitted.

"You're torturing yourself needlessly."

"Am I? This really yanked the rug out from under me. Which version of the facts is the right one? Or are they mutually skewed, with some truth on each side? Is it all a matter of interpretation?" Dan scratched his blond mop. "I keep thinking about Praedar's comment on the Old Ones—that from their point of view, maybe what they did to the N'lacs wasn't evil. It's tough, getting inside someone else's head . . ."

"Yes." The Terrans started. Praedar stood an arm's length away from them. Neither had heard him return to the room. "You accurately summarize the essence of xenoarchaeology and of truth seeking."

Following the logic, Dan nodded. "We have to be careful when speculating on another race's motivations. Huh! I can't even guarantee that members of my own family aren't tailoring facts to suit their memories and egos. It's arrogant to assume I'd be absolutely correct in pegging a nonhuman's reasoning."

"Indeed. Yet our work demands assumptions." The felinoid's crest bristled, revealing his irritation. "But it is divisive to use assumptions to attack colleagues who offer data interpretation varying from one's own." He held out an object for the Terrans to examine.

It was a stick-on badge. Manufacturers had passed out a number of those at the opening ceremony—sticky buttons, puffing their products. This button had obviously been made in a hurry on an expedition's specimen-tagger. Four words jumped at the reader: SAUNDER SPELLS SUPERIOR SELECTIVITY!

"So much for the 'Amity of Science' theme!" Kat exclaimed.

"So counterattack," Dan said. "Make up a slogan to balance the scales."

"Such as?"

He mulled the possibilities. "How about 'SAUNDER SPELLS SPURIOUS SELECTIVITY'? Or is that too low?"

"Not for me," another Terran voice cut in. Joe Hughes leaned against the door jamb of his roomlet and rubbed sleep from his eyes. "It's exactly what the Saunders and their pushy staffers deserve," he said.

Praedar turned the offending button over in his big palm. "As you say, a counterattack. Appropriate. Is it possible?"

"Sure," Dan said. "We've got a tagger."

"And a friend on Imhoff's team can get me a supply of badge blanks," Joe volunteered. "Let's get to work!"

Dan participated with enthusiasm, hoping the game would occupy his mind and help him forget that bombshell Feo had dropped on him. It was a tight race to finish the counterattack ammunition before the day's sessions began. Within minutes after the T-W 593 team arrived in the main building, they'd passed out their entire supply. Not every attendee who took one of the badges was an ardent supporter of Praedar's expedition. But all of them resented the 'SAUNDER SPELLS SUPERIOR SELECTIVITY!' buttons the other side was sporting. The tactic had backfired. Numbers were now almost equal in these badge wars. Stalemate.

The contest had been an amusing diversion. However, it was time for far more serious business—the Assembly.

Ramdas of Earth, a dean of Terran xenoarchaeology, gave a keynote address. Lectures and presentations followed. Vid monitors and a bottomless supply of cheap translation devices made it possible for guests to look at the exhibit halls and manufacturers' displays and still keep abreast of everything going on in the meeting rooms. But many attendees, including reporters, were eager to see presenters in the flesh. They queued up before each session and jammed the program items.

There was considerable cautious circling. Dan had seen hundreds of similar sizing-up routines on dozens of worlds. Terrans assessed each other. They and aliens studied their opposites. The questions didn't vary much. What was the other being *really* like? What did he *really* want? Was the translator device working as an intermediary, rendering words and phrases accurately, with all the nuances? Caution was a tool for survival in a potentially hostile universe or at a scientific conference.

Because the Assembly was hosted by Terrans and attendance was predominantly Terran, the main agenda matched their bio clocks—three hours of morning sessions, a midday break, and three more afternoon sessions. T-S 311's hours were shorter than Earth norm, but not so much that adjustment was a problem. Diurnally oriented Vahnajes and the marsupial Rigotians liked the schedule. Nocturnally oriented, polyphasic Whimeds and Lannons added night programs for their tastes, a secondary session track within the main one.

"The Amity of Science" was the theme, but chauvinism was running the show: *inter*species chauvinism and *intra*species chauvinism; clashes between Whimeds and Vahnajes, Rigotians and Lannon; and hostilities between Ruieb's "Progressive Research" faction and lutrinoid "Conservative Antiquarians." Loyalists of one institution of higher learning bickered with those of another. Jealousy flourished between conflicting attitudes toward digging, analyzing, and interpreting—"lumpers" versus "splitters."

The friction separating the Saunder group from the T-W 593 expedition was complicated by the multispecies makeup of Praedar's team. The visiting xenoarchs were an embodiment of the Assembly's motto. They pleased the media. They could make solid contact with three of the conference's five racial representations. And Praedar's team now had a Saunder-McKelvey on their side. They used Dan and his name as weapons. He marveled at the results. The media still were susceptible. Dan braced himself every time a news hound approached. But usually they were only after a PR quote—how his family had always been in the fore-

175

front of human endeavor, or how pleased he was, as a Saunder-McKelvey, to participate in this conference.

In many ways, the Assembly, like a dig, was composed of strata. The surface was a straightforward, five-day meeting for presentations of papers, exhibitions, models of the more important sites, and manufacturers' displays. Beneath that layer, there were deeper, hidden facets of cooperating and undercutting, angling, and seeking status. The methodology varied, according to species and long-held cultural patterns, but the attendees' goals were remarkably similar. The media, too, were wheeling and dealing to outmaneuver their competitors. Science publication reps were very much on guard against Rei Ito, the reporter from a powerful general network. The scene encapsulated millions of years of evolution. Five species, five stellar civilizations, in all their diversity, were intent on ensuring that *their* kind would lose no ground in this arena. Now and then there were outbursts of raw emotion, thinly disguised in polite words. The mood in lecture rooms and meeting halls often became downright acrimonious.

Whenever possible, Dan maintained a low profile. He was here to help his team impress its sponsors and to learn. Verbal brawls were risky. But it was impossible for him to avoid rubbing elbows with the attendees' likes and dislikes. Even in the exhibit halls he was constantly overhearing nasty exchanges.

". . . Hamada? Boring! I'm boycotting his presentation. We know what he's going to say. He's been dribbling out those 'preliminary papers' of his for years."

"Hell, he *can't* publish. His dig's a dead end. All he can do is fake it . . ."

The comments troubled Dan, as Feo had during that private chat at the opening ceremony. ". . . *a failure like Juxury. Sooner or later—maybe at this conference—his theories will come crashing down in ruins.*" And they might, if the Saunders convinced Praedar's sponsors and supporters that they were backing the wrong team.

Dan tried to shake off that depressing possibility. He viewed exhibits and attended sessions, soaking up info. Some of the papers were too esoteric for anyone but specialists in those disciplines. Many, though, held Dan's interest to the end. His stints in his home team's vid library paid off. By now he understood the jargon pretty well. Displays further whetted his appetite for knowledge. Projects he'd only read about in journal files came to life. The scientists who headed those digs were here in person. Their findings were on view, and sometimes attendees were allowed to handle sample artifacts and get a solid feel of other worlds and long-dead cultures.

The Sueh-Bou expedition presented its intriguing discovery of a six-limbed, six-eyed race. The gems of that vanished civilization were its singing rocks, mementoes of a species that had committed mass suicide. The Vahnaj scientists theorized the rock singers had reached perfection and ended their line to prevent eventual degeneration. Was that truth or Vahnaj stereotypes imposing themselves upon extinct aliens?

Svejar of Whimed explained his hyperbaric gestation project. Dan attended that lecture with Joe, getting an expert's insight along with the presentation. The before-and-after holos of primitive catlike females and their offspring complemented Joe's work with the N'lacs. Dan hoped that would help later on, when Joe made his presentation.

Dr. Jarrett, Getz's chief rival, staged an eye-opening show of an effigy cult with *real* effigies—humanoid figurines with intricately carved faces, hands, feet, and genitalia. In the question-and-answer segment, Getz got into a furious argument with Jarrett, delighting the news hounds.

The scheduled midday break wasn't long enough for a decent nap; by the afternoon sessions, Dan was feeling badly sleep deprived. He punched up his med patches and struggled to stay sharp.

Throughout the afternoon, the Saunders were ubiquitous in the session rooms, exhibit areas, and the manufacturers' hall. Shaking hands, bowing, and conversing, they were always smiling. Their PR machine ran full throttle. Even Dan came in for a share of their backslapping.

Rei Ito, too, seemed to be everywhere, popping up unexpectedly, cornering people, and wheedling interviews. Her lens pendant zoomed in mercilessly again and again. Dan felt it picking him out of the crowd and he waited tensely for the reporter to pounce on him. Did she know about the blacklist and the starhopper's registration? Was she on Feo and Hope's side, or Praedar's?

She didn't pounce. Neither did any other news hound. Dan got the impression they were toying with him, lulling him until he let his guard down. *Then* they'd swarm in for the kill. Anticipating that and concentrating hard on the job Praedar had handed him sapped energy. Dan drifted, following Praedar's, Kat's, or Joe's lead. Assembly shop talk swirled around him, filtering through the translation receivers he was wearing.

Praedar woke Dan out of an eavesdropper's fog. "We will visit the manufacturers' display. I require your opinion."

The booth offerings ranged from frivolous to essential. There were newer models of insta-cells, easier to transport and assemble, sturdier in adverse weather than the T-W 593 complex. Clothing recyclers were displayed that could incorporate style changes—as if a working dig had time to waste on such nonsense. Dan lingered over a display of advanced tools and vehicles, checking manuals and questioning sales reps, while Praedar listened in.

As they left the hall, Dan said, "We sure could use a couple of those super dredgers and the remote sensor rigs. But the prices!"

"Yes. Not easy to arrange at current exchange rates," Praedar admitted. "Yet it is well to be informed. That is why I wished our xenomechanician to assess. It is possible grants will permit us to enlarge our equipment expenditures in the future. You can best decide what investments would serve us."

Dan studied the Whimed sidelong. There was promise as well as wistful desire in the words. The boss was hinting that Dan might have a permanent place on the dig—if he wanted it. "Do you really think that kind of funding will ever materialize for us?"

Praedar shrugged, an almost human motion. "It occurs. Not often. But it occurs." Abruptly he shifted mode. "We will meet now with Jon Eckard."

That was all the warning Dan got. The Chartered Settlement Planets Councilman was waiting in one of the numerous small caucus rooms. He and his aide shook hands with the T-W 593 team members and swapped small talk.

Eckard steered conversation around to his connections with the Saunder-Mckelveys, and Dan remembered where he'd seen the man before—with Adam, years ago, when the young officers had visited Reid and Fiona on Alpha Cee.

"Your brother's a good man," the Councilman was saying jovially. "Hard, though. I never did figure out how he knew where all the upper-echelon skeletons were buried." Eckard's bland mask slipped a trifle. "That's probably why Adam ended up with a sector command while I got kicked sideways into a civilian post. Yes, sir, used to be real chummy with him and that pretty ensign he married. Those were the days."

There was an edge to his voice. Jealousy! Dan hadn't realized his brother had fought for Trina Wheeler's heart and hand. Eckard was still sore from that battle two decades ago. This situation would have to be handled carefully. The former Fleet officer was C.S.P.'s rep to the Terran-Whimed Xenoethnic Board, a counterpart to Anelen, its felinoid chairman. The two of them held a near life-and-death power over renewal of dig permits and desperately needed credit allocations—and they could upgrade the N'lacs' status, protecting them from exploitation into the foreseeable future.

"Your grandmother was Jutta Lefferts, right?" Eckard asked. "I knew it. Why, one of my committees works with the Lefferts and the Wyoma Foix Medical Foundation. Wonderful job they're doing back on Mars and the Mother World . . ."

Breathing easier, Dan said, "It's a family tradition, that project. You know the Wyoma Foix group saved my grandfather, after the second FTL experiment disaster."

"Genius. That's what Morgan McKelvey was. Just like Ward Saunder . . ."

Eckard rattled on, repeatedly stressing his tenuous links with Dan's relatives. It was almost as if he were trying to impress the younger man, rather than the other way around. That amused Dan.

The meeting ended with nothing accomplished, as far as Dan saw. Praedar made a point of shaking Eckard's hand firmly. As the Councilman rushed off to another appointment, Dan muttered, "How did we do?"

Praedar eyed him curiously. "I thought perhaps you could inform *me*. He is a member of your species." Dan couldn't tell if the alien was joking or not. His gaze distant, Praedar said, "These matters are difficult. I dislike the dependence upon the whims of a remote group. We beg for hearings and are given few answers. It is a degrading procedure." That was the closest he'd ever come to griping about the necessary bureaucratic wrangling his profession demanded. The complaint made an already charismatic being even more likable.

The day's main program tracks had ended. Diurnal species were straggling out of the Assembly building, heading for their quarters. Dan's team joined the crowd. The region's regular nightly rains hadn't begun yet, but a bracing wind swept off the surrounding forest. The blast jolted Dan awake, reminding him what he had to do. As his group passed the vehicle park, he turned aside and pulled a scooter from a rack. "I'll be back soon," he told the others.

They halted, startled, and Kat demanded, "Where are you going?"

"To the ship. Have to check her..."

"You did that this morning," Joe said.

"I'll check her as often as necessary!" Attendees stared, and Dan lowered his volume. "We can't let our guard down. And I can't be predictable. The Saunders and any repossess artists have to see that I may show up in Port at odd hours. I think I'll boost the ship's protective gear while I'm there, too. We aren't out of these woods until we're in outer orbit and making the FTL jump."

Kat smiled and shook her head. "You have an absolute gift for inventing and mangling metaphors."

"Thank you, I think."

"You need sleep," she scolded.

Praedar, though, took another tack, saying "Do what you must. Go."

Dan did.

The chore took a lot longer than he'd hoped, possibly because fatigue was eating at him. Driving back to the Assembly Complex in the rain was an ordeal.

A noisy welcome awaited him. Karl Imhoff's multiracial team and Praedar's were having an impromptu bull session cum party in the corridor and both suites. Dan wearily begged off joining the fun, and Kat and Joe helped him escape, making his excuses for him. While the friendly debates raged around him, Dan gobbled a late-evening snack, then locked himself in his sleeping roomlet and dropped into bed.

The next thing he knew Joe was shaking him and cheerfully exhorting him "Rise and shine!" Dan groaned and burrowed into the bedding. The xenobiologist nudged him again. "Come on. Roll out. We let you sleep as long as we could. Sessions are

180

starting. Praedar wants you over in the main building, circulating and playing the name game. Up! Up!"

Dan dragged himself into a sitting position. "All right. Jus' don't expect me to be coherent."

Actually, he wasn't in that bad shape. Logging zees had helped a lot, though he hadn't fully recouped on the sleep deficit. Half a liter of caffa, a few stims, and a med patch boost put him in fairly taut order. At least he no longer looked like a refugee from a week of battle status. He took a sonic shower, remote-checked the extra antitheft system he'd installed in the ship the previous evening, and headed for Assembly Hall.

Today promised to be a repeat of yesterday. And yesterday he'd managed to make it through numerous encounters with news hounds, scientists, and one of Praedar's sponsors with no major glitches. With luck he—and the team—might pull this off yet.

The morning program was a fascinating bag.

Dr. Azim's expedition's report on their dig described a hellish picture. A war, twenty thousand years before the present, had all but destroyed the planet, leaving radioactive residue and climatological obstacles that would defeat most researchers. Azim's group had established their camp on the world's moon and descended to its primary for brief excavating trips, measured in hours. Despite those restrictions—and several deaths among their crew—they had compiled a stunning record of the saurian civilization that once ruled that part of the sector.

York's team, sponsored by the Saunders, presented a thorough update on their investigations in the Beno system. Dan attended that session with reservations, but he had to concede York knew his stuff. The exhibits and holos were breathtaking. The presentation was marred for Dan, though, by York's frequent praise of Feo and Hope as his 'inestimable benefactors'.

A lecture by Armilly's fur-kinship aunt showed the other side of that coin. Tawnay of Hoyoo owed nothing to the Saunders. She had a heavy reputation in the xenoarch community, and she drew a standing-room-only crowd. The audience was willing to put up with the inconvenience of translation devices to hear her lecture. The Lannon's topic was 'observational luck'. Before she finished, many listeners were visibly upset. One of those was Feo Saunder. Why, Tawnay asked, did certain scientists spend decades in the field and fail to make a significant and lasting contribution? Others stepped onto a dig world and practically fell over

181

artifacts that altered xenoarch forever. While Feo fidgeted, Tavares whispered soothingly in his ear, no doubt telling his mentor that Tawnay's opinion counted for nothing. The audience's reaction suggested otherwise. Finally Feo couldn't take any more. He rose and left, creating a wave of murmuring comment in the hall. Had Armilly's aunt hit a Saunder sore spot? Dan hoped so!

The midday break, again, wasn't. Dan spent the recess on stage, in effect, being introduced to scientists and would-be investors in the T-W 593 project, speaking to eager young grads who were shopping for just the right expedition to join, and trying to sound like a highly educated, typical Saunder-McKelvey. Often Dan felt like a fool. The important thing, however, was that these people actually seemed happy to meet him.

So far, things were going well. Either Feo wasn't willing to rip aside his kinsman's disguise, or he was waiting for a more vulnerable moment in which to do so—perhaps when Dan flatly turned down that earlier offer to become part of the Saunders' expedition.

Quas-Jin's presentation was the highlight of afternoon sessions. The lecture put Dan in an awkward corner. The Vahnaj scientist was closely connected with Varenka's New Earth Renaissance projects. Further, Feo and Hope had virtually "adopted" Quas-Jin for the duration of the Assembly, making him their personal house guest and catering to him. Balancing that was the fact that Quas-Jin was Ruieb's old buddy. They had studied together and belonged to the same progressive faction of the Vahnaj Alliance. Family ties and loyalty to Praedar's team pulled Dan in opposing directions. He had to admit that Quas-Jin's report *was* interesting. The Vahnaj had brought recent holo-modes of Saunderhome. Varenka had been busy since she'd recorded that appeal for funds. The changes were astonishing. Varenka, with considerable help from Terran and alien associates, was turning the clock back to 2040. Eventually the original HQ of the Saunders would look exactly as it had more than a century ago.

In addition to the Saunderhome material, Quas-Jin ran holos of Varenka's now-complete cloning experiment. All the details, from preparing Jael Hartman Saunder's cryo-preserved genetic essence through high-tech gestation of the fetus to the finished product. The baby girl was visually suspended beside Quas-Jin as the Vahnaj recounted Saunder-McKelvey past glories. The infant's dark eyes reflected a promise of brilliance and keen ambition, qualities her predecessor had been famous for—some would say notorious for. Dan suppressed a shudder. He wasn't sure, as Quas-Jin seemed to be, that this child was a magnificent gift to the human race and her stellar neighbors.

Kat was sitting beside him, and Dan murmured. "What does any of this have to do with xenoarchaeology?"

"You disappoint me," the brunette said in the same muted voice. "To an alien, Earth's past *is* xenoarchaeology. Varenka did Quas-Jin a big favor when she invited him to join her project."

"For a whopping fee in Terran-Vahnaj exchange credits, I'll bet," Dan growled. "Varenka and her nephew Feo are just using alien interest in the family's affairs to puff their own reps."

"It's your family, too," Kat reminded him. "And Varenka is making an invaluable contribution to history. These are genuine achievements—rebuilding Saunderhome and cloning your line's founding mother . . ."

"Maybe," Dan said, unconvinced.

His last assignment of the working day was playing co-host at the team's exhibit. Praedar was expecting his second major sponsor, Anelen, to drop by the booth, and he wanted Dan to meet the man.

Compared to adjacent displays, T-W 593's exhibit was spread rather thin. The Saunders', for instance, took up an entire wall of the area. Nevertheless, Praedar's expedition was drawing a respectable crowd. The dig's stay-at-home members and attending representatives had put together a varied sample of their work. There were Rosie's reconstructions of "demons," with vivid tridis of the "demon-smashing" ritual, and Kat's years'-long record of Sleeg's tale-telling as related to N'lac village life in general. Joe's hyperbarics data included impressive visuals of intelligence testing and med stats on Chuss and Meej. All had contributed to the exhibits on display.

Quite a few visitors to the booth wore 'SAUNDER SPELLS SPURIOUS SELECTIVITY' badges. *That* was encouraging!

The Saunders, accompanied by Tavares and Quas-Jin, moved through the hall, holding court. They paused at Praedar's exhibit and gave it a cursory lookover, paying a few backhanded compliments, then started to go on.

Quas-Jin, however, wasn't ready to leave. He zeroed in on

Dan, bowing and bobbing. "Urr . . . Hon-orable Dan-iel McKel-vey. Greetings! Fel-i-ci-tations!"

Taken aback, Dan recovered quickly. "Most esteemed Quas-Jin, all Vahnaj is in awe of your scholarship, your devotion to science."

Bow.

Bob.

The lutrinoid was so anxious to converse that he bypassed most of the usual lengthy courtesies his species practiced. "I am . . . urr . . . de-lighted to ob-serve you . . . urr . . . in flesh. Your kins-woman Var-enka . . . urr . . . Saund-er-Nicho-lai-ev . . . much af-fection . . . urr . . . young mem-bers her fam-ily. My im-mortal an-cestor was . . . urr . . . the Ir-replaceable Quol-Bez . . ."

"Ah!" Dan exclaimed, brightening. "The Vahnaj Alliance's first Ambassador to Earth! Yes! My own ancestor, Morgan McKelvey, praised Quol-Bez greatly in his memoirs. The Ambassador was a being unborn generations will revere, with much reason . . ."

His own volubility surprised him as he found himself pulling these fancy phrases from childhood and adolescent training, from Morgan McKelvey's biography, which Dan had read dozens of times, and from years of living on the Saunder-McKelvey fringe, rubbing elbows with aliens, and knowing what Vahnajes loved to hear.

Bow.

Bob.

"I see . . . urr . . . . . . the great-ness of your kin in . . . urr . . . you . . . as I have seen it with-in the . . . urr . . . won-der-ful re-pro-duction of Jael Hart-man Saund-er . . ." Quas-Jin chirped.

By reproduction he meant the clone. Again, Dan suppressed a shudder.

"We must be going, Quas-Jin," Feo cut in rudely.

Hope fussed with Dan's collar and put on a friendly show for the ever-present reporters' lenses. "No wonder Quas-Jin is so taken with you, Danny. Fiona would be proud, as I know Reid is. Such strong, successful children! You, Adam, Zoe, Naomi." She patted Dan's arm and said, "Feo and I, we . . . we made the decision to devote our lives completely to our work. At times like this, seeing you, we almost wish that . . ." She broke off, sniffling poignantly.

Dan bit his tongue. He was tempted to reply that Hope already had a spiritual heir in Nathan Saunder, Terra's most popular actor!

The news hounds adored the scene. Feo, though, was getting impatient. "My dear, we *must* go . . ."

With the reluctant Quas-Jin in tow, the Saunders edged away. As they did, a group of Whimeds approached T-W 593's exhibit from the other direction. Their hawk-faced leader slammed to a stop, staring starburst daggers at Quas-Jin. Then that awful gaze darted toward Praedar in silent disapproval.

Anelen couldn't have picked a worse time to arrive.

The team's sponsor wheeled, his aides following him in lock-step, and disappeared into the milling crowd.

As the press parted to give them room, Dan saw Rei Ito. The Pan Terran reporter had been lurking behind the Whimeds, watching that stillborn encounter with Anelen. Like Dan, she obviously regarded Anelen's reaction as a mockery of the Assembly's "Amity of Science" theme. Ito smirked, then hurried in the Saunders' wake.

"Damn," Joe Hughes said bitterly. "The Saunders, Quas-Jin, and that media snoop, all at once."

Praedar muttered, "Anelen has been difficult in this matter before. At each grant renewal, I must persuade him that Ruieb-An's abilities in xenolinguistics are invaluable to the project. Some Whimeds are unable to overcome ancient enmities. My grandsire suffered greatly from the esper attacks of Vahnaj spies. Yet it did not distort his respect for sincere and peaceable lutrinoids." That was strong criticism. Praedar sighed and told Dan, "I wish, however, that he had not seen you speaking to Quas-Jin."

"Sorry about that . . . "

"It was not your fault. Do not apologize. You behaved most ethically. Anelen Usru Ialeen does not, at all times." Praedar shook his head in weary resignation. "It is done. We proceed."

There were no more such incidents for the remainder of the afternoon sessions. Gradually meetings ended. Rooms began to empty. Servos scurried about, cleaning and preparing for the nocturnal attendees' evening programs. Exhibit booths shut down and crowds retreated to their quarters.

Since a thunderstorm was threatening, Dan's team crossed from the main building via the skywalk. In their suite, snug and dry, they discussed tomorrow's agenda and compared notes on completed program items. The conversations reminded Dan of the indie haulers' gossip and news-swapping grapevine.

Kat ticked off the upcoming schedule. ". . . meet the sponsors at noon and then tour the Saunders' dig."

"Well, at least, if it rains, we won't get wet, not under that dome of theirs," Joe said.

"How nice. Excavating in their own private indoor site." Kat commented with sarcasm. "Day after tomorrow, we make our presentations in the morning, the Saunders that afternoon . . ."

"We are ready," Praedar said, nodding.

Dan wished he felt as confident as the boss sounded. He had no illusions about his own shaky position at this conference. Just because nobody had yet demanded he produce proof of his non-existent formal education or the ship's sale papers was no guarantee someone wouldn't do it. He didn't know how he'd handle the situation when it arose.

For now, he tried to relax and soak up patterns while his teammates exchanged opinions. Some of them had attended sessions that others hadn't. They combined their experiences, assessing, trading accounts of chats with potential supporters and opponents. How much progress had been made on the expedition's behalf? How many setbacks?

During a lull Dan remarked, "It's the same all over, isn't it? I used to think scientists would be special, different. No wheeling and dealing and lobbying behind the scenes. Serious, unbiased research. But now I know you have to scratch backs, too."

"And how!" Kat agreed. "It begins when we're students. Which faculty connection can hook us up with the digs we really want to join? What foundations do we need to butter up to get funding? Who has the power? What important figures' pet peeves are . . ."

"Human or alien," Joe put in, "the rules don't vary much."

"I guess it goes with being stellar cultures," Dan said. "If we didn't have the drive to scramble for status and reach, none of us would have lifted off our origin worlds in the first place."

"Indeed," Praedar said. "Status is inescapably necessary to our species. Feo Saunder responded poorly to Tawnay's lecture because the Saunders are not noted as finders. They have never made a discovery that they can claim entirely as their own."

"They even stole the T-S 311 site from you," Kat added.

"Dif-fi-cult." The Terrans and Praedar turned to Ruieb-An. "The . . . urr . . . mat-ter of our species . . . urr . . . mix-ing. It is

186

...urr...prop-er en-deavor, to seek truth. De-cipher-ment of N'lac lan-guage. Op-portuni-ity to this per-son. How-ever..."

"The brawl," Joe said, helping the Vahnaj. He explained to the others, "Ruieb and I saw a near-riot at one of the morning sessions. Ugly. Imhoff's people and York's. No punches thrown, but damned close." He shut his eyes, looking tired. "That's far too typical of all us humanoids. Chauvinism within our races, until we mature sufficiently, then xenophobia until we develop further. Imhoff's expedition, like ours, is a target because we're both multispecies teams. One more example of—"

"Who do you think you're kidding with that philosophical crap?"

Getz's challenge stunned the rest. The effigy specialist paced restlessly, waving his arms. "Lies! Trying to build a sweetness-and-light image for us. Well, you don't fool me! I know what you're up to! I suspected it weeks ago! Months! And I came prepared. Brought all my records, my key specimens. I knew I'd have to get out when the time was right. The wonder is it took me so long to come to my senses!"

He rushed into his room and grabbed his bags, which were packed and sealed, and moved toward the suite's outer door, plainly planning to abandon ship.

By now his teammates were on their feet, staring at him in bewilderment.

Getz ranted, "Oh, don't think I didn't see it coming. You're backing Jarrett and his crew of reputation wreckers! Waiting for me to get up there and make my presentation with you. Then you'll throw me to those wolves! Like hell you will! Damned if I'll let you destroy my work and take me down with you when this stupid project collapses..."

"Bill! What are you raving about?' Kat cried. "Nobody's plotting against you. When we talked about wheeling and dealing, we didn't mean..."

Ruieb-An had fled to a corner, dismayed by the Terrans' wrangling. The Vahnaj wrung his three-fingered hands, chirring apprehensively.

Praedar's response was quite different. His crest was prickling, his starry pupils widening. He took a predatory stance, ready to jump in any direction if Getz went berserk.

"Liars! All of you! I'm joining an *honest* group, the Gokhale Institute..."

Joe tried to interrupt. "Bill, you signed a contract with the expedition, as you're so fond of reminding us when it suits *you* . . ."

"Eat your damned contract! I'm not obligated to cheats and traitors like you!" Getz kicked his bags across the corridor. They bounced off the wall opposite and the door to Imhoff's suite opened. A few of his team members poked their heads out warily, watching the spectacle.

"It is unlikely the Gokhale Institute will wish to associate itself with a researcher whose data are in question," Praedar said icily.

"Under question!" Getz squeaked. "Only by you! I had to be out of my mind to ally myself to you. A *Whimed*, for God's sake! A Whimed and his crack-brained misfits. The final blow, Juxury, was when you took in this ignorant lout who thinks he's a self-taught genius . . ." Getz thrust an accusing hand at Dan.

"I thought I was supposed to be the Saunders' spy."

"Maybe you are!" Spittle flecked the older man's lips. "You did your best to encourage Juxury's insane ideas. He already has the others believing those fairy tales those subhumanoids spout. Nonanthropomorphic invaders from the stars! Ludicrous! And then you had the nerve to tell them my effigies are some idiotic alien technology. Concocting data. Twisting selectivity to—"

"Twisting selectivity?" Kat was outraged. "What gall! We all know what rotten science you've been conducting, pretending to catalog fluidics elements as effigies, when you must have—"

"Shut up! SHUT UP!"

Praedar took a heavy step toward Getz, then regained control of his temper. He loomed over the suddenly frightened Terran and said, "I have studied and worked with your species for many years. Chen showed me the best that humans could be, as Joe, Kat, and Dan, have done. Yet I learn. You astonish me with your lack of ethics."

"Go to hell!" Getz blustered.

"You can't just walk out," Kat said. "What about your students back on T-W 593? They trusted you, depend on you . . ."

"They can go to hell, too! All of you can, especially you, McKelvey. They say blood is thicker than water. I hope it is. I hope you sell them out to the Saunders. They deserve it. They're losers, just like you . . ."

Getz staggered into the hall, stumbling, grabbing his luggage. The cases bumped against walls as he made his way out of the wing. As his footsteps faded, there was a breathless hush. The only sound Dan heard was the mournful slash of rain on the window.

CHAPTER TWELVE

Doubts

Shock wore off. Imhoff's people crossed the hall and came into Praedar's suite to commiserate with their fellow multiracial group. Vahnajes soothed Ruieb-An. Whimeds huddled with Praedar, helping boil off his accumulated tension. Terrans sympathized with Joe, Kat, and Dan. Dan nodded mutely, still reeling from Getz's parting shot.

Loser! That again!

What if the man was right? Was the project a loser, as Dan himself had been, all too often?

No! He wouldn't take Getz's say-so for that. This was a scientific war for survival, and his team was going to win. It *had* to.

Praedar emerged from his huddle and Imhoff told him, "One never knows how a colleague will stand up to the challenges of the field. You must not take this too much to heart."

"I do not," Praedar replied, very serene now. "But I must strive to understand."

"What set him off?" one of Imhoff's people wondered.

Another volunteered, "I saw Getz talking to Tavares earlier

today. Whatever Greg said, it definitely shook Bill . . ."

"Perhaps Tavares pointed out what Getz already knew—that Jarrett will dissect him if he dares to present his material . . ."

"I ought to have seen this coming," Kat said. "With my background in sociology, why didn't I recognize the patterns? Bill's always been abrasive, but . . ."

"It's the Daust Effect," Joe noted. "Trying to duplicate past triumphs and becoming desperate enough to falsify his data."

"Was it so?" Praedar asked, scowling. "Did he see only what he wished to see and hide the truth? We all must be wary of that temptation. It is not possible to avoid all bias. But we rise above it."

"Bill didn't," Kat countered. "Isolated on T-W 593, he was able to fake it. Here, surrounded by other experts in his own field, everything fell apart for him. He's being judged by a jury of his peers and found guilty. I'm afraid his career's over."

"Maybe the Saunders will take him in, if the Gokhale group won't," Imhoff's chief aide said. He looked concerned for the Whimed's team. "He might hurt you, though, through Feo and Hope and Tavares. They could use the implications of Bill's desertion . . ."

"Nope," Dan argued. "Feo won't back a dying horse—or a discredited xenoarch. From what you say, that's Getz. The professional roof is falling in on our erstwhile effigy expert."

"Erstwhile?" Kat cut in. "Where did you pick up *that* term?"

Dan feigned dull-wittedness. "Dunno. Musta read it someplace."

"Huh!" Kat hugged him and laughed. "A lot of someplaces. What a faker you are!"

Imhoff's people didn't get the joke, but they laughed with her. After a while, they headed back toward their own quarters, leaving behind a mood of camaraderie and lightened spirits. The sense of belonging, of being a part of this community affected Dan. Not all his kindred had snubbed him after his father's financial ruin. But from that point on, much of the family closeness he'd formerly known had vanished. The lack was an unhealed wound. Now, out on the borders of explored regions, he had found a new family, one linked to him not by genes, but by affection and purpose.

Thoughts of that purpose, and the damage Getz might do to it,

191

sobered him. "How are the other attendees going to react to this?" he asked. "Won't it look bad for us?"

"Not necessarily," Joe reassured him. "This isn't the first time something similar has happened to an expedition, and it won't be the last. Stress and ego problems and personality quirks can throw a lot of xenoarchs off base, especially when they're stuck on a remote field dig. The other teams will guard their mouths. They won't hit us, because they may have to deal with the same thing, eventually."

"Getz . . . urr . . . er-ror of mind func-tion," Ruieb said. He wasn't as spooked as he had been, but was still noticeably upset. "Cor-rection . . . urr . . . must be sup-plied."

A logical attitude for a Vahnaj, even a progressive one. The lutrinoids exercised tyrannical control over aberrant citizens. Terrans had learned, belatedly, that Quol-Bez, the first Vahnaj Ambassador to Earth, had been deliberately maimed in crucial mental and emotional faculties before he had been sent to the humans. The Ambassador had voluntarily accepted that crippling; it assured that he could never reveal his species' secrets to a then-unproved alien race. Such drastic corrections were common in his Alliance, particularly among the mentally ill. Unlike Quol-Bez's sacrifice, most corrections were demanded, not undertaken willingly. It was natural that Ruieb-An, born in that culture, expected that Getz's flaw would be fixed, with or without Getz's cooperation.

Patiently Kat explained, "Correction will be supplied if Bill wants it. In Terran law, Ruieb, mind error isn't automatically crushed."

"At least not on the highly developed Settlements," Dan said softly. Kat and Joe shot him warning looks and he didn't elaborate. They were right. There was no point in telling Ruieb how some back-of-nowhere Terran planets handled their aberrants. Basically they didn't. Those settlers were far from modern psychomed aid and too busy battling hostile environments to pamper noncontrib citizens, even if the illness wasn't the disturbed person's fault. Exile was the usual answer. And exile, on an untamed world, was a death sentence. Getz, a product of sophisticated circles and honored for his past achievements, would be treated more gently.

Dan tried to turn the subject. "Well, it looks as if it's just the five of us from here on. So what's next, Praedar?"

"We adjust. We proceed." It was flat. No wasted breath would be spent on matters that couldn't be helped.

Praedar's determination inspired his remaining teammates. They figuratively picked themselves up and prepared to go on.

Bad news traveled fast. They had to run a gauntlet in the Assembly building the next morning. Saunder supporters, news hounds, and general attendees pelted the group with questions as soon as they arrived in the hall. Even while Dan and the others were straightening out the mess Getz had left when he'd yanked his "effigy specimens" out of the exhibit, the vultures hovered, sharpening their claws.

"This must be an inconvenience, Juxury, to say the least . . ."

"May we have a comment, Dr. Olmsted?"

"Are you sure you want to stay with such a dangerous project, Hughes? Obviously, working under those harsh conditions does serious harm to one's brain . . ."

"McKelvey, Getz says you have no valid credentials. Care to confirm or deny?"

Like his colleagues, Dan fended off the attackers. In his case, he cloaked himself in that mantle of Terra's uncrowned royalty, playing the Saunder-McKelvey princeling for all he was worth. "One must make allowances for mental infirmities, mustn't one? We shouldn't be too hard on the afflicted . . ." He tried to let pitying disdain for Getz blunt the critics' barbs.

Some gadflies didn't give up easily. A pro-Saunder reporter continued to badger Dan, digging hard into the matter of formal education and degrees until Ramdas stepped in. The revered dean of Terran xenoarchaeology sniffed at the news hound. "Degree? Hardly an essential. Read Harte's thesis. *Experience!* That's what counts. A willingness to get out there and dig. If you'd ever done any of that, you'd understand." Then Ramdas rounded on a scientist who was nagging at Kat. "Nora! I'm ashamed of you, my dear. When were you last on a field project? You're safe and sound at Saunder Institute on Mars, running lab checks. That's background science, not the cutting edge. I fail to see why any of you have the presumption to challenge your colleagues who are taking the risks . . ." The old man's presence daunted the vultures. One by one they crept away, before he turned his scorn on them. Ramdas winked and nodded to Praedar.

"Score one for our side," Kat whispered.

As the crowd shifted off to other interests, Joe said, "I heard an update from one of the Gokhale team. They *are* taking Bill in—temporarily. They've agreed to transport him as far as Alpha Cee and drop him at his old university. I gather Bill's holed up in Gokhale Institute's shuttle right now, refusing to come out for fear of traitors."

"What thin partitions," Dan muttered. Kat nodded.

She wasn't the only one who'd overheard him. Tavares was walking past the exhibit, and he paused and commented, "Maybe Getz isn't paranoid or crazy. There are a lot of backstabbers at the Assembly . . ."

"You ought to know," Dan retorted.

Tavares flushed, but stuck to his guns. "Look at it this way. Perhaps it's a blessing in disguise, Getz's data being so obviously flawed, or he might have resigned when he realized he was attached to a go-nowhere project. You do have a talent for attracting the . . . uh . . . unstable elements of our field, Juxury . . ." Satisfied with his telling counterthrust, Tavares made himself scarce.

He wasn't the last of the gloaters. But the amount of jeering tapered off as Assembly business began.

Jarrett, Getz's professional rival, expressed his regret to Praedar's team. The xenoeffigy specialist seemed genuinely sorry that a fine researcher had come upon hard times. "Causal awareness. Bill forgot that," Jarrett said. "He refused to see what he was looking at. I knew as soon as I saw those specimens that he was in trouble. Effigies! Ridiculous!" The scientist studied Dan and went on. "He mentioned your theory that those pieces of glass are some sort of electronics. True?"

Dan glanced at Praedar for guidance, fearful of putting his foot in his mouth and hurting the expedition. The Whimed indicated he should explain. "Not electronics." Dan said. "Something like that, yes. It's just a hypothesis, so far."

Jarrett was encouraging. "I'll be looking forward to your future presentations on the subject. Sounds interesting. The next Assembly?"

When the effigy specialist moved on, Dan let out the breath he'd been holding. "How did I do?"

Kat's smile eased his worry. "More than all right. You're learning the game nicely. When in doubt, hint that you'll be publishing—later. *Much* later."

Imhoff's presentation took up the bulk of the morning's programming. The format was a preview of tomorrow's scheduled sessions by the T-W 593 team and the Saunders. Imhoff, like Praedar, was a broad-overview xenoarchaeologist and his group was multispecies. However, he'd been able to bring two dozen of his people to the Assembly; eight of them were reading papers covering numerous subject fields. It was a crowded three hours, punctuated by lively question-and-answer sessions. Imhoff himself delivered his team's general summary of findings, and finished with a sharp poke at certain attendees. "Judgments from those who have not dealt directly with a site are always suspect. Before one can obtain an accurate view of a dig, one must be in the field and operate in the milieu of the dedicated excavator."

That brought an outburst of applause and some negative grumbles from splitters and die-hard lab denizens.

Praedar had insisted on his team's sitting in on Imhoff's sessions, both out of courtesy and interest. But the length of Imhoff's material meant that the T-W 593 reps had to hurry to get to their midday meeting with the sponsors on time.

Their rush was wasted. When they arrived at the room the Teran-Whimed Council had reserved, they found a previous meeting was running late. Praedar's group was forced to cool their heels for nearly half a local hour. Finally they were shown inside by a stony-countenanced Whimed staffer.

"You do not bring the Vahnaj Ruieb-An?" Anelen hit them with that when Praedar and the Terrans were halfway through the door.

Praedar returned Anelen's stare levelly. "No." He didn't bother adding that Ruieb was conferring with his fellow Vahnajes and wouldn't have had time to be at this gathering anyway. Anelen appeared to take Ruieb's absence as a victory, as if his disapproval had kept the lutrinoid at bay.

Both Whimeds at the table agreed to dispense with translation devices and speak Terran English, the language of the Assembly. That was no strain for Praedar, who was fluent in the alien tongue. Anelen wasn't. His accent was thick, his syntax abrupt and tortured. Dan wondered if that might not cause misunderstandings.

Jon Eckard toyed with a min-vid file recorder. "I don't suppose Ruieb's attendance is necessary. Besides, it'll save us a lot of messy sparring," he said, glowering at Anelen. The beefy former Fleet officer patted the file. "We've entered your requests,

Juxury. The formalities. Naturally, we'll be attending your presentation to get a feel for your project's update. No decision here. The usual time lag. Full Council hearings won't be for another two Earth months . . ."

"You have starship," Anelen broke in.

In the best of circumstances, a Whimed in a bad mood tended to worry a Terran. Now Dan's gut went cold.

"Our scheduled transportation was unavoidably delayed," Praedar said in a calm, reasonable tone. "Replacement was required."

"Makes sense to me," Eckard agreed, wanting to push on.

"Credits. You buy ship? Not in budget," Anelen said. His burning gaze shifted to Dan, Kat, and Joe. All of them tensed.

Who had told him about the starhopper's registration? Feo? Tavares? A news hound? Ito had the sources. She could have ferreted out the ship's shadowy status easily.

"Required," Praedar repeated. "A temporary title transfer."

Jon Eckard winked at his aides. "So that's the deal. I kind of wondered, but that spells it out. The old stunt, huh? Well, as long as there's no fallout, no problem."

At least *he* was being cooperative! The man was a spacer as well as a bureaucrat. He knew the little fictions settlers had to use to get along out here.

Anelen, though, wanted to quibble. "Illegality?"

To Dan's surprise, Praedar lied like a trooper. "No. Payment was made. Arrangements for extended purchase. No budgetary difficulty."

The Whimed sponsor's eyes dropped to the vid file holding Praedar's request for dig license renewal and funding. It was a none-too-subtle threat.

Praedar counterattacked, and Dan saw why it had been crucial for the boss to attend this Assembly in person. The felinoids reverted to their own language, a low-voiced, growling, rapid-fire exchange. Anelen and his staff reacted strongly. Their starburst eyes widened as Praedar apparently hammered home his reasons for "buying a starship"—and why that must not alter the Council's decision regarding the expedition. Anelen listened with jaw agape, looking spellbound.

Suddenly all the Whimeds were on their feet, going into a convulsive though amicable huddle.

Obviously Praedar's charisma worked just as well on his own kind as it did on non-Whimeds.

Eckard moved his chair slightly away from the whirling mass of felinoids. "I'll let them thrash that out their way. I'm more interested in this thing with Getz."

Kat took the lead on that. "Dr. Getz's resignation was by mutual choice, Councilman. You might call it an internecine disagreement, one that won't affect the project's aims in the slightest. In fact, I believe we've gained ground, now that we have Dan aboard."

"Mm. Maybe so. Can't hurt, adding a McKelvey to your publications' rosters . . ."

The huddle broke up as suddenly as it had started, and Anelen rushed toward the Terrans. He came to a halt with his nose scant centimeters from Dan's and examined the pilot minutely. "McKelvey. Yes. It is balance. Saunder-Nicholaiev. Saunder-McKelvey." Praedar smiled enigmatically. Dan hoped that meant he'd done his part at impressing Anelen.

Eckard skillfully channeled talk onto other matters. Why had it taken so long for the project to get its equipment in working order? That drew an angry response. The Terran councilman grunted. "Hmm. I see. Well, these things happen. Dirty work at the cross vectors. Never can prove anything. You scientists ought to be above such stuff, but I know you aren't." He leaned back, his expression veiled. "By the way, can you estimate when that planet of yours might be available for general colonization? Our staff is getting a lot of developmental proposals. Wozniak Corporation in particular has put together an impressive package . . ."

Dan sensed this was a spot where family connections might do the job. "Wozniak," he said, pretending to search his memory. "Ah, yes. That's a division of Saunder-McKelvey Interstellar. Don't they already own some major territory in this region?"

"You mean T-S 311?"

"Among other worlds," Dan replied, gauging Eckard carefully. "I imagine the Council has to stay on its toes in such cases. You wouldn't want a repeat of the Sixth T-W Sector fracas . . ."

The former Fleet officer grimaced. "Hell, no! We can't afford any more blowups like *that*! If Nakamura Kaisya or the Société Famille gets a whiff of undue favoritism toward your kin . . ." Dan smiled, communicating his empathy with Eckard's worries in that regard.

Kat added, "The Council's watchdog committee assigned us specifically to guard the T-W 593 aborigines. Any large-scale influx of offworlders would smack of exploitation, and . . ."

"Feo and Hope Saunder say those natives are subhumanoid. That'd take them out of the nonexploitation clause." Was Eckard rattling their cages to see if they'd yell?

"The Saunders are incorrect," Praedar said flatly.

"Remains to be proved, doesn't it? As I say, Anelen and I will be paying close attention to your presentations—and the Saunders'. Have to consider all the arguments. I mean, the Council's allotment isn't open-ended, you know. We have to pick and choose our projects for the best prospects of success." Eckard tapped the vid files once more.

Anelen's lips peeled back in a frightening leer. "You are McKelvey. Feo Saunder your kinsman. You opposed." Dan could almost hear wheels turning in the alien's white-crested head.

"I support Praedar Effan Juxury," Dan said, "in his search for ethical truth, *Irast*."

The Whimed's nasty grin widened. It wasn't reassuring. "Contest! We witness. Tomorrow!" Anelen's chin jerked down hard into his chest in a curt nod. "Is all. Bring next persons."

His Terran counterpart didn't soften that blunt dismissal. In moments, Praedar's team was outside the room and another group of wary applicants was filing in.

"Just like that," Dan muttered, irked.

Joe gripped his shoulder. "It was a fairly friendly sizing up, compared to some of our previous appeals for funds. You and Praedar were very effective."

"Are you sure?"

"As sure as one can be," Praedar said, "when Anelen Usru is involved." His gaze was remote and angry.

Their schedule had slipped still further by now. Terran members of the team grabbed a fast lunch. Then they rendezvoused with Ruieb-An and hurried to collect their passes for the Saunders' dig tour. They were admitted to the passageway connecting the Assembly building with the enclosed site south of the complex. Other beings were making that short trek, as well. The weatherproof arcade was crowded with scientists and the media.

Coming out into the sheltered excavation was a shock. Dan looked up at the ultra-expensive, arcing roof that covered the entire dig. This was an ostentatious display of wealth—with a vengeance! Saunder staffers were on hand to play tour guides. They greeted Assembly attendees emerging from the passageway and separated the mass into manageable segments. Praedar's group rated special treatment. A top aide paged his bosses as soon as he saw the T-W 593 team. Almost immediately a scooter car buzzed up one of the dig's paved paths and Feo and Hope stepped down to welcome their guests.

"We were beginning to wonder if you were coming," Feo said. "Caucusing with your sponsors, I suppose?" He knew damned well they had been! With all the staffers—also known as spies—he had running around the complex, Feo had to be in touch with everything that was going on at all times.

"Anelen is a strange person, isn't he?" Hope asked with a syrupy smile. "Most difficult. But one must deal with those types, when one is dependent on their largesse."

"Most xenoarchs have to go that route," Dan jabbed back. "You wouldn't be expected to appreciate that tradition, though, not with your elitist advantages."

"What would you know about traditions?" Feo snapped. "You arrogant young—"

Praedar said, "We are here. Let us begin."

Nearby, Greg Tavares was escorting a group of reporters, warning them, "When we stop at excavations, don't step on string markers or stand on the backfills." Several of the news hounds scowled at him. Rei Ito was particularly annoyed. Plainly the Pan Terran rep didn't like being patronized any more than Dan had when Kat had treated him to the same lecture, weeks ago.

The Saunders led their guests to the scooter car and helped them aboard the back-to-back bench seats. Feo drove, moving slowly along kilometers of neatly engineered lanes, parking at key points. There, Praedar's team alighted and were shown the dig's fine details.

From the air, the sheltered dig had seemed immense. Up close, it was overwhelming.

This was Saunder wealth, running riot: the great sun-filtering roof; on-site labs; refreshment canteens and creature comforts galore; excavating equipment polished to a sheen; and a superb clime-control system.

The dig was also a museum. There were neatly presented showcase excavations, with stacked tools nearby and striations labeled. Other exhibits were a partially opened trench, a cleared one containing numerous artifacts in situ, and a precisely cataloged array of extracted finds, cleaned and restored.

Gaggles of scientists and reporters wandered through the maze like tourists. Saunder aides hovered proudly, boasting, discussing field strategies, context surveys, topographical data, urban placement extrapolations, ecodisruptive factors, and standards for a crisis-free dig environment. The xenoarchs had little trouble keeping up with the docents' pace. The media reps were made of weaker stuff; they had to stop frequently at the canteens along the trails and soak up restoratives.

"I hope you're enjoying the tour," Feo said. "I think you'll agree we haven't done too badly in a mere six years here. You *did* get the jump on us, Luxury. We both saw those Explorer reports from Fleet's mapping division, back in '42. But you filed first. Besides, back then, Hope and I were deeply involved in our dig on the Eta Gamma Ulisorian worlds. We simply couldn't start our operations on T-S 311 right then . . ."

These busy, filthy rich xenoarchs were able to select at leisure where they'd excavate next—and muscle in on rivals with less power and funding.

Dan was torn between exasperation and awe. The dig was too fancy, too immaculate. It was also stunning.

If only Praedar had this kind of money! He, too, could free his people from dust drift, heat, cold, and equipment breakdowns. He, too, could attract armies of staffers and eager investors.

Money alone couldn't do it all, though. Feo and Hope had worked their tails off to create these results. Dan had to concede them that.

"This bulk demonstrates local construction techniques," Hope said, gesturing to a dirt wall extending the length of a large excavated plaza.

"And that building was their administrative center," Feo added.

Dan was elsewhere, elsewhen, seeing through the eyes of a being yet unborn—of a species yet unborn. He was on Earth or any one of dozens of Terran planets, digging, probing into mankind's forever time. *Homo sapiens*, whose sphere of influence had spanned parsecs, was gone. Its traces now were being uncovered by another race.

Would those future xenoarchaeologists be able to re-create the history of a stellar civilization from such pitiful scraps? Would some of them develop mistaken theories and fiercely debate colleagues who differed with them?

Another daunting idea flashed through Dan's mind. Did non-anthropomorphic species share that humanoid hunger to know? Not even all humanoids obeyed that drive. But they all had a portion of that seemingly universal push to investigate the past and speculate about the future. Dan tried to imagine the Evil Old Ones within that framework and failed. Praedar probably could envision such a concept. The newest member of his team couldn't—yet.

The Saunders led on, explaining the obvious. ". . . and these materials are firm-dated to two thousand years before present . . ."

"Right on the dateline when the N'lac culture fell," Kat said.

"Presuming the inhabitants called themselves N'lacs," Feo commented with a smirk. "We've found little evidence that this civilization was related in any way to those primitive creatures on T-W 593 . . ."

Dan ignored the byplay, thinking hard. Was it significant that certain features common at Praedar's dig were missing from this one—domed structures, jerry-rigged solar furnaces, glass elements, and windmills? Only the last could be excused, on the basis that this wasn't a desert world and water supplies weren't a problem. The other absences tended to support Praedar's theories and the N'lacs' legends.

There *were* remarkable correspondences between the dig on T-W 593 and T-S 311's—plazas, structures with inward-curving walls, and the same public paintings and writings. Ruieb-An pored over the squiggles, while the rest admired familiar parades of golden-eyed, elegantly robed star rovers, marching into oblivion.

Feo was saying "Hope and I got our quota of calluses here, but it's been worth it. I don't suppose you've been able to excavate such a large area or have done as much reconstruction as we have, mmm? One must accept limitations, when one operates under handicaps. Particularly given unpredictable aspects, as with your . . . mm . . . eclectic team. Judging by poor Bill Getz . . . Whatever are you going to do with those so-called effigies he was allegedly cataloging?"

"His collection is useful," Praedar said. "Alternative interpretations are being developed." He didn't elaborate.

Behind the Saunders' backs, Kat smiled at Dan and mouthed, "Fluidics!"

One of the tour's highlights was Hope's "baby"—a fully reconstructed N'lac colonial dwelling. Dan felt like an intruder there. He half expected to turn a corner and come face to face with Chuss' ancestors. The scientists were poking about dead aliens' property, pawing through their middens and ferreting out secrets the N'lacs might have preferred left in limbo.

The next stop was a cemetery. There were graves, grave goods, attendant ritual objects, and carefully preserved N'lac corpses, in excavated three-meter-deep mausoleums. The bodies were stacked in tiers of transparent cubicles.

Dan tried to maintain a scientific detachment. But he kept seeing his own forebears, disinterred and put on display for curious e.t.s. This topic had been argued loudly and often in the xenoarchaeological journals. Was it moral to disturb the dead, even in the name of knowledge? Earth's researchers had debated the point long before her first interstellar ship reached toward space.

If only the bones could speak and tell their finders whether or not they resented this exhumation.

"You haven't excavated *any* graves, have you?" Hope asked with her mock-maternal smile.

Joe flared, "You know we can't."

Feo was amused. "Oh, yes. Afraid of trampling on the sensitivities of those little primitives. I assure you, if such a nonhumanoid species existed here, it wouldn't deter us . . ."

"Would it not?" Praedar's stare lanced at the Saunders, taking their breath away for a moment. "Then you would make an erroneous assumption."

Dan picked up the ball. "Would you risk being proved wrong, decades in the future? We admire your conceit. Some of our ancestors, Feo, made some bad mistakes, counting on that same sort of conceit to carry them through. And a few of those mistakes cost thousands of lives. They also earned the Saunder-McKelveys big black marks in the history vids."

His cousin's color had become very high. "Don't preach to me, you—"

The Saunders' tour was being crossed by that of Tavares. Rei Ito stepped aside from the rest of the reporters and tuned her lens pendant to peak function, listening to the Assembly's hosts and Praedar's team.

"What about Varenka's cloning of Jael Hartman Saunder?" Dan demanded. "Your aunt refers to Jael as our noble ancestress. But what if Jael's critics were right? Varenka may be fostering a monster..."

"I will excuse your impertinence on the grounds that it's misplaced loyalty," Feo snapped. "Since we're posing difficult questions, I have one for you and Juxury. In your own published data, you admit you haven't discovered a spacecraft used by those 'escaped slaves.' Doesn't that suggest—strongly!—that *you* are the ones making erroneous assumptions?"

"The means of transport will be found," Praedar said, yielding nothing.

Hope simpered. "Could it be that such a vehicle never existed except in imagination? If there was no escape ship, and no link between those subhumanoids and this glorious civilization," she said, waving to the re-created grandeur around them, "where does that leave your theories?"

Her husband scraped at the wound she'd made. "A dig is meaningless, Juxury, unless it fits into a cogent, general scheme and sense-making arrangements. The dictum we all learned in our first institutional lectures..."

"We are also taught to avoid bias," Praedar reminded his host. "One strives to avoid the trap of presumption and overconfidence. Obvious answers are often illusions. At times, a solution must be found by approaching the material at an angle, employing new techniques and breakthrough concepts."

Spluttering, Feo exclaimed, "That's the sort of hazy reasoning that cracked Getz. He couldn't deal with the fact that he'd been working himself into a dead end by espousing your theories..."

"That's right," Hope chimed in, her voice abnormally shrill. "When will you see you're chasing phantoms!"

Suddenly it was as if Praedar's merciless gaze had burned away the Saunders' shells. Dan saw clearly the fear within them.

Dead end. A go-nowhere project.

Snide gossip, in Assembly session rooms and the exhibit areas, whispered that the Saunders were buying their way to their professional reputation, capitalizing on other xenoarchaeologists' discoveries, and using money to steal others' dig territories, as they had Praedar's rights to this stellar region.

And yearning, all the while, for their peer's respect—not their staffers' fawning praise, or bought and paid-for congratulations, but honest respect for hard work and solid findings.

What if Praedar was proved right? Disaster.

There would be hidden laughter, and mutterings throughout this scientific community that the Saunders had reaped what they had sown.

Everything Feo and Hope had fought and plotted for and spent their fortunes achieving would go dribbling through their fingers like dust drifting through a N'lac's paws.

A tinny sound jolted Dan out of his reverie. He grabbed at his wrist min-vid as Kat asked, "What's that?"

"Alarm! Someone's trying to get into the starhopper!"

Greg Tavares, conducting his guided tour for the news hounds nearby, turned and sneered. "Trouble, McKelvey? What are you concerned about? Supposedly it's Juxury's ship, not yours." The Saunders frowned at their protégé, disturbed by his comment.

Dan was turning toward a scooter car, seeking fast transportation. But he detoured and lunged across the path, seizing Tavares' jumper and shaking the man. Tavares was caught totally off guard.

"I told you that if anyone messed with the ship, they'd be sorry," Dan said. "I hope whoever you sent to do your dirty work has a strong set of neural channels." Spitting a curse, he hurled the redhead to the ground and loped for the car.

Praedar was waiting for him. Dan took the driver's seat and warned, "Hang on! I'm going to bend some rules," and they careened in the direction of the Assembly Complex.

CHAPTER THIRTEEN
◇◇◇◇◇◇◇◇◇

Challenges

At the Complex, they traded the tour car for a much faster road scooter. Dan put readouts in the red. The little vehicle swept through curves, racing toward town. Praedar clung to the safety bar, a predatory grin splitting his face.

Halfway to Saunder City, they ran into rain. Dan cued the scooter's scan systems to max, maintaining his speed, risking a skid. The scooter's bubble top didn't keep out all the wet and the wind stream. The blasts flattened Praedar's crest.

Scanners showed they had a tail—another scooter, far to the rear. Without remote lens capability, Dan couldn't tell who was pursuing them and he didn't much care. Right now, getting to Port was all that mattered. The team's ride home was in danger.

The vehicle whined in agony as he tore along Saunder City's sole main street, dodging pedestrians. The rain was slackening when they reached the Port's tarmac. Dan roared through the gate and swerved sharply, aiming for the end of the line of parked shuttles. Bright sunshine lay over the landing strips, drying the puddles.

A crowd was gathering near *Praedar's Project*—port personnel, human and alien pilots, mechs, and civilians. As Dan slid the scooter to a stop just beyond the mob, the Port's manager spotted him and yelled, "Clear a lane, boys! Let 'em through!"

Praedar and Dan squirmed through the confusion to where the manager's staff had cordoned off a space. They were keeping the curious well away from the expedition's ship. A man was lying beside the debark ramp access panel. His hand was pinned inside the control cowling.

Caught in the act!

Parameds were kneeling over the victim. Dan disengaged his antitheft device and the would-be tamperer's hand dropped limply. "How much juice was in that?" a medic asked.

"Not enough to kill him. It packs big volts, but not many amps."

"Cute!" a second paramed commented. "He'll come out of this with a wowser of headache, though. Did you concoct that zapper?"

"Yeah. I'm thinking of taking out a patent."

Praedar chuckled nastily. "Indeed! Did not your distant father, Ward Saunder, do so, and earn much wealth?"

"And how!" Dan said. "That was the start of the whole Saunder-McKelvey fortune. Maybe I'm his reincarnation. Recreating my ancestors is in vogue nowadays . . ."

"Move, you cretins, move!" Greg Tavares bulled past the mob of spectators. So *he* had been the one riding that other scooter! The scientist slammed to a halt, staring in dismay at the unconscious thief.

"Too bad," Dan taunted. "Your man didn't get the job done."

Another new arrival was at Tavares' heels. "Kimball, Pan Terran Network," he introduced himself curtly. The man was toting an ultrasophisticated remote link, focusing its lenses on the drama near the starhopper. Kimball spoke *sotto voce* into the audio tie-in, "Rei? You there?"

"On line, with Saunder." The woman reporter's image—and Feo's—appeared on the relay box's tiny screen. "I knew posting you in Port would pay off. Nice work, Kimball."

"We've got a scoop. No other news hounds here."

Tavares stammered, "I . . . I can take care of this, Feo. No need for you to . . ."

"Be quiet, Greg." The young man's face stiffened as he heard the menace in Saunder's words.

The Port manager was looking very unhappy. All this was bad publicity for his division. Dan played to the manager's fears. "This sort of crime might give a Settlement a rotten rep. Breaking and entering visiting spacecraft. I think I ought to put in a call to my brother. One of his Fleet Inspectors could check out this local setup." The manager paled.

Parameds were lifting the zapped man into their emergency scooter. Tavares, on the defensive, pointed accusingly at Dan. "You assaulted my aide! I intend to bring charges!"

"You admit this man is your associate?" Praedar asked with deceptive mildness.

"He . . . I . . ."

Dan demanded, "What was he doing sticking his hands in where they didn't belong?"

"Investigating! Checking your credentials, McKelvey, and Juxury's ownership rights to this ship!"

The ambulance howled off toward town, and its siren chilled Dan for a heartbeat; the ululation was very similar to a N'lac's cry of terror.

As the area quieted again, Feo said, "Ed?" The Port manager braced to attention. "Was Greg's student seriously injured?"

"Uh . . . no, sir. Just a little scorched, the meds say."

"Good. Good. Then give us some privacy. Remove those spectators." Port staffers hurried to obey, herding the crowd out of earshot.

"I've got this under control, Feo," Tavares said, selling his case to the image on the vidder. "Once I get hold of their onboard files . . ."

"You will do no such thing. Thank God the Pan Terran people were on top of this and informed Hope and me of your hare-brained plot. Where did you get the idea that we would condone criminal actions?" Feo threw a stern aside to the reporters. "All of this is off the record. Remember that."

Shaken, Tavares argued, "McKelvey's been blacklisted by the Terran dispatchers . . ."

"Because you bribe-buried our cargo, you bastard!" Dan clenched his fists and took a heavy step toward the redhead. Praedar interposed himself, preventing a fight. Dan shouted over

207

the Whimed's shoulder, "You hijacked our transport tickets, too! What *else* were you planning? A frame? A—"

"I'll squash you and Juxury both," Tavares said. "I'll get this ship repossessed and make sure you never launch . . ."

"No, you will not," Feo contradicted. "You have done quite enough damage already to our organization and to this conference. Your unprofessional behavior ceases right here. Don't bother returning to the Complex, Greg. Hope and I will make your excuses. I believe you're overdue for a sabbatical."

"The hell I am!" Tavares exclaimed. "You know damned well I was only doing what *you* would have if you'd been able to operate freely."

"Be still, or resign yourself to becoming another Bill Getz."

The redhead gulped, choking on his rebellion. The money and power that had protected him was now a weapon turned against him. Feo's message was plain: Cooperate, or be reduced to a nonperson within the scientific community. In an oily, persuasive tone, Feo went on. "Regan's Foundation needs a junior faculty member. I'll see if I can arrange an appointment for you. It would be a good training experience."

Tavares radiated frustration; he was trapped, as Dan had been by the blacklist. "That would set me back years! How can you . . . after all I've done for you . . ."

Feo's glare smothered his former protégé. Saunder turned to the woman sharing the broadcast booth with him. "This affair need not be spread any further, I trust?"

Rei Ito smiled enigmatically. "Of course. For the 'Amity of Science.'" Dan smelled sibling rivalry. Rei's sister was engaged to their mutual boss, Cameron Saunder. And Cam was Regan's son. Tavares would be farmed out to Regan's Foundation with Cam's news hound helping Feo suppress a scandal that might be hurtful to the xenoarchaeologist's standing. Rei, even more than her sister, was in the driver's seat, jerking around Saunders and a McKelvey.

Dan snorted. "For the 'Amity of Science.' Sure. And for your reputation, Feo."

His cousin nodded. "I'm glad you understand, Danny. I know Juxury does."

Praedar cocked his head. "You expect to be forgiven much."

"I'm forgiving *your* lapses, as well, don't forget," Feo retorted. "Employing a blacklisted pilot. Passing off my unlettered kinsman as an accredited scientist. Oh, yes, Danny. Don't imagine your little fraud fooled me for an instant. Only my goodwill stands between you and complete ridicule—ridicule, I might add, that could affect Juxury's status. So you'd be advised to keep your mouth shut. There is also the matter of generating an illegal document on an indebted spacecraft..."

Dan cut in, "How do you figure any of that cancels out a blatant sabotage of a rival's expedition?"

Feo's eyes narrowed. "I'll tell you once more: Be still, or you'll be sorry. I'm being far more charitable than you deserve. Call it interest on those loans your father refused to accept years ago. I'll insure that your ship isn't repossessed while it's on T-S 311. And you'll receive a fuel top-off before you leave. Not enough to allow you to tour the sector at my expense, but sufficient to guarantee your safe return."

And no more. Dan was keenly aware that his kinsman was putting shackles on the starhopper—and on his rival. Once back on T-W 593, Praedar would have to whistle and wait for outbound transport, at Feo's leisure; without extra fuel, *Fiona/Praedar's Project* would be as good as grounded on the N'lacs' home world.

Rei Ito spoke up. "Just for Cam's private information, do I have the situation straight? Dr. Juxury agrees not to press charges on this incident, the delayed cargo, or the prepaid tickets. And you acknowledge that Tavares carried out his plots in your name, Saunder..."

"I admit nothing of the sort," Feo growled. "And if there's a leak, you'll find I have *my* ways of reaching out, right into Cam's network staff. Is that clear?"

For the first time, fear shone in Ito's dark eyes. "You ... may rely on Pan Terran to be discreet, sir. No one but Cam will see our report." The news hounds were covering their asses. They'd probably get raises and a nice boost in rank out of this, even if they couldn't go public with the story.

Dan grimaced. "That's it? You damned near wreck Praedar's expedition. You bend and break Terran laws, and a few Whimed ones, too. Now you hush it all up with money. So much for xenoarch's high principles."

His cousin had the grace to look somewhat uncomfortable. But Feo didn't contradict the assessment, and his guilt didn't last long.

Praedar said, "Such practices are not uncommon, Dan. In the Whimed Federation, it is known as *hasju-aytan*—a necessary warp of ethics to achieve a desirable goal. One strives to avoid this. One does not always succeed. We maintain our progress toward the larger goal. History will judge us right."

"I admire your confidence and dedication, Juxury," Feo said with a sour smile, "if not your faulty selectivity."

The two faced one another through the medium of Kimball's remote vidder. Feo Saunder and Praedar Effan Juxury were peers, both established xenoarchaeologists. Both labored to fathom the past, and both stubbornly clung to opposing views of that past. They looked across a gulf light-years wide, divided by millions of years of different evolution, custom, and background.

"It's not over yet," Dan said wonderingly. "Just this phase of it."

Feo favored him with a tolerant sneer. "You *do* have promise, my boy. Perhaps Juxury didn't err in taking you onto his team, despite your pathetic lack of education." Tavares nodded, appreciating company in his underdog's misery.

"There will be no more obstructions," Praedar said.

"Yes, yes." His rival waved a hand impatiently. "You have my word on it. These reporters are our witnesses. Henceforth, we meet on even ground, Juxury—the intellectual battlefield of tomorrow's presentations. May the best team win." Then he spoke to Tavares. "Stay in town, at the office. Hope and I will meet you there, later, when the Assembly concludes. We'll discuss plans."

Tavares was whipped and he knew it, crushed by a Saunder steamroller. He had nowhere to run and no one to back him in the Terran sector, if he defied his one-time mentors.

Feo wasn't through chastening upstarts. His gray eyes became steely. "Dan, you won't need that spacecraft, once you finish piloting Juxury's team back to their dig. I'll make certain you never haul another cargo. You had your chance to work for me, and you slammed the door in my face. Hope and I have no forbearance for kindred who try to shame us."

The tarmac had been shot from beneath Dan. He hid his panic with bravado. "You mean those who refuse to crawl and beg. I thought so! You lied about my dad turning down your loan. You didn't make the offer, because he wouldn't grovel to you."

"This conversation is ended," Feo snapped, and the screen winked off. Well, that was *one* way to win an argument!

210

Dan's brief moment of revenge was swept away by despair. Feo's blacklist would make the dispatchers' look like a love pat. Praedar was no indie hauler, but he seemed to sense what had happened. He communicated with touch, grasping the Terran's shoulder sympathetically.

Gradually Dan awoke to his surroundings. Kimball had switched off his equipment and was following Tavares toward town, probably seeking an interview—though what the news hounds would do with it, Dan couldn't guess. By now spectators were scattering. Dan and Praedar stood alone by the ship.

With a sigh, Dan got busy testing the antitheft device and resetting it. He said, "I doubt this is necessary. Feo doesn't need to bother siccing repossess artists on me now."

"I am sorry," Praedar said softly. Then he nodded. "Matters are now stalemated on both sides, for the moment. We must proceed."

That dogged resolve kept him still plodding ahead. "Okay," Dan agreed without enthusiasm. "And just hope the Assembly is amenable to reason, even if we don't have all that Saunder money backing us."

Rain clouds descended again as they drove back to the Complex. Tours were continuing in the covered dig. However, Praedar's team had seen everything they wanted to see in the posh dome and had adjourned to their suite. They spent what remained of the afternoon and the entire evening mapping out strategies.

Dan sat on the sidelines, feeling like a push prop on an FTL craft. He could contribute moral support, but not much else at this juncture. He'd be sitting on the sidelines tomorrow, too. Dan harbored no illusions that the glamour of his name could affect the scientific debate favorably. That game had run its course, even if Feo didn't keep his promises.

From dawn onward, diurnal species streamed across the rain-drenched skywalks to the main building. Nocturnally oriented attendees were already staking out good seats in the auditorium. Saunder staffers, anticipating big crowds for this, the Assembly's starring event, had raised walls and enlarged the central area to accommodate everyone who wanted to see the confrontation.

Those who couldn't get admission to the hall watched the presentations on monitors throughout the exhibit sections and manufacturers' rooms.

Feo's students handed out transbuttons to every attendee who wanted one, and a few who didn't. Dan noticed that the devices bore the familiar Saunder-McKelvey Enterprises logo. That struck him as ironic. Ward Saunder and his son Todd had perfected the original Terran universal translators. Now Todd's great-grandson and Ward's great-great-grandson stood on opposing sides of this multispecies war of xenoarchaeological theories. Their teams would present their arguments to Terrans and non-Terrans alike through those S-ME transbuttons.

Somehow things always circled back to the Saunders and McKelveys. No matter where Dan traveled, he remained within his family's grasp. As the press was fond of saying, the Saunder-McKelveys were humanity's representatives, her reigning dynasty, a distillation of her brightest and best. Bitterly Dan added, "And her sneakiest and most ruthless."

The audience was quietly attentive during the T-W 593 expedition's holo-mode segments. Everyone knew why so many of Praedar's team weren't attending the Assembly in person. Dan handled the tri-di projector, making certain absent teammates' work was tuned to lifelike perfection. One after another, the specialists appeared on the dais, reading their papers, displaying artifacts and specimens: Sheila; Drastil; Rosie; Armilly; and Chen. That last, posthumous presentation affected the attending scientists deeply. Even the Saunder faction was subdued.

It was a hopeful lead-off for the rest of the program. Joe was up first. His exhibit materials had been samplers. Now he brought out his big guns, including remote-probe postmortems of N'lac graves. Hughes compared the bodies of recently escaped slaves with the corpses of later N'lac generations, showing a steady deterioration within their home planet's environment. The recital left nonmeds queasy. Hearing about polycythemia rubra, paracental scotomas, hypoxic vasodilation, and mesenteric venules was one thing; seeing graphic tissue holo-modes was another. The xenobiologist worked his way through the facts methodically. At one point he contrasted a living image of Chuss and his stats with those of a N'lac youngster of the same age who hadn't enjoyed the benefits of hyperbaric gestation and growth. Dan thought it was a rock-solid lecture. *That* ought to squash the critics!

He was wrong. The question-and-answer session following Joe's presentation proved that it wasn't easy to sell a bunch of big brains who were locked in a particular mind set. The Saunders' supporters hammered Joe with challenges.

"Similar tampering at the Vahnaj dig on Outi produced genetic monsters and mass deaths, Hughes!"

"You're interfering with those subhumanoids' lives!"

"Unethical!"

"Immoral!"

Joe parried adroitly. "If you recall, the Outi Gestation Project rendered its subjects sterile, among other ill effects. My experiment has produced four live births and thriving young. The eldest child is now ten years old, nearly mature for his species, and a leader of his tribe. The data confirm the Level Three humanoid capacity of this race. I suggest this offers a new and exciting field of xenobiology, as did the Whimed Federation's work on Eaunda..."

Hope Saunder, backed by her sycophants, commented loudly, "That underlines our argument; the Eaundas are subhumanoid!"

Joe struggled on until his time ran out. Shaking his head, frustrated by his opponents' obstinacy, he yielded the floor to Ruieb-An.

Vahnajes chittered and tweaked the gain on their translators. Ruieb might be a maverick and an oddball to his scientific fraternity, but the lutrinoids respected him. His presentation was very involved, crammed with esoteric xenocryptography material. The question-and-answer session was a blur of in-group exchanges, leaving nonexperts far behind. The Saunders' specialist in that discipline put in only token protests, apparently not eager to lock horns with an acknowledged master.

To compensate for their mild resistance against Ruieb-An's theories, the enemy camp gave Kat a very rough time. To Dan, her paper on N'lac social patters and mythology sounded thoroughly convincing, as it had when he'd heard her explain it weeks ago. But when she finished, a storm erupted in the hall. Praedar's friends and his rivals' shouted like brawlers, standing in the aisles, close to trading blows.

"Ridiculous!"

"... agrees with massive bodies of proof from every humanoid culture!"

"Swallowing that primitive mumbo jumbo whole!"

"Can't expect precise patterns from a people struggling simply to survive..."

"Getz warned us Olmsted was a typical Harte-taught näive . . ."

"*There*'s a wonderful character witness for your head-in-the-sand position—Getz!"

Dan didn't envy Praedar. The boss had the team's clean-up spot, following Kat. He waited until the crowd had calmed down and had resumed their seats before he began. His presentation was yet another demonstration of why it had been absolutely vital for him to attend the Assembly in person. It demonstrated more than his spellbinding presence, more than his ability to switch fluently from Terran English to Vahnaj to Lannon to his own language and back again. No holo-mode could have duplicated his power over an audience. The Whimed's charisma was at full throttle. He reached into minds, probing, stimulating, demanding that his listeners think and consider ideas their emotions told them to reject. He was a skilled manipulator, playing them, leading them down the paths he chose.

"Observe. Data checked and multiple-checked for accuracy. Continuous N'lac habitation of this locale since five hundred Terran years before the present. It has been suggested this species is not directly related to the culture that built the cities. I point out that no two species may occupy an identical niche simultaneously. We must inquire if it is possible that after a supposed dominant humanoid race mysteriously vanished from this world, the N'lacs could have developed speech, an intricate social structure, and an elaborate mythology within one and a half Terran millennia. I submit this is quite unlikely. If it were true, the N'lacs would qualify as a unique phenomenon, and they would be cherished for that achievement alone . . .

". . . the hard-learned lessons of our discipline's earlier errors must be remembered, with all the difficulty your predecessors had in grasping the importance of sexual dimorphism and the vagaries of xenoarchaeological allometry. We are now capable of realizing that the pressure of a hostile environment, notwithstanding a possible genetic alteration by captors, could significantly disturb anatomy and mental capacity. The evidence offered by my esteemed colleague Dr. Hughes demonstrates this fact admirably . . .

"A hypothesis need not refute every challenge in order to be valid. In the last analysis, a theory must satisfy the *majority* of unanswered questions regarding the material . . ."

Praedar's attention locked on the team's sponsors, seated in the front row. Eckard was visibly shaken. Even Anelen appeared edgy, as if he knew he wasn't Praedar's equal in the game of burning stares.

"Judgments by those removed from a site should not be the sole purview of decision." Throughout the huge room, human and alien field workers nodded earnest agreement. They understood exactly what Praedar was talking about. Why should the "go no-go" power rest with stay-at-homes in institutions, foundations, or the Terran-Whimed Xenoethnic Council? To those secure types, a dig's perils and its discoveries were abstracts. For Praedar and every other scientist on the scene, a site was the past, present, and future, with its own rich sensory elements and a *feel* no distant licenser could appreciate.

"Certain factions in the civilized sectors insist that any newly discovered, nonstellar race must be quarantined for its cultural protection—that starvation and a naturally induced extinction are preferable to contact with offworlders, no matter how benign that contact." Among the Vahnajes, there was twittering dismay. Progressive antiquarians frowned at their fellow Vahnajes, the most prominent espousers of the "no exceptions" hands-off policy Praedar had mentioned. The Whimed went on. "Others hold that incorporation, which may destroy a primitive people's right of individuality, is a necessary result of galactic exploration. Indeed, a privilege of the ruling races . . ."

It was the turn of other factions of the audience. Eckard, who'd admitted that aggressive planet colonizers were pushing his Council hard, ran a finger around his collar. Anelen blinked, his expression unreadable.

Praedar leaned forward, using all his mesmerizing arts. "I repeat—we who are in the field with intelligent primitives must judge the situation. In the case of the N'lacs, this expedition is firmly convinced that it would be unforgivably immoral either to sit with folded hands or forcibly to change their way of life."

He continued into a broad summary of his project, tying up loose ends and foiling the quibblers before they had a chance to get their credits' worth in. From Dan's point of view, it was one hell of a sales pitch. Praedar talked just long enough and quit. He left listeners hungry for more.

Praedar's opponents refused to stay down, though. The question-and-answer session was such chaos that Dan didn't understand how Praedar could hear himself think, let alone cope with what his challengers were yelling out at him. The translators, which had smoothed any jerkiness from Praedar's speech, converting Whimed abruptness into hypnotic eloquence, went into overdrive. Somehow, Praedar made sense of the mess, maintaining his serenity, and Dan's awe of the alien rose several more notches.

The Saunders dug in on one of their key points: the lack of grave excavations on T-W 593. A large number of attendees seconded them. There was a current popularity for analyzing xenoarchaeological remains, and the Saunders rode that wave for all the momentum they could get. Praedar repeated his reminder that *his* team was dealing with a living race, and desecrating the graves of their ancestors would be an offense.

"...may I note that the grave dates the Drs. Saunder have published coincide precisely with those we have obtained by remote probes and nonintrusive investigations. Given the correspondence of these dates, are we to accept that a civilization appeared, full-blown, on T-S 311? No earlier artifacts than the two millennia prior to the present date have been offered. Did this culture thrive for less than a Terran century and vanish as suddenly as it came into being, with no indication of a natural or humanoid-made disaster?"

That triggered another explosive round of approval and rebuttal. The Assembly's official timekeepers had to step in and stop the uproar. The debate shifted to the exhibit hall. As the midday break neared, numbers shrank. Eventually the combatants dwindled to a precious few and gave up. Praedar had obviously relished the clash. His teammates, though, needed a recess.

The break seemed all too short. A couple of hours later, they were back in the packed auditorium, sitting in the audience, this time, as the Saunders began their presentations. Dan sat to the far left near the front row, studying faces around him and gauging reactions rather than listening to his relatives' familiar arguments. Not too surprisingly, there were more SAUNDER SPELLS SUPERIOR SELECTIVITY badges than the counterattack ones in the crowd. This was, after all, the Assembly hosts' big event.

The media attended in force. Rei Ito sat apart from the science publication staffers. Dan wondered if she was being ostracized as a network reporter. Not that it mattered. He doubted any of the news hounds were going to be impartial in this war of theories.

Saunder-McKelvey money always added impressive weight to whatever project the affluent family members were involved in.

There was considerable whispering about Greg Tavares's absence from the platform. Maybe that would balance out Getz's defection from Praedar's team.

Unfortunately, Feo and Hope had plenty of reputable associates to fill the gap left by their protégé's disgrace. Saunder team players paraded to the dais, presenting their papers. It was apparent they'd rehearsed for months—possibly coached by an imported PR expert. Speeches were honed and polished, delivery crisp.

Discouraged, Dan gave his seat to one of the many standees and retreated to the rear of a room. He overheard a xenoarch remark to her friend, "Not spectacular, but Saunder's a decent scientist, I'll give him that," and his spirits sank.

The question-and-answer sessions were heated. But they were the same, familiar arguments, the same ground being gone over yet once more. After a while Dan tuned them out, surveying the hall. Praedar was sitting beside their sponsors and occasionally eyeing Eckard and Anelen calculatingly. Was the Whimed fearful, as Dan was, that all the hard work and the team's devotion to the N'lacs had gone for nothing? What a tragedy, if the project and the N'lacs died because of such petty things as Anelen's dislike of non-Whimeds, his disapproval of a shady starhopper ownership shift, and Eckard's unwillingness to stand up to powerful colony developers.

Kat slid her hand through Dan's crooked arm. He glanced down as she leaned against him, seeking comfort. "Why can't they see?" she murmured. "It's so important, for Chuss' people, for the truth."

Attendees turned, scowling, fingers to lips. Dan disengaged his arm and wrapped it around Kat, holding her close. They listened to the reminder of the presentations in gloomy silence.

Dan wasn't really hearing the people on the stage. Visions marched through his mind's eye: N'lacs, affectionate and sharing; offworlders, digging until they were exhausted, seeking the proof that too few of their fellow xenoarchaeologists would believe; the mural, portraying a civilization's reach for the stars; and a handful of slaves, escaping, fleeing . . .

Kat's grip tightened around his waist and Dan came out of his daymare. Applause was filling the hall. Feo, quite wisely, had let

Hope handle the summary for their team. She hadn't canceled out good impressions by being too long-winded. Dan and Kat joined the clapping politely, as the Saunders had for their presentations. Even in a battle, courtesies must be honored among humanoids.

Would they be, by creatures as alien as the Old Ones?

The rest of that day and most of the next was a wearisome anticlimax. Praedar had more bases to touch, more flesh to press, more points to make. Dan's job, however, was bound up with the starhopper. He skipped the final morning's minor programming —given to the field's newcomers and a few less important papers. While that was going on, Dan was at the Port, prepping the craft, getting that top-off fuel package Feo had promised, and loading it. The manager apologized for the short unit. Fear of Commander Adam McKelvey was still gnawing at the local personnel. Dan, in a black mood, did nothing to reassure them. Let them chew their nails. His team had been doing that ever since they'd arrived on this damned planet.

In the afternoon, most Assembly functions began to shut down. Exhibits were dismantled and readied for shipment. Feo and Hope, ever the gracious hosts, provided staffers and vehicles to assist their guests. This time Praedar didn't argue. He accepted the help. Even so, transferring the specimens was a bitch. Dan pumped his med boosters again and again and hit the caffa heavily. It took them till dark to get all the materials—except Getz's —stowed.

Then there was one more ordeal to get through before they could go home.

Each of the Xenoarchaeological Assemblies concluded with a formal. It was intended as a pleasant social gathering, a relaxing wind-up to days of intensive intellectual activity. This one, though, was going to be an additional tension-causer for Praedar's team.

As Dan emerged from his roomlet, Kat said, "Hey, that's nice." She walked around him, examining the tunic suit he'd exhumed from *Fiona*'s lockers. "Chic. You look every centimeter the Saunder-McKelvey princeling."

"At least it still fits," he said sourly. "Good thing these basic styles are back in. That's all I could afford, the first time these clothes were available. I couldn't afford this good nowadays." He returned Kat's compliments, admiring her glittering gown as she pirouetted for his inspection.

"This isn't particularly up-to-date or expensive, either," she said.

Joe Hughes chuckled. "Ah, but businesslike simplicity is always in fashion." His formal suit was very similar to the one Dan wore. They exchanged self-congratulatory grins and Joe said, "We'll do fine. We aren't the only impecunious field diggers here. Just think of it this way. The Saunders have to spend big credits to achieve the charming plainness we've come up with. Besides, a lot of our colleagues were never interested in fashion trends. No matter what the occasion, they look as if they slept in their clothes."

"Appropriate," Kat said, "when one's mind is millennia in the past."

Dan muttered, "I wonder if the N'lacs partied, just before the roof fell in on their civilization?"

"Quite possible," Praedar replied, then gestured toward the suite's outer door, urging them to move.

The T-W 593 group made a striking quintet—if Dan did say so himself—as they arrived at the fast-filling Assembly hall. Ruieb-An's floor-length metallic robes caught and magnified light. Praedar's spectacularly patterned skin-tight jumper matched his black, silver, and red crest. Dan and Joe bracketed Kat, doing their best to look confident and elegant.

Media reps waylaid them frequently, taking holos. The team was small enough to fit nicely within a single focus, and the multispecies nature of the five added spice.

Rei Ito greeted them. Her gown was much fancier than Kat's, but Dan thought Kat was far more attractive. For this occasion, the Pan Terran reporter had decorated her lens pendant with a circlet of ornate gems. The effect blinded her subjects while she was capturing their images.

Without any prior discussion, the group decided to stick close together. An old phrase, safety in numbers, popped into Dan's head—not that they could claim many numbers!

Like the opening socializer, this affair tended to split along racial lines. There was only a modicum of mingling. Most Vahnajes gravitated toward the enclosed, private refreshment islands set aside for their use. Ruieb-An, though, chose to stay with his team. Praedar huddled with Whimed colleagues when they approached him. But when the encounters ended, he rejoined Dan and the others.

The crowd eddied, forming pools where friends conversed or rivals rehashed differences. The room wasn't as jammed as it had been for the earlier ceremonies. Many humans and aliens had already left T-S 311. They had appointments to keep elsewhere, or they were dissatisfied with what they'd accomplished at the Assembly and wanted to get away and lick their wounds. Were Tavares and Getz among that latter segment? They certainly weren't in the hall. However, Praedar's presence here showed his enemies that *he* hadn't run.

Anelen and his aides walked briskly toward the five. Ruieb and the humans prudently stepped aside. The Whimeds went into a snarling huddle for a few moments, then separated, facing each other, panting. Anelen and Praedar traded clipped, guttural words.

Ruieb frowned, trying to follow the alien chatter and not succeeding. Dan glanced at Kat and Joe. They shook their heads. Kat said, "It's dialect, and rattle-fast, at that."

The confrontation stopped as quickly as it had begun. Anelen hurried away, staring angrily at a group of Vahnajes as he did.

Praedar was motionless, his expression frozen and tense. Slowly he roused himself as Kat asked tentatively, "Did he . . . ?"

"No reply." The Whimed's eyes were shimmering mirrors, reflecting the room's shifting overhead illumination. "He has not temporized so before."

Dan winced. That sounded bad—bad for the expedition and bad for the N'lacs.

When they bumped into Councilman Eckard a short time later, he was no more encouraging than his felinoid counterpart had been. "You mustn't push, Juxury. You know we have a lot of irons in the fire besides yours. Smuggling operations that have to be quelled. Coordinations with the Terran and Whimed Fleets. Settlement establishments. Colony applications. Trade affairs. All sorts of topics. We'll be convening in . . . oh . . . about twelve Earth weeks. I'll get back to you when I can." Eckard and his staff strolled on, to deal with other grant and license seekers.

The disappointment of those two meetings was but one strain in an evening crammed with them. Dan dodged one question after another concerning his credentials. Maybe Rei Ito was keeping a lid on her info, but other reporters and scientists had their own suspicions, and wanted to dig. Kat fought to hang onto

220

her temper as Saunder supporters scoffed at her xenosocio theories. Joe and Ruieb-An and Praedar had to cope with critics, too.

And always the media circled, their lenses probing.

Feo and Hope toured, receiving congratulations. Royalty, saying good-bye to their subjects.

The Saunders beamed, pressing the flesh. "So grateful you could attend. We wanted our friends to have a taste of home, as it were . . ."

Late in the affair, drawn together by an invisible magnet, the two groups met in the center of the hall. Rei Ito and the rest of the media revolved in orbit around them.

The initial contact was peaceful enough.

"Your presentation went well, Juxury. You're an incredible speaker. Where did you learn Terran English? You put most humans to shame," Hope gushed.

"Thank you. It is a flexible language. Chen taught me its nuances," Praedar said. "Your material was well received, was it not?"

"Oh, yes. No complaints. No, not at all." The Saunders noted Kat's gown and scattered polite praise on Joe and Ruieb-An. "And did you enjoy yourself, Danny?" Feo asked.

Dan forced a feeble smile. "Was I supposed to? I thought this was a working session, not a Saunder-McKelvey gala."

The inane grin slid off his cousin's face. "You're taking this interpretation of data disagreement entirely too seriously, my boy."

"No, he is not," Praedar said, his crest stiffening. "Unlike you, Dan knows that the eminence of your family will continue only so long as its members do not cling to stagnant havens at the cost of truth and progress."

"Really!" Hope exclaimed, bristling. "We do not feel driven to rush blindly into wild hypotheses . . ."

Kat leered. "Maybe that's because you're too wrapped up in preserving your reputation, not in finding the facts. We," she said, mimicking Hope, "are willing to take risks. We put our lives and reputations on the line to uncover the true history of this stellar area . . ."

Worried Saunder staffers were flocking around their bosses, trying to hold the reporters at arm's length. They couldn't. Rei

Ito, in particular, was devouring the exchange, collecting more juicy gossip for her network's boss, soon to be her brother-in-law.

Feo drew himself up haughtily. "Very well. I don't feel this is the place for such sordid discussions, but . . . what *is* this area's 'true history,' as you put it? How did this supposed enslavement of those primitives' ancestors take place? According to your own materials, the existing civilization destroyed all its spacecraft. Do you doubt Ruieb-An's translations of those data? Do you have any explanation of how those people were allegedly removed to some . . . some anthropomorphic species' slave camps? And how did the primitives—the escaped slaves—return to T-W 593? Did their shaman wave a magic wand?"

Dan had held his tongue during the earlier scientific debates. Now he jumped in with both feet. "That's what an alien technology often appears to be, Feo—a magic wand. When the Vahnajes made contact with us, humanity was stuck in its own solar system. The Terrans of that era believed that FTL was impossible. They refused to accept that it existed until the Vahnajes' spacecraft shoved the reality in our faces. And it took a lot of sacrifice and work before your grandmother and my grandfather proved Terra could build its own stardrive. For all we know, the nonanthropomorphic race that conquered the N'lacs used a technology even farther beyond our comprehension than FTL was to mid-twenty-first-century humans."

"That's right," Joe said. "Even if we don't know how the populations were removed, they were. Eventually we'll discover the method. The fact is, the N'lacs vanished from T-S 311 in the same time frame that they did on their mother world . . ."

"*Colony* world," Feo corrected him.

"Mother world," Dan insisted.

"What do you know about—"

"He knows a great deal," Praedar cut in. By now his crest was a spiky flag. His calm voice contrasted with that emotional barometer. "Dan listens. He learns. He does not blind himself to data for selfish reasons . . ."

"What does *he* have to protect?" Hope snapped. "Don't be deluded by his name, Juxury. I think you're the one who's blinded. Dan hardly qualifies as a typical member of our family, someone worth paying attention to."

"I'm no fat cat, if that's what you mean," Dan said. "You

seem to forget that our ancestors didn't start with a bottomless supply of money, Feo. You're using your fortune to buy a career. But how will the future generations of Saunders and McKelveys view you? As a pioneer, an innovator? Someone who wasn't afraid to take chances and test brand-new ideas? That definition fits our grandparents. Does it fit you? Or are you and Hope dilettante offshoots from the main tree?" He adopted Kat's tactic and aped a future vid historian, lecturing: "'Feo and Hope Saunder had all the advantages. They should have made a significant contribution to xenoarchaeology. Instead they played it safe and went nowhere . . .'"

Both groups hurled accusations.

"The graves! You didn't excavate . . ."

"And *you* haven't located any graves on T-S 311 beyond the invasion date, or any earlier than a century before . . ."

"No reconstructions. You're concocting your theories piecemeal to describe the impossible . . ."

"But what have you actually *done* here? What's your purpose? To manufacture a museum without any substance of the culture that created the objects?"

"How did these so-called N'lacs . . . ?"

"*Search!*" Praedar's basso thundering choked off the Saunders' arguments in midbreath. The Whimed's crest was a crown, but he was very much in control of himself and the situation. "Visit. Observe our site. Investigate our findings *in situ*, as we have had the courtesy to do for *your* work."

The challenge stunned the Saunders. They gaped at him, speechless. Rei Ito sidled past Saunder aides, moving in close on the argument. "That's a very interesting proposal." She looked around, soliciting seconds, and got them. The Saunders were becoming aware that dozens of scientists had gathered to watch the show. Like the news hounds, they awaited the Assembly hosts' response.

"Really, this has been a most unseemly . . . " Feo began, back-pedaling.

"Come on. It's a fair point. They've visited your dig twice now, Saunder, and you haven't been to Juxury's planet even once."

"Bad for xenoarch," Imhoff put in. "You ought to put up or shut up."

Feo and Hope were shoulder to shoulder, looking harried at the barrage of comment from all sides. Dan said, "For the family rep, you may have to accept Praedar's invitation."

His cousin shot him a bitter glare. "You're enjoying this."

Dan shrugged. "Whether I am or not, there's justice here. Well? As Ito said, it's an interesting porposal. Have you got the guts to confront our evidence in the field?"

The Saunders were in the middle of the room, but they were cornered. Hope threw up her hands in a gesture of defeat and Feo spat, "Oh, all right!" He bowed mockingly to Praedar. "*Irast*, we are at your service."

Praedar had never appeared more alien—his crest softening yet spiky, eyes oil-on-water colors, his lips parted in a feral smile. "Anticipated. When?"

The Saunders weren't going to be let off with vague promises. Their rival insisted on specifics.

Affecting an offhand manner, Feo said, "Oh, that's difficult to say. We have to wrap up the Assembly, of course, then we have some publications to tend to . . ."

Dan broke in. "Let's not let the appointment drag on too long. That's happened too often, in science and in our family. Feuds and duplicated efforts have wasted both parties' time. With common sense and cooperation, two expeditions could produce a unified picture of this ancient civilization, instead of quibbling endlessly over details."

"Logical," Ito agreed. She didn't give the Saunders any chance to rebut. "What's the date? You have the cream of science pubs here. We can all put it in our journals and vidcasts . . ."

Was the Pan Terran news hound getting even for Feo's cracking the whip on her? Whatever her motive, at the moment she was Praedar's ally. Other reporters took up her theme, pressuring the Saunders relentlessly.

"Three weeks," Feo said suddenly, surprising everyone, especially his wife. Hope gawked at him as he went on. "That will entail considerable interruption of our work. However, there apparently is no other way to end this ridiculous stand-off."

Ito turned expectantly to Praedar, ready to record his reply.

"We await you," the Whimed said. A relieved murmur ran through the crowd.

"Good. Kimball and I will accompany them, if you don't object," Ito announced.

Praedar didn't. Dan suspected his kindred did, but were afraid to make any more of a scene.

Praedar nodded. "I am content. Whatever you learn on T-W 593, you will witness what has occurred and know that the history of the N'lacs holds significance for all humanoid species. Truth will be served."

CHAPTER FOURTEEN
⊙⊙⊙⊙⊙⊙⊙⊙⊙

Nontriumphant Return

Dan knew the trip home was going to be far tougher than the outbound ride. He longed to cut short the formal affair, retreat to the ship, and launch. Praedar, though, was still building bridges with influential people at the Complex. So his team wore their bright smiles, shook hands, and continued to chitchat into the small hours of the morning. A number of new acquaintances like Imhoff and Jarrett took the trouble to talk to Dan at length. They all expressed hopes of meeting him at the next Assembly and told him not to take his critics' comments too much to heart. Dan answered them noncommittally, painfully conscious of his uncertain future and that of the expedition.

When the social finally ended, there was no rest. The team had to rush to change from their formal clothes, collect their personal luggage, and head for Port. The original schedule had set them up for a predawn window. However, traffic kept stalling. Dan wondered if that was yet another petty tactic by his cousin. The hours stretched on. Pilot and passengers boosted meds, trying to stay alert. Clearance came almost at midday.

Dan was grateful for his years on the starlanes. He needed that experience now. This was an ordeal demanding he operate on automatic.

Launch. Atmospheric flight. Increasingly higher orbit. Kilometer marks ticking past. Reaching. Feo's and Hope's planet shrinking...

It must have shrunk thus on the N'lac ships' screens, as they departed from T-S 311 two thousand years ago. They, too, had been going home—to permanent enslavement.

FTL point, and they were on their way across the light-years, with vector logged and locked.

Dan wanted to crawl into a hole and brood over the setbacks they'd suffered on his kinsman's world. He knew his companions felt the same. In a single-stage starhopper, however, privacy was impossible.

Praedar did his best to pull them out of their depression. He took the long view, putting the Saunder-hosted Assembly in perspective. This wasn't the first such conference, and it wouldn't be the last. No, the team hadn't scored an unqualified success, but it had made some converts. They'd knocked out Feo's dirty-tricks man, Tavares. They'd squeezed a promise from the Saunders to pay a courtesy visit to T-W 593.

"Time will prove us right," Praedar said.

They tried to believe. And they tried to forget. Most of all, the Terrans and Ruieb-An yearned for sleep.

Ordinarily, once he'd completed in-flight checks, Dan soaked up as much sack time as he wished during a starhop. Now, weighted by the responsibility for four other lives, his stints in his web were fitful, disturbed by bad dreams. When he awoke, he was still tired. Station-tending chores had never seemed so tedious.

To walk in planetary gravity on *his* planet; to breathe air filled with dust devils, not the smell of rain forest and rotting vegetation; to see purple foilage, not yellow; to be among friends, human and alien—to be . . . home . . .

Days crept by, full of introspection and regrets.

If only . . . if only . . . if only . . .

And then they were going sublight and dropping into real space.

Dan beamed a terse ETA message ahead and fed figures to the comps. They retraced their outbound passage. In a few hours the ship was descending from high vacuum and blackness, entering a blue-green atmosphere.

On final orbit, Dan took manual control. This might be his last opportunity to be a pilot for a long, long time. As he lined up on the approach leg, zoom scans showed him a crowd of vehicles and beings gathering at the northwest edge of the mesa. A welcoming committee! A warmer one, he hoped, than what they'd met on T-S 311. He adjusted braking to stop them well short of that waiting mob and went to touchdown phase.

Praedar's Project taxied to her slot. The herd of desert trucks and rovers bucketed toward her. The sight boosted the travelers' morale a lot. They hurried through tie-down procedures, eager to debark.

Halfway down the ramp, they were engulfed by laughing colleagues and N'lacs amid a chaos of bear hugs. Everyone was talking at once. Whimeds huddled joyfully. Vahnajes bowed and touched gently. Armilly whooped and roared. Childlike, webbed fingers clutched Dan's, and piping native voices rose above the storm of offworlders' conversations. Chuss and Meej flung their skinny arms around Dan in an exuberant imitation of a Terran embrace. "Kelfee! Kelfee! You come back in fly-fly! Bring all friends back! You home!"

A lump filled Dan's throat. He said huskily, "That's right, you fellows. All home home," and he returned the youngsters' clumsy hugs.

Truth from the mouths of funny-faced, goggle-eyed e.t.s! This was home, though not one that Varenka's New Earth Renaissancers could ever love. It took a settler, a true child of the stars, to feel that way about a planet parsecs from Earth. But knowing he belonged here, was wanted here, twisted Dan's emotions powerfully.

How long would T-W 593 *be* home, for any of them?

"Hey, how did it go?" Sheila bellowed. "Damn you, McKelvey! You tied us in knots down here! That was the barest-boned naked-ass ETA message I've ever heard! Why didn't you tell us anything?"

"Yeah!" Rosie cried. "Sadists!"

Others spoke up, the clamor deafening.

"Was Imhoff there?"

"What about Retur?"

"Did Quas-Jin report on the Saunderhome restoration?"

Kat shouted, "I took plenty of candid vids. You'll see them all . . ."

Joe added, "And I bought all the recorded wafers of the sessions I could, so you'll have the flavor of the program . . ."

"Was Jumapili's update on the Eridami dig . . .?"

"How did Bill handle Jarrett and the effigy aces?"

Realizing Getz wasn't with the other returning travelers, his top student exclaimed, "Where is he?"

Apprehension replaced elation. The stay-at-homers' fears were obvious. "Not another accident, another death!"

Praedar ended the suspense. "Dr. Getz resigned. He has joined the Gokhale Institute."

"What! He *can't*!"

"He did," Joe Hughes said flatly, and he snapped his fingers by way of illustration.

"I understand the trigger," Kat put in. "Jarrett ripping his data to shreds, as we figured he would. Bill might have simply opted out of the presentations, saying he'd decided his paper wasn't quite ready. He could have resigned later on. The fact is, he deserted us, right in the middle of the Assembly."

Nodding, Praedar said, "His action, coming at such a crucial time, hurt our group's credibility with the sponsors."

Getz's students were devastated. Several wept. Others swore.

Baines growled, "What a guy! Never mind about the team!"

Someone else yelled, "Traitor! That's what he is!"

"He never *did* fit in . . ."

"Everything for his project, nothing for us."

Getz's most loyal student said defensively, "That's not fair. We don't know what caused him to . . ."

"Don't we?" Baines countered.

"If McKelvey hadn't pushed him so hard . . ."

Joe shook his head. "It's looking more and more as if Dan was right about those glass elements. And Bill *knew* he was."

Dan didn't have time to relish the praise. He was busy helping cooler heads restrain quick-tempered types. When things calmed down a bit, Praedar told Getz's students, "Your instructor did not appear concerned for your situation. You are welcome to stay with the expedition. You have been good team members. This dig offers opportunity to young xenoarchaeologists. You may discover you wish to work with specialties other than xenoeffigies."

"Y-yes," the most senior student said. "We . . . we appreciate that. I could study with Armilly . . ."

Another volunteered, "And I'm interested in fluidics. I took my minor in frontier-world glass manufacturing. Maybe I can assist Dan."

"Good." Praedar dismissed that topic and jumped to another. "How has excavation progressed in our absence?"

Joe said, "You must have plenty to show us."

Sheila grabbed the cue. "Oh, we do. A real mixed bag. Some good stuff, some dead ends, some itchy snags." Chuss and his fellow N'lacs wrinkled their noses and shuddered. Sheila went on. "But we want to hear what you did at the Assembly first. Give!"

As the stay-at-homes nagged, Dan eyed them warily. How were they were going to react when they got another nasty kick in the shins? And they would—the story of their representatives' triumphs and failures.

Ruieb-An said. "Is . . . urr . . . need-ful re-turn . . . urr . . . all speci-i-mens to lab-or-a-tory . . ."

The reality of that ended all demands and counterdemands for the time being. The recent travelers got off light. They readjusted to gravity while their colleagues transferred exhibit cases and luggages to the vehicles. That done, everyone piled aboard and the caravan started for N'lac Valley.

Dan gazed across the familiar landscape of dark mountain ranges, thickets of tendrilled trees, and dutos riding thermals. Clouds of oony spun aside in the the vortices left by the trucks, then regrouped in crimson, humming swarms. The scene should have put him at ease. It had all the right sights, sounds, and scents.

But . . .

Something was wrong.

Hardly aware he was doing so, he was scratching the backs of his hands, his nape, his thighs, and his arms. He had company. N'lacs and offworlders all were scratching, the N'lacs more frantically than expedition members. With difficulty, Dan mastered the impulse. A few minutes later the scratching urge disappeared as suddenly as it had begun, and he realized that his impression that something was out of kilter with the landscape had vanished when the bugs-under-the-skin irritation stopped.

Weird! This wasn't like his instinctive reaction to an alien environment. Anyway, the N'lacs had felt the peculiar urge, too.

"Well, now you've had a taste of it," Sheila said. Chuss, looking badly spooked, hung onto the back of her seat. The blonde patted him reassuringly. "That itch has been driving us nuts ever since you left."

Dan didn't want an elaboration. Kat and Joe didn't seem to be in a hurry to hear the details, either. Were they, like him, half afraid further mention might set off more scratching episodes?

"Any more quakes?" Kat asked.

"Several." Sheila's expression was grim. "And still no epicenter Baines can pin down. No more deaths, though, thank whatever deities are in charge of such things."

Trucks and rovers rolled into the valley and collected in the parking area, whining to a stop. Dan heard numerous malfunctions in that dying chorale. He'd have to get back to work on vehicle maintenance. Obviously that had slipped in his absence.

Offloading kept everyone busy for the next couple of hours. But it took far less time to restore exhibits to their shelves than it had to pack them neatly in the starhopper's hold. When the chore was done, the stay-at-homers renewed their plea: What had happened on T-S 311?

Praedar didn't reply. He stared at Hanging Rock, and for a moment Dan thought the Whimed would go to Chen's grave. Instead Praedar headed up Dome Hill at a ground-eating pace. The rest tagged after him—except for the N'lacs. Sleeg was squatting near the dud pits. One daunting glare from him, and Chuss and the other young villagers halted and sat beside him meekly.

When Dan reached the top of the slope, he saw that the home team had made good use of his instructions about operating the dredge. They'd moved a small mountain of sand and rubble. Both domes and the painted ramp were almost completely uncovered now. Another structure had been revealed, too—a low, sand-strewn tunnel connecting the two domes. That ought to make investigating the interiors easier.

The smaller dome was Praedar's goal. There wasn't room inside for everyone. Stay-at-homers waged a brief, noisy argument and verbally drew straws to see who'd play tour guide. Sheila, Armilly, Rosie, and a couple of others escorted the travelers through the maze of string markers and the door Dan had opened earlier, into the muraled chamber.

The pictorial history of N'lac enslavement bothered him even more now than it had when he'd first seen it. Something about those fragmented figures, swimming across space and time, gave him a cold feeling in his gut. He turned his back on the images and followed the team to the far side of the room.

Ruieb-An was engrossed in a batch of recently revealed writings alongside the inner door. Other scientists crowded around Armilly. The Lannon's remote scan monitors danced with ghostly schematics traced by his electronic probes. "Tunnel go down in hoosh then up sawoosha to there."

Sheila talked under his garbled Terran. "We coordinated these advanced look-sees with some exterior surveys. We pulled core samples. The usual—dating, materials analysis. We didn't try to bore on through, of course. We don't want to damage anything inside. That's probably irreplaceable. Armilly's giving us terrific views of what's in there, though—frustrating ones. You know. We want to see and touch. Everything's been hanging fire until McKelvey fixes this lock."

"Aaa!" Praedar said. "Our xenomechanician. Yes."

The team turned hopefully to Dan. He was happy to be relied on. But he wasn't sure he could perform the miracles Praedar was expecting. This lock looked different—tougher—than the one at the other door.

"Xenomechanician, huh?" Rosie said, chuckling. "So that's what he is. I'll bet that made the taxonomists at the Assembly scratch their heads."

Dan was peering at the door and its mechanism. "The wall's still intact here. No broken pieces hanging out. That makes putting it back in gear touchier. I may have to remove a section."

"It is approved," Praedar muttered. He leaned over Armilly's scanners, staring hungrily at those shadowy glimpses of treasures beyond the locked portal. "Do so. We must view."

Kat said, "The N'lacs tried hard to maintain a link between the domes. Yet they abandoned them. Now that we're opening them again, after all these centuries, Chuss' people seem to be wavering between reverence and terror. Why? What's in the big dome?"

"Machineroo thing," Armilly offered. He cued his monitors. Outlines of a bulky object filled the screen. Tracers blocked out angles.

"Big, whatever it is," Dan said. "Octagonal? And some kind of paneling or cowling running around the base of the structure. Just that one huge glob, right in the middle. Can't figure it."

"None of us will, until you get us inside," Sheila growled.

"Power thing hummy register and make squiggle chart move," Armilly noted.

The blonde grunted unhappily. "And how! A screwy, low-level energy output, according to his gear and ours. Most of the detectors claim that the energy source is there—and that it *isn't* there. A few tracks agree it's there, but refuse to record the wavelength. And one track told us that, because the stuff doesn't match known configurations, we should ignore it."

"We will not do that," Praedar said firmly, and the Terrans smiled.

"Hell, no!" Sheila said. "It's all up to you, handsome. Get this fornicating door open, or we're stuck."

Kat made a face. "Be reasonable, Whitcomb. The door isn't fornicating anything. It's just sitting there minding its own business."

That triggered a round of tension-releasing laughter, then attention shifted back to the show-and-tell session. The stay-at-homers described work they'd been doing while the team's reps were at the Assembly: imaging; cataloging; recording the murals on holomode; and warehousing all the artifacts in the small dome's entryway. They'd accomplished quite a lot. In fact, it appeared nearly all the ground had been covered and everything was hanging fire now, waiting for Dan to solve the mystery of the locked door.

"We'd have got more done," Sheila said, "if the damned quakes and itching would ever let up."

"Another matter to be examined and answered," Praedar said.

"Don't we hope." Rosie sounded aggrieved.

Abruptly Praedar swung around and headed out of the dome as rapidly as he'd climbed the hill. Again the rest trailed after him, curiosity getting the better of them. Dan had a bad moment of *déjà vu*; this was exactly what they'd done the day Hanging Rock fell and Chen died.

Was Praedar thinking the same thing? As he emerged from the ancient structure, he took a hard right and hurried across the valley toward his friend's museum. Few of his colleagues followed. They waited on the path, watching from a polite distance while the Whimed knelt by the boulder. Praedar remained in that position a long time, his gaze unfocused, his spidery hands splayed out against the stone. It was a moving scene, the essence of a being remembering, preserving the truth of a dead friend's life.

At last, Praedar shook off his grief. He rose and trotted back to the others. Sheila hesitated, as if wanting to be sure the Whimed was fully back in the real world, then said, "We've taken to calling it Chen's Rock. Okay?"

Praedar smiled sadly. "Appropriate. Chen would be amused.

He would say that place names are as ephemeral as the species that bestow them."

For some reason, the comment made Dan shiver.

"Shelter," Praedar went on, gesturing to the insta-cell complex. "Heat oppresses you Terrans and Vahnajes. Let us adjourn there. We have seen your work. We will show you ours."

Nobody needed a second invitation. Offworlders trooped toward the complex. Chuss and his friends scampered after them. Other N'lacs joined them. Sleeg disapproved. He shrilled warnings after his people. They pretended not to hear. They obeyed his rules when it came to the domes. But apparently they regarded the insta-cells as safe.

The cook shack was a cool haven. Scientists and N'lacs swilled liquids and savored the clime-controlled air blasting from the vents. Vahnajes were so relieved to get out of the sun that for once they expressed only minimal disgust when the other species wolfed snacks that the camp's cook was passing around. Kids of four races climbed onto adults' laps and shoulders. Team members settled onto benches, chairs, and perched atop tables. Some sat on the floor. Others stood, forming a circle as Kat cued her candid holo projector. The N'lacs were as eager as the rest to see the show. They were familiar with tri-dis, and whether or not they thought the process was magic, they weren't afraid of it. They giggled and muttered, pointing at the strangers' images forming in the holo beams.

The Twelfth Xenoarchaeological Assembly unfolded with lectures, panels, exhibits, conversations, and interviews. Kat's amateur souvenirs and the professionally recorded wafers Joe had bought were shown. This was the cutting edge of their science, and the stay-at-homers reacted volubly.

"Did you hear that? Imhoff told the Saunders that their cataloging and dates match our findings precisely. With *his* rep to support us, how can the Saunders deny. . .?"

Kat had included segments on the reporters covering the Assembly. In one, Rei Ito was quizzing the Saunders and then Praedar's team. The audience shouted, "Is that Miwa Ito the Scandalmonger's sister? Hey! Your future in-laws, Dan!"

"So the rumor goes," he conceded, sighing.

Images flowed on. So did the comments. As more and more discouraging tri-dis were shown, the onlookers' mood darkened. There were fewer cheers and uglier curses.

Dan slouched, nagged by guilt. Had he done everything he should have, could have, at the conference? They'd been hurt there, perhaps mortally. The starhopper was as good as grounded, and so was he. Anelan was disenchanted. Eckard was waffling.

The Vahnajes were chirring unhappily as they watched the holo-modes. The Whimeds huddled compulsively again and again and glowered fiercely. Terrans grumbled louder and louder. Armilly hunched into a large, furry ball, his manner unnaturally solemn. The N'lacs were increasingly anxious, eyeing the off-worlders uneasily. The e.t.s looked as if they wished they'd listened to Sleeg and stayed clear of this gathering.

"Damn the Saunders! Even with our evidence right under their noses!"

"Urr . . . *kunta nesanle* . . . urr . . . urr . . . URR!" Ruieb's bunch griped.

Whimed topknots were bristly. Drastil stood braced for battle, his large head thrust forward belligerently as he watched the show. Terrans and Vahnajes edged away from him.

"Pig-stubborn data jugglers!"

"Playing blind, deaf, and dumb to our data! How could you let them *do* that to you, Kat?"

"What was I *supposed* to do?" she retorted hotly.

"Quas-Jin. Oh, hell! There's extra ammo for the Saunders."

Ruieb protested, "Is not so! Is . . . hon-or-able being."

"And crammed with prestige, which he rubbed off all over the Assembly's hosts."

"What could we expect?" Sheila cut in. "After all, the Vahnajes and the Saunder-McKelveys go way back, eh, Dan?"

He wished she hadn't brought that up.

"Can't get away from your damned kindred *anywhere*!" Rosie cried. Then she grimaced and added lamely, "I—I know it's not your fault, Dan, but . . ."

Baines pointed at the holos. "Jarrett? Saying he sees no basis for unnecessarily mythological explanations of alien cultures! Whose side is he on, anyway?"

"He expressed his view of the truth," Praedar said, his voice tightly controlled, conveying calm.

It was a small drop of oil on an agitated sea.

As the holos replayed the final night's formal affair, Kat said, "If Feo and Hope actually follow through on a promise you'll hear them making, we'll have to watch our language and manners more than we've been doing here. Mustn't step on our guests' toes."

"What . . .?"

"Shh!" from several dozen intent viewers. They listened to the challenge and Feo's unwilling agreement to a fair exchange of visits.

Beams winked off. Kat stored the holos and closed the projector. The cook shack was remarkably still. Then Rosie said incredulously, "The Saunders? Here? Is is possible?"

Almost as one, the team turned to Dan. "Why are you putting me on the spot?" he demanded. "I'm not responsible for my kin."

"Are they coming? Are they really coming?"

"Yes," Praedar said. "They have much to prove. And Feo gave his word. He is not without his ethics."

"Oh, he's sure demonstrated that," Dan retorted with withering sarcasm.

Praedar argued, "They are careful scientists. The fact that their selectivity and interpretations are in error will not affect their agreement to observe our site."

"Maybe. Hard for them to back out," Dan said, "since there were all those witnesses and Ito invited herself in. Okay, so they put up. But I'll bet they won't change their attitudes one damned bit."

"They killed us at the Assembly," Sheila spat. "Dammit, you let 'em get away with murder! Our project is a watershed in xenoarch research, and you blew it for us."

Joe refused to take that. "We did it very well, all things considered. If you think you could have done better . . ."

"Damned right!"

Tempers exploded. Long-nursed resentments and personality conflicts had been brewing for months. Fatigue, despair, and frustration all erupted at once.

Terrans, Whimeds, and Vahnajes swapped angry words. Armilly banged on the cook shack wall, shaking the partition alarmingly. N'lacs were running around, panicking, ducking under tables, and tripping offworlders. The whole thing threatened to disintegrate into a wild multispecies brawl.

A human threw the first punch. Peacemakers attempted to break it up and got dragged into the clashes that were starting all over the room.

Dan struggled to separate Baines and Getz's senior student. In the confusion, a misaimed blow rocked the pilot back on his heels. "Fine!" he yelled. "Let's play it that way, then!" He grabbed handsful of both men's jumpsuits, catching them off balance and hurling them headlong against the dining tables.

Baines came up swinging. "I'll get you for that, McKelvey! I always knew you were on their side!"

"STOP!"

The command stunned everyone. People went rigid, then turned, seeking the source of the deafening roar.

Praedar stood atop a Vahnaj privacy eating booth. His mane was a crown. His fingers clawed air.

"We are *scientists!*" he reminded them.

Those who had fallen groaned and pulled themselves upright or were helped to their feet by others. Sheila disengaged her opponent's hands from her braids and backed away from the woman. "Uh . . . sorry, Barb. I didn't mean that."

Terrans whispered sheepish apologies. Vahnajes straightened rumpled clothing and fluffed their sideburns. Armilly looked oddly deflated. Whimeds combed their disheveled topknots and fidgeted, energy levels still at a peak.

Kat and the team's socio specialists crawled among the N'lacs, soothing and coaxing them to come out of hiding. Chuss and Meej were the bravest, though they remained on guard, ready to take to cover again if the offworlders went crazy once more. Eyes wide, the villagers stared at the bigger humanoids.

"It is uncivilized," Praedar said. "This must cease. It is stupid." People avoided his angry glare. "We must not oppose each other. Ignorance is our enemy, not our colleagues. Conflict hampers the discovery of truth."

An ashamed murmur rippled through the crowd.

Kat cuddled N'lac females and their children, speaking softly to them. She glanced up at Praedar, then at the mob standing below his platform. "I think this has been proof that we're overdue for a pit fit."

That set off a buzz of conversation. At least the team was discussing options now, not throwing punches.

Chuss sidled close to Dan and tugged at the pilot's sleeve. "Is okay, Kelfee? Is be okay?"

"I sure hope so." Dan patted the N'lac's bald pate. "None of them fellow is mad at *you* fellow. Not really mad at each other fellow."

Chuss wrinkled his tiny nose, uncomprehending. "Is bad feeling from temple. Bad stuff."

237

Dan shrugged, uncertain what Chuss meant. "Could be."

"Pit fit! Right!" Sheila shouted. "You said it, Olmsted! Overdue and then some!"

Joe chimed in. "It's been months. More than half a year. With this mess we've just been through, here and at the Assembly, we were bound to crack. And we will again, if we don't loosen up."

A chorus of agreement rose. The proposal had seized everyone's fancy. They turned to Praedar, clamoring. In response, Praedar turned to Ruieb-An. "You will accept this? I know it is distasteful to you."

The lutrinoids chirped and swayed, a sober row of gray-faced figures in rumpled diggers' clothes. Ruieb-An said, "We . . . urr . . . ac-cept. We have . . . urr . . . al-so felt such . . . urr . . . need."

"Armilly?" Praedar asked. The Lannon heaved a great sigh and nodded.

The Whimed straightened to his full, impressive height. He peered down at his team. "It will be. Each species will provide its preferred alterant. What site shall we use?"

Baines had been hanging his head, looking anywhere but at Dan and Norris, Getz's student, his sparring partners. The xenogeologist recovered a bit of his composure. "How about the dud pits?" he suggested. "That way we won't mess up any ongoing digs."

"And they aren't deep," Norris said. "So when we fall down, we won't get hurt."

"Or hurt anyone else," Kat added under her breath.

Praedar dropped from the eating booth, landing lightly. A mischievous grin split his bony face. "Very well. It is agreed. Collect. Aja roots . . ." and the Whimed scientists brightened in happy anticipation. "Po fruit for our Vahnaj colleagues. Armilly will bring his eshi. The Terrans will bring . . ."

Sheila led the humans in a rousing cheer: "Binge juice!"

CHAPTER FIFTEEN

✪✪✪✪✪✪✪✪

Nightmares Walk

Chuss loped alongside Dan, getting in the pilot's way. "You fellows have big fun fire party, huh huh?"

Dan moved crabwise, trying to maintain his grip on a slippery container. He was helping Baines and other burly types carry a still full of "binge juice." "Yeah, yeah, big party."

"It will be, once we get on the outside of this stuff," Baines corrected.

The muscle men maneuvered carefully through the cook shack's door and toted their burden to the dud pit flats at the bottom of Dome Hill. Twilight was falling, and the valley was cooling off fast. No one minded the temperature drop, though. People were in a jovial mood, forgetting that less than an hour ago some of them had been at others' throats.

Sheila supervised the fire-building squad. They spread brushwood piles in a snaky line between the shallow excavations. "Good thinking, Whitcomb," Kat said. "Distribute the illumination, so we'll all have light to see by and find our way to the juice." The blonde touched off the tinder, and soon brush was

239

burning brightly, showering sparks into a darkening sky.

A carnival atmosphere took over. Team members brought food, musical instruments, bedding, chairs, tables, and portable vids from the insta-cells. N'lacs were infected by the spirit of the occasion. A steady stream of the e.t.s traipsed back and forth from the complex to their village. The natives emptied their larders and their clay beer pots into the communal party stores. Spits were set up. Lizards roasted, scorched skin and fat sizzling as they dropped into the flames. Gradually a dizzying array of refreshments was assembled—something for every species and every taste, with both alcoholic and nonintoxicating beverages to wash down the edibles.

N'lacs and offworlders wandered down the line of pits, selecting their spot for the evening. They had plenty of choices. Dozens of the depressions lay scattered on the half-moon apron between the insta-cells and Dome Hill. Excavations ranged in size from holes barely big enough for Chuss to fit into up to jumbo models. None was over a meter deep. Most were less. Dust drift had carpeted the bottoms, creating soft landing pads for any who overindulged and toppled inside.

The Vahnajes had staked out their claims early and were settled in. Dan had rarely seen lutrinoids so relaxed. They'd dipped deeply into their preferred mood alterant—pickled fruit called po. They were definitely feeling no pain. In fact, they were giggling inanely.

The Whimeds were chewing their favorite hallucinogenic roots. The substance had stained their lips bright red, and their eyes were starry opals. Drastil and Yvica were exceedingly giddy. The married felinoids shook with silent laughter, enjoying an intimate joke.

Armilly sprawled in the deepest pit, loudly inviting passersby to share his cakes of "hooshi best eshi stuff." He wasn't offended when they declined; that left more for him.

"Over here," Rosie called, beckoning to Frank. The cook was hauling trays of mugs and cups to the pit area. Terrans ran to help, then yelled advice as Frank tapped the still.

"Hurry up! I can almost taste it!"

"Stuff ought to be potent enough to cure a lot of ills . . ."

"It's been brewing since . . . since when?"

"Since forever! Pour, Frank!"

Sheila handed Dan a brimming cup. "There you go, handsome. Let's get a Saunder-McKelvey's opinion on T-W 593's private stock."

He sniffed the mug's contents while the cook protested, "Hey! Don't be so generous with that."

"Oh, stop it, Frank," Kat jeered. "No one in his right mind swills binge juice. Besides, there's plenty."

Joe slapped the still's side. "Hear her slosh! Must be thirty liters in there."

Dan took a small sip. A river of cool fire slid down his gullet. For a second he couldn't utter a sound or even inhale. Finally he whispered, "That's . . . that's impressive."

"Made from the very best native vegetatives," Rosie bragged. "And a hell of a lot of ingenuity."

"Every xenoarch field group has its own recipe," Kat said. "But ours is the best."

"This isn't . . ." Dan wheezed, took a deep breath, and tried again. "This isn't what you pass around at the tale-telling."

"No chance!" Joe chuckled. "We save this for times of direst need, and tonight qualifies."

Not certain how hard the alcohol would hit him, Dan walked carefully, following his friends to one of the larger pits. His stride remained steady, reassuring him. The juice's effect seemed to be subtle, despite its potency. He joined the rest, sitting on the rim of the excavation, watching them for cues. What was standard behavior at a pit fit?

Humans and Whimeds stretched their legs into the depression's center, bumping boots. Dan imitated them, making contact with Joe and Rosie. Kat and Sheila got into their act, and the five of them traded clumsy, harmless kicks in a game of foot-sparring. A group of N'lacs, including Chuss and the adolescent female he was nuzzling, perched in the next pit and laughed at the off-worlders' horseplay. Praedar wasn't huddling. Nor were other Whimeds. Oiled by their red roots, they were looking remarkably like humans with funny hairdos, arms around each others' shoulders, swaying and singing off-key. Several of them were jabbering enthusiastically. Dan translated enough to know that they were swapping dirty stories.

He leaned toward Kat and said, "Did you ever hear the one about the spacer marooned on an asteroid station with seven Rigotians . . .?

To his surprise, she hadn't. Firelight accentuated Kat's blush.

She swatted at him, a phony, chiding slap. "You ought to be ashamed of yourself!"

"Why?" He waved at the Whimeds. Kat listened a moment, then blushed even more deeply.

"Sure, take it easy," Sheila advised. "That's what this is all about."

"Oh, I'm sure *you* think of it that way," Kat snapped. But she didn't move away when Dan put his arm around her.

Some celebrants were teetotalers, for medical or ethical reasons. But they didn't put a damper on the festivities. On the contrary, they joined in wholeheartedly. Unlike Fleet troopers on leave or indie haulers with credits to burn, team members who indulged weren't interested in wiping themselves out fast. They set a leisurely pace, balancing intoxicants with snacks, horseplay, conversation, music, and a lot of pit hopping. There were few mean drunks. The tone was what everyone had hoped for—a generalized release of tension.

Armilly chanted Lannon poetry, whether or not anyone was listening. Vahnajes owlishly reminisced, their heads waggling atop their long necks. Terrans, Whimeds, and N'lacs snake danced around the bonfires. A number of tipsy felinoids tried to embrace everyone, including Vahnajes. Dan saw very little of the interspecies standoffishness that had been so obvious on T-S 311. He wondered if Imhoff's multispecies dig crew was equally able to throw away those chauvinisms dividing the races at their pit fits. This was the way things should be, throughout the sectors— humanoids, sharing, cooperating, putting aside those age-old fears of beings who were somewhat different from themselves.

For a while Dan was part of a slap-happy chorus line, dancing between Praedar and Kat, then Joe and Sheila, then Armilly and Rosie, stumbling and weaving in a silly, impromptu folk stomp. Those on the sidelines cheered them on.

A second and then a third refill of binge juice shot Dan's coordination to pieces, as it did most of the partyers. They retreated to the pits, though some of the Whimeds continued dancing for another half hour.

Terran, Whimed, Vahnaj, and N'lac children stuffed the... faces and played together until sleep overtook them. The kids curled up in the pits, safe and close at hand while their parents reveled.

The flicker of the fires, the camaraderie, the food and drink all lent a dreamlike quality to the celebration. Dan floated on waves of conversation. Kat talked with Rosie about a prank the two of them had pulled in their student days. Drastil and Praedar argued, without rancor, the fine points of Whimed philosophy. Sheila and Joe tried to outdo each other with graphic medical anecdotes. Rosie and Baines exchanged raunchy stories and prodded their hormones. A number of couples were doing that.

The mood hadn't quite reached the romping stage yet, however. Someone started a singalong, and the majority of the pits joined in. Whimeds and Terrans led the show. But Vahnajes, N'lacs, and Armilly often chimed in. The result was a jumble, both pleasant and discordant. Did Terran music mean any more to the aliens than their music did to humans? Who cared? Or . . . no matter, as Praedar would say.

Dan contributed his baritone to the musical stew—an assortment of what he thought of as camp ditties.

There were a dozen verses of the perennial complaint:

> "So excavate on the double-quick!
> Shovel and haul! Dig, dig, dig!
> We think this stratum's too damned thick,
> What a hell of a way to do re-search!"

Then they took a poke at the expedition's long-suffering galley master:

> "Soup! Soo-up! Behave yourself, digger,
> Or it's wonderful soup!
> Don't gripe at Frank's cooking.
> Don't say that it's foul,
> Or he'll feed you fried bugs and say with a growl
> That you'll get . . .
> Soo-up!"

Kat shouted, "I've got a new one!" And she ripped at the team's rivals:

> "Feo Saunder has a project
> That impresses man-y.
> He and Hope are selling hard,
> But we're not buying an-y!

> Won't acknowledge others's data,
> Nev-er listen to us.
> Some folks say the Saunders won it . . .
> But I say they're spur-ious"

The final line brought groans, chuckles, and loud demands for more verses. Diggers improvised with wretched rhyme and worse meter. No one criticized. Each crude stanza triggered fresh laughter.

N'lacs, not understanding what was so funny, but wanting to participate, shrieked gleefully.

Dan felt as if he were two persons, one cackling idiotically, the other viewing all these intoxicated scientists from a lofty and detached position. Why were they all fooling themselves this way? Tomorrow the problems would still be there, staring them in the face. Getting drunk wasn't going to make their troubles vanish.

But . . . the problems could wait.

Tonight they'd enjoy a timeless festival.

Eventually the silly songs drifted into nostalgia. Ruieb chanted a maudlin hymn to a long-dead Vahnaj hero. It left his fellow lutrinoids drippy-nosed with sorrow. Not to be outdone, the Whimeds offered a ballad extolling one of *their* epic giants. Armilly droned a lament for a motherless cub, searching the stars for his home world. Chuss, grasping the tone, led his people in thumping, melodic recital of their escape through the Big Dark. Inspired, Dan jumped in when the N'lacs' song ended. He didn't introduce his donation. That wasn't necessary.

> "We've ranged across the light-years.
> Been to planets near and far.
> > From Earth out to our distant stars,
> > From sector fringe and back to Mars.
> And when our days are ended,
> No matter where we've roamed,
> We know we'll die on Terra . . . because . . .
> > Every planet is our home."

Raggedly at first, then ever more strongly, humans blended their voices with his. The words were less than a generation old. But in that time they had been adopted as mankind's unofficial anthem. The song touched hearts everywhere in Terra's sphere of influence, with rare exceptions, like die-hard New Earth Renaissancer proponents. Those born on Mars Colony, Kruger 60, Settlements Clay, Vaughan, and Hung Jui sang and wiped tears away. It wasn't the best rendition Dan had heard, but it was one of the most affecting.

> "Some of us come from Old Earth,
> Or from Polk or Alpha Cee.
> > Some never leave their planet base,
> > And others live their lives in space.
> Yet when our days are ending,
> No matter if we've roamed.
> We know we'll die on Terra . . . because . . .
> > Every planet is our home."

The verses went on for a long time. The Terrans had plenty of emotion to get out of their systems.

As the singalong began to falter, Dan noticed Sleeg sitting at the edge of the dud pits. The shaman refused to participate in the gathering. But he insisted on hanging around, scowling at Chuss and other merrymaking villagers. Dan could imagine the old e.t. mumbling "Nothing good will come of this carousing with offworlders, mark my words!"

No one paid any attention to the N'lac wet blanket. They were rehashing past triumphs and shortcomings, their memories made fuzzy by intoxicants and the night.

More and more beings were dropping out. Tired parents were taking sleeping kids to the complex or the village. Some people snored, waking with a start when neighbors poked them and told them to tone it down. In many of the pits, inhibitions had been lowered far enough that sexuality was taking the reins. Praedar and one of his Whimed students were embracing passionately, the erotic nature of the encounter apparent even to non-Whimeds.

Some team members, though, wouldn't let go of scraps of lingering anger. That had to burn out before they could relax completely.

"Remember that fight over lab assignments?"

"Kroo-ger! What a brawl!"

"A third of us packed quarters and moved up the valley, that time. Thought the whole expedition would come apart."

"Almost did . . ."

"And it still might," Kat whispered.

Dan leaned close, speaking in her ear. "We won't let it."

She peered up at him. "Keep telling me that. Please. I want to believe we'll win. I *have* to. But it's so difficult . . ."

"We'll win," he said obediently, wanting to make her happy.

"When you say it like that, I think . . ." Kat forced a weak smile. "That tech specialist confidence. I can hear it. Must be part of that hidden reservoir Chen saw in you, those depths not even you thought you had."

"Good ole Saunder-McKelvey genes," Dan joked, slurring the words.

"The best of them." She tilted her head back against Dan's shoulder. "What you said that last night at the Assembly—about the high principles, the true spirit of your family . . ."

"I don't remember saying that," he muttered, chuckling. "It was probably somebody else. Maybe a reporter."

"No, no, it was you," Kat insisted. Her words were slurred, too. "You know, you've become my fav-favorite xenomechanician."

He laughed, amused that she'd had trouble with "favorite" but none pronouncing "xenomechanician." Alcohol made humans silly and erratic. Dan's arm tightened around her as he said, "And you are my favorite xenosocio-socio-sociologist."

Kat nodded absently. She was trying to spot someone in the shadows, hampered by the bonfires' unsteady glow. Praedar and his romping mate were barely visible in the dark recesses of the pit. But Kate saw them. She gazed at them intently for a long moment, then turned away quickly. "Make love to me, Dan." Her arm stole invitingly around his neck.

Rambling discussions and a leftover song session in nearby excavations became white noise, melting into the background. At this stage of the celebration, Dan couldn't separate drunken fancies from basic sexual drives, and he wasn't at all sure he could perform. However, his hormones prodded him to try.

He and Kat slithered farther down into the pit. Other couples —and one trio—were doing the same. Firelight stabbed into the shallow openings, reflecting on sparkling eyes, bare skin, and Whimed crests, fluffy with excitement. Somewhere in the distance, Vahnajes cried in either pain or passion. Sheila was exhorting her partner of the night: "Come on, I'm not delicate . . ."

In his memories, Dan heard the blonde making another statement: *"I'll tell Olmsted what she's missed and send her your way. She needs to cut loose. And she's not going to get that from Praedar, not the way she wants it."*

Had Sheila done that? Sent Kat his way?

The thought evaporated as Kat kissed him passionately. He gave himself over to sensation, refusing to wonder how they'd arrived at this time and place together.

"I'll hate myself in the morning." Kat giggled. "I'm drunk."

Dan caressed her. "So am I. We all are. Loopier than a Fleet scout on planet leave after a year-long tour. Wasn't that the idea?"

"Yes," Kat agreed softly. She giggled again. "But we'll have sand in the most inconvenient portions of our anatomy."

"It's worth it, and I'll be glad to help you remove yours . . ."

Then he quit wasting breath on talk.

To his dismay, the alcohol *did* get in the way. He was running as fast as he could and making no headway. Oddly, the same nerve-deadening side effect blunted his pride, so that the situation struck him as absurd, rather than a blow to his masculinity. He'd hoped for more intensity, higher peaks. But he couldn't complain. It was fun, romping along like this.

Kat, unlike him, was getting somewhere very fast. The binge juice had opened sexual and emotional floodgates for her, and Kat's desire bore them both on that high water. Fuzzy-brained, Dan was enjoying a series of small highs, gratified that Kat had no complaints about his end of the deal. This was a good start. Another time, now that the ice was broken, they'd meet halfway or better in a thoroughly terrific coupling.

It was a strange setting for lovemaking. Bonfire heat cooked one side of his exposed skin, and desert cold chilled the shadowed side. Other rompers of several species were nearby. Dan was mildly surprised at his lack of embarrassment. This was a semipublic arena, and ordinarily he didn't go in for that sort of thing at all.

Kat was gasping in ecstasy, murmuring in delight. Icy shock dashed the fuzz out of Dan's head.

She had spoken Whimed.

He didn't understand all the words. He got the gist, though. With difficulty, Dan kept himself looking into the darkness, seeking his rival.

Flashbacks! On a ride home in the skimmer, Praedar had grieved that he would not live long enough to witness the completion of this dig. And Kat had stroked the alien's crest, petting him as if she were his lover—as if the two of them were alone in the flyer. Dan had felt like a voyeur on that occasion.

Sexuality across species lines happened. Every major Settlement had places where exotic practices could be bought or arranged among consenting legal adults of different races. There were always rumors that a certain diplomat, merchant, or spacer had an appetite for romping with alien beings.

Dan had no inclinations in that direction himself. He'd thought he was free of bias against those who did.

Apparently he was more prejudiced than he realized. Sheila's blithe attitudes about polygamy raised non-Krugerites' eyebrows, Dan's included. But he'd handled that okay. Besides, she'd been talking about multiple *human* sexual partners; and the Kruger 60 citizens weren't the first *Homo sapiens* to experiment with those mating patterns.

Trying to envision startling alternatives, Dan pictured Kat and Praedar embracing . . .

He reacted physically to the concept. Kat stiffened in his arms, asking what was wrong.

"N-nothing," Dan muttered. He'd been slammed into a mental wall and was trying to recuperate.

"I . . . what did I . . . did I say something . . . ? Dan?"

"Nothing," he repeated, working hard to rationalize his feelings.

Kat didn't have a crush on just any Whimed. Her unrequited love was aimed at a unique, admirable being. In fact, her ideal was admired by damned near everyone on this dig, males as well as females. That didn't mean they were all quirky!

The important thing was, Kat hadn't sought out Praedar tonight. She'd chosen to make love with a Terran male. Dan's being too drunk to fulfill his part of the arrangement didn't figure in. If he'd been sober enough, he'd have made her forget fantasies and give her total attention to the man with her.

"It's fine, fine," Dan said, salvaging his ego. Gradually Kat relaxed, accepting his assurances.

They lay together among others in various stages of sleeping, cuddling, drunken singing, and romping. Dan's thoughts were a-reel, dulled, sinking fast toward a half-doze. He decided he didn't care that Kat was attracted to Praedar. Whimeds had that effect on a lot of Terrans. Under these circumstances, isolated and thrown together by common purpose, it was inevitable that a susceptible Terran woman could convince herself she was in love with the expedition's leader.

The shallow pits didn't conceal much. Dan became conscious of his partial nudity and a twinge of modesty made him rectify the condition. Kat was straightening her clothing, too, shivering a bit. They clung to one another, sharing body warmth and soaking up heat from the fires.

As couple after couple were sated, a drowsy mood fell across the excavations. Humans laughed softly or snorted; Whimeds purred; Armilly grunted happily at who knew what; N'lacs made comical "wheeple" noises; and Vahnajes twittered.

Then something nudged at that somnolent, drifting attitude. Dan frowned, resisting a growing pressure within his skull. It crawled through his ears and eyes, an invisible probe, increasingly hot, increasingly painful. Pressure turned to hurt, rousing him.

And a maddening itch gripped every square centimeter of his body.

He wasn't alone. Praedar, Sheila, Chuss, Joe . . . they were all scratching—the entire expedition.

Those who hadn't indulged in mood alterants weren't immune. They also rubbed their temples and dug at their flesh. That urge was a juggernaut now, sweeping in, hammering, relentless. Dan drew blood, raking with his nails frantically. He had to stop this damned itch! It was like . . . like an invasion, an enemy, attacking them.

The invader took material form.

It weaved, advancing in an erratic zigzag, as drunk as the revelers. Dan squinted, straining to focus on the object.

Spindly appendages were tipped by splayed, metallic feet. Metal limbs . . . tentacles? They were wispy, flopping things.

How many legs and tentacles? Eight? Ten? More? Dan couldn't be sure.

The invader rocked crazily, staggering, sometimes moving in reverse or far to one side. It looked like a mechanical vid clown.

But Dan's reaction wasn't laughter. Fear tightened his gut into an agonizing knot. Gooseflesh rose, warring with the itch.

The thing was as big as Armilly. Its hide was a piebald patchwork of gleaming plates and rusty excrescence.

Battered by the pain in his head, Dan groaned. It was a fight to keep his eyes open now and follow the invader's unpredictable approach course. If only there was some feature to nail down and identify—a head, optical apertures . . .

Suddenly the intruder was on top of the pits, tottering wildly, occasionally slipping off the edge of an excavation and stepping on people.

People fled, froze, or gaped open-mouthed in dumbfounded disbelief.

The hurt and a buzzing filled Dan's head. He pounded his palms against his temples, desperate to shut out the assault.

Baines stood on the rim of a pit, roaring defiance at the metal object. The xenogeologist was mother-naked and very, very drunk. The woman he'd been snuggling with grabbed at him futilely, begging him to get down and hide.

Dan nodded, then winced at the new stab of pain the motion brought. The woman was right. They shouldn't draw the invader's notice. It would be best to get out of its way. That's what he wanted to do.

But he couldn't move his legs. They seemed paralyzed.

The intruder rocked past him, less than two meters away. One of its splayed feet dropped into the pit, striking the Whimed female Praedar was with. She shrieked, writhing. Uncaring, the metal object lurched on.

Joe Hughes, on all fours, crouched on an adjacent dud pit apron, staring at the apparition in astonishment.

Sheila was outdoing herself for profanity.

A Vanhaj ran by, wild-eyed and gibbering.

Somehow, Dan finally willed his legs to function. He got out of the pit and to his feet. He stood there swaying while Kat used him as a living crutch to pull herself upright beside him.

Praedar was making the same heroic effort. He paused, his big hands curved into humanoid talons. Like Dan, Kat, and others, he was gawking incredulously at the invader.

N'lacs were loping madly in circles, setting up a terror-stricken, ululating howl. Some were so panicky that they ran directly in front of the invader, barely escaping being crushed by its damaging feet. Chuss' shrill voice blasted Dan's eardrums: "Demon! *Demon!* The Evil Old Ones' demon!"

CHAPTER SIXTEEN

○○○○○○○○○

Ancient Enemy

Nausea turned Dan's insides to an acid boil. His body was a leaden weight, his head an explosion about to happen. Was that the aftereffects of the binge juice—or of this party crasher?

He felt bugs under his skin, itching intolerably, and his eyes wouldn't work right. His gut was in a mess . . .

The pit fit had seemed like a good idea at the time. Now alcohol addled his wits and made it nearly impossible to think, move, or be sure that what he was seeing was real.

Goaded by an unknown compulsion, Dan put one foot in front of another, forcing himself to follow the metal thing. Praedar was doing the same. More slowly, Kat and others followed them.

The invader was heading east, leaving the dud pit area. They had to hurry, if they were going to catch it.

Why the hell did they want to catch it?

For some reason, Dan knew he had to try to do exactly that.

Panic reigned at the pits. But Sheila and Joe were remembering their paramed training and starting to get into gear. "Calm down and give us a hand here!" the blonde yelled, bending over an injured Whimed.

And always, Chuss and his brother Meej, galloping in circles, continued to cry, "Demon, *demon, Demon!*"

The pandemonium faded as Dan plodded farther from the fires. Every instinct told him to find a hole and bury himself in it. And yet, over and above that sense of self-preservation was a burning need to find out. He and Praedar trudged ahead, still struggling against the itch, pain, and lingering partial paralysis. Others trailed them.

Solar storage lamps alongside the trail bloomed to life as the pursuers neared. Ten meters beyond Dan, the spindly-legged intruder's metallic skin reflected the lamps' gleam. Beyond, Chen's Rock loomed, a dark presence set against the eastern cliff. To the left of the grave marker, in the N'lac village, frightened screams rang through tendrilled trees. The natives who'd returned early from the pit hadn't escaped this walking horror.

Abruptly, unexpectedly, those agony bands holding Dan's skull fell away and the maddening itch stopped. Hardly daring to believe he was free, he broke into a run. So did Praedar. The Whimed ate up ground, with Dan right at his heels. Farther back, the rear guard shouted encouragement to them, promising help.

Help? What kind of help? None of them was armed or knew what the intruder was capable of. It could be a bomb, one that might detonate before they figured out how to defuse it.

And still they chased it. Curiosity was an unquenchable thirst.

Dan stumbled, blinking. Illumination was poor. This end of the trail had few solar lamps. But there was no doubt of what he was seeing. The intruder was walking straight up Chen's Rock, and over its top.

Grimacing, determined to close in, Dan raced around the boulder. They had it! They'd head the quarry off, trap it! He met Praedar, who'd gone around he opposite side of Chen's Rock, on the far side.

There was nothing between them but cold night air.

Moments later, their fellow team members crowded around them, babbling questions. Kat pressed Dan's arm demandingly. "Where did it go?"

"Didn't you see?" He sketched out the intruder's feat with a sweeping arc of his arm.

"That's not possible!"

"None of this is . . ." Rosie complained.

Baines hefted a metal bar he'd picked up somewhere along the trail. "Dammit. I wanna pound tha' thing . . . poun' it inta junk." The drunken xenogeologist seemed unaware of his nudity and the fact that he was shivering until his teeth chattered.

"No," Praedar said. "No destruction. Analysis."

That brought a noisy outburst of opinions. Dan stayed clear of the argument, thinking hard. On impulse, he looked up, pointed, and roared, "Look!"

Praedar echoed him, having seen the same thing at the same instant.

Silhouetted against one of T-W 593's moons, the intruder perched atop the cliff. Several of its wispy tentacles waved, seeking purchase. Finding it, the visitor finished its ascent.

A heartbeat later it was gone, over the rim, and out of view.

The scientists craned their necks, staring at the empty spot where the nightmare had stood.

"How could it . . . ?"

"It *couldn't*!"

"Right up the side of the rock, and then right up the cliff!"

"*Nothing* can do that!"

"Some machines can," Dan said, surprised that he sounded so unexcited. "Telorobots . . ."

"Tha's in space," Baines countered. "Couldn' do it here."

"It just did," Dan reminded him. "We saw it. Or does binge juice produce hallucinations?"

"Maybe," one of the rear guard muttered. "Maybe the nonhumans saw something else . . ."

"They saw *something!*" Kat protested. "Dan's right. This can't be the result of intoxicants."

"Chuss' people identified the object," Praedar said.

Dan felt rather than heard a collective intake of breath. He seconded the Whimed. "Yeah. They called it a demon, just like the model they smashed and the paintings in the small dome . . ."

"But this was three times the size of the models," Rosie said, her voice cracking. "Four times!"

"Did their legends reduce it to something they could handle without tonight's terror?" Kat wondered aloud. "It fits. It fits."

Everyone tried to talk at once. Thick-tongued, still giddy from intoxicants and adrenaline, they tangled, words colliding.

"What a discovery! The N'lacs' myths. Proved! They're not fairy tales. Wait till the Saunders hear this!"

"Sleeg's magic didn't work. Supposed to keep th' Evil Old Ones and their demons at bay..."

"The significance!" Kat exulted. "Why has one of the Old Ones' demons returned here after a two-millennia absence?"

"If wha' we saw was one o' their robots," Baines said sourly.

"How can you deny it?"

"I'm s'drunk I'm not sure who I am, let alone tell wha' happened here. Coul' you?"

"We aren't *that* drunk," Rosie said, offended.

Praedar broke in sternly. "This accomplishes no good. We go back. Colleagues and N'lacs are injured."

The statement chastened the enthusiastic and helped sober the drunks a trifle. Shame replaced argument, and the group began retracing it steps. Now and then one of them glanced back at Chen's Rock and the cliff.

Halfway along the cross-valley path, Dan overheard Praedar mumbling "Must find, must find..."

And what would they be up against if they did?

Nightmares, akin to the intruder, babbled from the darkest depths of Dan's brain. Nonanthropomorphic conquerors and their robots existed. And the robot demon was still on the prowl for humanoid slaves—to punish the heirs of those who had escaped, and to press new humanoid species into its masters' services.

No! That invasion had happened millennia ago, in the forever time.

According to Feo and Hope, it hadn't happened at all. The stories were mere primitive fantasies.

That thing that had reeled through the pit fit and climbed the cliff was one hell of a damned real fantasy!

Baines pounded his arms against his body to stimulate blood circulation. Dan empathized, though he didn't share Baines' state of undress. One didn't have to be naked at a time like this to feel ice seeping through one's bones and soul.

As the servant, so the masters? Were the Evil Old Ones mere parsecs away, awaiting a report from their robot? Was history about to repeat itself on T-W 593 in a new attack, with a much wider scope than the original invasion? Not only a handful of N'lacs would be swept up in this slave-catching net. This time, the roundup might include the Whimed Federation, the Vahnaj Alliance, and Terra.

Dan shuddered. What a night this had been!

Kat stumbled off the path, sobbing a curse. Dan steadied her and she said, "This is so . . . so stupid. The whole thing. Getting drunk. No sleep. Running after that thing like a bunch of . . . of maniacs . . ."

"We're only humanoids," he said. Her laughter was heavy with suppressed tears.

"Humanoids," Praedar put in. "Like the N'lacs." His calm tone was a facade. When the group reached the bonfires, Dan saw that the felinoid's crest was a bristly thorn bush. So he, too, had been badly spooked by this past hour's events.

The scene at the dud pit resembled a battlefield after the defeat. Victims were moaning and retching. The broken still lay on its side, its contents soaking into the sand. Pieces of clothing, tufts of hair, and spilled food were strewn over a midden of mug shards.

Praedar attempted to backtrack the intruder's course, hunting footprints. To his disappointment, most markings had been obliterated during the panic.

"I wish someone had been alert enough to use a vid cam when that thing was coming through here," Dan said. The boss favored him with a wry look and a nod.

Parameds and good samaritans were helping the wounded. The returning chase team hurried to aid them. Baines detoured long enough to locate his clothes and put them on. Unlike the wounded offworlders, who were scattered all over the dud pit area, the N'lacs had gathered in a bunch. Kat bent over them, concerned. The e.t.s shrank from her touch.

Joe said, "I checked them earlier. No serious damage. Just scrapes and bumps, mostly."

"But they'll suffocate in that pile," Dan said, worried.

"No, I've seen them do this before, when they're badly scared," Hughes replied. "They'll come out of it, eventually."

Chuss bared his tiny teeth. "You fellow go away. We okay."

They definitely weren't okay. They were a quaking heap of wrinkled red skin and wide golden eyes. But any effort to pull them apart obviously would only add to their trauma.

The N'lacs were still there when the last of the injured scientists had been removed to the cook shack. By then Dan had quit worrying about the e.t.s suffocating. Instead, he was afraid they'd freeze; the bonfires were dying out fast, and predawn temperatures were sinking.

Joe, on his way to the village to see how things were going there, stopped and spoke to Chuss's gang once more. Whatever he said finally penetrated. Slowly the N'lacs untangled themselves. Then they scuttled ahead of Joe on the trail. Sleeg, though, stayed put where he was—at the foot of Dome Hill. The tale-teller was spellbound, gazing unblinkingly at the structures, mumbling charms to ward off evil.

Sheila and Joe had converted the cook shack to an emergency med station. They'd progressed far enough in the mop-up that they could split their attention. Joe took care of the villagers. Sheila finished treating patients in the complex. She dosed out painkillers liberally, drafted muscular types to carry sedated co-workers to their sleeping quarters, and completed a tally of casualties. Luckily, there were no critical injuries. The most serious involved broken arms, legs, ribs, and a concussion. The rest were an assortment of sprains, abrasions, and bruises. Many people admitted they would have escaped the intruder unharmed if they hadn't been so drunk; in their fright, they'd run right across the thing's path.

Reasonably whole expedition members stoked up on caffa, stims, and hangover remedies and debated what to do next. Bleary-eyed, queasy, and aching, Dan put his credits' worth in.

First, they had to agree on what had taken place.

With four different species, four different varieties of sensory inputs, and four different cultural styles of observing and interpreting, that was tough. Stir in mood alterants, and it was a miracle any of the team members' accounts meshed. Even teetotalers offered wildly conflicting versions of what they'd seen, smelled, heard, and felt. Dan was grateful the N'lacs weren't participating in this rehash. They would give yet another viewpoint.

They argued it around and around, sifting testimony, questioning, proposing, and theorizing.

Slowly they arrived at a consensus, or as much of a consensus as they were going to get.

Praedar ticked off their conclusions. "It is metal. No apparent visual or auditory orifices. Thin, multiple upper appendages. Ar-

257

ticulated lower ones, with splayed, footlike bottom sections. No detectable scent. No detectable sound . . ."

"Or none we could hear under those chaotic conditions," Rosie corrected.

Nodding, Praedar went on. "To Whimeds, its silvery color luminesced. To Vahnajes, it radiated an aura, possibly an effect connected with the itching compulsion that we all suffered to a degree, the cranial pressure, and the temporary paralysis some were prey to . . ."

"And I'm betting it's probably the source of those quakes," Baines added. He looked like hell, but he was considerably more awake and less drunk that he had been. "Remember that we felt that same scratching urge when that quake shook loose Chen's Rock. And we've felt it during each subsequent seismic disturbance. The tie-in seems too strong to be coincidence."

"One more reason to pull its plug," Sheila growled.

Praedar resumed his summary. "In all respects except size, the intruder duplicates the demons described in N'lac legends and artifacts. Although it demonstrated an unanticipated ability to scale sheer rocks and cliffs in apparent defiance of gravity, its major method of locomotion was irregular, creating havoc for those unfortunate enough to be in its way."

"It's a miracle no one was killed," Kat said.

"Yet," Cavanaugh added.

Praedar turned to Dan. "Does our xenomechanician confirm that these data suggest a robot?"

"Yes, one capable of interstellar travel." Dan had everyone's full attention. "The ship's monitor tracked an unknown blip entering T-W 593's atmosphere weeks ago. At the time, I assumed it was space junk. Now I think what the detectors picked up was our visitor, spiraling in for a landing."

Ruieb-An asked, "Urr . . . is search probe? Like Vahnaj?"

"Huh uh. Not like the one your race sent to welcome mine into the galactic community, over a century ago. This one is probably a slave scout."

All of the scientists had been mentally circling the same ominous idea. They stared at Dan, silently begging him to come up with technological reasons why what they feared wasn't true. He did exactly the opposite.

"It's tricky to extrapolate about an alien machine, but . . . working on the basis of what *our* servos can do, that thing holds

258

some deadly potentials—recording images, analyzing, and identifying our five species as a particular type . . ."

"Humanoid," Rosie whispered. "Slaves."

"It might also be programmed to send a message back to its home base regarding what it's found," Dan said. "There's one bright spot; the way it's acting, its programming's badly messed up, maybe bad enough to prevent coordination and any message-sending. That could be why we're still here and why no Old Ones' spaceships have arrived to round up us and the N'lacs and haul us off to unknown stellar regions—and the slave camps."

Another pained silence fell. Armilly broke it, saying "If catcher, did not try catch. Stomped. Broke inside."

"As Dan theorizes," Praedar agreed. "Indeed. It is very possible we owe our present freedom to this robot's state of disrepair."

Dan massaged his temples. "Yeah. It's drunk, in a way, as we were. Drunk from too much spacing. I suspect our intruder is a quick and dirty expendable. The Old Ones could send out scouts by the kiloton, primitive, simplistic servos, in their terms. It makes sense. The N'lac legends hint at an enormous alien empire, thousands of millennia old. Such a species wouldn't waste its time personally searching this galactic quadrant's Terrene worlds for slave stock. So, send out fleets of intruder models. Most of their searches would come up empty. Or they'd get wiped during planetfalls or passages through radiation and magnetic belts. But if only one in centuries hit a humanoid gold mine, it would be worth it. We humanoids do the same thing; we prospect by remote servos in asteroid belts and hunt for habitable planets. Stripped robots are ideal for that kind of work."

"Simplistic with some nasty fillips," Sheila said. "Terror tactics."

Praedar summarized, "We have assumed the N'lacs' demons were policemen. Were they instead such scouts?"

Dan nodded. "This one's damaged. Imagine one in better shape, landing in an isolated geographic region of T-W 593, two thousand years ago, flattening the locals, and sending a report back to its masters. In effect: 'Come and get them!' "

"Yes," Praedar said, very thoughtful. "Was this valley that isolated region? We may have erred in postulating this was a capital city. Such a discovery will require correction of our hypothesis."

Baines spoke up. "Hey, the quakes could be a form of detection as well as a terror device. Subsonics, to spot living beings . . ."

"Enough theories and hypotheses!" Sheila cried. "We know what we're up against. How could we not, after all the years we've worked with the N'lacs! We're in a war for humanoid survival. And this expedition is on the front line!"

Dan sighed. "Do I hear Captain Derek Whitcomb's daughter talking? You sound like Adam, straight out of the Space Fleet's battle manuals. Hit 'em hard before they hit you. Hit 'em with what? Where? How? We don't even know if the Evil Old Ones still exist. They could have died out centuries ago. This robot could be the final gasp of a dead race . . ."

"And if it isn't?" the blonde retorted. "How the hell can we postulate such an alien species' life span? Or their motives?"

"Exactly! You want us to strike half-cocked, with no info at all?" Dan said.

"We have to stop that thing before T-W 593 is invaded again!"

"Urgency must be tempered with reason," Praedar said levelly. "All of us share Sheila's apprehension. Time is of the essence. What will the robot do next?" he asked the team's xenomech.

Dan wished he could wipe the cobwebs and fog from his mind. "Self-repair. A *lot* of self-repair. I'm betting it's already done plenty of that, during the weeks it's been on this planet. Remember, indications are that it's gone through hundreds of landings and launches. It's amazing it's still functioning at all. If we're lucky, it'll never achieve its original readiness—"

"And if we're lucky," Kat cut in, "you're right about the Evil Old Ones being extinct. But . . ."

"If they're not, pray that robot doesn't get itself glued back together sufficiently to send them a message and show them what it saw last night."

Rosie stammered, "Is—is that possible? Sector Fleet scouts have ranged parsecs beyond this solar system. The Old Ones' stellar regions must be very far out. Could even a brand-new robot of that type send a coherent message such a distance?"

"Yes," Dan said flatly. "Some of Terra's servo scouts have subspace capability. No bets on what an alien technology may have put into that thing's guts. Compressed holo signal systems . . . anything! As I say, I hope it's too messed up to mend itself. If it does, it could throw something a hell of a lot heavier at us the next time we meet it."

"How long will this self-repair require?" Praedar wanted to know.

"Maybe if I get a close look at it, I could tell you. We're dealing with systems no humanoid engineer or inventor has ever seen," Dan said.

"Except in a slave community," Kat reminded him.

"You shall examine it, yes." Praedar's gaze was unfocused and remote. "To preserve it. To study it." His teammates eyed him with alarm. "You are the only one here with the requisite knowledge to analyze this object, Dan. You must instruct and advise us."

"If we could examine it . . ." Rosie murmured dreamily.

Dan retorted, "You'd better catch that perambulating accident zone before you make plans to exhibit it—or before the Evil Old Ones' spaceships start arriving."

"He is correct," Praedar agreed. "The long view. First we must locate the robot."

"Where do we start?" Baines demanded. "The plateau measures at least fifty square kilometers . . ."

"It could have gone in any direction . . ."

"If it left footprints . . ."

"Hey, yeah! Let's get up on the cliff!"

The group split up along specialty lines. As it did, Dan noticed Kat and Sheila conferring in whispers, smiling conspiratorially. An utterly human reaction intruded on his concern about the robot. What were the women discussing—comparing notes on their mutual lover? His ears burned. He exited the cook shack in a hurry, following Praedar to the skimmer hangar.

Early-morning sunlight was streaming into the valley now. Sleeg was maintaining his vigil below Dome Hill. Chuss and Meej had returned from the village and sat beside him. The shaman glared at the offworlders. The adolescents, though, were oblivious to anything but the ancient structures. Their rigidity was a striking contrast to their earlier hysteria.

Dan had to run to match Praedar's pace. Then the Whimed stood by, fidgeting, while Dan ran obligatory checks of the skimmer's systems. Minutes later they lifted, swooping from the hangar and climbing steeply. The scene beneath them was a humanoid hive. Scientists prowled the dud pits with recorders and casting materials. Joe and volunteer aides were busy in the village, soothing the N'lacs. Armilly and a team had reached the top of the cliff from the access road. Dan hovered, watching them unload gear. The wind hadn't disturbed the robot's tracks much yet. Telltale marks leaped from Armilly's monitors to the interlinked screens aboard the skimmer. A trail! For a few minutes the cliff-top team and those in the flyer exchanged words, coordinating plans. Then Praedar pointed to a splay-footed, weaving trace farther to the southeast on the mesa. "To find. To examine," he ordered.

"We'll do our damnedest," Dan agreed.

He tracked the spoor at low speed, giving scanners a chance to soak up every scrap of data. Time was of the essence, but so was information. The intruder's drunken behavior hadn't improved after it had scaled the cliff; its trail was a reeling zigzag. Dan corrected course constantly to stay with it. That was one sick machine, and it had hours of head start on them. How far had it gone while they were tending the wounded and debating options?

Twenty kilometers from the landing strip, the tracks ended at a gray-black expanse that reached to the mountainous horizon.

Praedar slammed a hand on the skimmer's control panel. *"Aaa! Lava flow! Bruska ji!"* He played a symphony on detector gear. So did Dan, dipping into alternate search systems. Terran, Whimed, Vahnaj, and Lannon science all came into play, sweeping the alien terrain. After a time, Praedar conceded defeat.

"Shielded," Dan announced. "It's absorbing our signals, not bouncing them. In fact, it could use them to detect us." He hastily shut down the hunt beams. "Xenoarch equipment isn't built for this job. We need one of my brother's military eyes in the sky, preferably armed with an ultra-modern disruptor..."

Praedar scowled, disapproving.

"I'll do a broad sweep," Dan said. "We'll eyeball check. Maybe we'll see where it left the flow."

They didn't. They crisscrossed, circled, and circumnavigated the badlands. The rugged outpouring was full of crevices where a sick machine could hole up.

Reluctantly Praedar decided to abandon the search. He brooded as Dan flew a beeline back to the cliff and landed. The two of them stepped out into a rapidly heating oven.

Scientists were on their hands and knees, staking out string-marked grids, dividing the section where the robot had been into individual territories. They'd taken casts of the prints. And they'd holo-moded those splay-footed indentations. Armilly had collected some minute fragments that appeared to be metal. The labs would have to break them down—if they could.

Time! They needed time to analyze and to track the enemy.

As Dan was thinking that, another tremor shook the valley and mesa. Team members waited it out stolidly. When it ended, Baines said, "So it's still sending those out. And I still can't find any epicenter."

"If you could," Dan said bitterly, "locating the thing would be easy."

Praedar walked to the cliff's edge. Dan joined him there, and they both gazed down into N'lac Valley. The xenomech didn't have to ask what commanded the boss's attention. Three tiny bodies—Chuss, Meej, and Sleeg—continued to sit on guard duty near the domes.

"Not even that quake shook them loose," Dan said. "They don't dare leave their post, trying to hold back a repetition of the forever time . . ."

"They tell us what we should have realized," Praedar murmured. "The large dome, in particular, is the focus. Answers must lie within the temple of the many-fathers-ago. The secrets must be revealed."

Dan smiled ruefully. "Yeah. And that's up to me, isn't it?" Other scientists as well as Praedar were looking at him, once more putting all their hopes on his shoulders. He'd wanted to be a full-fledged member of the expedition. Now he was—with a vengeance. And inwardly, he knew he couldn't guarantee results on the trust they had handed him.

CHAPTER SEVENTEEN
ΟΟΟΟΟΟΟΟ

Outside Interference

Five days later Dan was still sweating over the lock mechanism. As he had feared, the thing differed considerably from the one controlling the door between the entry area and the mural room. In addition, the N'lacs' ancestors had done their best to jam this portal to the tunnel. And the lock also contained some odd, glistening filaments, totally unfamiliar to Dan. The stuff appeared to be annealed to the fluidics elements, and he was having no success in figuring out what the substance was.

Quakes didn't help his work or the work of his teammates. Tremors continued to strike, coming, according to Baines, from several points of the compass simultaneously. The constant tension of anticipating those shocks rubbed nerves raw. When Dan was in the insta-cell complex, he could sense the increasing friction scraping at tempers. He escaped most of that in the dome. That enclosed space intensified the quakes' effect, but isolated him from arguments and debates raging in the insta-cells.

"How's it going?" Sheila spoke with forced cheerfulness and set a food box down beside the xenomech.

He leaned back from his work at the door and sighed. "Thanks. I tend to lose track of time in here. No night and no day. But lots of ghosts." He gestured at the mural. Chuss, Meej, and their adolescent buddies squatted in front of the painting. Over the past few days a number of scientists had come and gone, asking questions Dan couldn't answer and offering help he couldn't use. The N'lacs were there all the time. Now that the youngsters had dared to enter the temple, they seemed obsessed with the place.

As Dan munched and swigged the lunch package, Sheila regarded the N'lacs. "The best Kat and Praedar can get out of them is that they have to watch the door to the Big Dark."

"Or the entrance to hell," Dan muttered. He washed down the last of the food and returned to his task.

The blonde leaned over his shoulder, studying the equipment he was using. "That some of the stuff you cannibalized from the ship?"

"Yeah. Wish I'd thought of it when we were tracking the robot—not that it would have helped much there." Dan played a probe across the opened panels, watching readouts. "This isn't what the gear was built for. It's all a jerry-rig, like half the tools and vehicles on this world."

"You ought to know," Sheila said, smiling. "You put it all back in operation. You weren't kidding when you said you could do other things besides pilot."

"Feo made sure I won't be piloting again soon," Dan said. "Not that it matters, if our visitor . . . hah!" He peered eagerly at the cobbled-together scanner. "An anomaly in that range? Huh! Fine! We'll just . . . ."

Engrossed, installing fluidics elements to replace ones he'd guessed wrong on earlier, he didn't hear Sheila leave. He did hear her come back, accompanied by Praedar, Kat, Ruieb, Armilly, and a dozen other scientists.

"This may be another false alarm," Dan warned. Why did they pounce every time he found a new tack to take? Hadn't they learned, after these past few days, that most of his tinkering led to dead ends? This discovery, though, proved successful. He was as surprised as the rest when he felt a subliminal tingle in the wall. Chuss and Meej, shivering, turned from the mural, staring at him fearfully. "Hang on . . ." Dan said, fine-tuning the installation.

"Do we need any more proof his fluidics theory is right and Bill Getz's wrong?" Kat asked, sniffing.

A ready light warmed to life. Unlike the one at the outer door, this one shimmered. Its surface was strangely faceted, resembling an insect's eye.

Armilly had brought extra deep-probe equipment in anticipation of this. Now he scanned conditions beyond the door. The Lannon had already collected volumes of readouts on the same area. But Dan approved such caution. "Is air stuff comings," Armilly said.

"Pressurizing?" A glance at the screens confirmed that. Dan frowned. "I guess I woke something more than a door."

"Open. Open!" Praedar urged.

Dan hesitated for a second, then touched the ancient trigger. The portal whispered ajar, the gap slowly widening. There was no abrupt shift of air, no draft. Dan shoved equipment out of the way, clearing access to the entry. Ahead, in the tunnel, light panels dormant for centuries were energizing.

How? The solar panels that once had fed them had long since torn away in T-W 593's sandstorms. There had to be a storage technology, a separate connection, one dismantled by Chuss' ancestors and now reborn. Because Dan had repaired the lock? Was that a key to the entire system? Or . . . was the system being tuned in on by a hidden robot? Activating the door mechanism might well be cross-switched with alien remote devices. Feedback upon feedback.

Praedar led the team inside. Armilly assured them the way was clear. No clutter. No "importants" they might step on. The tunnel was bare. Warily, each step an adventure, the offworlders advanced.

The corridor was fifteen meters long. Like the small dome, its walls were covered with decorations and writings. Ruieb-An homed in on the latter, translating. "Place of . . . urr . . . *hallway* of many-fathers-ago. We . . . urr . . . re-turn . . . is ours . . . is Home of N'lac . . . urr . . . where we may . . . urr . . . live. Seal . . . urr . . . broken. Is not to . . . urr . . . for-get. Fear. Temple of . . . urr . . . Old Ones. They who . . . urr . . . were al-ways. Sacri-fice is . . . urr . . . *was* made. No more sacri-fice. Urr . . . stay not here. Death . . ."

The paintings were a visual feast. Portraits, perhaps, showed the escaped slaves. They weren't as pop-eyed and flushed as the current villagers. Dan felt sure that if Joe were able to look into the portrait subjects' retinas, he'd find far fewer hemorrhages caused by soroche than he did in Chuss' people. The collision between genetic alterations and a hostile environment hadn't yet taken effect on the N'lacs in these paintings. In places where later portraits had been added to the earliest ones, deterioration of the species was very evident.

"They preserved," Praedar said reverently. "They feared the large dome and this tunnel opening to it. But they did not forget it or destroy it."

"Even when it had been buried for God knows how long," Sheila said. "When we arrived here, they called this the Valley of the Many-Fathers-Ago. And they practically pointed Armilly at this hill and told him to scan for buried structures."

"And here we are," Kat said softly, gawking.

The corridor was musty with age. Had Dan thought the mural room held ghosts? This was worse. There was a twisting ache in his belly that he hadn't felt since he was a kid, terrified by a scary vid drama. What he was responding to now, though, was no fiction.

"They couldn't forget," he said. "Not after what the Evil Old Ones did to them."

Some of the paintings were of Old Ones and their robots. That was a daunting reminder of the demon haunting the planet's surface.

But where, dammit?

Xenoarch machines were designed to analyze minutely and scan within ancient monuments and graves. There were confining limits to the amount of conversion Dan could achieve on such gear—limits that in effect made searches for the robot futile.

If the starhopper had military capabilities, he might be able to spot the intruder from orbit. But it was useless to speculate. The little ship's fuel was so low he couldn't launch. He'd get her to geosynch orbit—and then what? Park there and observe and report to the team, and wait for his life support to run out? A successful reentry was very doubtful, with such a skimpy fuel reserve.

Damn Feo, anyway! Vengeful cheapskate! Starving Dan and his expedition, as Feo had starved his cousin Reid, years ago.

But this time, more than a branch of the Saunder-McKelveys

was at stake. And the crisis confronting humanoid life forms was a hell of a lot more terrible than bankruptcy.

"Is bad bad place." Chuss and Meej had left their companions and crept into the tunnel. The brothers cringed, glaring at the paintings of Old Ones and robots. Chuss' lips peeled back in a fierce snarl. "Bad place! Evil! Kill demon!"

"We'll pull its plug," Dan said. "That's as good as killing it and them." Chuss ran to him and clutched at the Terran, peering nearsightedly at him, pleading. Rattled, Dan turned to Kat. "Why don't you explain it?"

"I've tried . . ." She bent over, on an eye level with the N'lacs, talking in their tongue. They didn't buy the plan. They wanted the robot—*all* robots, and their masters—dead.

Suddenly Chuss and Meej whimpered and dropped to the floor. They flung their skinny arms over their heads. From the mural room came more shrieks, other N'lacs, also reacting with terror.

Twenty seconds later, there was a quake.

When aftershocks ended, Chuss and Meej scampered back to the comparative safety—in their viewpoint—of the mural room. The scientists watched them go. "Sensitivity," Praedar said. "They feel the robot's functions before we do—before the terrain does."

"Canaries," Kat said. "Earth peoples used to use pet birds to detect lethal gases in fossil fuel mines. Small avians were much more sensitive to the gases than humans. If a bird died, it was a warning for Terrans to make themselves scarce. What we have here is a N'lac early alarm system."

Rosie was appalled. "That's outrageous! You can't . . ."

"She didn't mean it literally," Sheila said. "It was an analogy, like handsome's mangled metaphors. You didn't think Kat was proposing to use N'lacs as a siren to tip us off when a quake was due?"

"I wasn't so sure. The callous way you recounted that, I thought you were planning to give Baines extra time to tune his seismographs . . ."

"We work together," Praedar said firmly. "Offworlders and N'lacs. We protect them. We do not exploit them. No one suggests we shall."

Cavanaugh broke in. "Dan and Sheila have both mentioned

contacting the Fleet, and we all know what that would mean for the N'lacs . . ."

"I'm more aware than you are," Dan said. "If it comes to that, I'd prefer working with my brother, rather than those greedy planet developers who are pressuring Eckard to give them access to this world—or my cousin, who thinks the N'lacs are subhumanoids. But we have to look beyond T-W 593. If push comes to mash, the rest of the humanoid sectors have got to have a fighting chance to defend themselves against a new invasion by the Old Ones. Otherwise, history will repeat itself, and the knowledge will be swallowed up for millennia—again. I don't know about you, but I want our species to get off that slavemobile!"

"Things up through," Armilly said.

That stopped the argument cold. It took several moments for non-Lannons to figure out what the procyonid meant. He jerked a hairy thumb at his scanners, then at the far end of the tunnel. Dan and Praedar glanced at the screen display, then hurried along the corridor. Another locked door barred the way. Armilly shuffled forward, playing his detector probe across the wall and portal. "Things. Make stirs little."

"Faint indications of activity," Praedar paraphrased.

"Whatever's going on inside, it isn't making much headway on this lock mechanism," Dan said. "This looks like another patch assignment. How many damned doors are there in here, anyway?"

Praedar probed the barrier with his spidery hands. "That is to be determined. Answers. Armilly?" The Lannon pointed to his screens. "A small room with a door that may be linked to this one. A pressure chamber?"

Dan, peering narrowly at the lock, nodded. "That would fit with the general arrangement, given the difference between the aliens' worlds and the one the N'lacs evolved on . . ."

"Beyond the airlock, one large room—the end of our quest."

"Maybe the end of more than that," Sheila said, "if we don't watch our step."

The scientists huddled around Armilly's gear, fascinated by the shadowy images he was extracting from the dome's hidden interior.

"Look at that huge platform in the center!"

"Platform?"

"Must be. You can make out the shape . . ."

"It's enormous!"

"Was that where the Old Ones held court?"

"A pressurized slave market! Built to keep the visiting masters comfortable until they returned to their spaceship."

"No wonder the N'lacs treat this place with dread and awe. This is where it all began and finished for them and the only place the escaping slaves recognized. During captivity, they must have tried to hang onto legends of their home world. But the sole constant was the Old Ones' pressure chamber; everything else had changed—the climate, the city, decayed and buried in dust drift . . . The dome was a haven, even though it was a symbol of their hated masters."

"Stow your philosophy! Just consider the size of that central enclosed platform!"

"If the Old Ones stood there . . . are they *that* big . . . ?"

"As much bigger than we imagined as that marauding robot is bigger than the model demons the N'lacs smash."

"Kat said it. Sleeg's myths reduce the enemies' sizes, so his people can cope. Dealing with a monster that huge is . . ."

"Horrifying!"

Dan headed out of the dome. The discussion interested him, but he needed additional tools to unlock the latest barricade blocking access to the temple.

When he was halfway down the hill, Kat caught up with him. "Wait, Dan! I want to . . ." As he turned to face her, the brunette ran into him. He braced her to keep her from falling. She gulped and blurted, "About the pit fit . . ."

"That again?" Exasperated, he started to move on.

Kat held on to him. "You dodge me every time I approach this topic."

"What's there to talk about? We had fun, even if it all blew up because of our intruder."

"*My* problems occurred before the robot appeared." Kat was no Whimed, but she was damned good in universe-class staring games.

She gathered her courage. "I . . . I've rarely been that drunk. I dislike losing control of myself."

"Your control seemed perfect, to me," Dan said lightly. "You've got superb physical reflexes."

She looked torn between the urge to bawl or belt him. "I know I-I said something, gave you an idea that . . . I . . ."

270

"That you're in love with Praedar."

He expected her to blush. Instead, Kat went ashen. "Y-yes. It's not unusual for young field workers to have a crush on the dig's leader. But normally that leader is of the same species." Kat sagged in relief, now that she'd put things out in the open.

"I thought you'd be . . ."

"Blasé? The trained xenosocio, well versed in the biosexual customs of all humanoid species? I am, in the abstract. It . . . it's very different when it involves personalities. I-I haven't handled the situation at all well, and I'm ashamed." She touched Dan's face gently. "I would have continued to shove my feelings into a buried reservoir forever, if you hadn't come along, and if Sheila hadn't pushed me, as she's pushed for years, to bring me to reality."

"Our friend from Kruger 60," Dan said, embarrassed. So the women had traded confidences, before as well as after the pit fit. "Sheila's quite a manipulator, among other things. Talk about mixed-up personalities."

Kat laughed nervously. "She's a very generous being."

"I take it then that you don't resent her throwing you at me?"

The brunette's jaw dropped. "I thought she was throwing you at me!"

Dan embraced her and they shared a laugh. As their tension eased, he said, "I'm not complaining about that night. If you're not, we're fine." Sobering, he added, "Anyway, we don't have time to bite our nails over minor, personal snags."

"I know." Kat had regained her normal, brisk tone. "That's why it's essential to clear away emotional clutter. I-I've been a fool. I recognize that now, finally. Years, wasted on a hopeless fantasy. Praedar doesn't . . . won't ever. . . . ! I'm grateful, really, that you and Sheila put me on . . . What do pilots call it?"

"A correct vector." The spacers' phrase was salt on a wound.

Sensing his pain, she said, "It's rotten, what Feo's done to your ship and your license. The bastard."

"Oh, he's legitimate, right down to old-fashioned legal forms in quintuplicate. Main branch Saunder-McKelveys are very fussy about that, for inheritance reasons." Dan sighed and said, "I've accepted the situation, like you with Praedar. I have to. Even if this uproar with the robot hadn't happened, I'm stuck. Feo saw to that. Either the expedition takes me on as the resident xenomech, or I'm a charity case, taking handouts from my brother, or Feo."

"Of *course* we—"

"Dan! Dan!" Norris, Getz's former student, ran up the hill toward them. Spurts of dust flew from his bootprints. The young scientist panted to a halt beside the crates and bent over, his hands on his knees as he sucked in air.

"Take it easy!" Kat exclaimed. "It's too hot to run . . ."

"Message. On the com recorder. Feo and Hope . . . on their way here . . ." Norris wheezed.

"They can't be!" Dan and Kat chorused; then Dan added, "My cousin said they'd need at least three weeks to tidy up leftover business from the Assembly."

Norris waved toward the complex. "Dunno. The message came in about an hour ago. Maybe two. None of us noticed it then. We were all busy. I just happened to go past the com room and saw the recording light. When I checked it . . ."

Kat ordered the winded student to sit down and catch his breath. She lectured him as sternly as any paramed.

"I'd better notify Praedar and the others," Dan said, and headed back to the domes.

Half a local hour later, nearly the entire camp's personnel had jammed into the insta-cells, eager to see the message. The crowd filled the labs adjacent to the com room and overflowed into the cook shack. Dan fed the signal to monitors throughout the complex, so that everyone could witness the news simultaneously.

The Saunders' images formed on the screens. The signal was extremely sharp, particularly when compared to what T-W 593's equipment could put out. Subspace static and shimmer was reduced to a minimum.

"Amazing what you can do when you can afford top-grade com gear," Dan muttered.

"Hello!" Feo said. "We're sending this while we're en route to your dig. In fact, our crew informs us we're nearing the T-W 593 system right now. Hope and I realize this is a bit sooner than we promised to arrive. But we decided we've owed you a visit for so long we might as well advance the date a trifle. I trust you won't object . . ."

"You mean you wanted to foul up our work schedule," Sheila retorted.

Dan halted the playback momentarily, then let it roll once more.

". . . wanted to pay our courtesy call while the media were in

272

attendance. We know you'd want a complete record of the exchange . . ."

"Media," Kat said bitterly, and again Dan interrupted the playback until she'd finished speaking. "Pan Terran network, he means. Read 'Rei Ito.' Keep it in the Saunder-McKelvey family . . ."

"We don't need any of them," Rosie grumped. "They'll just get in the way."

"That's what they want to do," Dan said. "The Saunders will fulfill their promise, catching us with our pants down, and they'll have reporters to sop up every awkward thing we say and do. Or so they plan. The idea is to make us look like unorganized amateurs, and the Saunders like expert professionals."

"Indeed," Praedar said. "I understand. Chen was wise in the manners of Earth. Feo will verify he is ethical. He has kept his word. He will attempt to expose our flaws."

"A PR stunt," someone in the labs shouted. "Dirty tricks!"

"However, the situation has altered since the invitation was extended," Praedar said.

No one else chimed in, and Dan cued the playback. Hope, front and center, was putting on her best maternal act. "You mustn't go to any trouble for us. We're well aware of the demands of field work on remote planets. We'll bring all our own food and housing. It's the least we can do to facilitate matters. After all, we're in the same profession, and we must have some feeling for our colleagues' inconvenience . . ."

That brought a noisy round of catcalls. The backtalk made Dan grin. Even sophisticated humanoids tended to argue with vid images that displeased them. Not even techs were immune to the impulse, though they, more than most, were keenly conscious of the time lag differential in a message like this.

Praedar didn't join the sassing session. He stared inscrutably at his rivals' faces. It struck Dan that the boss and Chen had been a truly odd couple. Reversed stereotypes. A rubber-visaged, voluble Terran Oriental. A Whimed, a species noted for its impatience and intense emotional reactions, who specialized in cool rationality.

"Our arrival time . . ." Feo turned from the lens, speaking to someone out of frame. "Captain Topwe? Ah!" Saunder read off the ETA.

That created consternation on the receiving end. "Ouch!"

273

Sheila yelped. "That's . . . that's *tomorrow*! Less than twelve hours from now!"

"We're looking forward to seeing you . . ." Hope gushed.

The rest of the message was a formal sign-off by Feo's "Sparks." Dan did some fast calculating. Allowing for a space yacht's fancy com gear and Feo's A-One broadcasting priority, the call had been made deliberately late. There was no reason it couldn't have been sent days ago, when the Saunders were still on T-S 311. Instead, they'd wanted to surprise their competitors and virtually drop in out of a blue-green sky.

"Warn them off," Dan said. "They can still turn back. They've got plenty of fuel reserves. That's no problem, for *them*," he added, thinking of how Feo had all but emptied *Fiona/Praedar's Project*'s reserve package.

"We will accommodate them," Praedar said. His team protested. He waited out the arguments, then went on. "Dan will inform his kindred of the situation. They will be given the opportunity to retrace their course. I do not believe they will."

"Hardly!" Dan agreed. He frowned, studying the Whimed. "I'm beginning to see your angle. You're thinking the Saunders will wield a lot more influence with the C.S.P. Council and Space Fleet than we can, if this robot hunt turns really ugly. Come to that, the Saunders probably pack more clout with the Whimed section of the Xenoethno Board than we can. You figure they'll be useful, on that score? Dubious. Prying open their minds may be tougher than getting the door to the main dome cracked."

"Inform them," Praedar repeated. "We will demonstrate to Feo and Hope that there is far more to our dig than we ourselves knew when I issued them the invitation to visit us."

CHAPTER EIGHTEEN

Collision Imminent

Like *Praedar's Project*, the Saunders' personal ship was a single-stage starhopper. However, her top-of-the-line design put her light-years beyond any ordinary indie craft. Sleek and powerful, *Lady Belvedere-Saunder* poised as if she were still in flight, not parked on the mesa. She was a luxurious big sister of the well-worn smaller ship nearby.

A parade of aides and flunkeys was offloading luggage and portable housing units to the local expedition's trucks. Feo and Hope certainly didn't intend to rough it while they were on T-W 593. In fact, they were flaunting their wealth blatantly. They'd brought their own press corps, as well; Rei Ito and her aide, Kimball, panned their lenses across the landscape, recording. Expedition members who'd interrupted their work to drive out to the landing strip and fetch the visitors watched the show sourly.

Praedar's welcome had been polite, not cordial. The Saunders milked the formalities, effusively thanking their host repeatedly for his invitation, as if they'd wrangled it out of him, rather than having been cornered into accepting it!

Dan ducked out of that time-wasting exchange and spoke to the ship's crew.

"Thanks for those landing coordinates," Captain Topwe said. "Very precise. Good signal, too."

"Better than you expected from a nowhere Settlement like ours," Dan noted. The pilot didn't deny that. "About that request I made when you were in descending orbits . . ."

Topwe pulled a dupe wafer from his pocket. "Here you go. Full-spectrum scan. Five thousand kilometer radius sweep. What are you looking for?"

"A servo. One I'm not sure I want to find," Dan said. the yacht crewmen blinked at the cryptic answer. "Thanks for the search dupe. With *your* equipment, I know that if you couldn't locate the robot, nothing short of a battle-state Fleet intervention will."

Topwe glanced curiously at *Praedar's Project*. Dan read the man's thoughts. "She's bare-bones on fuel. Won't lift and get back intact. So I've yanked some of her packages for surface research work. That's why she's sitting there like that with her ramps and hatches wide open."

"Too bad," Topwe said. "She's a trim little craft. A shame to let her rot."

"I agree. But my cousin and I had a disagreement. And he's getting even with me through my starhopper."

The men and women of the yacht's crew sympathized. They understood.

Or did they? Half a year ago, Dan would have been devastated by the grounding and cannibalization of his ship. Now his mind and emotions were full of that bigger picture, and the loss of one inanimate possession no longer seemed so crucial. Far more vital issues were at stake.

Loading was complete, and the trucks and rovers headed westward. Dan drove the lead vehicle. As he steered around rough spots on the road, Feo leaned forward and commented to his kinsman and Praedar, "I invited Topwe and his crew to join us, but they declined."

"Naturally," Dan said. "Their ship's home to them. Non-spacers don't realize that."

"What were you talking to them about?" Hope demanded waspishly.

"Collecting a favor. Pilots' protocol," Dan replied, looking smug. His relatives were miffed by the cryptic retort. Whatever the future held, Dan would remain a member of the space fraternity. The Saunders could never take that away from him.

He was proud of the caravan's smooth, purring operation. His kindred took such things for granted. Praedar's team hadn't done so, until their resident xenomech had repaired their fleet.

The first sight of N'lac Valley sent the reporters into an orgy of recording. After his initial surprise, Dan saw that their enthusiasm was genuine. This was a first for them—an honest, in-the-raw dig, very different from that sterile, enclosed museum the Saunders were creating on T-S 311.

A second welcoming committee of sorts was on hand in camp, starting another round of introductions. Those who'd complained the loudest yesterday about this visit now lined up to meet the Saunders. Dan couldn't fault his relatives' behavior. They were in their gracious, noblesse oblige mode.

Joe Hughes led Chuss and Meej forward. The e.t.s had been expertly coached. This recess from their vigil in the domes was doing them good. Both N'lacs were cheerful, eager to shake hands. Feo and Hope were strongly taken aback by this face-to-face encounter with a species they'd dismissed as subhumanoid. Chuss bowed and bobbed, as elegant as a Vahnaj diplomat. "You fellow come see our Home. See Pwaedar's Home. Happy meet you fellow. We show you valley. Dome place. Village. Catch you much meat for supper."

"Impressive command of an alien language for Level Two, isn't it?" Kat asked archly.

The Saunders managed to recover their poise and thanked Chuss warmly. They *did* seem impressed. Maybe, with the N'lacs' help, the expedition could dent Feo and Hope's stubborn opposition. They weren't stupid. But were they bendable?

Chuss and Meej scampered a few meters away from the new arrivals, sat down briefly with their backs to the offworlders, then turned and hurried back to greet them again. It was a charming display. Kat and Joe had to restrain the youngsters from welcoming the Saunders *ad infinitum*.

"You will wish to refresh yourselves before you begin a tour," Praedar suggested, gesturing to the insta-cell complex.

"Oh, they're not tired," Dan said. He couldn't resist a jab at his kindred. "That yacht's equipped with artificial grave and all the planetary comforts. Terra's royalty always travels in that fashion, unlike us ordinary hardworking xenoarchs. I'm sure they and their pet news hounds are straining at the controls to see our dig—and sneer at it." He touched his cap to Feo in mocking deference. "I'd love to tag along, but duty calls."

"Don't be rude, Danny," Hope scolded. "It won't hurt you to be sociable and . . ."

"Not possible. I'm the only xenomech here," Dan said coldly. "And what I'm doing won't wait. I don't have an army of students and flunkeys who can take over my work in my absence," he added in a final thrust. He spun on his heel and walked toward Dome Hill.

Kat was standing near the dud pits. As he passed her, she said softly, "Lighten up."

"Why? If I hadn't needed to get this orbital scan chip from their pilot, I wouldn't have wasted time out at the landing strip at all," Dan growled. "Don't forget to read them the camp rules and tell them they've got to be out of here in forty-eight hours."

"Stop it!" Kat snapped. "Remember why we invited them here in the first place. And come to that, another visit by the robot, and we may be grateful that they—and their ship—are here. We might need a way to transport our injured and children offworld in a hurry."

A faint tremor punctuated her words and wiped away Dan's petty concerns. "Yeah, I know," he muttered. "I just . . . I just yielded to the temptation to kick them back."

She nodded. "You've had more provocation than the rest of us. The ship, your career . . ."

Her pity made him uncomfortable. Dan hurried up the trail, determined to crack that lock. He'd spent too much time today in childish oneupmanship games.

Inside the tunnel, he settled himself in between Armilly and Ruieb-An. The Lannon, coordinating frequently with Praedar, kept his constant scans of what lay beyond the barrier updated. The Vahnaj was amassing small mountains of translations from the walls. Ruieb complained that the writing here, close to the main dome, was a complicated dialect of the N'lac dictionary he'd painstakingly assembled. His work, like Dan's, was going slowly.

Dan read through the survey wafer the space yacht's captain had given him. It was a good scan—and it told him nothing he didn't know. Wherever that robot was hiding, it was well shielded and impervious to prying offworlders' eyes and most of their tools.

That check done, Dan got busy on the door mechanism. He'd made little progress so far. More and more, he was thinking in terms of brute force, either on the airlock or straight through the dome's wall. He had made several plans along that line, and one proposal. Praedar had turned the alternative down flat. No destruction! It would wreck priceless data. Dan's arguments that time pressures might demand they resort to blasting their way into the dome met with stern repetitions of that "No!"

During the day, team members dropped in to see how the tunnel crew was doing. Each friend supplied a running commentary on the Saunders' tour. Dan listened absently, preoccupied.

"Won't believe *anything*. It's like talking to rocks!"

"How can they just ignore our injured and scoff at those robot tracks we collected . . ."

". . . have to give them points for stamina. They didn't get winded even when we went kilometers upstream to early dig sites . . ."

". . . if they patronize us one more time . . . !"

In the hottest part of the day, Dan, Armilly, and Ruieb-An were alone. Other offworlders were in the insta-cells. The tunnel was a similar haven, musty but cool.

Methodically Ruieb-An plowed through layers of inscriptions. He fussed over nuances within the writings, looking for clues, precious keys that could point the way to a solution of the dome's mysteries.

". . . is Big Dark place . . . urr . . . to . . . world . . . thing . . . forever going . . . urr . . . we came here . . . our . . . kindred . . . urr . . . from other world thing came here . . . we were taken . . . urr . . . one, one, one, one . . . to the forever time room and . . . urr . . . urr . . . to the Big Dark . . . urr!"

Dan and Armilly looked up from their fluidics elements and remote scanners now and then, listening worriedly to the Vahnaj's droning recitation. The death of the N'lacs' civilization was reduced to a handful of phrases on a tunnel wall.

Did its account forecast the death of other humanoid cultures as well?

By late afternoon, exterior temperatures had moderated enough that the stream of visitors resumed, with reports on the tour.

"Should have heard the debate in the cook shack. Hope almost got a box of Chen's museum relics dumped on her head!"

"Feo made a crack about us wasting credits on costly vehicles, until Praedar set him straight. The Saunders didn't want to admit that our trucks and tools are wrecks, and that *you*'re the reason they run so well, Dan . . ."

". . . seeing the N'lac village really shook them. The Saunders dug in their heels, still trying to claim Chuss' people are subhumanoid, but it's getting tough for them to do that . . ."

Between those reports, Dan cleaned fluidics elements, studied Armilly's probes of what lay behind the door panels, and installed the elements. He noted each failure, recorded what had functioned, retested, checked probes, and tried again.

There was a disturbing aspect of his effort. At times, parts of the long-unused mechanism appeared to heal themselves, without any contact. Increasingly he had a feeling that he was an ignorant participant in a mutual repair line. What or who was his partner? Why were those elements—different from fluidics—suddenly coming back into the alien circuit? It certainly wasn't because of anything he'd done.

The Saunders arrived at the domes. The commotion in the mural room distracted Dan, though Armilly and Ruieb-An seemed to blot it out. Dan secured his gear temporarily and went back along the tunnel.

A confused scene awaited him. N'lacs were kneeling in fearful adoration before the painting. Sheila and some of Getz's students were describing the intricacies of the ancient glass oven to Kimball and some of Hope's aides. Rei Ito was recording, while Praedar, Kat, and Joe pointed out implications in the mural to Feo and his wife.

Chuss divided his focus between the painting and the offworlders' conversation. "Is old time. See? Here. Many-fathers-ago. Here come Evil Old Ones." Chuss sidled below the images, waving to particular sections of the pictorial history. "Bad time. They take us away through Big Dark to Old Ones' world. Change us. Make us into hands."

The Saunders listened courteously. Did Dan detect a crack in their facade? At least they weren't being rudely scornful, as they had often been at the Xenoarchaeological Assembly. Chuss' intelligence and fluency was kicking hard at their long-held prejudices, though Dan had little optimism that any breach there would be permanent.

The N'lacs' young leader patted his chest. "Many-fathers-ago escape. Look there. Much danger in the forever time. They come back through Big Dark." With a broad sweep of his arm, he traced that flight. "Many far aways. Many strangers. N'lacs not see. Not smell. Not feel. Is nowhere. Go there-here blink blink . . ."

The tale interlaced with the one Ruieb-An was compiling from ancient N'lac writings. There were connotations between Chuss' words and the lines of Ruieb-An's dictionary. A startling concept stirred in Dan's mind—an idea he'd toyed with for weeks, subconsciously, and refused to meet squarely.

Matter transmission!

No! It couldn't be! That theory had been tested again and again and again, by Terra, by the Whimeds, Vahnajes, Lannon, the Rigotians, and the Ulisorians. It simply did not work. Impossible!

How would Praedar counter that? "Impossible in humanoid technology. We do not deal with humanoids."

Voices droned on. Dan didn't hear them.

What if there was no spacecraft? What if there had never been a spacecraft? Praedar had pointed out that the expedition might have made incorrect guesses about the demons of N'lac legends and about this site's having been a capital city. They'd all made assumptions as well about the legends of the slaves' escape.

Dan had ignored logic—because the obvious conclusions ran counter to every technological law humanoids were taught and believed.

He envisioned a desperate handful of frightened N'lacs, plotting how they'd break free from their monstrous captors. For the first time, Dan saw all the objections to that theory.

They were not the objections the Saunders had thrown at Praedar.

This had nothing to do with claims and counterclaims of which dig world had been the colony and the N'lacs' planet of origin or with differing schools of xenoarchaeological evidence collection and interpretation.

The concept was so shocking, so radical, that it threatened to upend a lot more than the opposing ideas of the scientific teams.

And if Dan was right, considerably more was at stake here than the survival or failure of his expedition.

Voices were arguing about trivial details. "You've observed the N'lacs in their home habitat. You must admit they're humanoids . . ."

"Possibly a backward remnant of the former ruling species on T-W 593. Rather like a pocket of Neanderthalers, on Earth . . ."

"How can you . . .?"

"This mythos won't do, my dear Kat. You're a trained socio. You know how isolated primitives—and even civilized peoples under stress—sometimes adopt and pervert facts and artifacts. The South Pacific cargo cults of the twentieth century, those metal-poisoned Mars Colony miners and their tales of canyon critters existing along the Valles Marineris . . ."

"You can't argue away an entire social legend by . . ."

"Oh, there are potentials here, Juxury. Perhaps we could work out a cooperative arrangement to assist you. A small grant from our Foundation? I'm sure Anelen is giving you trouble. He's notorious for credit-pinching Whimed scientists who work with nonfelinoids. But we suffer from no such chauvinism. And Eckard will be no problem. He's fawned at the Saunder-McKelveys' heels for years . . ."

"Don't listen to them, Praedar. They're trying to muscle in, take over our dig, make us their flunkeys . . ."

"You would alter? Select to accommodate your own theories? Is the price of truth so small, Feo?" Praedar demanded.

"Of course not. We suggest a pooling of resources . . ."

Sheila cut in with withering scorn. "And who will get the final credit? You and Hope! Surprise, surprise. T-W 593 and T-S 311 become a joint project—under the magnanimous control of the oh-so-benign Saunders. No, thanks!"

"That accusation is completely unjustified . . ."

Rei Ito approached Dan. "While they're debating these fine points, could you fill me in on the N'lac slaves' technology? This fluidics stuff? In pop science layman's terms, naturally . . ."

When he didn't respond, other conversations faltered, then began to die. He didn't rouse himself from his trance, though, until Praedar gripped his shoulder. "The door? You have its secrets?"

"Huh? Oh. Maybe. Or it has mine. It's repairing itself, in a way." The xenomech frowned and shook his head. "I don't like it. But I'm even more worried about what Ruieb-An's translations and Armilly's probes are turning up. Something's going on in the dome's interior. I think it involves the N'lacs' forever time. It's machinery, gradually coming back on line after centuries."

"What function does this machinery serve?" Praedar asked.

"Transportation."

"The pieces of the spacecraft the slaves used . . ."

"No."

Praedar's crest rose. The alien plainly was startled and intrigued. He gestured for Dan to continue.

"Everything we've found confirms the N'lac tales that the Old Ones are nonanthropomorphic, exoskeletoned, totally nonhumanoid. We humanoids have been thinking down similar vectors— because our technologies are basically very similar. Our inventors all followed remarkably parallel routes to high civilizations and the stars. The Old Ones may have taken some of the identical paths—discovering fluidics, for example. But nothing says they had to match us, step for step. In fact, it's damned sure they didn't. They could have found things we missed—or gave up on because we thought they were impossible.

"Kat says the majority of folktales are based on reality. Forget cargo cults and canyon critters. Look at the mural. What do we see?"

"The history of the N'lacs," Praedar said. "Development, stellar expansion, conquest, enslavement, escape . . ."

Dan pounced. "Escape. How? In a spaceship? Piloting such a craft is complicated. Where did slaves acquire the knowledge? Where did they get the freedom and the open hours to launch and plot a course for a world none of them had seen? They lacked all the skills. And in a spaceship technology, it would have been easy to capture them and cut them off cold. Forget that FTL ship we postulated. You're not going to find it."

Aggrieved, Rosie said, "I can reconstruct from even the tiniest . . ."

Dan shook his head. "It never existed. Trust me. This is my field of expertise. I blinded myself to the truth. Chuss' ancestors escaped via the same route the Old Ones used to take them into slavery . . ."

Feo frowned impatiently. "Which is? Quit spouting tech-mech

mumbo jumbo. If you have a hypothesis, let's hear it."

"How about it, McKelvey?" Kimball, Ito's assistant, said with a smirk. "I can see where you're headed. And you're crazy."

"Quick judgment, for someone who just landed here and knows nothing about the N'lac culture and their history," Dan retorted.

"Never mind," Hope said. "Feo's right. What are you hinting at?"

"Matter transmission. That's what that gigantic shape inside the main dome is—a transmitting chamber. The N'lacs' door into the forever time," Dan replied.

He got no further. The Saunders were snickering at him. Kimball was laughing out loud. Most of Dan's teammates, however, weren't. They mulled over this new, shocking theory.

"That is the most absurd . . ." Feo broke off, scratching frantically.

So was everyone else. The torment had hit them hard and so suddenly that the N'lacs hadn't given the scientists and news hounds any warning. Just as suddenly as the itching had started, it stopped.

Simultaneously, the ground shook. Somewhere outside the domes there was a muffled "whump!"

Baines loped for the door. "*That* wasn't a quake. I'm going to get my seismo gear . . ."

Offworlders and N'lacs left the domes, the complex, the village. Puzzled and uneasy, they stood in the warm, late-afternoon sunlight, gazing about. "There!" Dan yelled, pointing east.

On the mesa, a fireball and smoke column spiraled upward. Indistinct, misshapen, and blasted objects tumbled in the seething cloud, arcing and falling.

Dan felt sick.

Baines emerged from the cook shack. He said, "Not a fault acting up, but one hell of a surface shaker . . ." He froze, gawking at the hideous smear in the sky.

"Get rovers," Praedar ordered. "We will see . . ."

"No," Dan warned. "There'll be lingering radiation for a while. Besides, we can't help them. The yacht crew's dead." He was the focus of attention as he said, "That sort of fireball is unique. It's the result of a deliberate power feed overload in a starhopper's propulsion system. The same thing killed Geoff

Saunder and the other passengers in the '47 *Ad Astra* disaster. I saw a similar blowup on Morgan Settlement a few years ago, when the rebels committed suicide, rather than surrender. Tie down a ship's main circuit, boost her oscillator to the top, and she'll take out everything within at least a kilometer's radius— including whoever pushed her trigger."

CHAPTER NINETEEN

∞∞∞∞∞∞∞

Death Song

Joe, Sheila, and the Saunder team's biologists insisted on riding up to the plateau in hopes of finding survivors. Baines, toting radiation detectors, accompanied them.

Silence blanketed those awaiting their return. By now the valley was preternaturally quiet. The only obvious sound was the faint hum of the reporters' vid lenses. Dan glared at them. He didn't get a chance to tell them what to do with their recording gear. The samaritans were coming back.

It was much too soon for them to have gone very far. As they climbed down from the rover, their faces told the grim story. Dan's expert guess as to what had happened was right on target.

Joe's sorrowful confirmation sent the Saunders and their aides into grief-stricken moans. Hope, sobbing, leaned on Feo. "Not Topwe! No! They couldn't be . . . no, *no!*"

"Hush, love," Feo soothed, his own eyes full. He looked pleadingly at his cousin. "I-I'm sure they didn't suffer."

Dan put rivalries aside. His voice husky, he said, "No, it was quick. Nanoseconds. They never knew what hit them."

He hoped it was true. There *was* a doubt, a horrible vision. The crew, dimly aware of their fatal actions, yet helpless to halt their trip to death.

Rei Ito was trying to maintain a detached, professional attitude. She didn't succeed. Kimball was more cold-blooded. He zoomed his lenses at the mourners. Everything was grist for him, including tragedy.

Dan grabbed the man's jumper, pulling him off balance. The news hound shouted angrily. Dan tightened his grip, choking the protest. "Shut that thing off, or I'll make you eat Cam Saunder's expensive vidder gear."

"This . . . this is news," Kimball squeaked. "You can't . . ."

Ito stopped the fight before it got any worse. "McKelvey's right. Shut it off. At least for now."

Dan was saluting her sardonically when Praedar bored in on him. "You have said the crew did not know what hit them. Chen made me acquainted with that Terran colloquial phrase. I wish elaboration. What *did* hit them?"

Feo and Hope chimed in. "Yes! Tell us! Are you insinuating that Topwe and his people are . . . were . . . suicidal maniacs, like those Morgan Settlement rebels? Then why? How?" Hope channeled her emotions into gestures. She wiped fiercely at her tear-stained cheeks with the backs of her hands.

This pair had made Tavares their scapegoat without hesitation. A typical, head-over-heart Saunder-McKelvey power move. However, Tavares was still alive, and his career was only temporarily on hold. The yacht crew was dead. The Saunders wanted answers—and revenge. Dan appreciated that. Topwe and his people had deserved better.

"No, it wasn't suicide. Not in the normal sense. They were *made* to trigger that overload," Dan said. The Saunders were at a loss, but Praedar's team picked up on the implication immediately. They nodded as he went on. "The scratching was a tipoff. That's what the robot does when it goes into gear. I don't know how . . ."

"Stimulation of nerve endings," Joe supplied. Sheila agreed.

"Okay. That's one of its tricks, along with quakes and who knows what else. I told you it would try to repair itself. This is proof that it has done so, at least in part. It's graduated from party crashing to murder. The *Astra* was destroyed by human saboteurs. The yacht was blown up by an alien machine. It obviously controlled the crew's minds, using them as its slaves."

Kat gasped. "The N'lacs were forced to blow up their space ships, too!"

"Exactly."

"The Old Ones—" Praedar's bass rumble sent chills down Dan's spine. "—most probably employ extrasensory powers. Their robot is so equipped, as well."

Dan looked toward the dissipating smoke that marked the yacht crew's pyre. "It's starting all over again, after two thousand years. A robot scout, setting up humanoid slaves for its masters."

"That's . . . that's ridiculous," Feo said.

"You saw our injured and the castings of the robot's prints," Sheila retorted. "You laughed and said we were faking the whole thing. Who's laughing now? How did you think our people got hurt?"

Baines added, "And what made Hanging Rock fall and kill Chen? A random quake, generated by the same robot. It's resorting to nastier terror tactics . . ."

"Taking out the spacecraft is brilliant," Dan said. "My brother would approve completely, from a military standpoint. Our escape route is cut off. In case nobody's noticed, we're stranded. The yacht was parked next to *Praedar's Project*. It's gone, too."

"Oh, Dan, your ship . . ." Rosie cried.

Hope stammered, "This—this fantasy about an alien robot . . . you can't expect us to . . . to swallow . . ."

"It is the truth." Praedar was at his spellbinding best. He nodded to the distant smoke. "*That* is the truth. What we explained to you about the N'lacs' history is truth. What reason have we to lie?"

"Your reputation in xenoarchaeology," Feo shot back. "Eleven years of work on this planet wiped out, if you're proved wrong . . ."

Dan wanted to shake his cousin until Feo's teeth rattled. "Listen! I'll give you the benefit of the doubt because we're all reeling. But, dammit, get this through your head! We are not on stage at your Assembly. This is no interview for your PR staff or Ito's Pan Terran Network. Topwe and his crew are dead. Chen is dead. That robot's responsible for their murders. And we're trapped here. Is that soaking in?"

The Saunders paled and Feo stammered, "We—we can summon help, alternate transport. Our crews on Wolf or Arden . . ."

"What makes you think our mechanical enemy—or the Old Ones—are going to wait until they arrive?" Dan demanded. "And if any more ships land before we've solved this, their crews will die, just as Topwe's did."

"There has to be a way out," Rei Ito exclaimed, a bit shrilly. Her pose as a cool, detached reporter had developed enormous cracks. Kimball was no longer so cocky. Apparently he wasn't so callous about his own imminent demise as he was about the fates of others in this war zone.

"No way out—for us," Dan said. "However, you'd better pray that self-repairing machinery in the dome does its job slowly—or the Old Ones may have a way in. And then we're done for."

"You . . . you weren't kidding," Kimball said, flabbergasted.

"Welcome to the real universe. No, I wasn't kidding. And I wasn't pulling my theory about a matter transmitter out of thin air. It answers all the transportation questions. All of them and a hell of a lot more."

"If we are destroyed," Praedar noted, "we will not be the first humanoid species to become extinct. That is the ultimate end of every species."

"But not ours," Dan said. "Not this time. This time, we have to win."

Feral hunger gleamed in Praedar's starry eyes. "Indeed! I do not intend to yield easily. There is too much to be learned."

Hope murmured, "But . . . but there's only one robot . . ."

Dan rounded on her. "An alien robot with capabilities we can barely guess at. We're in trouble. Big trouble."

"The Fleet!" Feo oozed warmth and persuasion at his kinsman. "Your brother Adam. Call him. Hope and I will back you, of course. You and Juxury can count on our complete cooperation . . ."

Under other circumstances, Dan would have guffawed. "Kind of late, cousin. I'd love to hold you up for ransom—bottomless funding for the expedition, a new starhopper, and your full endorsement and admission our interpretations are right and yours wrong. But none of us has the time for any of that." He punched the air, burning off accumulating tension. "What we need is time, Feo. That's one thing you can't buy."

"Surely a call to the Fleet, assistance from Adam's armed cruisers . . ."

"That's a big universe out there." Dan jabbed a thumb skyward. "Thanks to your dirty tricks, this dig is poor. No fancy com equipment, such as you're used to. The one decent subspace rig on this planet just went up in flames. If we send an S.O.S. to Adam right now, it would take hours to reach him and hours more in time lag exchanges for you and me to convince him to come here—if we could convince him. A local day and three-quarters for his fastest ships to get here. Plus, there's no assurance that damned robot can't reach into orbit and knock a warship out, as it did the yacht."

"We do not know when the machine will strike again," Praedar said.

Galvanized, the scientists tossed ideas around, thinking fast.

Dan wanted to push and prod. Time . . . *time* . . . *TIME!* Ticking away.

The discussion had barely begun when another crisis hit.

The Whimeds were the first to sense it. Praedar snarled, "What occurs?" and Drastil, Yvica, and the other felinoids peered around anxiously.

Offworlders gawked as a living river flowed past them, moving westward.

N'lacs were on the march—hunters, diggers, gardeners, mothers with infants at the breast, and children. Chuss was in the forefront, with Sleeg hobbling in the rear. Like puppets, the N'lacs stumbled forward, obviously being drawn against their will. Sleeg's quavering voice rose, keening.

"That's a death song!" Kat said, gasping.

The e.t.s fought whatever was manipulating them. Occasionally one would break free for a moment and grab a stone or a brushwood club, as if he hoped to attack their unseen foe.

Like a massive blow, the same force driving the N'lacs smashed into the scientists. It was an agonizing pressure in the skull, a fear that sapped the will, and a violent urge to scratch until one bled.

The Saunders, their aides, and the reporters were hit hardest. Praedar's expedition, more familiar with the sensation, resisted it. But that invisible puppet master was tugging them in the

N'lacs' wake, making them all follow the e.t.s' entranced exodus.

"Loor! No!" Joe Hughes' medical training overcame the manipulator. He tore free, pushing through the mass of N'lacs, shouting "Sheil! Help me! We have to get her back to the hyper chamber! She's in labor!"

The same humanitarian impulse goading Hughes helped the other parameds. One by one they pulled away from the throng and managed to separate Chuss' mother from her people. The parameds bore her toward the village, while Loor continued to paddle reflexively with her feet, still obeying her orders.

The rest of the scientists, inspired by the medics' example, braced against the pain. They grabbed at N'lacs, trying to halt them.

"Wait!"

"Stop!"

"Where are you going?"

"There's nothing over there!"

Doggedly N'lacs plodded on, descending the banks of the ancient, dry riverbed and crossing the rough terrain. Sometimes offworlders succeeded in wrestling a couple of villagers to the ground and pinning them there. The flood simply parted and moved on past them as if the obstacle weren't there.

Chuss was far ahead of his tribe by now. Dan abandoned his attempt to corral minor members of the N'lacs and made an end run, hoping to head Chuss off. Praedar did the same thing. They lunged down the dusty slope, dodging jumbles of boulders deposited there eons ago. Losing his footing, Dan slammed into a small island of packed soil and jagged pebbles. Stunned, he shook his head, then renewed his pursuit.

A dozen young N'lacs were scaling the far bank. Their small feet and hands didn't disturb the loose earth much. They had no trouble making the ascent. Dan, though, scrambled for purchase, impeded by the crumbling slope. He yearned for an Ulisorian's platform or antigravs. Finally he reached more or less level ground—the valley plain.

Chuss' gang loped onward, shrieking insanely: "Demon! Kill!"

Behind them, near the complex, along the riverbed, the offworlders fought maddening itches, pain, and the mesmerized N'lacs.

Praedar and Dan raced to block Chuss and his adolescent cronies from further flight.

"Oh, my God," Dan panted.

The robot was parked out there in the open, less than seventy meters ahead!

The xenomech's curiosity glands were salivating. How much they could learn from that machine! A whole new technology!

Just a bit farther!

N'lacs closed in on their tormentor, throwing rocks, bashing the robot with clubs. The villagers would have to be kept at bay, of course, while offworlders dismantled the thing . . .

A terrible new wave of pain hit Dan hard. He fell flat on his face. Half senseless with shock, his vision dancing with lights, he lifted his head. Praedar lay a few meters from him. The Whimed thrashed wildly, like a hog-tied big cat.

Red-faced mites, the N'lacs, swarmed over their metal foe. It flailed with its tentacles, knocking them aside. Its motions were clumsy and uncoordinated, as if certain circuits weren't working right. Had it burned out vital components when it killed Topwe's crew? There might be hope yet.

Why was it here, west of camp? Could it transport itself? Was that why none of the searches had located it?

Pain pounded at Dan, pinning him. Through a blur of tears, he gazed at the unreachable target. It was daylight now, and he wasn't drunk. He tried to absorb details, even though the setting sun partially silhouetted the object, obscuring some features.

A power pack, there? Eight, nine, ten limbs. The xenoarchs specializing in Procyon Five's octopoid culture would love that fact. There were dents and numerous signs of bad landings and micrometeroid strikes. And . . . were those glittering facets at the narrow part of its upper torso optical receptors?

The N'lacs thought so. They tried to cover those insectoid apertures with their paws, believing if it couldn't see them, it couldn't hurt them.

Another wave of agony smashed into N'lacs and offworlders alike. Those who were still upright fell, whimpering.

Chuss, however, was held erect, a red-skinned doll, turning at the machine's whim. It made him raise and lower his arms and cock his head as it probed its specimen. *Was this the species the masters hunted? A final test must be made*. Chuss was clutching a sharp stone he'd used as a weapon. Now he was forced to turn the lithic blade inward, slashing bloodily.

Dan, bound by a mind-grip, watched impotently as Chuss flayed himself.

CHAPTER TWENTY

∞∞∞∞∞∞∞

The Door into Forever

It was nightmare incarnate. Chuss' death was Dan's—was *every* humanoid's.

Fiery tendrils in the brain relaxed, their hold becoming weaker.
He could move!

Killing Chuss had demanded too much from the automaton's crippled systems. It couldn't maintain its control over so many beings.

What remained of Chuss was on the ground, life ebbing fast. The lethal stone tool fell from limp fingers.

And at that moment, Dan and Praedar leaped to their feet. The rocky plain gave them plenty of ammunition. Dan threw a skull-size rock as hard as he could. The machine lurched, ropy tentacles swaying. An even larger stone, hurled by Praedar, crashed into its other side, skewing the killer on its axis.

Two more hits ripped the robot over—and short-circuited its remaining hold on its victims. Released, the N'lacs attacked their ancient enemy in full force. Dan and Praedar had to cease fire for fear of hitting the e.t.s. Chuss' people wrenched tentacles out of moorings, battered the insectoid eyes, and crushed panels and metal feet, wreaking havoc with stones, clubs, and bare hands. If only the machine could suffer, as their young leader had suffered!

Praedar moved among them, begging "No, please, stop. It is disabled. It is information we must have . . ." But he couldn't put much power into his orders. Like the N'lacs, his shock was linked with rage.

Finally the N'lacs turned away from the demolished invader and gathered around Chuss' corpse. Sleeg had made his way painfully across the river. Now he hunkered beside his murdered apprentice and chanted sorrowfully. The sound echoed countless laments down the long ages of humanoid civilizations. A life had been snuffed out. Survivors mourned their loss.

Dan still held a rock he'd had no chance to throw at the hated robot. He slammed it into the ground so hard it bounced; he roared, "Dammit, dammit, dammit!" Physically and emotionally drained, he dropped to one knee, choking on tears and grieving for a dead friend.

Offworlders and N'lacs were one, stricken. Somebody offered to summon the parameds, then abandoned the thought. There was no point. Joe and Sheila could do nothing for Chuss, but they might be able to help Chuss' mother.

The news hounds were recording. Dan didn't object, this time. Their tri-dis were proof this had actually happened. Eventually the expedition might need that evidence, to convince a Space Fleet Board of Inquiry or C.S.P. Council that this whole tragedy wasn't a mass hallucination.

Feo was murmuring "Terrible, terrible . . ."

Hope, sharing her rivals' pain, was weeping. Death upon death had affected her deeply. "It . . . it has to end. It has to. So . . . so unbelievable."

Dan rose and nudged the robot's wreckage with his boot. A tentacle toppled against the bashed, bulbous torso with a tinny clink. "Unbelievable? What? Admitting you were wrong?"

"Don't." Feo groaned. "Not at a time like this, Dan. Don't be unfair. We . . . we concede we may have made errors . . . But now we have to . . . to pull together . . ."

"I agree," Dan said. "But I don't think you grasp, even yet, exactly what we're up against. This isn't over. It's just beginning."

Meej's voice hung in the twilight breeze. Sleeg's lament was a drone beneath the boy's pidgin Terran. "Forever time! We all go back to forever time! Evil Old Ones come again. They take us to temple, to the place to be gone. We fellow, them fellow friends —all gone to forever time . . ."

"The scout. The forerunner," Praedar said. "The invasion will arrive from the temple."

Dan nodded. "The dome."

Praedar's expression was a taut mask of agony. He looked much as he had when he was picking himself up after Chen's death. The Whimed pointed to the pile of junk and asked Rosie, "Can you re-create? It may tell us how to defeat the Old Ones."

"I-I'll need help," Rosie said. Her face was dust-stained and streaked with tears. "This technology . . . Dan will have to advise me. We've got ten years' worth of reconstructed model demons, but *this* . . . It will mean re-creating a tech manual as well as the object."

"I'll assist you when I can," Dan said. "I think I'd better tackle that door into the main dome now, though. It's our first priority. I just hope to hell we've got enough time . . ."

Feo was shivering. "You . . . you can't mean that these Old Ones, these legends, might possibly still exist?"

Kat snapped at him and Hope. "Can you assure us they don't? If you're wrong, it won't mean a tarnished professional reputation; it'll mean the enslavement of six humanoid sectors."

Very solemnly Praedar said, "Speculate on today's incident magnified. Not the much damaged and impaired mechanism the N'lacs disabled—after grievous loss—but the beings that designed this robot, and perhaps other robots far more deadly."

"That chamber that shows up on Armilly's scans," Dan added. "The anomalies in the readings. I told you something's waking up in there. We'd better pray it's not too late to head off whatever's coming—as we were too late to save Chuss." He broke off, his throat thick with anguish.

"It's a death race," Baines said. "Not just our lives are at stake, but every Terran's, every Whimed's, every Vahnaj's, the Lannons, the Rigotians, and even the Ulisorians . . ."

Praedar was looking at the N'lac funeral. "The manner in which the robot dissected Chuss! As we would dissect a plant specimen or an insect . . ."

"Why?" Hope exclaimed, aghast. "Why would they do that? And why would they come here themselves . . . if . . . if they exist? Why not send more . . . more . . . Spirit of Humanity help us! More robots?"

"You ask the motives of beings alien beyond our present knowledge to understand," Praedar replied. "I cannot tell you. I can only repeat Kat's warning—we must not assume that the Old Ones will *not* choose to come here. There are too many undiscovered data."

The Saunders struggled to cope. As ranking members of Earth's First Family, they could have squandered their lives in hedonism. But they'd chosen to devote their vast fortune to science—and not all their acclaim in that career had been purchased. They had been contributors. Now they used that intelligence to adjust, trying to keep up with Praedar's leaps of reason and with their kinsman's view of what might confront them.

"You . . . you actually think matter transmission . . ." Feo gulped.

"We've run out of alternate explanations," Dan said.

"We felt it." Hope's words were almost inaudible. "We saw it. Topwe's crew, that poor N'lac . . . they're really dead."

Resisting, Feo was arriving at a terrifying conclusion. "If . . . if Dan's right . . . my God! *Living* abominations, controlling the powers that murdering machine wielded!"

"The robot was crippled," Dan reminded his cousin. "We can expect its masters to be in full command of their faculties and even more ruthless."

"They . . . they must be stopped!" Feo cried. "Even if we must destroy them. They can't be allowed to invade Terra, the sectors . . ."

Dan eyed Saunder with grudging admiration. He wasn't sure he could have made such a complete shift in stubbornly held convictions as Feo was doing. "You learn, cousin," Dan said. "You really do learn."

"Let . . . let me help you with the reconstruction, Rosie," Hope volunteered. "I have some experience in that discipline." The older woman was being modest. Hope Belvedere Saunder was the dean of xenoarchaeological re-creations.

"How can I assist?" Feo offered, surprisingly humble.

A lingering suspicion nagged Dan. Was the Saunders' new attitude genuine or a temporary necessity forced upon them by crisis? Would they revert to their former ways when—and if—they got out of this mess?

Praedar took Feo's offer at face value. "Your organizational skills will be most useful. We have much to do. Your work in such matters on the Eridani asteroid dig was superb."

"I . . . thank you. That's very generous, considering . . ."

The Whimed shrugged off his rival's gratitude. "If we survive, no doubt we will have future disagreements. At present, we must deal with our problem as a unit."

Problem! Praedar had a talent for understatement!

As the N'lacs carried Chuss home for the last time, Rosie and Hope began collecting the robot's components. Dan headed for the domes.

The reporters tried to be everywhere at once. Ito ran alongside Dan, asking nervously, "What can we do?"

"You mean you aren't going to stand on the sidelines and collect vids until the universe collapses around our ears?"

"If the Saunders are convinced, so am I," the news hound retorted irritably. "That . . . the ship blowing up, that native's death . . . dammit! Tell us what to do!"

Dan stopped and spat orders. "Get Kimball busy on the expedition's com. You two are the only ones here besides me with some background in that technology. Soup it all you can. Borrow from your equipment. Feo will pay you back, and you know it. When you've got as much power into it as you can, get a message out. Work with my cousin. Notify anybody and everybody. Warn them."

"The Fleet?"

Praedar was waiting nearby, listening. He frowned at Ito's question. But he didn't turn the notion down flat.

"I think you'd better get word to my brother, yes. If what I have in mind fails, Fleet's going to have to come up with an alternative—maybe wiping this planet out of the sector." Ito's ashy color revealed her panic. Dan touched the reporter's arm gently. "It's a once-in-a-lifetime chance, Rei. Your sister's never going to cover a story like this one. You can do it."

She steeled herself and nodded. Then she and her aide hurried toward the complex.

Dan glanced at Praedar. "I know. I don't want the Fleet here, either. I've seen what can happen to primitive peoples on worlds administered by the planet developers and their military adjuncts. But . . ."

Feo was tagging along with his rival, asking Praedar for guidance in their organizational efforts and taking notes on his wrist vid. Now he said, "That sort of thing won't be allowed here, Dan. I do have some influence with both the C.S.P. and the Fleet's civilian administrators. There will be no exploitation of these little humanoids. They have suffered enough . . ."

"If you mean that, thanks," Dan muttered. "I'll hold you to your word—assuming we get out of this with our lives and our freedom."

The next two hours were an ordeal for Dan, working with the alien lock mechanism barring the way into the main dome. Ruieb-An was close by, offering a stammering, running commentary, translating nonstop, correcting his earlier decryptions, refining and giving the new data to Dan as well as Praedar, who was in and out of the tunnel constantly. Dan tried to ignore the distractions, and he willingly put up with Armilly's bulky monitoring gear and the Lannon's huge, hairy, strong-scented presence in these close quarters. The procyonid's advance glimpses were invaluable.

Outside, things were happening fast. Injured and family groups being transported onto the mesa—avoiding the still "hot" yacht wreckage—to the Vahnajes' sulking camp. Everyone knew that if the Old Ones won this battle, there would be no safe spot anywhere in the galactic quadrant for humanoid life. But moving the weak and vulnerable members of the Settlement to a distant shelter was an action both teams felt they had to take.

The N'lacs refused to leave. In fact, they seemed almost fatalistically resigned. Sleeg's doom-sayings had come true. Chuss was dead. The robot was "dead," too, but the N'lacs' legends warned them the demon was only a prelude to the full invasion— an invasion those same legends told them they couldn't stop.

Only Meej exhibited defiance. He crept into the mural room and then into the tunnel. Eyes wide, a brushwood club gripped in his small hand, he squatted, waiting in the shadows a few meters behind Dan, Armilly, and Ruieb-An, for a chance at revenge. He would strike at the masters who had killed his brother—or die in the attempt. Nothing Praedar, Kat, nor any other offworlders said moved him.

Kimball, a convert personality now, was laboring his ass off and pushing his training to its edges. Like the scientists, he was constantly in and out of the tunnel, setting up vids and relay monitors and interconnecting the complex with what was going on at the door to the temple. Whatever happened, the news hounds were going to capture it all on holos and chips. More, they were enabling every team member to witness the discoveries while they were taking place.

Feo reported that an initial message had been sent to Adam—or rather to the nearest Fleet base, for instant relay onward with better, faster subspace equipment. There was no answer as yet, naturally. There wouldn't be one for some time. By then, help from Space Fleet—from *anybody*—might well be academic.

Again and again Dan was forced to lean back and take a breather. His eyes burned from unshed tears and memories of Chuss' death. His hands shook. Tension ate at him. He couldn't afford to make any mistakes now—better to pause and regroup than do that.

He had Kimball set up a min-vid scanner on the wall nearby and zoom it in on the lock mechanism. Dan wanted everything he did recorded. He especially wanted tri-di samples of that odd, glistening material that was linking up with the fluidics elements. When he was able, he extracted minute specimens. Teammates took them to the labs for analysis.

Test! Recheck! Install a fluidic element! And look at Armilly's monitors. How were the mysterious self-repairing gadgets beyond the door doing? Far too well, it seemed—better, Dan feared, than he was.

Test . . . check . . . recheck . . . install . . . and watch the glistening organic repair substance grow, crawling and making connections Dan had only speculated about.

As often as not, his speculations were right. And the shiny stuff saved him the trouble of repairing that particular damaged part of the smashed lock.

But he wasn't sure he wanted to have his tech-mech skills confirmed by a slimy, alien . . . thing.

The more it repaired out here, the more it might be fixing in there. The door into the forever time could be back in full operation and shipping through slave masters before Dan could get them inside where they might have a fighting chance to defend themselves.

His mind was hurtling down several tracks and options—plan B, in case plan A hit the wall. He seemed to hear Adam reciting from Fleet manuals, years ago: "Never lock yourself in a corner. Always have an alternate angle of attack."

Then, Adam's serious sermonizing on military tactics had struck Dan as silly. War plans! Not out here in space, though maybe back on the stagnating Mother World, with all its woes. For spacers, wars were obsolete. Nothing but small-scale skirmishing had taken place in the open sectors for centuries. Distances were too great. The risks of interstellar conflict and mass annihilation too real.

Those rules didn't apply to nonanthropomorphic enemies. Who knew how they thought? Would they abide by the sanity that had kept the humanoids coexisting with each other for these past centuries?

Doubtful! They were alien, totally alien, a species which built scout robots that caused pain, blew up escape ships—and their crews—and made a helpless humanoid captive dissect himself for their uncaring examination.

The odds weren't favorable, not favorable at all.

And time was ticking on relentlessly.

A light! Another faceted, inanimate insectoid eye glowed in the recesses of the ancient mechanism.

None of the people watching—Praedar, Meej, Ito, Feo, Kat— had seen that telltale gleam. But Praedar heard something. And Armilly detected the change on his monitors. Both of them edged forward. Praedar asked Dan, "It functions?"

For a moment the xenomech leaned his forehead against the door. He boosted his stim patch, shoving dosages into danger zones. He was so damned tired! But there could be no rest, maybe not ever again.

"Yeah," Dan said wearily. "It functions. We can open it, and take a look at the past—or our future."

CHAPTER TWENTY-ONE

∞∞∞∞∞∞∞∞

The Temple

The door's operation was whisper-smooth. That was ominous. This was working entirely too perfectly. That organic material repaired things—with Dan's help—with terrifying speed. He hoped a matter transmitter, being a far more complicated project, would take it considerably longer. If it didn't . . .

The escaped N'lac slaves had done their part, five centuries ago, by smashing everything in sight. Within the airlock, light panels and cycling mechanisms had been shattered. Like the lock mechanism, they were healing. Not quite up to peak efficiency, but close. The systems woke as humanoids poked their heads into the tight little passageway, then began altering pressure. It shuttled the offworlders and Meej through into the dome, two at a time.

A bad omen. Was the MT repair equally advanced?

Inside the main structure, other light panels, facing the upper, inward-curving walls, hung in broken sections. Dan saw more of the glistening stuff "growing," gluing shattered pieces back together. The same thing was happening in the lower wall sections.

Cowling, shielding alien circuitry and relays—was growing, healing itself.

Praedar sniffed. "Air is heavy. Analysis."

Dan nodded, shifting some of Kimball's vidders inside the dome, cueing them. "You get that?" he asked the scientists watching from the complex. "Tie together with the data Armilly's assembling."

"More equipment," Praedar ordered. "Everything must be studied."

"We don't have time . . ." The Whimed's burning glare made Dan sigh. The boss was going to get them killed with his felinoid passion for gathering every scrap of the truth! "Okay, okay! Baines," he said, addressing the vidder's all-seeing lenses. "Ask for volunteers for a brief tour. Set up the surveyors in here. Move it fast. We might have to get out in a hurry."

"Will do."

The atmospheric heaviness Praedar had mentioned was more obvious now. "It's building up," Dan muttered, "making things cozy for the Old Ones."

Kat glanced at him. "They'll come through themselves, instead of sending robots?"

"It is a door they have used in the past," Praedar said absently. He was wandering slowly in a circuit of the dome, trying to see everything.

He probably could do that easier than the humans. The lighting was too dim for them—dim and hurtful. Ito adjusted her lens pendant, as Dan was doing with the remote vidder, trying to filter out the painful spectra. Praedar's umbralaca pupils contracted to pinpricks. The humans squinted, unable to screen out all of the alien glare. "How interesting," Feo murmured. "Fascinating!" Praedar nodded, agreeing completely.

The offworlders circumnavigated the dome's single, central object—an enormous octagonal box. On Armilly's monitors, the thing had been a ghostly form, its dimensions and details mapped by probes, but lacking the impact of this direct contact.

The chamber was remarkably insubstantial-looking to be capable of doing what Dan was sure it could.

The central object was freestanding, its top a scant two meters below the dome's highest point. A noticeable bulge was near the center of seven of the object's lattice-patterned exterior panels. The eighth side was open. Through that, the humanoids saw tiny, sparkling solar systems, wheeling and orbiting in midair, forming rainbow comets' tails. Again, the light from those dancing miniature suns and planets hurt the eyes.

"They are large," Praedar said. "Consider the capacity of the chamber."

"*Very* large," Dan amended. "Godawful, in fact."

In a faint voice, Kat reminded them, "Sleeg said they were big."

The tale-teller's words rang in Dan's memory. *"Evil Old Ones. No bones. Bones outside. Round. Tall. Tall tall!"*

Meej had hunkered in front of the open-sided section of the box. "Many-fathers-ago tell us. They like there." He jabbed a webbed finger at the adjacent panels.

Kat stepped back, trying to get an overall view of the thing. "It's . . . they're abstract depictions of the Old Ones. Look! The lattices form two-dimensional exoskeletons. You can see the tentacles, suggestions of thrombosed veins in the soft body parts, and . . . are those eyes?" she wondered, staring at a spot high up on the nearest lacy panel.

There were more sparkling, hurtful movements and hovering illusions of insectoid optical receptors.

Dan shuddered. He wasn't the only one in the dome doing that.

"Are you recording this, Rosie?" Kat asked the remote vids. Her friend's affirmative reply sounded unusually soft, as if something within the temple were smothering voices. "What a wonderful find! Now we know the N'lacs' tales were right! Vivid representations of the Old Ones, apparently in one of their own alien art forms," the xenosocio crowed.

"*Evil* Old Ones," Dan corrected her. "I don't care if we're supposed to be scientific and not make judgments about them. After what they did to Chuss . . ."

"Were desert lizards intelligent, they might feel we are evil," Praedar said. "We kill and eat them."

"That's different."

"Do the Old Ones consider it so?" Praedar wondered. "This is knowledge, to be preserved and studied."

Grimacing in exasperation, Dan said, "The knowledge will be lost, if those studying and collecting it—and the civilizations that produced them—are enslaved."

For a long moment Praedar considered that, then, with obvious reluctance, he nodded. "Balance. The longer view. Humanoid history and survival must be weighed against the acquisition of new and invaluable data."

"Invaluable in more ways than one," Dan said. "Even if we manage to come through this intact, that's no guarantee there aren't other temples or matter transmitters elsewhere in the star regions beyond the known sectors and other ways the Evil Old Ones could emerge from them. Everything we find out might be a crucial defense weapon in the future. As Sheila said, we're on the front line."

"Glad you've come around to my side, handsome," Sheila said, speaking from a monitor. Like Rosie's voice, the blonde's was oddly muffled.

"How's Loor?" Kat asked.

"Still in labor, but making progress," Sheila's tiny image replied. "The reporters set up a relay link for us here in the hyperbarics chamber, so we'd know what was going on out there." She hesitated, then added soberly, "We . . . we didn't tell her about Chuss yet. I don't know how we will tell her, when we have to. I don't . . . I can't deal with it myself . . ."

Dan and the others understood fully. However, they had little time for grieving. They were circumnavigating the alien chamber, visually exploring, thinking. Those lattice-shaped representations of the enemy kept calling to mind Sleeg's descriptions of the Evil Old Ones: no bones; tall; round. They were huge, living versions of the robot, enormous exoskeletoned insects—no, probably not true insects. The square-cube law prevented their evolution to such a size, surely.

At least . . . such creatures couldn't have evolved in a terrene environment. Those genetic alterations the captors had made on the N'lacs showed that the Evil Old Ones didn't inhabit a strictly terrene environment. Yet with appropriate medical manipulation, it apparently was one in which humanoids could live.

If Dan needed any further proof of the Evil Old Ones' world, the dome's self-repairing mechanisms supplied it; they were fast converting the interior into a stone-metalline tank filled with muggy air.

"Watch pressure and atmo composition closely," Dan warned.

A remote observer in the complex responded, "We're watching. It's crazy stuff. Heavy on oxygen and some stuff we've never seen before. Our analyzers are gibbering . . ."

305

"Can we breathe it okay?" Ito wondered anxiously. Feo eyed her with contempt. He was the scientist, depending on his fellow scientists—though they had been his competitors—and treating a layman's fears with contempt.

"They'll tell us if we can't," Kat said. The comment didn't reassure Ito.

Neither did the next relay from the labs. "Increasing rapidly in there. At that rate, you'll have to vacate in ten more local minutes, or risk decompression . . ."

"*Terrans* will do so," Praedar muttered, unconcerned.

Ruieb-An was translating ancient N'lac graffiti covering the room's lower panels and puzzling over a totally unfamiliar language inscribed higher up. The Old Ones' writings? That possibility set the Vahnaj atwitter. What a scientific opportunity! "Re-cord!"

"They are doing so," Dan assured the Vahnaj.

Meej craned his neck and pointed to two big panels framing the matter transmitter's open panel. "Is see thing. To look at the many-fathers-ago. Evil Ones see through Big Dark. I stop! Break!" and he hurled his club into the right-hand panel. It rebounded, hitting Meej, making him whimper.

"Plainly it'll take something a lot stronger than that to break it," Feo said unnecessarily. "Look at it. Not a scratch."

"He said they can watch us," Dan muttered. "Damn. I didn't expect that. They could be watching us right now, comparing us with a garbled message that robot sent . . ."

"This is so?" Praedar wondered absently.

"I don't know." Dan thought hard, checking local time, mentally plotting star maps. Where was the planet's rotational line and orbit at this time of the year? How did the time factors coordinate with the unknown stellar regions beyond the Terran-Whimed fringes? "It might depend on straight-shot transmission," he said, "of subspace com—or whatever they're using. And maybe of matter transmitting, too. They might have to be precisely aligned in order to travel . . ."

Ito was no longer a disinterested journalist. "Zap it!"

"Yeah! With what? And get zapped back?" Dan snarled. "If they can fold space that superbly, who knows what else they can do?"

"It seems beyond reason," Feo said. "That such a species . . . Why didn't they follow their escaped slaves centuries ago?"

Kat didn't want to take her eyes off Meej, but she rounded on Feo. "Think! The N'lacs certainly did. They smashed these machines as they smashed the robot. And their legends speak often of the damage the many-fathers-ago left behind them, on the Old Ones' world—sabotage of a sort, a delayed fuse or something. That's possible, isn't it, Dan?"

"Mm. In most technologies, sure. Makes sense." He nodded, as absorbed as Kat was in keeping an eye on Meej. "A lot of sense. Blow up the door on the other side of the Big Dark—and scramble its settings, so that the masters couldn't know exactly where the escapees had run to . . ."

Praedar said, "Many, many planets. Humanoid life. So many species seized as prey. To the Old Ones, it is likely humanoids resemble one another, no matter how individual we seem to ourselves. Yes. By destroying opposite entries to the Big Dark and destroying the data by which they might be located, the many-fathers-ago guarded their freedom."

"Until we got unlucky," Dan finished. "If that robot had missed this solar system, this world, the N'lacs might still be safe—and so would we."

"Five minutes . . ." a watchdog in the complex noted. "Atmo count is going up. Better get ready to abandon the dome . . ."

"We can't!" Kat wailed. "We've just begun to . . ."

Sheila broke in. "Dammit, Olmstead, I'm seeing the same readings they are in the complex. They're not kidding. You've got to get out of there. You wouldn't like decompression. Not a bit!"

Meej was ignoring the exchange. Suddenly he pressed his hands against the side of his head. "They come for us. Evil Old Ones. Come see. They see us hands and come to take." He dithered, running into the room's shadows, then bravely venturing forth again to sit directly in front of the "see thing" panels, as if he were posing, acting as bait, despite his terror.

"Yes!" Praedar repeated, a gleam in his starburst eyes. "They wish to satisfy their curiosity. *Aaaa!* Perhaps they are not so alien, in that regard. They will look. Then they will come."

"We don't know that, Juxury," Feo argued. "Whitcomb's right. Be sensible. Assuming these aliens exist, it's folly to remain here, at their . . ." Had he intended to use the word "mercy"? That didn't seem appropriate, in view of Chuss' death and that of the yacht crew.

"I will receive them," Praedar stated flatly. His mind was made up.

Dan was aware, even as he participated in the frantic attempt to dissuade the boss, that they weren't going to budge him. Kat begged, "Don't throw your life away like this. You saw what it can do. We have to get out of here, make plans . . ."

"No time," Praedar countered, imperturbable. Softening a bit, he smiled at the Terrans. "I will not die."

"Get out of there!" Sheila yelled faintly. "You'll get the bends . . ."

"Not Whimeds," the expedition's leader retorted.

"You, too, if the atmospheres build high enough," she threw back at him, furious with his stubbornness.

Feo said, "If we join forces, we can remove him bodily . . ."

The look Praedar gave him froze Saunder. None of the felinoid's teammates were so rash as to second Feo's suggestion. Praedar talked to the relay monitors. "Sheila, bring an injector gun. Extreme potency. Drastil, bring me my *oryuz* and a pressure suit." The paramed resisted, briefly, before yielding. Drastil didn't quibble for even a moment. Praedar turned to Armilly and Ruieb-An. "You preserve special knowledge. Kat preserves. Dan does. You will withdraw. It is possible I am wrong. You will reinterpret the data and present it. Generations to come must be informed of the truth."

The peculiar air was flooding the dome now, plainly entering from the matter transmitting chamber.

Near tears, Kat exclaimed, "Don't, please don't . . ."

"Remove! Terrans, Vahnajes, and Lannon."

Dan had to carry Kat into the airlock and push her and Feo on through into the tunnel. Armilly, Ruieb-An, and Ito had preceded them. Instead of following the crowd, Dan temporarily sealed the door, locking himself in the dome with Praedar and Meej.

On one of the monitors, he saw tiny figures under the glow of solar lamps. It was full dark in N'lac Valley by this time. Sheila, running, met Drastil on the dud pits apron. The blonde handed the Whimed a med kit. Drastil added it to an armload he was already toting, then hurried up Dome Hill. He passed Kat and the other observers, who were on their way out of the temples. They clustered near the painted ramp wall, talking excitedly.

"Terrans must leave," Praedar said. "The atmosphere is becoming inimicable to your species." He darted a disapproving glance at Dan.

"I've still got a few minutes. I need to talk to you—while I can. Face to face, the way you want to meet the Evil Old Ones. You plan to capture one, don't you? With that injector gun." Dan grimaced. "That's insane. Hell, we don't know if humanoid medicines will have any effect on those things at all. Kat's right. You're going to let your curiosity kill you."

"I will not die," Praedar said tonelessly.

Drastil cycled through the airlock and brought his superior his burdens. Praedar methodically began to don his pressure suit. The shorter Whimed stood by, an orderly attending his general, who was about to engage in a life-or-death battle.

Dan stared at a silvery crest cap Drastil was holding. "That's the *oryuz* device, isn't it? A Whimed anti-esp defense."

Both felinoids glowered at him, unhappy that he recognized the gadget. "How do you know of this?" Praedar growled.

"I saw it in your office, weeks ago. One of my kinsmen, Anthony Saunder, discovered the *oryuz* when he became involved in the Whimed-Vahnaj secret war, around the turn of the century." Praedar nodded, mollified by the explanation. Dan went on. "It works for you, sure, against the Vahnajes' mental power-force enhancers . . ."

Reverently Praedar lowered the silvery cap onto his crest. "The device belonged to my grandsire. He used it ethically. I will do so, as well."

"Injector guns!" Humanoid anti-esp devices!" Dan said, frustrated. "Those aren't going to work against nonanthropomorphic beings."

"That is to be established," Praedar replied, with a smile. He took the pressure suit helmet from Drastil and prepared to put it on.

"We need a backup plan," Dan said a bit desperately. There was an intensifying weight on his chest—the strange air was oppressing him.

The Whimeds met his stare. The minute stretched into eternity. Then Praedar said, "You are correct. This is what you proposed earlier? To smash the wall with the dredge? That also puts you at risk. It would cause explosive decompression. You would be seated at the dredge's controls, vulnerable to the results."

Dan was astonished, scarcely believing his ears. The Whimed

was amenable! He hadn't turned the plan down flat, as a desecration of xenoarchaeological treasures. Praedar acted as if he'd accept the backup scheme. He wasn't beyond reason—and he wasn't being blindly suicidal.

"I-I'm willing to take the risk. I'll wear a suit, too. It'll offer some protection," Dan said.

Praedar held up a cautioning finger. "Only if I fail."

"Okay! Okay! I promise!" At that stage, Dan would have agreed to damned near anything. He felt weak with relief and wondered why. His backup plan was no guarantee of success. None of this was. They might still end up in the Evil Old Ones' slave camps—they and untold other humanoid millions. "Look, if the injector gun and the esp headgear don't work, try to hang onto your initiative," he said. "Try to get out of my way. I'll watch you on the monitors, and if you're in trouble, I'll come through about here—in a hurry."

"If I fail," Praedar reiterated. "Only if I fail."

"What about Meej?" the xenomech asked. The N'lac continued to crouch before the matter transmitter's door—waiting for revenge, or death.

Praedar regarded the boy fondly. "He remains. You and Drastil go. But Meej is the leader of his tribe now. He has the right to decide on their behalf. The child of slaves must defy those who enslaved his people."

CHAPTER TWENTY-TWO
∞∞∞∞∞∞∞

To Destroy the Ages

The area was far too crowded, in Dan's opinion. People stood outside the complex, spilling across the dud pits, looking toward Dome Hill. The excavation apron along the crest was full of more observers and helpers. They divided their attention between Dan and an assortment of vid monitors. The scientists, with Kimball's guidance, had set the things up everywhere. No one, in or out of shelter, was far from one.

As Dan squirmed into a pressure suit he, like the rest, kept watch on the scene inside the main dome. Praedar and Meej were waiting. The Whimed was fully suited and helmeted, the injector gun at the ready. Meej knelt facing the matter transmitter's door. Neither felinoid nor N'lac seemed bothered by the steadily increasing atmospheres and the alien air's composition.

"Tough people," Sheila commented. She, Kat, and Baines were assisting Dan into the borrowed spacesuit. His own, of course, had been atomized in the explosion. Sheila frowned at the monitors. "Tough and crazy people. Whimeds are a lot stronger than Terrans, sure. And N'lacs have never fully readapted to the

311

local air after those genetic alterations the Old Ones inflicted on them. So presumably Meej is geared for the alien pressure. But if you smash through that wall . . ." The blonde tugged on a suit seal, testing its closure, her face set in a fierce scowl. "Come to that, I don't think you can take that. This outfit was made to protect humans in a vacuum, not explosive decompression side effects and flying metalostone."

Dan shrugged. "So keep your fingers crossed. Maybe the injector gun will work fine. Praedar will nail his specimen and we'll all celebrate. Maybe Feo's right, for once, and this is a false alarm. Maybe there are no more Old Ones. Or maybe they can't get their matter transmission coordinates lined up as they used to. Two millennia is a long time. Precession of the equinoxes, galactic rotation—lots of things could prevent them from coming . . ."

"Huh! And maybe if I flap my arms, I can fly," Sheila said.

"Sorry the suit doesn't fit better," Baines apologized. "I'm the closest to your size in camp, though, so . . ."

"It's fine. I'll try to bring it back in one piece."

"Bring yourself back in one piece," Kat said. She glanced at the vid shots of the dome's interior. "And bring them back."

"I'll sure as hell try . . ."

Armilly had reestablished his remote probe station near the ramp. Now he boomed, "Energy thingoo inside big box. Changes stuff . . ." Kimball cued zoom closeups of the scene. Dan saw that the little suns and planets suspended in the matter transmitter were accelerating. The hurtful glare was sharpening, as well.

"We've just run out of time," Dan yelled. "Get clear. All of you!"

"We belong here!" Kat exclaimed defiantly. "We're staying! *Whatever* happens . . ."

Sheila nodded. "Damned right! We'll see it through. You go, we all go. And if either Praedar's scheme or yours works out, somebody's going to need a paramed. That's me, for damned sure!"

"What did you say about crazy people?" Dan asked sarcastically. He broke into a run, jamming the suit helmet down on its neck ring. Praedar's voice hissed from the helmet's audio circuits. The face plate was open.

As Dan loped toward the dredge, Sheila's parting shot competed with the Whimed's dispassionate, scientific running account of events inside the dome. "Give the fornicating bastards hell! Go get 'em! Kroo-ger! Go *get* 'em!"

Minutes before, Dan had driven the vacuum dredge onto the sandy triangle between the ramp and the tunnel. The rig waited for him there now, ten meters from the dome. That wouldn't give him much of a momentum-building ram run, but he intended to bypass certain safety factors and add to the machine's striking power.

The bulky suit made him clumsy. Dan boosted himself up into the cab with a grunt and slid behind the controls. Feo was already there, sitting beside him. "What the hell?" Dan muttered. "Get out of here. This is my job."

"I know, and I'm not trying to take anything from you." Saunder's expression was pinched. A sickly green glow from a full-range bank of dashboard monitors added to the effect. It was plain that Feo was scared. Dan didn't blame him. "I-I have to talk to you. Just for a moment. I *have* to . . ."

There was an earnestness about him that got through to Dan. Feo had been stripped of pretense and prestige. This was the man, down to his basics. The unspoken reality hung between them—that this might be their last chance to exchange words—ever.

"Okay. Make it quick . . ."

"I-I may have been mistaken about you, about Juxury, and about your father."

Dan was splitting his attention among the array of onboard monitors Kimball had arranged, showing every angle on multiple screens. A tracery of data updates crawled at the bottom of the frames: pressure analyses; air composition; audio tracks of Praedar's incoming accounts; biomed stats on the Whimed and Meej; and the time factor.

Despite those compelling demands on his mind and emotions, Dan turned aside for a second, peering at his cousin.

Feo nodded. "I've been thinking about that, ever since the Assembly. It . . . it *could* have been a matter of misconceptions, of crossed interpretations, like Hope's and my dispute with Juxury, all these years. There's so much to regret. Looking back, I can see that . . . I didn't mean to hurt Reid. Spirit of Humanity, no! None of us realized how serious his financial situation was until . . . and then . . . He was proud and offended, understandably. If . . . if we get out of this, I'm going to try to make it up to him. And to you."

"I'll hold you to that," Dan said, trying for a light note. He didn't make it. His focus darted back to the monitor boards as he said, "You're a bigger person than I thought. I've misjudged you, too. You're right. Let's not go into this hating each other."

"I've never hated you," Feo said. "I . . . what Kat and your other teammates have told me . . . I didn't know how capable you were. It's a crime you've been hampered by lack of funds. You're another Ward Saunder, Dan. You ought to get a chance to show the entire sector your talents . . ."

Praedar's running descriptions came from the helmet speakers. A dozen other voices were on the monitors, along with the data flow printout. Dan absorbed them all and savored his kinsman's words.

So he was a full-fledged member of the T-W 593 expedition *and*, at least in one man's eyes, a full-fledged member of the Saunder-McKelveys.

Dan wished this acceptance had come at a more auspicious time!

"Yeah, that's me. An inventive genius in a tech-mech's suit. I'd love to introduce this matter-transmitting alien technology to the humanoid civilizations. What a joke! Leapfrogging into our own future, using a nonanthropomorphic species' devices." He paused, listening intently to some of the flood of reports, then added, "But our species and theirs have worked together before. Humanoids built the Old Ones' machines. That robot was built by descendents of Chuss' ancestors."

"His own kindred," Feo murmured, appalled.

"You and I, cousin, could end up in the same cage. Our Saunder and McKelvey descendents could build robot demons to enforce continued slavery on our however-many-times-removed grandchildren."

"No! Never!" Feo cried.

On the monitors, Meej was saying excitedly "Smell thick thick! Not like place Joe make for our mother. Old One smell! Soon soon!"

Sheila's face filled one of the screens. "He's not kidding, Dan. There's a big increase in pressure . . ."

Dan held out a hand and Feo took it in a firm, encouraging

grip. "Thanks, for what you said about Dad. Better make yourself scarce now. I'm going to be busy..."

Saunder jumped out of the cab and ran back as far as the ramp. He stood there with the other daring observers, waiting to pick up the pieces—or face utter defeat.

Kat, Sheila, Baines, Armilly, Ruieb-An, all the expedition's Whimed members, Feo, Rosie, and the two reporters...

Dan had to give the latter credit. Like the Saunders, they'd found reserves in themselves they probably hadn't known that they possessed. Ito had screwed her courage to the sticking point. She was speaking softly into a candid vid pendant, assembling an in-depth eyewitness report for the Terran network. Kimball simultaneously maintained a survey on the dozens of monitor relays and fine-tuned his master holo camera, intent on capturing all the action.

"Meej see them fellow come soon soon! See them fellow die!" the N'lac piped, waving his little club valiantly.

A red-skinned, golden-eyed David, ready to slay his Goliath!

In fact, compared to even a tall humanoid like Praedar, the indications were that every Evil Old One was a Goliath.

But would the famous legend follow the same happy-ending pattern this time around?

The data feed showed that pressure in the octagonal matter transmitting chamber was near the maximum feasible for its structure. Dan slammed shut his helmet's face plate and cued the dredge. The giant rig trembled beneath him, straining to be released. Readouts leaned into the red. "Not yet. We give Praedar his crack at them first. This is immortality for him, whether he lives or dies..."

Praedar and Meej were waiting, two humanoid Davids.

Telltale scale lines showed a momentary hiccup in the matter-transmitting chamber's energy field. Armilly's monitors indicated that the latticework box was bulging, its metalline sides stressed.

Had those organic, self-repairing processes combined as well as they should have with the fluidics elements? Maybe they'd lost some of their efficiency after two millennia. In that case, there might be no need for the injector gun, Praedar's anti-esp device, or the dredge. A transportee materializing in the chamber could be met by an overtaxed terminal and sudden death as the box collapsed.

Why not wish for a magic wand, while he was at it?

Praedar provided a steady vocal anchor to Dan and other observers on the outside. ". . . The gases are filling the dome. They do not appear to affect Meej adversely yet, nor am I having breathing difficulties . . ."

"Shut your helmet, dammit," Sheila muttered on an adjacent audio channel. "Quit using your lungs as guinea pigs."

Kat chimed in. "You've picked up Dan's penchant for mangled metaphors. She's right, Praedar. Don't be foolhardy."

Praedar didn't break the flow of his tour-guide description, but he did take their advice, securing the pressure suit's face plate. "Extensive exposure to such an atmosphere would impede other humanoid life forms, as would this pressure level. However, I am not noticeably stressed, as I believe the medical data will prove."

"Cocky," Dan growled, envying the Whimed's awesome strength and his species' evolutionary advantages over *Homo sapiens*.

"Your assessment of the time factor was quite accurate, Dan," Praedar said. "It would seem the cycle has neared . . ."

Something was happening.

Popping noises and a peculiar hiss overrode the audio's carrier wave. Praedar, unruffled, announced, "I can see a form. It is amorphous, indistinct—in sections. Interesting. Transmission is apparently not instantaneous. Note that."

"Okay, okay," Dan said through clenched teeth, his hands poised on the dredge's controls.

Meej and Praedar were finally getting a chance to meet the enemy face to face.

No, not face to face. There *was* no face, in humanoid terms. There was a swirling mass, coalescing in the octagonal box. The huge body gradually replaced those little hovering solar systems, a slimy, glistening blob encased in a chitinous dark exoskeleton. No true features showed, only randomly placed insectoid eyes shimmering near the being's middle. It looked fragile, tendrilled. Things undulated sinuously, like alien hair.

Dan's gorge rose. He wanted to look away, but didn't dare. The reality was far worse than his nightmares. This was the N'lacs' foe, fed on the food of nonanthropomorphic gods and become a hideous, living giant.

Praedar was still speaking for the records. "My measurements suggest certain esper emanations. I am activating the *oryuz* and preparing to fire the sedation darts. The alien has assumed complete form at twenty-one oh eight, local meridian time. . ."

Monitors spewed figures. Data poured from the dome to the complex's labs and storage banks—the truth, undeniable.

It was an Old One in the flesh, the species Praedar insisted must not be called evil, because its motivations could not be accurately compared to those of humanoid races.

In Dan's mind's eye, Chuss' bloody corpse hurled a defiant contradiction of that idea. That excrescence in the matter transmitter *was* evil.

"We're less than insects to them," Dan whispered. "Unfeeling toys, servo hands made of organic materials . . ."

The Old One swayed, almost filling the towering, boxy "altar" within the ancient temple. It was a personification of malevolent danger.

Meej shrieked and clutched his head. The N'lac had been lifting his club, moving to strike at his brother's killer. Now, unseen claws ripped at him, smashing the e.t. to the floor. Meej writhed in agony.

Nanoseconds later the same force hit Praedar. The Whimed staggered, gasping, his flow of scientific description interrupted.

"Fire the injector gun!" Sheila bellowed. "Now!"

Praedar did. He held the pain at bay, his *oryuz* device shielding him, for the moment. The med stunner spat its supply of darts, point blank. Zoom lenses showed the needles embedded deeply in the quivering, exoskeletoned monster. Dosage levels read empty. The Old One had absorbed the entire charge.

To absolutely no effect, except to accelerate the Old One's assault on its humanoid gadflies!

Meej jerked and danced pathetically. He raked at his skin, drawing blood. Praedar dropped the injector gun and grabbed at his helmet, undogging seals, pulling it off. The *oryuz*, now useless, encircled his erect crest as the Whimed screamed, his back arched, and he began tearing off his protective gear. In moments he'd be flaying himself, as Meej was doing.

Near the ramp, below the hill, in the complex, and in the village, humanoids shrieked as a massive mind attack swept over them. Dan felt tendrils probing his mind, twisting, torturing.

A single Old One, wielding incomprehensible esper weapons, was crushing the will of potential slaves.

The N'lacs, caught totally unaware, had never had a chance.

Maybe . . . just maybe . . . this time, forewarned and fore-armed, humanoids could fight back.

"Hang on, hang on," Dan pleaded, tears of pain filling his eyes as those intrusive, invisible knives lanced at his gray matter. "Praedar! Hang on! Get Meej! *Move!* To your right! *TO YOUR RIGHT!*"

He didn't wait to see if they did. He slammed the dredge into full engage. Fifteen metric tons of vehicle, its treaders whining in overdrive, thundered forward.

Readouts pegged all the way into the red. Power systems keened.

Dan was nearly hurled out of the cab. He continued to roar at the monitors. "Move to the right, Praedar, move to the right!"

Then he was flattened, helpless, sprawling, barely able to breathe. Dan gazed dumbly at the screens. Had Praedar heard him? Could the Whimed somehow find the will and strength to act?

Yes! *Yes!* Praedar tugged at Meej, edging to the right.

Slowly . . . so *slowly!*

Time moved in nanoseconds.

Dan whimpered, on fire, roasting on the Old One's esper spit . . .

It didn't matter. The dredge was on automatic. And there was no leisure for that alien to absorb and control the intricacies of humanoid technology. It had disabled the driver, but the dredge was impervious to its assault.

The dome loomed, dominating Dan's universe. It seemed to hurtle toward him as the dredge plunged along its preset course.

Fumes boiling from its cowling, the rig smashed through the curving wall and into the dome, through the lattice-walled chamber—and its occupant.

A tiny, still-functional fragment of Dan's mind prayed: *Please, let the alien gases cancel out the oxygen factor. No fire. Please, don't let there be a fire . . .*

Its kinetic energy drained, the dredge lurched to a stop with its intake hoses buried in the opposite wall of the ancient building.

Dan was hit with a barrage of ricocheting debris. Chunks of metalostone hammered at the cab, shattering the screens and pelting him. Steel-sharp shards, puncturing the pressure suit and cutting the face and body within.

The alien esper tentacles were gone!

He was free!

Gobbets of still-pulsing viscous flesh and exoskeleton clung to him, mingling with Dan's blood and the tatters of his suit.

Groaning, he turned his head, squinting through a seething fog of powdered stonite, metalline, and alien.

Beyond the spot where the transmitter had stood—to its right —lay two bodies. One was tall, lean, and crested. The other was small and red-skinned. Both were bleeding. And both were moving—feebly, as Dan was, in obvious distress—but moving.

They were alive.

And the Old One wasn't.

Shouts, outside the jagged hole in the dome wall, came from a rescue squad. Sheila was giving orders and assembling a crew to assist the wounded.

Fine! Let them take over now.

Praedar had done his job, buying them time. And Dan had done his. They'd earned a rest. He abandoned his struggle against unconsciousness and sank in dreamless—nightmareless—darkness.

CHAPTER TWENTY-THREE

ⵔⵔⵔⵔⵔ

The Long View

There was a dull ache in Dan's head, his arms, and his legs. A haze of soft noises and voices came from an adjacent area. The solidity of a bunk or cot was beneath him.

He was swimming in free fall. Where was his safety tether? He had to get back to . . .

Not to the ship. It was gone.

To home, N'lac Valley, and his friends.

Where *was* that tether?

He had hold of it. It felt remarkably like a hand, strong and masculine. He struggled to get his eyes open, then winced in the sudden glare of bright room lights.

The face looking down at him was his own, grown older. Dazed and blinking, he said faintly, "Adam?"

"It's about time you woke up," his brother replied. The tone wasn't nearly as stern as Dan remembered, and the big blond officer sitting beside the cot was grinning. "Whitcomb said she thought keeping you sedated this long assisted the healing, but that you'd mended enough." The Commander took a deep breath.

"What the hell were you trying to do? Be this generation's Morgan McKelvey?"

Morgan, their grandfather, crippled in a failed FTL experiment and terribly burned by alien energies . . .

Dan's universe snapped back into sharp focus. He hurt. It was a muted, all-over ache, though, not the searing agony of burns. He struggled to sit up. Adam helped, steadying him until the trembling in Dan's muscles eased.

"Not . . . not Morgan. There wasn't a fire, was there?" Dan asked.

"Not according to the footage I've watched," Adam confirmed. He leaned back, studying the younger man. "That was an incredible stunt you and Juxury pulled. You're both due for the highest commendation Terra and Whimed can give you and medals from the other sectors, as well."

"Praedar? How is he? How's Meej?"

"Both alive," a familiar, sassy female voice said. Sheila entered the room, wielding a med scanner, checking Dan out. "Not that the three of you have any right to be. Forn! You heal fast! You're a credit to Joe's and my efforts."

Dan groaned, rubbing the back of his neck. "I feel as if the dredge fell on top of me."

Memories! He brushed reflexively at the invalid's jumper he was wearing, half expecting loathsome scraps of the Old One's flesh to come off on his fingers. There was none.

"Yeah, you were a mess," Sheila said. "All of you. I told you that you were going to need parameds." She patted her racks of supplies. "Good thing, though, that the Commander's chief surgeon came here with all the latest mending goodies—for Terrans and other humanoids." The blonde sighed tiredly. "The important thing is that you're in a lot better shape than our late, unlamented invader. Rosie and Hope have their work cut out for them—trying to reconstruct that oversized glob of ugly . . ."

"It . . . it seems like something that happened to someone else," Dan said. "Something I saw on a vid."

"You *can* watch it on vids," Adam noted. "Your expedition's vids, and the news tri-dis those reporters put together. It's the best evidence package ever. Everything is on holo-modes." He leaned forward, pressing Dan's shoulder. "You're going to be famous, you and Juxury. All the data your team collected makes the Fleet's job easier, to boot. Astrophysics division is backtracking right now, using that line-of-sight vector you figured out. We can pinpoint the area of uncharted space they came from. I've got our preliminary defenses in place and on the lookout. We'll be ready for those scouting robots, if any more try to get through. And the mapping comps are searching the planetary records, checking for matter transmitter sites—now that we know what they are."

Relief was a stimulant. Dan managed a smile. "Sounds good, Adam. They won't catch us off guard. Not ever again."

His brother shook his head in fond amazement. "Thanks to you and your scientific team."

Dan learned that he'd been out of it for six days. Sheila and Joe had used deep-sleep healing therapy to keep him zonked and give his injuries a chance to knit. Adam's Space Fleet rescue squad had responded quickly to Feo's frantic appeal; the troops had been on T-W 593 for nearly three days. By the time they'd arrived, of course, the danger was over. They were cooperating with the expedition to mop up now, using those kilotons of information gathered during the crisis.

For another day, Dan did little but shuffle around the infirmary, getting his strength back. Praedar and Meej were doing the same, as restive as he was to be out and about. Sheila, however, was holding them down until she was certain they were sufficiently recovered from their ordeal. For Dan, the confinement was softened by a steady stream of well-wishers and updates. Outside, the cleaning up was well underway. The invalids wouldn't be participating in that, of course; they'd earned a rest.

When Sheila gave him his conditional release on the following morning, Dan walked out of the insta-cells more or less on his own. He *did* welcome Adam's supporting hand. And he was still shaky enough that he didn't try to go far—no farther than the dud pits. Adam helped him to sit down on a stack of storage crates there, where he could soak up the sun and look around.

Dan's first interest was Dome Hill. The scene had changed radically. The main structure had collapsed in on itself. A Fleet vehicle, temporarily converted to civilian uses, was winching a big piece of the ruined dredge out of the debris. Scientists and military personnel were all over the area. Dan was gratified to see that the uniforms were obeying the expedition's rules about not stepping on any "importants." Adam's people treated the string-marked grids the xenoarchaeologists had set up as if they were guarded by plasma weapons. Baines was in charge, this shift, and the O.D. of the hilltop squad took orders from him without question.

Adam saw Dan's surprise. "My personnel will coordinate with yours absolutely. This is Juxury's Settlement. We're here to aid, not administer. Dr. Olmstead, Sheila, Hughes, Rosenthal . . . they all insisted that was the way Juxury wanted it, and Feo agreed fully. Any assistance we can offer is yours. Once Dr. Juxury's back on his feet, we'll be turning our total attention to the defensive astro sweep." Commander McKelvey looked skyward, his jaw setting in a firm, angry line.

The man in charge of the humanoid outer defenses was on the job and eager to go.

For a moment Dan was tempted to tease and say "Iron Fist!" He didn't. That urge to one-up his brother was gone. Ever since he'd seen Adam's anxious face above him, the rivalry and resentment that had ruled their relationship for so long had vanished. Dan wondered if it, like so much else in his life these past years, had been a case of flawed selectivity and interpretation. From now on, he'd be better able to step into another being's skin and try to see the universe from that angle.

They were all humanoids. And in the long view, that had proved infinitely more important than their differences.

Sheila had followed her patients from the complex and kept a close eye on them. Kat, too, was watchful, making sure Meej didn't overdo. Like Dan, the boy was savoring the morning. He sat by the dud pits, strawbossing as Sleeg guided N'lac adolescents in creating a magic sand painting. Colored figures showed the Old Ones and their demon robots shattering into fragments. In a large circle around them were N'lacs and offworlders, stick arms linked in a united front against the ancient enemy. In a closer triad, contacting the foe shapes, were distinctive representatives of Dan, Praedar, and Meej. And in the middle of the ruined Old One was a crude rendering of the vacuum dredge.

"We'll need another dredge," Dan murmured.

"We'll get it," Kat assured him. "And an entire fleet of brand-new equipment. Feo's promised that. He's already put through the call to the manufacturers."

"Yeah, I think I remember him telling me that yesterday, but I was kind of fuzzy. . ."

Adam said, "Feo's going to turn the lobbying screws on the

Pan Sector Council, too. Cam Saunder's reporters will provide the clincher—all those holo-modes. When they're through, there won't be a humanoid for two hundred parsecs who doesn't know Juxury's name and yours, Dan. You're heroes."

"So's Meej," Dan murmured. The boy glanced around at the mention, grinning happily. Straightening, Dan asked, "Where *is* Feo? I saw Hope, earlier today, but not him."

"He has departed for Pan Sector HQ Central."

Moving carefully, Dan turned and peered at Praedar. The Whimed was leaning on Drastil's arm, as Dan had leaned on Adam's. Drastil eased his boss down onto a crate opposite the one Dan sat on. The two wounded warriors regarded each other. Praedar looked five times worse than Dan felt. The protective suit, the *oryuz* device, and the felinoid's stamina had saved him from death, but hadn't shielded him completely from the effects of the Old One's esper powers and explosive decompression. Raw gashes marked Praedar's bony face, arms, legs, and chest. There were scabbed patches where parts of his crest used to be. His starry eyes were blackened and swollen.

"Feo's gone?" Dan said, puzzled.

"He exceeded his visitor's pass." It took a second before Dan spotted the telltale twinkle in those bruised eyes. A pained smile twisted Praedar's mouth. "He serves us best at present elsewhere, at Pan Sector Central and at the Terran-Whimed Xenoethnic Council. He will coordinate to ensure that the facts of these events are known and understood."

"Can we trust him?" Dan asked, old suspicions stirring. "Now that the danger's past . . ."

"You can trust him," Adam said. "He . . . he told me about that conversation you had just before the blowup. And he wants to make amends, to Dad, to Dr. Juxury, and to you. I . . . I think he and his wife have undergone a major change of opinion."

"Yeah . . ."

"Much has altered," Praedar said. "For us. For Feo Saunder. We have discovered that we are not adversaries—not in the long view of history. We are allies."

Dan chuckled, then winced as broken ribs complained. "The next Xenoarchaeological Assembly is going to be considerably different from the one we just attended. If Feo backslides, all the data will put him on track again. Yeah. Much has altered. Your theories have been proved, Praedar. With Feo's influence and fortune supporting us, this dig's going to be one in a million. A very special site. We'll have to keep tabs on my cousin, just in case, but . . ."

Kat's dark eyes glowed. "You said he could learn. He has done so." She turned to Praedar. "The messages are already starting to come in. Offers of funding. More funding than we ever dreamed of . . ."

Sheila put in, "And student applicants, up to your crest. We'll be selective. Kroo-ger! No more Bill Getzes! Strictly hardworking xenoarchs with plenty to contribute—in the best Praedar Effan Juxury tradition. Speaking of contribs and pulling one's own weight, Commander, you promised that your people would be shifting operations out to orbit—and out of our hair—by the end of this week."

"That's right. I'll be cutting the order today, now that Dan's okay." Adam saluted Praedar. "Your license and your expedition are secure, Dr. Juxury. Depend on that. You have a Fleet officer's word on it. You won't be bothered by planetary developers or other butt-ins—not your people or these e.t.s you're protecting."

The Whimed looked from Dan to Adam and back again and smiled. "Yes. I depend upon that. *Aytan*. You are both *aytan*. As is Feo."

"*Now*," Dan muttered, in a last jab of fast-fading doubt.

Praedar went on. "Saunder-McKelvey. Terra. You have taught your kinsman what it is to be Saunder-McKelvey and Terran. To be what your family is capable of."

"That's right," Kat said. "Get back in top fettle in a hurry, Dan. Hope and Rosie expect you to help them with the robot's reconstruction. I think your brother's science staffers want to pick your brains, too."

"And how!" Adam exclaimed. "A matter transmitter! Do you know what this means, Dan?"

"Sure. Some new patents under the Saunder-McKelvey name," Dan said with a grin. He forced himself not to laugh. "Overdue. The family's been loafing along, technologically, for a while—since Morgan McKelvey and Brenna Saunder made the FTL breakthrough, seventy-five years ago. I think it's time for another big jump, huh?"

The admiration in Commander McKelvey's expression erased years of bitterness and misunderstanding. Adam nodded. "And I'll make damned sure all the sectors know who deserves the credit. My kid brother! This century's Ward Saunder."

Sheila pointed at Meej. "You fellow get strong strong again, huh huh? Got baby sister fellow take care of now, show how to think smart . . ."

"Loor's baby," Dan said softly. Sorrow for a dead friend tightened his throat. Then his spirits lifted. Chuss was gone. But Chuss' people would survive. With Feo's money and prestige and Adam determined to twist the right arms in the military divisions, the planet grabbers had no chance. The N'lacs' future—and the expedition's—looked very bright.

Adam studied him slyly, then winked at Sheila and Kat. "You may be a groundbreaker for the family in *another* regard, I suspect. Shall we say, a potentially fascinating experiment in Saunder-McKelvey genetics?" He didn't appear at all upset by the polygamous implications of that. The officer's grin rivaled the morning sun. "Well, I'll butt out for now. I know you and Juxury have a lot of scientific stuff you want to discuss."

Once more, pride filled the commander's face—pride for the kid brother who was definitely no longer a loser.

Adam hurried away, climbing Dome Hill to assist the combined mop-up team there.

Praedar tilted his head back, peering above the western horizon, where a few faint stars resisted the sunlight's onslaught. He seemed to be searching for distant worlds that no free humanoid had ever seen.

"You found the truth," Dan said. "You found it and preserved it." Uncertainty flickered across the alien's expression. "Yes, we had to smash the dome, the MT, and the Old One—to save our species. But we can rebuild them as harmless replicas and retain the knowledge they have shown us."

"It is not *all* the truth," Praedar protested mildly.

"No, I suppose we never get all the truth," Dan admitted. "If we did, we'd stagnate and get lazy. That's not the humanoid way—not for the Saunder-McKelveys of Terra, and not for Praedar Effan Juxury."

The Whimed lowered his gaze to the landscape of N'lac Valley, the home of the T-W 593 Project, rescued from the forever time. Rescued, too, were the beings—N'lac and offworlders—who lived and loved in this place.

"It is so," Praedar said. "The long view. That portion of the truth which you and I will be remembered for *was* found, *was* preserved." He was content.

Dan held out his hand. Praedar took it in friendship and in partnership. They smiled at one another, bridging the chasms of evolution and time and space. Kat and Sheila, supporting them, looked on with approval.

"Someday, eons down the line," Dan said, "our species will be dust. We'll all be projects for other, future expeditions to dig up and study. Now, though, for our time, and for our descendents', we've won."

ABOUT THE AUTHOR

Juanita Coulson began writing at age eleven and has been pursuing this career off and on ever since. Her first professional sale, to a science fiction magazine, came in 1963. Since then she has sold fifteen novels, several short stories, and such odds and ends as an article on "Wonder Woman" and a pamphlet on how to appreciate art.

When she isn't writing, she may be singing and/or composing songs, painting (several of her works have been sold for excessively modest prices), reading biographies or books dealing with abnormal psychology, earthquakes and volcanoes, history, astronomy—or almost anything that has printing on it, gardening in the summer and shivering in the winter.

Juanita is married to Buck Coulson who is also a writer. She and her husband spend much of their spare time actively participating in science fiction fandom: attending conventions and publishing their Hugo-winning fanzine, *Yandro*. They live in northeastern Indiana in a house crammed with books, magazines, records, typewriters, and other paraphernalia.